Danger 9b

and his

Goddess

of

Fortune

by
Richard J. Hatch

ISBN: 979-8-218-37989-6

You now have this book with all the great extras.

Now bring Jill, Rick, and the whole gang to life

with the recorded 14 hour theatrical audiobook

production version.

It features music by the Beatles and others with full sound design, and international voice talent.

"Danger 9b and his Goddess of Fortune"

Find it at:

Danger9b.com

Table of Contents

Dedication

To my children and grandchildren and all their descendants – so you might get a glimpse into my life in the 1960s. And to all my crushes over the years. First, there was Jill – oh yeah. Then, in no particular order, there were all those who kept me on the straight and narrow: Annette, Marilyn, Lorraine, Paula, another Paula, Kathy, Cyndi, Pam, Vicky, another Cindy.

Then, God saved the best for last, Julia.

Introduction

It was 1964 and a tense time in the world. The USSR, the Union of Soviet Socialist Republics was a menacing threat with a huge nuclear arsenal. Their space program and the race to the moon seemed well ahead of ours. It was the 'cold' war. The Beatles and their music were exploding all over the world. Hula Hoops and long hair swooped into the headlines and the drug and hippie culture bloomed. But to us American and International kids living in Ankara, Turkey everything was groovy, well insulated from the troubles of the world. We had our own worries to contend with. For me – it was Mitch Alegre, but more on that to come. To me, Rick Foster, there are a lot of things not real clear in my mind about those times, but I remember Jill. So, I'll tell it like it was, or should have been, or just plain lie. I got to be pretty good at that. It's as if it were yesterday. I may not start right at the beginning.Stay with me, it all comes together.

I have a vivid imagination, but I don't have to engage it that much to remember those times, quite some time ago, and talk about Jill. Oh yeah, Jill. I'll leave it to you to sort out the real from the wish it were so. This is how it went down.

Danger 9b

and his

Goddess of Fortune

TURKEY
LEBANON
ISRAEL
SYRIA
JORDAN
IRAQ

Prologue
Do You Wanna Know a Secret?

Ankara, Turkey
Degil Trading Company Offices
23 October 1964 20:30 hrs
The Day of Disaster

Sales executive, Robert Foster, is about to call it a night at the office when his phone rings.

Mr. FOSTER: "Foster here."

The voice on the line is almost breathless, with a real sense of urgency.

VOICE: "Robert, your son has just entered the Soviet Embassy compound. Did you know about this?"

Mr. FOSTER: "What? The Red Zone? No, no, that...that... can't be."

VOICE: "And he's taken Colonel MacGregor's daughter, Jill in with him. Do you know why?"

Mr. FOSTER: "Which son? Are you sure it's my son and MacGregor's daughter?"

VOICE: "It appears to be your younger son. Confirmed."

Mr. FOSTER: "Alert team Red Feather. I'll ...I'll... take care of this."

He slams the phone down. "Rick, what in the world are you thinking?"

Episode One

O! Fortuna

Chapter One
Revolution

Ankara, Turkey
In the Russian Embassy
23 October 1964 20:30 hrs.
The day of Disaster

Jill doesn't say she wants a revolution, but then the shock wave hits the two of us. I stagger back and hit the wall. Jill is flung on her backside. An ominous cloud billows up like a native smoke signal and fills the windowless room.

"Ha. That was, how do you say it? Full-on gnarly," Jill states far too matter-of-factly.

A stench assaults us and reminds me of a bubbling volcanic Sulphur pit storming my nostrils. The lights start to flicker, then complete and utter darkness envelopes us. Then it hits me. Oh no, please, not here. Little Miss Arsonist strikes again.

What sounds like a heavy metal embassy gate rattles and clanks as it slowly descends over our room's exterior door. I'm guessing the maintenance czar has neglected to grease this gate's track for years. Straining my neck as if to listen more intently to a slow-motion car wreck, my ears ache with the anticipation of the final crash. A pathetic emergency light, high up in the corner, stumbles on to barely dim as if it doesn't know how. The echo of a screeching siren begins to wind up like a bellowing air raid warning. Am I bombing out that badly?

"Wow, man, this… this is... is... really hairy," I say.

Clattering boots on adjacent hallway floors reverberate through the building as if mustering a tap-dancing battalion. Yeah, they got rhythm, but I'm not clapping. I finally wince as the gate bangs shut, blocking any escape.

"Sorry. I didn't think *that* much would happen," Jill mutters.

"I… I…" I can't stammer out anything more. This is not to protocol. She did say, "Let's have some fun," but normal people don't freak out like this, especially in a foreign country. My thoughts look like ragged multi-colored underwear tumbling behind the window of a laundromat dryer. And she keeps feeding the darn thing coins. Why images of holey underwear? Mine? Does it mean poor me is being quickly exposed? Or maybe it means I don't want her to think of me as some panty waist or hear me whimper.

If I'm lucky, Jill will mistake my panicky mumblings as the muffled, incoherent shouts of soldiers leaking through the walls. Their accented grunts seem to curse at me. With my auto-translate mode turned on in my mind, it's confirming they are yelling;

Rick! You are an idiot.

The stink still lingers in the room. Honest Abe, Jill, it's not me. I'm dry. I stare at that single emergency light from the yellow bulb up high. The flimsy filament flutters as if a butterfly, flicking this way and that. It is so Jill.

Well, *Danger 9b,* how did you let her get you into this? Yeah, what got into you, Rick Foster? These pathetic questions now pound on me. She calls *me* a ten-piece puzzle, but *her*? I don't think a thousand-piece box can hold Jill. And there are no corners to start with.

"What are they yelling outside?" she asks as she grabs my arm.

I say nothing. I just stare at her. I mean, this is *Fortuna,* my goddess! Don't blow it. If any sound does come out of my uncontrollably contorted mouth, it would be as coarse as a barkless Japanese Basenji dog. What's going on outside these walls? Who knows? What's going on right here, inside of her? Outside, inside, it's all a jumble.

Has she no rules? Is her bag bodacious lawlessness? Rick, why are you just now asking yourself this? This is so her and so not you.

"Well, it's certainly getting more interesting. So don't be… is it… uptight?" she tells me.

Her unmistakable yank of personal gravity is beyond my control, speedily drawing me in like some space-age tractor beam. Patting my hand, she adds, "That was, what are your words? 'Far out.' I guess we got their attention."

I still stare at her through our dusk of confusion. What is this lure that draws me into her mysterious universe, churning inside this marvelous creation called Jill MacGregor? I began our date wanting to know. But now? I don't think this is gonna be all right. It's proving to be a disastrous day.

Come on. It was just a stick of gum.

I didn't know sweat is salty. I do now. My mind is whirling, searching, going back, back, back, reviewing where did I go wrong?

Chapter Two
Yesterday

**George C. Marshall Regional High School,
Ankara, Turkey, early September 1964
A few weeks before Disaster**

To me, Rick Foster, Jill MacGregor is a puzzle right from day one. My troubles might seem far away, but as Jill arrives, they may be here to stay. This strange thought hits me the first time we all see her. You gotta understand. A new body adding to our starving number of students at George C. Marshall Regional High School is almost as rare as seeing the trifecta of lunar events a – super moon, a blue moon, and a lunar eclipse in the same month. So, a strange face is a celestial delight, or as our Latin troubadour, Mitch Montealegra, indelicately puts it, a fresh piece of meat. Jill is on his grill as the new skirt in sophomore class this year. She moves in two weeks after school starts. Standing, or should I say, promenading in front of the whole class, like a fearless Joan of Arc, she announces,

"I am an American. However, Ich bin in Bern in der Schwiez geboren." And continues, *"J'ai vécu a Paris et internat a Londres."*

Seeing all our faces this day, it was like, huh? German, French. Yeah. Paris, London, and Switzerland are all in there somewhere. Most of us have been living overseas for a time, one place or another, but thishas been her whole life. Nora, our foreign exchange student from Germany and the class mirror warmer, squirms in her seat. I know right then things will be different.

"¿hablas español? Senorita?" Mitch asks, hopefully, his second language.

"Uh. Excuse me, bub," I tell him. "You're speaking out of turn here."

"Bug off," he growls.

"*Si, Un poquito*. I also speak the King's English, but I've never lived stateside," she answers.

Right off the bat, Mitch is pouring on his charm, like thick maple ooze on his fresh cut of bacon. He's emptying the whole bottle. Come on. It's not making sense. He has the knockout Nora chasing him. What is he doing? Nora will give him the stink eye. And she knows how to do it.

Jill is dressed this first day in a cute little Swiss outfit with lederhosen. It is like looking at a picture postcard from the Alps. The only thing missing is her Alphorn, the giant Swiss musical instrument,to complete the outfit and blow us away. Her sparkling red shoes and a little green pointed cap round out the picture. Okay. She was born there.It makes sense. It contrasts so strikingly with her fabulous red-blond hair and snowy skin and… well… I am told, and I can see for myself, that girls physically mature faster than boys at our age. Nora, or, as I prefer my name for her, 'the vulture,' is our best example. At sixteen, she is overly mature. Jill? Not so much. Can I say that? Yeah, we guys notice these things. Can't help it. Either way, it's okay with me.

Or course, this is how I see it. I take it from the yawns and stares out the window by my classmates, that I might be alone in my observations. So why is Mitch so interested? I don't know what to think.She is like looking at a tulip in the middle of our weed patch. She doesn't 'fit. For the first time, I want to stop and savor the sweet aroma of this rare bloom.

"My favorite authors are Shelly, Dickens, and Doyle," she continues.

Oooo… that Mitch. I want him to just flake off, but he pounces right on this one. It's his sense of conquest.

"Hey, nice and tender cut, wouldn't you say, Foster?"

He found a famous poem by her favorite British poet, Byron Shelly. Come on. The next day at lunch, he jams on his guitar and recites the poem in song. Okay, he can strum a guitar. He is not a rock and roller. His singing? It really hacks me out. Think of a Turkish nose whistle roughly in tune. Actually, it must be pretty good. The girls seem to swoon. I do, too, in pain. So here is what he 'sings' to this Shelly guy's poem. Then he copies it, written on a heart. Yes, printed on a red heart. I try not to freak out.

> *Music,*
> *When soft voices die,*
> *Vibrates in the memory –*
> *Odours,*
> *When sweet violets sicken,*
> *Live within the sense they quicken.*

Odours? Mitch can't even spell it right. I'll give you odors. He stinks, and I hate poetry. It makes one work too hard. So why do I care? Somehow, I do. Mitch hooks her with this stuff, and who knows what else. They are off and rolling.

For some reason, I find it hard to breathe whenever I am around Jill. What is this? Others around her tell me they suffer from a different kind of lung issue. They call it suffocation. Those rat finks can't stop repeating her comments.

In English class, we all hear from her:

"The proper pronunciation of either is not 'ee-ther.' It is 'ii-ther.'"

I suddenly lose my perfectly good pronunciation, *pa-tay-ta,* for potato, and start saying *pa-tah-toe* instead. What is this?

In history class, she exclaims:

"Alexander the Great lived here. I am his secret daughter from my previous life."

What? That's heavy. Maybe I am somebody else, too? Perhaps I'm a lost son of a great Greek philosopher, maybe Diogenes. Okay, I suddenly have a huge urge to study all things Greek and Macedonian.

At lunch, it is:

"For *some* of you, I will host a party at my house every Saturday night if you dare. Please wear party hats."

Her parties turn out to be legendary, but right now, I am pretty sure I am not invited. Dancing is not my forte. But just in case, I start reading how to do the new dance craze, the 'twist,' and how to make an origami paper hat. My initial hats look more like the twist, and my version of the twist is as contorted as my pathetic folded attempts at fedora hats.

And echoing out of the restroom the next day,

I hear Jill sing in the most angelic voice.

"Gaius Musonius Rufus is my hero."

Rufus? Who? I now have to know. Don't get me wrong. I do not *normally* lurk around the girl's bathroom. I'm sure there are anti-loitering rules or just plain common sense against the practice.

So, what is happening to me? I feel like a balloon whose opening has come loose and is fluttering wildly around my life. No one knows where it will land. I'm wandering far from me and my practical good sense.

Chapter Three
The Fool on the Hill

George C. Marshall Regional High School
25 September 1964
28 days before Disaster

A little cluster of balloons tied to the front doors is all that welcomes us to our new school. It's located outside the city on a considerable rise of land, a hill where a new military base is under construction. This is going to be my lot, silly foolish me, day after day. I'll need to try on a thousand faces, and maybe one will be loud enough to hear. Most of us live scattered around the city and have to take a blue U.S. Air Force bus to school. I can't help but hear the talk about Jill's parties.

"Could you believe her house?" Mitch whispers to a classmate, Dave. "Geez, I thought I'd have to show my passport to enter."

Then Tom, my best friend, adds, "Once I found the way to her kitchen, I thought the walk-in freezer was a winter playground. Wow, they even have their own private cook. They even have an intercom to find each other in the house. ''"

Mitch has finagled his way to sit by Jill and Marie, Jill's newly acquired best friend.

"Jill, I love your purse. So unique." Marie tells her.

"Thanks. I had it made to remember my grandfather."

Mitch's proximity to Jill really irks Nora. I can hear her feathers fluffing behind me. This day Jill sees me reading my 'Fundamentals in Chemistry' textbook.

"Oh Richard, you're such a... what do you yanks call it... you're such a square!" she tells me in a fake British accent. Then Mitch starts up the chorus, and the whole bus seems to join in.

"Oh Richard, you're such a..," and on it goes mocking me.

It's a common occurrence for me. Then, like the hair product commercials shot in slow-motion I had seen back in the states on the boob tube, I watch Jill shake the most glorious wild mane of reddish-blond rivulets of flowing, radiant, tempting, god-like strands of fleece that all float slowly and sink gently just past her shoulders. I have to buy this product. I need to touch this. I must! But I don't.

Then Nora, yes, the mirror warmer, calls out from her vulture's perch in the back of the bus, her wings stretching out to encompass her little flock of boys nestling around her. With her German accent, she proclaims, "No von look on her! She is Medusa! *Achtung*! Bevare der viggling red snakes of horror slither around das putrid vhite face and *das madchen's* evil eye," then Nora turns on Marie, " protected by *ihr kline slave*."

"Her *kline* slave"? Jill repeats. She knows her Deutsch. "My little slave?"

"That's just what Nora does. Ignore her." Mitch quietly cautions.

Marie has been through this kind of abuse before.

"Don't start anything, Jill. Sometimes the best revenge is just to smile, let it be, and move on."

"I'm smiling. It's just upside down. I'm not going to let her, what's the word, 'chop' you like this, Marie." Up she stands, swaggering towards me on her way to the back of the bus. Oh. Here's my chance to say something memorable to her. My mind races to the best thing I can think of. So, for the first time, I venture to talk to her.

"Ahh, excuse me." I point to the sign above our bus driver. "You're not supposed to stand on a moving vehicle." I'm sure it is a great first impression. Come on. I am concerned about her safety.

Ignoring me, she stops in the aisle right behind me and shakes that mighty collection of heavenly tendrils right over my head into Nora's

face. I don't look back. In no way do I want to vex the wrath of her flock on me.

"Ahhh. Save yourselves! *Ja.* Don't look on *das* monster! *Nein. Nein,*" Nora yells.

Then, right at Nora, Jill utters, "Huh? Nothing happening? Oh,that's right, *du alte Frau,* you were already chiseled of cold stone a longtime ago, missy." And she sashays back to Marie and Mitch. "I said it with a smile, Marie."

I know some mythology. I think this is right on. I'm smiling. I'm not sure Nora really catches her drift as her assemblage also cackles in confusing babble.

When we get off the bus, you can bet Nora and her flock are circling Mitch like he is dying meat ready to digest. Yes! He is going to have to pursue Jill with a bit more caution.

Could I possibly think of approaching her formidable citadel of confidence? Can I actually breach her impenetrable walls to get her attention? Am I that big of a fool? What puts this foolish notion into my head?

SHE TALKED TO ME. I 'TALKED' TO HER.

Chapter Four
Please, Mr. Postman

George C, Marshall Region High School
28 September 1964
25 days before Disaster

The passing of notes became so essential to jabbering on a constant basis. We all look and see, will there be a letter just for me? That's what we all hope. We have this cool way of communicating and protecting ourselves. It really started in eighth grade. We credit Billy B. Where do I start with him? Get a load of the note he wrote to his first crush, Aisha Venkataramanujam. It took a while, but I can spell and say her name now. She is stunning! She is a British citizen. Her dad is a diplomat withthe U.K. Her mother is a Brit from Africa, and, of course, with a name like that, her dad is from India, I guess. She has such a beautiful accent, a mix of English and Hindi.

Anyway, Miss Burnbom was our eighth-grade teacher. She grabs this note when we all are supposed to be taking a silent test and reads it OUT LOUD to the whole class.

Miss Burnbom bums me out. She smells like baggy pants.

But you, my Aisha,

Your eyes are like my mother's crystal glasses,

Sparkling, no matter how you hold them.

Your sweet voice runs smooth as strawberry jam.

Your hair is as exotic as the angel hair on my Christmas tree.

First of all, sweet and smooth don't work together, right? Is it supposed to be '*smooth* voice is as *sweet* as…? Whatever. Her hair is just fantastic, but it is NOT white like I remember Christmas angel hair.

It is a stark angelic black. It is almost iridescent - glowing. She continued reading.

Your skin is like my Snickers bar, all melty chocolate and delicious...

Stop! Billy B. What are you thinking? It is worse to read out loud. (I have to admit, looking back, I like his stuff better than Mitch's poems.) Aisha, I thought at the time, would be devastated. No. She just takes it in stride. I think she still feels a little sorry for Billy B. You can see what prompts the rest of us, more intelligent human beings, to adopt the practice of using code names when we pass notes. We are also far cleverer about when to pass our precious communications. Billy B. has never figured this out.

Yes, code names. I choose and am known only to my close associates as 'Danger 9b.' It sounds cool, and it comes naturally. Even back then, my pusillanimous self-wanted to be considered 'exciting.' However, great adventure, breaking the rules, or taking chances is not in my blood. I am now entering foreign enemy territory.

So, how is Danger 9b going to impress the new skirt, Jill, now known as 'Fortuna'? With a shaky lump in my throat and with Tom by my side for support, I get out a coherent question. "Jill, why did you pick 'Fortuna'?" This may be my third conversation with her. Then she starts up, in her mock British accent,

"Oh, Richard! You are such a bore."

Is that good? She is talking to me. Did she mean that feisty beast, considered fiercely independent and highly intelligent? Oh, wait, that animal is also very hairy and part of the wild pig family. I'd better go with its homonym. Wait. That's the yawning kind. Not so good either. I mean, 'ii-ther', whatever. She is using the dreaded 'B' word for me.

"Fortuna, gentlemen, is a goddess from Roman mythology," she states.

Then Tom pipes in. "Was she a sister to Sterculius?"

"Okay. Who was that?" I ask.

On cue, Tom lets a fake fart fly.

"God of poop and the privy."

We can't hold it in. In spite of our snickers, Jill just glares at us. And through her teeth, she grinds on us.

"Fortuna, you plebeians, is the goddess of fortune, good luck, and fate."

And that makes sense. It fits. For me, she <u>is</u> a goddess! And if I am so *fortunate,* with *fate* going my way and *good luck,* I can rise from my lowly plebeian class to be worthy of pursuing such a heavenly being. I am certainly going to need divine help to pull this one off.

"Our school doesn't offer courses in Greek or Roman mythology, culture, or philosophy. No one here even knows Musonius Rufus," she reminds us.

Rufus? Oh yeah, Rufus in her song. Okay. Right. She has us there. No clue.

But Fortuna? My mom has this record of a choir singing some HUGE chorale piece called 'Carmina Burana.' It starts out with the biggest sound you can imagine singing in Latin:

'O Fortuna! (big voices) Velut Luna! Statu variabilis'

Yes, she is that grand in my eyes. O Fortuna! Maybe I will talk to her again?

Chapter Five
All You Need is Love

In the Russian Embassy
23 October 1964 20:40 hrs.
Day of Disaster

"Aren't you going to say something?" Jill asks.

I need to say something. All I need is… not sure yet. There's not much I can say, but I can cram how to play her game. Is it easy? I mentally slap myself. Now I'm back to reality. I can barely see anything with the dull flickering of the emergency light again, reminding me of the imaginary butterfly flitting around my head. The iron gate still seems to be reverberating within my brain. I hear her mumble.

"I guess you can give me the sock now, sorry," she says.

"I think what you mean is 'sock it to me.'"

"Oh. Right. You can still give me your sock if you need to."

"That's not what it… oh, never mind. I'm solid with it," I lie. Again, I am so confused I have nothing more to say. I'm holding my dad's device. Jill is calling it a 'thingy.' It's still connected to my ear, just to calm and distract me. The guard then bursts back in. He has no idea this is all our doing. But he sees the mysterious contraption in my hand connected to the earpiece and cord protruding out of my ear. I see his eyebrows rise, his eyes flash, and his neck muscles ripple.

"*Что это?*" (What is this?) He grabs it out of my hands and head. "*Иди со мной*". (You come with me.)

He roughly grabs us both by the arms and pulls us through an inner door. We stumble down an interior hall, with him continually pushing us. Stopping at a hallway door, he rips it open, shoves us through the opening, and slams us in. Metal latches connect, and bolts slide into place, sealing our fate.

Jill uncharacteristically shudders just a bit. "Well, this is a little extreme. Maybe I should have thought this one through. And I don't think he liked that thingy in your ear."

She grips my hand tightly. In any other situation, this is heaven. We are touching. But this is not just any situation.

I know this is my time.

I have to step it up - for her.

"We're gonna die," I mutter.

"What?"

Oh. That's not stepping it up.

"I mean, we're gonna die from, from, laughing at this. Yeah, yeah. Someday we'll be history. Ah, I mean, it will be in our past. Not all your fault. We're going to… to… be fine."

I hope.

Now it becomes clear it was history class. I should have known.

Chapter Six
I Should Have Known Better

George C, Marshall Regional High School
10 October 1964
Thirteen days before Disaster

A tiny piece of tightly folded tin foil can really ruin one's life. Protruding like a two-pronged fork from the end of a rubber comb, this fantastic conductor of energy can generate a lot of attention. This only confirms my best instincts about Jill. Stay away! But I can't help myself. It isn't my fault. I can just flake off. But with a girl like her, canI use the excuse of 'I should have known better'? Right in the middle of Mr. Tenney's Crusades lecture, with his back to the class, drawingon the map board,

"And so, from their stronghold in the Kiz Kalisi fortress...

I watch as Jill folds the little aluminum wrapper that goes around a stick of gum. I think it is from a pack of Juicy Fruit flavors.

...the soldiers of the second crusade marched forth and ...

She creases it and folds it around the end of her comb,

...attacked Suliman's army from..."

and jams it into the room's electric outlet.

The flash is like a bolt of lightning, jutting up to the ceiling, a military-grade explosion. Talk about historical and so gnarly. The lights flick off. The windows even rattle. White smoke swirls up from the back wall, and an awful electrical smell, like a bubbling volcanic Sulphur pit, permeates the classroom. Mr. Tenney comes unglued.

"Students! QUICK. Take Cover!" He ducks under his desk.

Nora yells, *"Ach der Lieber! ",* rolls to the floor, and hugs Mitch's legs.

This is definitely against school policy, which may be found on page five in the rules manual or in article two. But it probably doesn't even have to be written down. I first see Tenney's eyes peek above his desk, swiveling back and forth like some undercover agent reconnoitering if the coast is clear. He slowly rises to see our class safe but in commotion. Nora climbs to Mitch's lap. Only I and maybe Mitch have seen it. There sits Jill, crossing her ankles and sporting an expression as if she is in some quilting bee.

"My goodness."

Her hands are folded reverently on top of her desk. "What could have happened?"

Before anyone can say anything more, and against all the natural instincts that scream inside of me to remain calm and unaffiliated, my limbs automatically hurl me straight up,

"Ahh. Yes, Sir. Sorry, Mr. Tenney, I… I… I accidentally brought my left-over magic trick in my lunchbox, and it accidentally went off, accidentally."

"Foster, take yourself to Bean's office. Tell him your sob story."

He's our principal at our school, overseen by the military.

I venture a smile at Jill on my way up the aisle, and she blows me a kiss.

Talk about far out.

<u>So</u> worth it. Mitch gives me an icy glare as I walk out the door. Might I possibly have a chance? Score a run for Rick. I triumphantly march down the hall to the office when it hits me like a foul tip into my catcher's mask. I jerk to a stop. Rick? What is this? What got into you? Really?

I now dub it, *The Jillian effect.*

It is the last period of the day. After I sit for a time, Major Bean enters his office and does a double take.

"What?" He is just as surprised as I am, sitting in front of him. "It was you? Robert Foster's son? Don't waste my time," he tells me. "Let's just start fresh tomorrow. Ok? And leave your magic at home from now on."

Funny, but I don't have to say anything but "Yes, Sir."

I head to my bus. I guess I will have to take up some real trickery if it gets me what I want.

Jill doesn't take the bus home this day. Nuts.

With Jill gone, Marie, her normal seatmate, unnoticed by me, is looking over the row and my shoulder. She sees my open textbook page, the one that says, *Property of George C. Marshall Regional High School.* It has the appearance of the wildest tattooed lady you canimagine, only using the letter 'J.' Almost completely obscuring the stamped label, **DO NOT DEFACE.**

"My poor Rick, you are pathetic. Are you suddenly emerging from your den? If you're going to get her steady attention, can I suggest you go bigger?"

The bus hits a pothole, and my head knocks against the rack overhead.

"Attention? Why would I want to do that?" She gives me that look and shoves my page up to my face.

"You tell me, Mr. Graffiti."

"How is he supposed to go bigger than today, Marie? I mean, for my best buddy, that was outta sight! Give me some skin, man," Tom exclaims, slapping our hands. I've known Tom and Marie for about two years now. We all arrived in Ankara at about the same time.

"Yeah. I guess that was pretty boss." I lie and rub my head.

"Taking the hit for her will definitely get you an invitation to her parties, guaranteed," she says.

"For real?"

"Are you allowed to dance?"

"Of course, silly. *Can* I dance is the better question."

"Great, then you better engage that broken noggin' of yours. This is your best opportunity. You really captured her attention. I was shocked. Not a bad start."

"You think so?"

"Usually, I'm the one steering her out of trouble. So, thanks. But you are something else. I heard that Major Bean was *more* than lenient with you. He certainly knows your reputation."

I twist and kneel backward on my bench, holding on tight to the support bar and staring Marie down, drooping my face as best as possible. Is it pathetic enough? "Why, why, why won't you tell me anything more about her? You're tight with her. What kind of best friend are you?"

"A loyal best friend. Besides, you'd call that rat finkery. Right? Consider it your quest to find out. But I'll give you one for free. She loves theater."

"Oo, Oo, That's good. But is that all you got? Come on. Did youtell her I was in the 'Wizard of Oz'?"

"No. Two years ago? You come on! That's your job. Oh, you were so darling. Oh please. Mr. Cowardly Lion, king of the forest, please say the lines for me."

"Not this again. Don't do it, Rick," Tom pleads, "you won't hear the end of it."

"Oh, pleeeeeease."

Despite what you may think of my reluctant self, I do have this undercurrent for the theatrical. I mostly keep it well-contained. After all, this role was in eighth grade. I give in and put on my character voiceand draw out my own classic lines.

What makes China's wall a world wonder? Courage.

What makes a blond go even blonder? Courage.

What makes the fire ant so hot to trot?

And who's now takin' a moonshot?

They got somethin' that I ain't got?"

"Ha! Courage. You got that right, mister," she immediately jumps in. "Time to step up your lion— r-r-rruff." She paws at me. "With that kind of verse, you can compete. Do you know how Mitch beat you out?"

"Beat me out? I didn't know I was even in the contest. Come on. Mitch is Mitch. But if this is something I can use, how did he?"

"Courage, dummy. He pursues her. At every point. All the time. Anywhere. Any place. It just might doom him, but he is all heavy on her."

"You're telling me HE is the lion?"

"Well, sort of, yes. Time for you to grow some claws and mane."

Sharp nails and more hair count as her advice? Oh. I get it now. Man up. Well, this day is a start, and my heroic act earns me my first note from Jill, as Marie predicted, delivered in a thrown paper wad in English class the next day.

Dear Danger 9b,

I think I may have misjudged you. Please come to my costume party this Saturday! Yes, costume. Surprise me. It will be so fab.

Fortuna

I go back to her comment on the bus. Does this most out-of-this-world, delicious female I have ever encountered in my long, almost sixteen years of life really think I am such a snooze fest, a real square? Ahhhrrrgg! She did use the 'B' word for me. (I am not a Bore. Am I?) Why isn't Mitch, my nemesis, not such a downer?

My lion is now crouched in the tall grass of the savannah, ready for the pursuit.

Chapter Seven
Got to Get You into My Life

Jill's Place
17 October 1964
Six days before Disaster

I'm alone. I get a ride. I'm not sure what I will find here. Am I meant to be near her? Is it easy? Got to get into it, man. Just be a LION. Yeah, man up. Courage. Go Bigger. Why? Am I really ready to storm the gates of the fortress, Jill? That's what is going through my mind as I arrive at Jill's palace this Saturday night. Ok, maybe not a palace, but it is a bastion rarely seen in Turkey. So, being October, she is throwing a costume party. I am ready. I really am a Lion. I still have my Cowardly Lion costume from the musical I was in two years ago. I have to cut space in the feet and paws just to fit inside. They sort of flop around myshoes and hands. I feel stupid climbing into it in the back seat of the taxi.

"What means this dress you wear?" asks my Turkish taxi driver, Bullet Head, "*çok ilginç*"

"Yeah, I know, very strange. We call it 'Halloween' in America."

"You all *deli*." He slowly shakes his head as he spies several other bedecked kids entering her gate, looking like a witch's parade of misfit toys, demons, and goons.

"*Evet*, you all *deli*."

I know I'll be in good company. Turks don't celebrate or understand Halloween. So, we have to keep it inside, or it will freak people out. I pull up the zipper on the side of my felt and wool cocoon getup with one last tug. It's the start of a lot of squirming.

"I guess it is *deli*, crazy, now I think about it. Yes, *evet*. Can you scratch the middle of my back?"

One might think I have leprosy as he gingerly uses his worry beads to lightly rub my spine.

"*Deli, deli, deli,* little Foster."

"Ahh. Thanks, also, for the ride."

I stand still, just outside the stone entrance walls of her… house?… and gaze upwards. The rounded turrets at the corners and a family crest over the huge, heavy wood door make it look like a crusader castle. All of us live in apartments scattered around the city. Not Jill. I was told this, but now it's for real. Her place is as formidable as my quest forher, a quest maybe as silly as Don Quixote chasing his impossible dreams, ignoring reality. What am I expecting, hoping? Well, at this point, I am more squirming from my itchy mane around my face to worry about it. In this getup, I am bound to get some attention, but I really have no plan. Boy, does she have the spread for a party! Someonehere has moola. Lots and lots of it. Now Mitch's pursuit of her is makingmore sense.

At least half the sophomore class, maybe thirty of us, are here, the ones who don't think Jill is Medusa. I must have moved up to the loser half of the class. Ok by me.

Spooks and specters, superheroes and super weirdos, hippies and yippies, and who knows what else all mass together, vibrating around the room as if Pandora has just opened her box of paranormal chaos.But there Jill is, a vertical sparkling halo arc about her head flaunting a flowing silk cape over a graceful, iridescent green dress. She wields a heavenly scepter made from a tennis racket. The goddess Fortuna has come to life. Stalking around her, as if trying to conjure up a love spell with some tribal voodoo magic, is a guy wearing red horns and a red cape with red pants. Guess who? It is so natural for him. Yeah, I check my pulse. It's like a drum solo. And then there is Nora. What? She is festooned as a go-go dancer with full-length black hip boots and a soft blue, thin halter top.

"Marie," I question. "Why is the vulture hovering here?"

Marie is little Bo-Peep, shepherd's crook and all.

"Jill is of the opinion to keep her friends close and her enemies closer."

"But why would Nora want to swoop so low to be with us?"

If Nora was jealous before, looking around this house is making her even more squeamish. This now seems like a pretty good tactical maneuver. And Mitch's attention to Jill is really getting to Nora. So, great. *Willkommen* Nora! She is probably regretting her attendancesince none of her flock is permitted. Well played, Jill. These party animals don't even fill Jill's spacious living room/dance floor.

Jill is playing songs from this great new band from the U.K., The Beatles.

"My dad won't let me listen to these guys at home," Marie whispers to me.

"You have a record player at home?" I ask.

"Yeah, but their lead singer, John, said The Beatles are more popular than Jesus."

"Oh, I didn't know Jesus was in the record business. That would nix at home for me, too. I guess my mom hasn't read the news."

They are huge around the world and much loved by us here in Turkey. We have a few dressed like them in the room. It is The Beatles' first record album, '*Please. Please Me*'. It spins with twelve hit songs we all obsess over as intensely as Cupid's embrace of Psyche. Jill hasa new turntable with extended speakers, and it can really blast out music. It's amazing what sound engineers can do in 1964 playing our vinyl records.

We are all in for a new kind of dancing. It's not like our parents. They would hold on to each other and throw the girl around the dance

floor as if circus acrobats. In the center ring of our big top is now the new 'rock and roll.' Everybody does their own thing, and you don't touch. No way! Like a fast-moving contortionist, the more gyrations of the body, the better.

"They all look like a bunch of the undead trying to emerge from the tomb," I admit to Marie. She giggles as one of our friends, Will, the only one of us that passe as an Adonis, the Greek god of beauty and attraction, but now dressed as 'Hercules,' grabs her for a dance.

"It's haunting time," she calls back to me.

The only objective of this kind of dancing is just to stay in the vicinity of your partner. If you stray too far, you whisk into a vortex of peripheral alien dancers, and someone takes your place. You don'tknow who your partner is half the time. It looks weird with guysbopping next to guys, especially those caught in the outer vortex, as I study the phenomena from my safe observation post in the library.

'Rick, you have to ask Jill to dance,' keeps throbbing in my brain. I just can't do it.

I talked with Marie and Aisha, Karin, and even Nora.

"Vat are you doing here?" Nora asks me.

"Hello, Nora." And I walk away. It is the safer choice. But not before I hear little Billy B. confidently walk up to Nora. He is dressed like a bumblebee, stinger and all. Billy B. got an invitation?

"How's about you and me, little lady, take a buzz on the dance floor?" he says as he thrusts his stinger at her boots. Whoa. This kid really is fluttering far from his hive. I hear Nora blast out what probably are numerous German expletives, sounding like a recording of a raging Hitler, including *'du kleine Schieße.'* "You little...." And I'll leave it there.

I find my way to Jill's library, trying to keep my six-foot flailing tail in control. I don't know what all this stuff is in the room, but it all

appears to be old and, I assume, valuable. I stop at a corner and slide up and down, trying to get some relief to my backside. Some things are mounted securely on walls or behind glass cases or nestled between a modest number of manuscripts. It has that musty, irresistible odor of old parchment and ancient cow leather.

I pull one volume off its prominent position on a shelf. It's hefty as a bowling ball and has a soft but tough cover that feels like the seats of a fancy vintage limousine. It reads, *"Historiae Alexeandri Magni"* by Quintus Curtius Rufus. Rufus? Not the same guy Jill was singing about. His name was Musonius Rufus. Maybe a cousin? I don't know what the book is about, but I recognize it to be in Latin. That's enough for me. Pretty cool. I put it back.

On a small table is a program from a funeral held only last month. Next to it is a small portrait perched on a desktop tripod of an old, distinguished-looking man,

The result of proud parents, there are bits of Jill's artwork in one little corner. Yeah, I see her portrait of Mitch in art class every day. Justglad it isn't hanging here. My tail then gets tangled in her plaster cast we all made of our hands. My tail pulls it off the table and lands in my pouch. I catch it before disaster shatters it on the floor. I'm thinking, aren't we required to keep these at school? Her artful mold is as gracefulas the ancient Greek statuary I had seen in Athens. I fully admire it as I place it back. My hand hesitates over it, then caresses the smooth curvature of her palm and then each individual luscious finger. This might be the closest I'll ever get to holding her hand. My mind really lingers on this one. So irresistible.

A curious domed helmet with a fine mesh screen hangs on one wall. A sword hangs above it. Below it is a trophy with Jill's name on the plaque and the writing in French. It sports a figure of a girl holding a sword in her hand. Maybe it's Jill posing as 'Joan of Arc'? Hmm. She's been in some kind of duel. Next to this trophy is another with a horse

figure on top. Again, the writing is in French, but her name is on the plaque. I guess she likes horses.

It all starts to gel into this solid image of her intimidating stronghold. She is rich. She can sing, she's an artist, rides horses, can wield a sword, and speaks a few languages. I can see she can dance and apparently likes theater, according to Marie. Oh, did I say she is rich? Then there is all the rest of her glorious and curious self. I pull back my lion mane from my head.

My Cowardly Lion is backing off big time.

Some of the things in the room are labeled. There is an old decorative parchment under glass with what appears to be Arabic writings, with a plaque that reads, 'The Timund Qur'an – Persia 15th Century" And whoa, there is one book I know, a very rare original, an 1830 first edition of the 'Book of Mormon.'

On a shelf, higher up, is a statue of a lady's head carved out of black stone with a neck almost as long as a swan. I carefully pull it down when all the lights in the library go red. A buzzer blares loudly, repetitively, in the room. I twist around, not knowing what to do, when in rushes Jill's mother, Mrs. MacGregor.

"Oh! I should have told everyone. This room is alarmed." She pushes a red button by the door, and all goes quiet. The soft library lights glow on again. A man in a black suit bursts into the room. "It's all right, Charlie. Just an accident."

And he walks away.

"I'm so sorry, Mrs. MacGregor." I met her earlier that evening.

"No harm done. That is an original bust of Nefertiti." She takes the statue from my hands and admires it. "For centuries, she has been the epitome of beauty." She turns it for me to see. "My father acquired it as a reminder for Jill. Nefertiti, in addition to her famed beauty, was one of the few Queens, over thousands of years, who became ruler of Egypt,

and essentially, all the known world in the 18th dynasty." She lets me hold it again.

"I guess Jill has something to aspire to."

Mrs. MacGregor laughs, "I hope."

"Who is the other statue?"

"You should know her, Mr. Lion. She's Aphrodite, the Greek goddess of love and desire. Not Jill's favorite. Why aren't you out there with your friends?"

"Oh, I'm sorry for the intrusion, but, this is far more interesting."

"That is completely acceptable. Jill loves this room as well. You are welcome. You're Robert Foster's son?"

"Yes, mam."

"What a good man. Let me thank you for being Jill's friend. It hasn't always been easy for her."

"I… I hope she considers me a friend. We don't know each other very well yet."

She stares at me, then tilts her head, "well, I think she may be missing out. We'll just have to see about that. Give her a chance."

Whoa. That is a leap. Do I have an ally in her mom? She takes Nefertiti from me and goes to replace her and stops. She takes down what may be a photo hidden behind the statue.

"So, this is where she hid it. Jill hates this picture," being careful not to show me.

"Why is that?"

"I don't think she is ready for anyone to see this or any of our early family photos. Sorry." She seems uncomfortable, so I quickly change the subject.

"Mrs. MacGregor, may I ask who this man is?" pointing to the portrait.

"That is my father, Pierre Fontaine. All these things and much more were his... hobby. Jill was his only granddaughter."

"I'm sorry for your loss. Were they close?"

"Oh, father was so worried about Jill. He doted on her continually while he could."

Worried? This strikes me as odd. No matter.

"I think Jill mentioned she has a brother?"

"Oh, Jacque. Yes... Ah... He's eight years older. He doesn't live with us anymore. Off doing his own thing, whatever that is."

I want to ask more questions, but she excuses herself to do her chaperoning, taking the photo, and replacing Nefertiti as she leaves. I look around a bit more and then wander into a nice little reading nook and sit down.

While getting up the gumption to ask Jill for a dance, up jumps her cat, Chuk, on my lap. Like Kipling's 'Jungle Book' snake, Kaa, the kitty's penetrating, radiant green eyes could almost hypnotize me. She also slithers back and forth over my costume's pouch. She then progresses to a paw 'march' on the same path, extending then releasing her claws into the felt of my costume, over and over.

"Oww, take it easy there."

As one feline to another, at least someone notices me. I give her a few strokes and get a nice purr. She seems to like the fluffy end of my tail and continually paws at it.

"Even if she likes yours, whatever you do, don't yank hers," Tom says. He is wearing his baseball uniform with his team's name, 'Indians,' emblazoned across the chest. As a fellow ballplayer, he doesn't have to stretch hard for that one.

"Why would I yank her tail?"

"Trust me. You don't want to know. Your baseball career would be put on hold."

"Is that how you got that lump on the side of your head?"

"No, not Chuk. Don't tell anyone, but yesterday I gave Karin a kiss outside her apartment building."

"She walloped you?"

"No, the building's caretaker whacked me. I forgot you don't do that stuff in public."

"Oh, you mean the *kapaci* did that? Ha! A public display of affection? You broke the no-no on P-D-A?" I nudge him with my shoulder, and he smiles with a confident nod. "How... how did it feel?"

"It hurt. What do you think?"

"Wise guy. You know what I mean."

"Don't tell me you guys don't believe in kissing?"

"I'm solid on kissing. It's just – well – that's not yet my expertise, Romeo."

"You should give it a try sometime. But you just might have to break the law," he warns as he rubs his head. He notices, then takes the stem of a red tulip out of the vase next to us and holds it up.

"Another redhead. Hey, did you know the Tulip was first cultivated right here in Turkey?"

I take a breath. Here Tom goes on what Tom does. "No, I didn't."

"The Sultan's headdress was the shape of the flower, so they named it after the Turkish word for 'Turban.'"

"I will congratulate the Sultan next time I see him."

Redheads. Yeah. Lucky for me, not everyone likes redheads. They get a bum rap. They scare some people because they look so flawed. And she scares folks because she acts so odd. Don't believe me? Try this.

When our bus drops her off at her stop, she does this weird dance as she moves down the sidewalk. She reminds me of a jumping goat that can almost leap out of its corral. She propels herself straight up, legs straight, then vibrates her legs in the air. Then hops on one leg, then another, continuing this pattern for as long as I watch through the window as the bus drives off. Maybe it has something to do with her Scottish heritage. No Turks would do this, so they just stand clear asshe waltzes or whatever down the sidewalk.

"I can't see why you're so stoked about her," Tom comments, "unless it's the money. Wow. There's more than one odd thing about her. For one, those eyes."

"I know. One blue and one brown. She's so choice."

"I didn't think that was possible."

"Tom, this is Jill we're talking about. Anything goes."

Jill, (ahhhh), just the mention of her name electrifies my senses. I'm pretty sure 'Jill' is the name of the song the Sirens sang to a tied-up Odysseus to try to lure him into a shipwreck. I think I'll need to have Tom bind me to a chair to resist her. No convenient mast is available. Jill, to me, is a Siren in disguise, an iridescently big-blue-eyed (and brown eye) earthly temptress. It's odd, but no boy thinks about her the same as I do. I don't think Mitch does, either. Can't figure him out.

Just then, Jill floats over to us. Her essence is like a bouquet of blooming Turkish jasmine or maybe the scent of a tulip. Anyway, the fragrant flow arrives in the air before she does, and I take it in deeply.

"What's that smell?" Tom asks.

"Quick, Tom, tie me down."

"What?"

Her dazzling sky-blue eye, adjacent to the soft, delicate, glorious glow of her angelic face and swan-like neck, looks down in pity on the two of us mere mortals. Tom stays put. He is not scared or affected by this Siren redhead. Of course, I don't *know* if her exquisite skin is soft. It sure looks like it. I really want to find out.

"Hi there, Chuky." She picks her cat up from my lap and strokes her. You lucky duck. "You know, she doesn't make friends with just anyone. You must be special." She pulls my fluffy mane headdress back up over my head and rubs it. "Love those fuzzy ears." She turns to Tom. "Hello there, Tommy, you naughty boy. Karin is looking all over for you."

"How did you know?" He quizzes her. She just winks at him.

"What are you both doing here, party poopers? Be fun, you two. Come on. Get up. And oh, Mr. Foster, you wild thing, you owe me a dance." She wiggles her hips and then flits away.

Whoa. Wow. Ok. That makes things a little easier. That is perhaps the second time she's talked to me. Things are looking up. Maybe her mom is at work on my behalf already?

"Do girls keep any secrets? And don't you call me Tommy."

"You told me, didn't you, lover boy?"

"All right, you nailed me on that one. But did you know redheads are so rare, they occur less than one percent of the time?"

"Yeah? Well, that redhead exists as less than one percent of the one percent," I say in awe as she turns in the distance and gestures for us to get up. "And that makes her the only one of her kind. Do you think they taste different?"

"Well, now you're talking my language. Maybe Mitch knows? Come on, Lion, time to untie yourself and stalk your prey," slapping me

on the back and pulling me up. "Let's get her into your life."

I think I will now wreck my ship on the MacGregor's rocks to listen to the Siren's song and figure out how to dance.

Chapter Eight
Back in the USSR

In the Russian Embassy
23 October 1964 21:05 hrs
Day of Disaster

"I don't know how lucky we are with these boys, but there are worse places to crash," I say as we look around our cell.

The room has a couch with a pull-out bed, a flower-pattern upholstered high-back chair, a nightstand, and a reading lamp. I see no chains or instruments of torture. Thankfully, there is a W.C., a small room with a toilet and sink through a door on one wall. The tiny bulb of another overhead emergency fixture provides our only light. We sit on the couch, huddled together. We hear a flurry of activity faintly through the building, alarms still blaring in the distance.

"How long can they keep us?" she whispers. "My dad will be so worried."

"My dad will be so furious. I might get grounded for life."

"I'll check for visiting hours," she coughs out. "Do you remember Major Powers?" I am hoping she will not remember because it is on my mind.

"Yeah. Well. It turned out alright for him, eventually."

"Wasn't he in the Air Force when he was shot down over Russia a little while ago?"

"He was flying a highly classified spy plane taking reconnaissance photos."

"How many years did they keep him prisoner?"

"Two. They exchanged him for a Russian spy about the time I arrived in Turkey."

"I can't afford two years. Does torture hurt?" she blurts out.

"What are you talking about? We're kids. They're not going to keep us." I assure her with a sudden burst of uncharacteristic nerve. She holds on to me even tighter.

"Listen, do you wanna know a secret?" I start to softly sing The Beatle's tune that got me into this mess. Yeah, I blame the song. She follows up with the next phrase, which talks about not sharing the secret with anyone else, and I end with one word of the next lyric, 'closer'. She hugs me. I shift uneasily, even squirm. A little voice in my head is yelling, so I quietly say, "Jill, I have to confess something."

Don't do it, Rick. Keep your cool.

"I know already. You are a terrible dancer."

Chapter Nine
Beatlemania

Jill's Place
17 October 1964
Six days from Disaster

From my perch in the library nook, I think everyone is a terrible dancer except Jill. What is cool about The Beatle's music is just about every song has something that reminds me of Jill. All of them are love songs. All of them. How boss is that? You can sing along and get away with telling someone (the right someone) that you like them, no matter how silly you look, without saying it directly to them. I then hear the Beatle's song loud and clear floating from the dance floor, entitled,

'Do you wanna know a secret?'

It rings through me like a hip heavenly chorus with a rock and roll beat. There it is. I got it. Now it just hits me. Secrets? I hear girls get jazzed about secrets. That's it! How about I have a secret? Do you wanna know *my* secret? This is the start of something big. Yeah, a big problem. It can buy me time. Thanks go out to The Beatles, I guess. So even though she invited me, I still need to call up the *nerve* to ask Jillto dance. Just maybe, the lion in and on me is emerging and shaking. I guess that's good for dancing.

Like entering the mystical land of Oz, this strange new world of relationships is perplexing. One thing I know tonight, I want a slow song to dance with Jill. Why? Because with a slow number, you have an excuse to dance close and hold hands. Yes, you can actually touch! And I want so much to touch Jill. Dancing slow I can fake. I'll be ableto test my earlier observation of heavenly softness, to actually hold Jill'shand and feel her close. That is my plan. I have to wipe the wetness from my lion paws as I gaze into the writhing pit of demons on the dance floor.

'*P.S. I love you.*' is the only slow song on the album. The lyrics are about letters and *love,* and it is my first big chance with Jill. We all love to write notes to each other on crumpled pieces of paper and pass them back and forth. This is the plan and the dance I aim to have with Jill. Slow, nice, and quiet so I can hold her close and *maybe* get the courage to sing in her ear, 'P.S. I love you' and get away with it. However, just when I have the song cued up and Jill on the dance floor with me, someone (MITCH) switches it to:

'Twist and Shout'

"*SHAKE IT UP, BABY, NOW*" comes blasting out. It is the most raucous song on the album. Not a love song. It's for the new dance craze, 'The Twist'. Jill is really rocking the twist, rotating her middle back and forth and leaning this way and that. Her moving hips are electrifying something in my brain. My twisting looks stupid, especiallywearing a fuzzy brown covering. Reading about twisting and doing it are two different things. Luckily, Mitch looks as silly as I feel, dancing right across from us with the vulture. His devil tail looks like a malfunctioning pressurized air hose with the end missing, waving all around. This is supposed to be my slow number. But I keep going, dancing in her vicinity, trying my best to copy what is going on around me. My fuzzy mane around my face isn't enough to dull the vibrancy of the blaring music. We get to moving when she steps on my tail, andI knock into her.

"Oh. Sorry!" she yells.

Twist and Shout!

I gather up my tail and hold the fuzzy end in my hand.

"Why did you wait so long to ask me to dance?" She yells.

Twist and Shout

I let go of an awesome sneeze into my fuzz and yell back, "Yeah, lions like to prance."

"Is that the thing you're doing, a prance?"

Twist and Shout!

"Take a chance? Sure, I'll take a chance," shaking that fuzzy end at her.

"Oh yeah? What kind of chance?"

I look down at my pant legs protruding out of my cut-off lion paws.

"I don't know what kind of pants, cotton, I guess."

Twist and Shout!

"No, silly, NOT PANTS, CHANCE. What chance are you going to take?"

I finally hear her clearly.

"Oh, yeah. A chance. With you!" I get brave suddenly. Jill does this to people.

"What did you have in mind? Hmmm?"

I'll hold to my theory she likes surprises. BAM! Just then, I am whapped in the face by a flying devil's flopping tail. Then body slammed a few feet away. I turn and see Mitch gyrating away.

"Oh, sorry there, Leo," Mitch yells out. Then the music ends. It's the last dance of the night. Jill glares at Mitch and walks away to gatherand say goodbye to her guests. I take a planned detour through the library. Object in hand, I head through the hall and take a right into the kitchen, where I see Jill entering at the other end. Ooo busted.

"There you are. You get lost in the savannah?"

I pull my mane off my head to hear better and straighten my hair. I shift from foot to foot, glancing anywhere I can but her. I keep my free hand moving to distract from the one behind my back. My eyes flit all

around at the cooking pans and shiny pitchers and other stuff adorning the walls and tables.

"Nice jugs…"

"What?" She says.

"Aah… ah… I mean pitchers, yeah, and pots," I quickly add, in various vocal octaves.

"Ok, Mr. Dance, take a chance in your cotton pants, man, I mean darling lion. What did you mean by 'take a chance'?"

She's actually talking to me, again, along with a good question. I feel as stiff as the Tin Man in Oz, but I manage to get out, "Well. I'd like the chance, some night soon, to… well, you heard that tune tonight, 'Do you wanna know a secret'?"

"Yeah. I love secrets."

Ah-Ha! This is perhaps the confirmation of the first piece thatmakes up the huge girl puzzle in my mind. They can't resist not knowing a *secret*. I take a deep breath, my heart pounding, palms still wet, and continue.

"Well, me and my cotton pants, we'd like the chance…" I stop. Suddenly, my mouth is a very dry savannah. I almost choke. I guess you don't sweat in your mouth.

"Yes?"

".. to share my greatest secret."

"Hmmm. Along with that cute fuzzy mane that was on your head, you are also getting interesting, Mr. Foster. I would love that."

We set the time for a date. This coming Friday.

I did it. Pow. Take that Mitch. And he doesn't even know about it. Finally, here is my 'in'. My Lion has roared or maybe just squeaked.

I'm not sure which. I can only imagine what kind of note I will get from Mitch once he knows.

Chapter Ten
Hey Bulldog

My Apartment, Ankara
22 October 1964
One day from Disaster

Can I really talk to her? I have. I can talk to her, finally. I feel like some kind of bullish dog! It's now Danger 9b, Fortuna, Mitch, and a secret. That's where it is, just hours ago. *Hoş geldin*, that's Turkish for 'welcome'. Welcome to my world. That is the situation I am pondering, okay, stressing about Thursday, the day before our first date. This makes it the day before yesterday since it's now well past midnight in our cell. How did it come to this? How is it that a few of us American and International kids are living here in Turkey, the land of baggy pants? Yeah. The old Turkish men here wear a weird fashion of oversized baggy pants. It's a look left over from the Ottoman empire.

"I've been assigned to our station in Ankara, Turkey. We leave next month," my dad exclaimed one day a few years ago.

"You gonna raise birds now?" I innocently ask.

There is such a country. The Black Sea is on our north, and the Mediterranean Sea borders our south. We are between Europe and the countries of the Middle East. For thousands of years, this has been the crossroads of conquest and contest. But, at this time, it's now a contest between Mitch and me. Yeah, a great battleground. I'm in the land conquered by Alexander the Great, occupied by the Byzantines, captured by the Romans, then invaded by the Crusaders, and seized by the Ottoman Empire of old. Enough of that. I get plenty of that from our history teacher, Mr. Tenney.

Our fathers are either in the military or are diplomats who work at the American, British, Canadian, or German (Nora's dad) embassy. Some parents work for corporations, mostly the giant oil firm of

Tumpane that finds oil for the Turkish government. Most of us live scattered around the capital city of Ankara, living among the 'natives' in apartments or, in Jill's case, a house, if you can call it that.

Since I am a baseball player, to keep track of Mitch, I decide to keep score, as they do in baseball. I call it my rivalry 'box score'.

I have penciled the box score on my desk in science class. I keep it simple, just lite lead on wood, a number under the headings Danger 9b vs. Diablo.

RIVALRY BOX SCORE:

Let's see. Mitch. One point for the poems. Not my judgement but Jill's. I'd dock him two. He was already up two for being her "boyfriend". But I get three points for taking the hit in class. And two, for telling her I am going to tell her my GREATEST secret. Even so, I may still be behind. But this is just the first inning.

Did I mention Mitch picked Diablo, Spanish for 'devil', as his code name? I won't argue with that.

Stealing the line from The Beatle's hit song, 'Do you wanna know a Secret?' Now weighs on me. Yeah. Why did I say I will tell her my greatest secret? I did not realize it would be the momentous tectonic shift in the whole course of my young career. Now *she* wants to know. And so do I. That means I must come up with one. Ahhhhhrrrgg! It's enough to freak me out. It's the night before our date, and I've got nothing. NOTHING.

I brainstorm. Am I a descendant of your Rufus? No, it won't work. I don't know any Greek. The Beatles have asked me to record with them? No. Dad will not let me grow my hair out. I like Brussels sprouts?Yeah, right. That's a winner. It goes downhill from there.

At home that night before my ordeal and after lights out, I am under my covers. I have a flashlight and the latest book of 'Hardy Boys'

mysteries. I think it out again. 'Okay, Rick, time for Danger 9b to take courage and step it up', my mind pounds into me. Yikes. It's all happening tomorrow. *Get attention.* Get her attention. Hmmm. I start humming The Beatle's tune, 'Do you wanna know a secret?'

Okay. Rick, go big or go home. Wait, I am at home. I don't want to be at home. I want to be with her. Hmmm. It must be something spectacular. What would the Hardy Boys do? They are like teen Sherlock Holmes. These two brothers in fiction stories help their detective dad solve mysteries and crime cases. It set my brain in full creative mode; Dad, Hardy Boys (don't be boring), Danger 9b, mystery (think fun), adventure, secret. (Don't be boring).

Ha! Got it! But, oh boy, will she really fall for it or just bug out on me? Will I really do this?

Can I really get away with it?

It's not that I am the most truthful guy in the world. However, I am taught to tell the truth. It is my nature, mostly. Mom tells me my tongue will turn green if I ever lie, and only she can see it. I try not to stick my tongue out around her. It makes eating a little difficult. But this is way out there. My tongue just might grow a forest with this one. I'm not great at pulling off a puffer. But it has to work. It just has to. Courage lion. You Bulldog you. Do it! This will be my own experiment in terror. I mean, she already has a boyfriend. I've only talked to her a few times. But now I have a plan, a date, and a made-up secret to share. I am putting my reputation all on the line, I must confess.

Chapter Eleven
Tell Me Why

In the Russian Embassy
23 October 1964 21:25 hrs.
The Day of Disaster

"About that confession, Jill."

Unwanted droplets form on my head, and I glance at the W.C. Do I need to?

"A confession? YOU? You did something wrong?"

Don't do it, Rick. Keep it together. Keep it going.

"Ah. Ah… a… yeah. It's about me. No. Nothing… wrong. I mean. Yeah, besides my dancing. Ah. This… ah …. Well, maybe it's no secret… this whole boy-girl thing. It's new to me."

Well, at least, this is the truth.

"Confession time? Ok. It is for me, too. Mitch is my first, ah, boyfriend."

"What? No."

"You hardly know me."

"Yeah. But, tell me why you… you and… and… Mitch?"

"Do you remember, I was kinda out of it, staring at you when you first told me your secret?"

"Yeah. I thought I had hypnotized you or something."

"Not far off. I was… thinking about us. And Mitch? Oh, he is interesting. But you? You are a ten-piece puzzle."

"Why just ten?"

"Any more than that, and I wouldn't try. Only, I don't have a reference picture to put you together."

"If I'm a ten-piece puzzle, eventually, you can work that one out. But girls? You all are a box of a thousand pieces, and all the corners are missing."

I do get a laugh out of her. But it's short-lived. The siren stops, and our table lamp flicks on. We hear our door being unbolted. A man with a mustache as large as his face, wearing a well-tailored suit, enters with our guard.

"You!" He points at Jill. "You vill come vith me."

Chapter Twelve
It Won't Be Long

George C. Marshall Regional High School
23 October 1964 09:30 hrs.
The Day of Disaster

It won't be long until she's with me. It's tonight! I'm freaking out. To cope, while I sit in class, I etch the letters a little deeper in the dark grooves on my wooden desktop, J-i-l-l, next to my box score scribbles. I know it's against school policy. What am I thinking? I'm not. It's like hearing Turkish for the first time. Confusing and alluring. It's a brisk October, but my clothes are a little damp. Am I just *deli?* How did I get to this point?

Jill turns to look at me, and I quickly look away. Is it in time?

She makes this shushing sound to catch my attention.

I look over, and she wriggles her nose at me. It would be her hips if she were standing. I check my pulse. Carelessly, she lets sail a note, folded like a paper airplane, which soars around and lands in the next aisle. Before Tom, who sits next to me in science, can pick it up, the note is scooped up by Mr. Tollet, our science teacher.

"Mr. Foster." Mr. Tollet's voice jerks me back to class. He slaps my graded homework on my desk.

"Yes Sir?" I stand up to the side of my desk as required of us.

"Do you even know how to use a dictionary?"

"Yes, sir, we have the latest 1964 edition of Webster's at home."

"Then use it next time. Your spelling is a-t-r-o-c-i-o-u-s."

"Average, yes, Sir."

He glares at me. "Average?" He just shakes his head, and the class snickers. "What is this nonsense?" He unfolds the plane. I slink down, ready for the beat-down. He reads aloud,

Danger 9b,

I am so looking forward to this night. So excited.

Fortuna

"Fortuna? Ha. Well, whoever you are, Danger 9b. I hope your Monday homework gets done. Sounds like this goddess' plans might just fry your neurons into a bowl of mush."

" Whoo-hoo," says the class almost in unison.

Fortunately, our note system works. We're not ratted out. It really is only a dozen or so of us with code names, so most of the class doesn't know either. No reason to flip my wig about it. That quirky little smile emerges from the face I just can't get enough of.

She is now expecting something exciting from me. I can see it in her gleaming countenance. She raised white eyebrows. Am I such a yawn? I try to reassure myself. No! Not after tonight.

Maybe I can do my Cowardly Lion bit for her? Oh, Marie, you know me best, why can't you just sell me? Ahhhrrrgg.

This place, to me, is as strange as the mythical land of Oz. I think Oz is really a Turkish word. There are families here with the last name of Oz. So, it all fits Turkey, Oz, and the classic 1939 movie and book. Jill arrives here in our Oz, red ruby shoes and all, to skip along our own yellow brick road with fellow foreign teens in a historical land with odd customs and wild landscapes.

Tonight, only my heart will be skipping along as we follow that yellow brick road. Not sure where it will lead. I keep telling myself. I AM NOT BORING. I'll use that mantra just to stir me out of my den and out of my forest of solitude. I am a LION. I'm strong and fierce

and, and, and, and... scared of... well, the unknown, maybe even myself under the Jillian spell.

I look over at Mitch. His attention is also *not* on science. He now knows I'm taking his girl out tonight. I so want to propel a well-placed spit-wad, delivered through a drinking straw, to catch him behind one of those flappy ears. Ooo, take a deeper breath, Rick. I'm sure there isa rule against flying projectiles either as notes or as weapon delivery.

Tonight, it's Fortuna and Danger 9b.

Chapter Thirteen
Things We Said Today

The streets of Ankara
23 October 1964 18:05 hrs.
The Day of Disaster

"Rick, she's going to remember all the things you say today. Don't blow it," Tom advises as I get off the bus, trying to calm me down. He doesn't know my real plan.

In preparation for the evening, I discover dad has again borrowed this cool device. It looks like a portable transistor radio, only much smaller and sleeker. People have transistor radios, but not like this one. At least, this is what I think it is. I've seen it once before. Do I dare touch it? But this night, I see his 'emergency' suitcase he keeps by the door is unlocked. This doesn't happen. And I need backup. I need legitimacy. This is it. I fish it out.

The device is really far-out, with a wire that connects a hearing piece to plug into your ear. This is boss, man. It's not the bulky headsets that have been around for years. This thing is tiny and fits into my ear, connected by a single wire. New. Maybe even secret. How does he have it? Well, more of that later. No one has these. I'm not supposed to have it, but I take it along with me to look cool this night on my date with Jill. I figure out how to turn dials to listen to distant radio stations.

As planned, I walked to her house. I pause and take a deep breath, gazing up again at the realm of ramparts of her heavenly abode. I push open the gate. Why I tiptoe down the long walk leading to her massive, solid wood front door, I don't know. The knocker reminds me of the face of 'Marley' from Dicken's 'A Christmas Carol'. Oh, that's right, one of Jill's favorites. My knock sounds to me like a bomb exploding, wreaking havoc through the entire house, given my heightened anxiety. She opens the door.

49

"Ricky!"

I don't know what she's done. Make-up, hair, earrings, necklace? I think I will melt right here. She'll have to stuff me back together. What hits me the most is that air of sweet, intoxicating jasmine and tulip that encircles me.

"Hello, Jameela." I manage to get out.

"Jameela? You got the right house?"

"It's Arabic for 'beautiful one'." Where did that come from? It was all so natural.

"You are a most surprising person, Mr. Foster. You know that?"

There are not many things international teens can do in Turkey for fun. And we normally do them in a group. I don't want to be with other friends this night. So, we go walking. It's daring of me. Walking is sometimes an issue for me. But Jill seems patient. It's a cool night. She wears a green turtleneck sweater. Oh, do I like girls in sweaters? Her hair curls all around and swirls in smooth sweeps over her shoulders. The red against the green is so striking. One side of her hair is pinnedup with a tulip-shaped fastener. Not as wild as usual but just as tempting.

"What's that thing in your ear?" she asks me.

"Oh. Check this out. Just a… a… something my dad has. Take a listen."

I hold it to her ear. It's a new tune from The Beatles, broadcast shortwave from the BBC station in England, thousands of miles away.

"Ooo. I like this one, 'I wanna hold your hand'," she sings along.

"This is the BBC? I used to listen to them all the time in London. *Wauoh, il est superbe,* a pretty advanced thingy and headset."

"Well, you know, got to keep up with 'things'."

"What else does it do?"

I need to think fast. I don't know. "Measures your pulse, transmits radio waves, records stuff."

"Records?" She turns it over to examine it. "What's your pulse right now?"

"Ahh. I haven't figured out that button yet. Probably fast."

"Impressive." She hands it back to me, and I pocket it. Our steps clicking on the sidewalk, like out-of-sync Broadway dancers, only intensifies how awkwardly silent I am. Then loudspeakers fire up from a mosque the next block over.

"Allahumma Rabba hadhihidda'watit-tammati…"

"Time for their evening prayer."

"I know that's not Turkish. What's he saying?"

"Yeah. Always in Arabic. The language of the Qu'ran. We were introduced to that last year. You may get it again at culture night."

"So, what's he singing about?"

"It's more of a chant. I don't remember exactly. Something about Allah and congregational prayer and Muhammed, their prophet."

"I'm used to it now. I'd better be. It's five times a day."

We pass a local policeman on routine patrol, a *becgi*, walking his normal route in the neighborhood. His wooden whistle bangs lightly against his Billy club. They use soft whistles at times throughout the night, each with a different cadence, to communicate all is well with other police on nearby beats.

"Iyi aksamlar memur bey," I politely say. (Good evening, officer)

"What did you say to him?"

"Good evening, sir. You are passing the goddess of fortune. May your days be so fortunate as mine and full of good luck." She nudges me with her shoulder. I stagger just a bit.

"Yeah, right," spoken with a rolling of those fabulous eyes. "I love this night you picked, Ricky. So romantic. And we're alone."

Alone is part of my plan. So important. I like her calling me Ricky. So intimate. Wait. Did she just also say, 'romantic'? This is getting good.

"What could be better than a cool, sparkling wet Ankara night in October?" she tells me.

Along with the gentle aroma and the freshness of the earth right after the rain, her own glorious scent continues to wash completely over me, rendering my prepared speech almost incoherent.

"Look at that golden light… uh… bounding off the wet streets. It matches your hair, reflexing… ah… like some Turkish Whirling Dervish." Reflexing? Bounding? Come on, I rehearsed and rehearsed something different well beforehand. It was supposed to come off as *reflecting* off the streets and *dancing* off her hair. What happened? *The Jillian effect.* Wait. I don't mean to imply her hair is a Whirling Dervish. Oh no. And the Dervish are dancing, not the light. Oh, never mind. It is better than most of Mitch's stuff.

"*Wauoh.* You are being funny and very poetic these days. And yes. My reflexes are good," She giggles.

Yes. She has the most luscious laugh. It starts low in the troposphere and soars up high into the mesosphere, stays there and swirls around a bit, then dips ever so slightly down to the stratosphere. I can float on this all night.

What? Did she say I'm funny? What's happening to me? This is not typical of me. Maybe it's a mistake to bring up poetry right now, too,

considering Mitch. Just then, a stray cat (there are a lot in Turkey) crosses our path. It stops, looks up at Jill, and meows.

"Oh, aren't you the cutest?" We both bend down to pet her when our hands briefly touch on the back of the kitty. Jill doesn't pull away. I do. "You and my Chuky would be best friends," she says as she cuddles and strokes him.

"I now dub thee 'Chairman Meow'."

"Oh, he's a Siamese cat?"

"She is now. *Zaijian*, goodbye, Chairman Meow." She gently places her on the ground, and off the contented creature goes.

"That's the only Chinese I know, besides hello, *Ni hao*."

I am envious of that cat. Jill's purse then slides off her shoulders to the ground. I stoop to pick it up.

"Cool sack. So soft."

"Not a 'sack'. It's a very rare leather purse. I had it made from my grandfather's gift of an ancient, exotic, cured hide."

"Oh. I saw your grandfather's portrait in your library and the funeral program. So sorry about him."

"Thanks. He was... the best and most generous."

I carefully place the purse back on her shoulder. I don't know what it is about girls and purses. What do they hide in there? It is a major unsolved puzzle piece. All I know is that it's *forbidden to look.*

Anyway, we continue our stroll, walking so close. It's cold enough to barely see our breath condense, then disappear. The cool, damp, and clean air fills our lungs and races my heart. I feel so alive, but why are my hands so wet? It's not from the air. I wipe them as secretly as I can on my cotton pants.

'Should I do it now? Is this the right time?' I desperately ask myself. I have not forgotten the lump on Tom's head. Affection in public is not the culture here. It offends most people. Not in my book. But it may be against the law. Wow, what do I do? It's dark, and the coast is clear. Okay, Rick. Go for it. Like a lion cub's first step onto the savanna, it is new territory for the Cowardly Lion. Check my pulse. My walking pattern is a little erratic, so it's a great excuse. My now exaggerated uneven steps slightly bump my little finger into hers.

"Sorry," I stammer. She smiles. I can feel the warmth emanating from her irresistible body. Our little fingers just barely touch again, thenshe intertwines our pinkies. Is this really happening? Something ticks in my brain and sends a wave of pleasure through my whole body. Yes, from just our pinkies.

Then she weaves her fingers through mine. Oh, well played, Miss MacGregor. Pow, Pop, Wow, ZZING. I think I've stuck my fingers in a 110-volt socket. It is lightning! It is so electrically charged I should be grounded. Did somebody just whack me? A distinct sense of new warmth, like hot chocolate racing through all my veins, just engulfs my body. I can hardly speak. So, I just try to smile to conceal my explosion of emotion. This is the first official time we've touched. Fess up, Rick. It's the first time you've really touched a girl on purpose. And yes, her skin is so soft. This is more than just neato. It's outta sight.

"This is nice, Ricky. My hand was cold," she whispers and just stares into my eyes. And stares and stares.

"Jill, Jill, you okay?" She looks lost, then jerks back into our moment.

"Oh. Yeah. I'm great. Just noticing you… your eyes."

I hope that's a good thing. I recall The Beatle's tune we heard earlier, '*I wanna hold your hand,*' and I start to sing it softly. She joins in. I guess she doesn't care one wit about our PDA.

"So, this big secret of yours, is this it?" She teases, swinging our hands.

"Well, this is no secret now, but no, it's not." I want to build up to it, but what other time would capitalize on this moment? The low, long whistle of the local police *becgi* echoes gently from blocks away, indicating all is well in his sector. It's a sign. Where we walk is a soft dark. Just the faint glimmers of a few porch lights from the houses above us cast speckled shadows through the remaining leaves of an overhead sycamore tree. The walkway reflects the gold and red leaves, caressing the wet ground as a mild mist swirls around us. Jill's jasmine-tulip essence, mixed with the clean, crisp air, was overwhelming all my senses, even my good sense. So, I charge ahead.

I stop and face her. I then back away a step. I take her other precious hand in mine. She looks down at our hands, then up into my eyes. Her delicate face, in the dim light, is full of anticipation. This better be good, Rick.

"Jill," I whisper, heaving out a big sigh for dramatic effect.

"I, yes, little ol' me – and **my** whole family… we're on a special assignment… " (big breath here)

"We're all spies for the U.S. government, members of an Air Force unit in the Office of Special Investigations."

Ka-Pow. Take that Mitch. Yes. Is this spectacular or what?

Now, I know what you're thinking. Spies? Really? That's the best you can come up with Rick Foster? Hey, this is the 60s. Spy stuff is boss, man. It's the grooviest. Besides, I think she digs it.

All she does is stare at me, expressionless. So I stumble onward, "My mission tonight is to stake out the entrance to the Soviet embassy. You want to… to… to help me?"

Now, I don't know what to expect, but she steps closer to me – staring at me again with her bedazzling eyes and an astonishing expression.

Nothing. She says nothing. She moves towards me. I think she is going to kiss me. Yes! Will I get my chance to taste her unearthly essence? I think she wants to. I want to. Oh yes. I don't know what to do. Maybe I can just hold still and hope her aim is good? She holds my face in her now warm hands and pulls me in for a very tight… hug. I feel the heat of her cheek on mine and the heavenly form of a female press and caress me.

"Yes. Yes," she whispers.

Bing, zing, Ka-Pow, Do wa Ditti, gum pum! Up the socket voltage to 220 my fingers are in. I mean. I am in ecstasy! Okay! And I think holding hands is great.

Now, I'm not of the belief I can get lucky by telling lies. Okay, well, it's working here. I am not sure she knows about the taboo on public affection. I don't care. This is night, we are alone, and it all adds to the excitement. She believes me!

"You have to promise me not to tell anyone, especially grownups,"

"Promise." she blurts out and hugs me again.

Not sure how I earn that one.

A guy walking past us on the other side of the street yells,

"*Çok Fina! Çok Fina.!*" (Very Bad!) Jill blows him a kiss. I pull her quickly up the street as she belts out our theme song, "*I wanna hold your hand*!"

I'm getting far more than I was bargaining for. So, I'm satisfied. I still wonder, will I ever feel our lips touch? My extreme anticipation reminds me of seeing my Christmas present under the tree I just know is a BB gun, only to unwrap a baseball bat. Ok. That's still good. I really

think she wants to kiss. I have an idea of maybe why she doesn't. Maybe she's a bit self-conscious. Or maybe she doesn't want me to get walloped by a passing guy.

Chapter Fourteen
A Hard Day's Night

The streets of Ankara
23 October 1964 20:15 hrs.
Thirty minutes from Disaster

The night is passing quickly. I've been working like a dog to keep this all going. With my potential head 'whapping' man, who was across the street and now far in the distance, she asks,

"So, what's a stake-out?"

"It's our target for the night. The embassy of the USSR, Union of Soviet Socialist Republics."

"Yeah. I know their name and it's just up the street. What do you want to know about the Russians?"

"Well, we watch a target, stroll around, observe, and take mental notes, watch."

"What's the fun in that?"

Ok, an interesting question that I'm not prepared for.

"It's all part of my assignment tonight. You get it. The Russians are our cold war enemies."

I am hoping that she understands that a stake-out is just what spies do. That is the whole of my plan, nothing more. Because it means I can hold her hand for that much longer and be with her, alone, without anyone else. This is a good plan. I have no other. My mistake.

The embassy is on a big piece of land with a bunch of buildings in the complex. Of course, it's surrounded by high stone walls. I know there is the main ornate structure just up from the front gate. My heartis still pounding, and this gorgeous female is holding my hand.

Rick, don't wimp out now.

We get to the embassy gate. She pauses. It's wide and high and of solid metal construction. Next to it, there is a speaker and a call button on the wall. Why do I mention this when we are to just walk by? Wait. This is Jill we are talking about.

"They sure put out a welcome mat."

She walks over and presses the speaker button. Yes. The Russian doorbell. Ding, dong, hello to our enemies up there. Obviously, someone is going to answer this call. Ok. 'Hello, what do you want' is what I expect. What is she going to say?

"Jill! I… I… " I am too stunned to say anything, still reeling from her hugs. The old coward in Cowardly Lion is starting to re-emerge.

Hello. She doesn't have to say anything because the gate just immediately creaks open.

"Look at this. I guess they're expecting us. Come on," she says and pulls me up the drive, "let's have some fun."

Now, I know I told you my name is Danger (9b). But now, note the added parenthesis to emphasize my modest rank. My body is saying,

> *"DANGER! Danger (9b), RUN AWAY!*
> *This is a job for a Danger 1 A special agent,*
> *Not a lowly 9b pretender."*

"Jill! Are you crazy?"

"Maybe a little."

"No one goes in here without official business." Ignoring me, she goes on,

"Look at this place. Are we 'staking out' yet?"

I know I'm walking, but I feel she is dragging my carcass on a bed of rolling pebbles, but that's just the sound of my teeth grinding away.

Don't say anything more, Rick. Don't do it. My mind races. Don't blow your cover story. You're in this now. I manage to spurt,

"Oh. You're, you're… doing great."

She continues to lead me up the driveway.

"Did you know the grounds of any embassy are deeded to that country? We're really in Russia! So exciting." She is practically glowing with enthusiasm.

Yeah. But, since they allow no tourists to visit the USSR, there is no reason for us to be here. This means, as we pass through the gate, yes, we are on Soviet territory, but now we're subject to Soviet laws. And oh, I forgot to tell you. Jill's Dad? And MY dad?

When is a good time to say this?

My dad is a spy!

Yes. It is true. Don't ask me how I know this. I'm not supposed to know this. How else would I have come up with such a spectacular whopper and gotten away with it so far? He is working undercover in counterintelligence for the OSI, the Office of Special Investigations in the Air Force. But Jill's dad?

He is the U.S. military Air Base commander, Colonel MacGregor. This really complicates things just a bit, don't you think? Trust me, it does. This is just now hitting me. Dad's words are now wildly firing off my synapses.

"Rick. We've talked about this. You don't talk about what I do. I'm a businessman. Got it?"

Arghhhh. So, there you have it. On the one hand, is a not-so-fun boy (according to Jill MacGregor) taking a huge risk, having a father with a sensitive government position. On the other hand, you still have this same hope-to-not-be-too-boring boy, taking an *unpredictable* military leader's daughter into, essentially, cold-war enemy territory.

Well, actually, she's taking me. I am pretty sure we are heading into big trouble, like Frodo Baggins entering the Dwarf's cave of Moria, probably swarming with Orcs. But – this is Jill. Here's my chance, Rick. There's still time to back out. You can confess right here and now.But no. I don't want to blow my chance with a goddess.

"Isn't this cool? Look at these wide sweeping grand stairs, like a French Napoleonic château!" she says gleefully, starry-eyed, and me fully petrified.

These stairs lead up to an imposing front door. Do you remember those guards in Oz, with the big coats and massive hats and spears marching at the Wicked Witch of the West's castle entrance? Well, as we get to the stairs, only a single guard hurries out to meet us. I'm not relieved. No. He has on a very impressive Soviet military uniform.

And he has an equally impressive sidearm. It may as well be a spear. I mean, it's a gun. He hasn't drawn it yet. He stops, looks at Jill, and is immediately slain by her irresistible presence. Bang! Yeah, buddy, I know how it feels. Then he comes to his senses.

что ты хочешь? He asks.

"What does he want?" I whisper.

"I'm sure he wants to know what we want, you know, 'vat do you vant'?" she says in her best Russian accent. Then she turns to him and goes right on in her best British accent,

"How do you do, my good man? Why are you Rush-in around? (She turns and winks at me) We're actually seeking the British Embassy." I quickly tell him, in my bad Turkish,

"*Üzgünüm. Üzgünüm. Onu Boshver! Onu deli,*" which in Turkish loosely means,

"I'm sorry, forget her. She's crazy."

Jill looks at me, still a bit surprised. She doesn't know much Turkish yet. Score! The guard doesn't know what to think, nor does he understand what she nor I am saying. He just gestures to us up the stairs.

"*Da, Spasibo,*" Jill tells him, then whispers to me, "It's the only Russian I know." The guard ushers us through the immense front door and has us pause inside a small waiting room. He then exits through an interior door. So, we sit. We wait. I'm trying to act cool. I don't say a thing. I take in a deep breath. I do it again and try to smile.

"Now, this is what I call a stake-out." I nervously nod my head in silent agreement. Jill looks around the room décor.

"So Bolshevik." We still wait. Jill gets up and walks around the room, and investigates a few of the plaques adorning the walls.

"Look at this printed Russian. I can't even read the words. What a weird alphabet. They're probably extolling the virtues of communist oppression." I still say nothing. Is there a law against this? Check my pulse now.

Don't blow it, Rick.

So, I take out my short-wave radio or whatever this thing is and plop my tiny speaker into my ear. Maybe I can figure out how it should measure a pulse or pick up another great tune.

"Now I get it. That's your dad's 'special' com set. Can you hear them?"

"Oh, well," I think I will just go with it. "I didn't want to say anything about it until you knew."

"Tell them we're waiting for further instructions."

Other than us, it's still quiet. She's done exploring the room and sits down next to me. She gets fidgety.

"Want some gum?" Jill hands me a stick of Juicy Fruit brand gum and unwraps the aluminum foil from around another stick for herself. For her, it's not for chewing.

It does not occur to me until it's too late.

Chapter Fifteen
Help!

**In the Russian Embassy
23 October 1964 21:16 hrs.
Disaster Hour**

So yeah, a stick of gum. That's how we got here. Help? Yeah, I'm gonna need somebody. Not just anyone. Then, the Russian's question jerks me back to our predicament. I should do something.

Jill doesn't move.

"I say you vill come vith me," the mustachioed man sternly repeats. She stiffens as the guard reaches for her. For the second time in my short lifespan, I have no control. My limbs just propel me up.

"No! We stay together."

Did I just say that?

"I'm the one you vant, ahh, want."

The guard grabs Jill by the hair. That does it. No one but me touches that hair! I knock his hands away.

"Hey Buddy, hands off." He flings me across the room like I'm a tin toy and pins me up against the wall.

"Nyet!" the suited man yells. The guard releases his grip on me.

"We're just kids," Jill blurts out. "What are you holding us for? All we wanted were some brochures for my school project on Russia." It is brilliant thinking.

"Vat is this?" the man demands, holding up my 'radio' set and earpiece.

"Oh, that. That's my birthday present – to him." She is so fast with another excuse.

"Vere did you get dis?" He demands again.

"The Pazar," I add, glancing at her, "the Ankara marketplace. We both saw it at the Pazar. A man was selling it."

"No. I don't believe you. Dis vould cost many rubles, dollars."

"Oh. I know. I have plenty," rubbing her fingers together, "family money – my grandfather's"

"Vat are your names?" We dutifully tell him.

"Vat work you fatter do?"

"My father works for the Air Force," Jill states calmly.

"Foster? Vat you fatter do?"

"My father? Ah, yeah. Toys. He sells toys."

"Really? ROBERT Foster? Toys? Dis, not a toy!" he yells, holding up the device.

"I told you. I bought it at the Pazar," Jill insists.

He commands the guard, who takes Jill's purse and dumps the contents on the nightstand. They spill all over and onto the floor. Whoa. All the forbidden items keep pouring out. My eyes go wide, I'm sure. Among all the stuff I can't recognize, there is one thing I do. Mitch's poem with the heart on it.

The man rifles through the items and mumbles in disgust. He looks at us with additional suspicion, then abruptly walks out, whispering something to the guard.

They lock us in again.

I head for the W.C. Jill starts to recover her trea sures.

"Are you alright in there?" she asks after a while. I hear her plainly and realize she has heard all my groanings just as well. I open the door.

"Yeah. Better. Slightly. Jill, they know my father." ·

"I noticed. Small world, I guess. But Danger 9b, you attacked a Russian soldier! Rarrrr." She paws at me. "You are truly a puzzle, Mr. Richard Foster."

"He was more like an Orc."

"Nah. Not that scary, but it does make for a better story."

"Jill, you gotta know, that wasn't me. I don't know what happened. But you were brilliant."

"Thankfully, that homework story worked."

"Miss MacGregor, I have wandered far from the real Rick Foster. Trust me."

"We'll work on that." She starts to fix her ruffled hair. I so wanted to help.

"There's a mirror in there," I say, pointing to the W.C.

"Ahhh, no thank you. No need to meet Sterculius just now." I turn red.

We're mostly silent for a time as we wait and wait. An hour passes, tick, tick, tick. I pace the room while Jill fiddles in her purse, endlessly rummaging through its contents. Another hour goes by, tick, tick, tick. I break our silence with,

"Jill. About your grandfather. I'm just curious. You mention him often."

"No one like him. Ever. He was a professor of History and Archeology. He was a Philanthropist of the highest degree. A man of adventure."

"So that's where you get it."

"What do you mean? Our money?"

"No, NO. I mean, your sense of adventure. Your knowledge of history."

"He was also a very mysterious man. I guess some would call him eccentric and quirky. Always full of surprises."

"What about your brother, Jacque?"

"Oh. A half-brother, really. My Mom was married before – a long time ago. We don't talk about him. He sort of went off the deep end."

All of this talk is a good distraction, but the reality is sinking in. Something more is going on, and the worry grants silence to our banter. More hours pass. Jill rests her head against my shoulder, jerking awake periodically as I struggle to keep my eyes open. Steps in the hall lead to metal moving on our door as it finally unbolts and opens. By now, we were guessing it was almost daylight. Our guard gestures for us to come out. We warily followed him back to the waiting room and out the main front door we had entered hours before.

… ati Muhammada-nil-wasilata wal-fadilata waddarajatar… The chant and call to Morning Prayer are already echoing in the distance. So, we know it's just about dawn. Believe me. I'm doing a morning prayer in my heart. What's happening?

Our guard leads us down the exterior steps when we see a dark limousine parked at the bottom of the drive near the gate.

This is it.

When the Soviets took over the Baltic countries again after World War Two, Stalin, the Soviet despot, secretly deported hundreds of thousands of people to deplorable camps in Siberia. They starved to death or succumbed to extreme cold. Stalin eventually starved millions of people - on purpose.

I think we're off to the gulag – the Soviet prison camps. I know about Soviet prisoner exchanges. You know, a spy for a spy? They're going to keep us for an exchange. After all, Jill and I 'invaded' their territory. One not-fun and terrified boy for one Soviet spy. Of course, it would probably take three Soviet spies to trade for a goddess, who, by now, is like a ragged doll, her hair mostly straight and her eyelids almostshut... I'm sure I don't look much better. Only I have witnessed her vulnerability. Somehow, this endears her to me and gives me more of what I lack – a bit of daring.

Jill takes my sweaty hand, and we move very tepidly down the driveway to our fate and the dark limousine.

69

Episode Two

Danger 9b and the Acrobats

Chapter Sixteen
I'm So Tired!

We reach the limousine at the bottom of the embassy drive. Our guard stands aside as the passenger door opens, and a U.S. Marine stepsout to open the back door and gestures for us to get in. His dress white hat and uniform have never looked so good.

We drop Jill off first. Mrs. MacGregor is waiting for us on the street outside her house.

"Thank God." She says as she opens the door. Jill slowly lets my hand go and mouths, "Thank you," as she exits.

Thank you? Never are two words packed with more possibilities. I'm sure I look like a sloth, barely hanging on and so tired. I haven't slept a wink; but my mind is still racing. Thank you for not yelling at me for almost getting us abducted? Thank you for protecting me? Thankyou for sharing your secret, for a nice, exciting evening (and morning), being my friend? My eyes are drooping. My clothes look like a wet sponge, drained on one end, and dripping on the other. And yet feeling so… alive.

Orange rays are just now bouncing off my balcony window when the limousine lets me out. Dad, the real spy, arms folded, his foot tapping like a wild drummer, is at our building's entrance. The veins in his neck are as big as Turkish worry beads. His face taught, not a lineto be seen. I want to shrink very small like a cat on broken glass andjust tiptoe past. It is not to be.

"What in the world were you thinking?" He says each word quickly, starkly, and direct. "I knew ten minutes after you arrived inside the Soviet compound you were there with the Colonel's daughter."

"But dad, it wasn't… I mean her… I didn't know…" His eyes are as blurred and red as mine, so I finally admit, "Yeah, pretty stupid. She had a school project on Russia. I was only… helping her."

His temperature only rises. "That's just not like you! It's created havoc for me – in more ways than one. You have no idea what it took to get you out of there. We'll talk later, young man. Go to bed."

It's worse only a few hours later when my door bangs open, and Mr. Espionage himself stands there, almost frothing.

"Where is it, Rick? Did you get into my case? I've told you that was off-limits!"

I sort of hear him and groggily try to answer, "Wwwhat?'

"What happened to it? Does this Jill have it?"

"You mean your little thingy radio?"

"No. No. No! This can't be. It was not a radio!"

I sit up a little and rub my face. "Ahaaa, they took it."

He stares at me for the longest time. Here come the worry beads again on his neck. I thought he'd have a stroke. Instead, he puts his fist through my wall.

"I'm toast," he mutters as he leaves my room and slams the door.

It's a little hard to sleep now. The hole in my wall is glaring at me. The Russians know my father's name. I didn't tell them. What do they know about him? It becomes clear to me now. I've really blown it for my dad. This time, the 'device' was in the suitcase he always keeps by our door. 'For emergencies,' he always says. I am never to mess around with it. My brother, Steve, then enters the room,

"Whoa, lover-boy, what did you do with that girl last night? My, my, aren't you the one coming of age." He gives me a thumbs up and leaves, singing a parody of last year's hit by the band, the Crystals, 'Da

Do Ron, Ron'. "I met her at midnight, and her name was Jill. Ya do run, run, run, ya betta run."

I don't see Jill for a time after that, or anyone else for that matter. I do NOT confess the specifics with dad, especially the bodacious, gnarly lie I am carrying. That's it. Grounded for being a dumb kid. Ok. I'll take that. He never says anything more about 'the thingy that acted like a radio and isn't'. I couldn't even go to school. But Jill does try calling. Dad does not let me speak to her.

O Fortuna!

I always wanted to know what stuff is between my walls. Now I know. It looks like my insides feel; raw and messy. I'm assuming his 'toast' is not good. Have I blown my dad's real cover? Is he now a target? My head starts to hurt, throbbing like it's trying to keep a beat with a drum set kick drum. But I'm stuck. How am I going to keep this charade going? It sounds stupid, I know. I get it. A dumb idea. But I came upon it naturally. A family of spies. What can be cooler? Only my brother could never pass the qualifying test. That's the truth.

We are off to a DOOZI of a start. I've no one I can really talk to about it. I am sure her folks will ban me for life after all the fuss. This is getting complicated. What did she just do to me? My poor lion's been knocked off the yellow brick road, lost in the forest. I'm in way over my mane. Can I really keep this going? I've just molded a new and very breakable image and a secret to protect. I will need to invent more adventures ahead for the new AGENT Danger 9b in Turkey, the land of baggy pants. I'm watching my pressure gauge needle bounce closer to the red line. Where to get ideas? Well, I've got my collection of 'Hardy Boys'– teen adventures to draw from. Maybe there. I've plenty of time to think.

And, of course, there is still Mitch. Long before our current contest, he picked the code name, 'Diablo', and wears it proudly. Yes, I've said it before, 'Devil'. Does that fit or what? This is now the official start of our own cold war,

Danger 9b versus Diablo.

It was game on.

RIVALRY BOX SCORE:

I am sure I am up 2 points over Mitch after this great adventure. Maybe even 3 points!

Chapter Seventeen
'Twist' and Shout

As if the new dance craze isn't enough for me, near the end of my grounding, my dad throws me a new move that is freaky far out.

"Rick, as dumb as that stunt was, I hear you acted admirably to protect Jill."

I think I'm still in trouble. I look at the hole in the wall. It matches my insides and my new place to store secret notes if I ever get any again. I haven't seen Jill yet. I am bracing.

"From what I heard. I think I like this girl."

What? Did his sound waves correctly reach my auricle cavities?

"I'm glad you are coming out of your shell. Do you like her?"

What? I don't know what to say. So, it comes out… "Yyyyeah… kinda. She's sort of a mystery, though."

"You just figuring out that girls are so enigmatic? Yes, sir, that is progress. It's about time you showed some initiative. You are well on your way. If you figure them out, let me know."

"Yes, Sir. I… I... I will keep you… informed." Wow, my dad has given me a new puzzle piece, *enigmatic*. Where's my Webster's? Then he adds,

"I think you should keep that friendship going, or whatever it is. You're only young once."

Whoa? What did he just say, and what did that mean? My possum brain is treading very slowly and carefully now. What does he know? He seems to know everything these days.

"You mean I'm not grounded anymore?"

"No. Just… I'd keep her close if I were you, ok?" My father is now a 'Chatty Cathy' doll. They're new. This is a toy where you pull the string on their back, and they say dumb stuff out loud. I think I need to rename dad 'Freaky Foster' or something. Pull his string and get free love advice.

"What about the toast?" I ask hesitantly.

"The what? Oh, yes. Well, let's say you have greatly complicated my situation. I'll handle it."

My head is spinning. Thoughts are tumbling all over like kids in a carnival funhouse. Is my dad giving me relationship counseling now? I mean, we've had 'the talk', and it was, you know, informative, but that was just general stuff. But this, this is getting personal.

"Keep her close?" I ask. "Ok. Yeah. Sure. That's a good plan." I still have not told him about the whopper I cooked up for Jill.

Really? Really? I am thinking. Dad just smiles. I think I just entered the ecstatic state of Nirvana, coming close to the ultimate good in life. Am I dreaming a fab dream? I have permission to spend *more* time with Jill? What opening in the great heavens is bestowing such a gift onme? O Fortuna! All the goddesses must be smiling at me, even Sterculius. I don't get it, but I'm not complaining. How are Jill's folks going to feel about it? Our apartment phone rings and Mom calls out,

"Jill on the line."

My heart leaps, and I fly to the receiver.

"Rick, are you okay?"

Oh, how I love to hear that voice.

"I'm all juicy fruity, Jameela."

She giggles. You know that giggle. I continue, *"The weirdest thing happened. My dad doesn't seem as upset right now and thinks you are peachy-keen."*

That was a new phrase going around.

Then she jumps in, *"That's why I'm calling. Even after our adventure, my dad says he likes you."*

"Wow. Really? Wow! That's Fab. Far out." I am stunned again. I've only met Colonel MacGregor once. *"He likes me?"* I pause, thinking, then add, *"Well, what about you?"*

"Oh, you know how I feel."

What I meant by that question is asking how she is doing. I am not bold enough to ask how she feels about me. Now that's just the problem. We, boys, don't know how girls feel. We don't even know what to ask, let alone interpret the reply. When we do ask, inevitably, it's the wrong question.

These facts are mixed in with those thousand puzzle pieces. I don't even know where to start. I've dumped them all out and just stare at the unbelievable complexity of the task. Well, maybe that's a second piece down, next to the *enigmatic* one, and in place; *they never tell you how they really feel*. I guess I'll get used to that. Talking to boys, girls never seem to come right out and say what they mean *unless they're mad*. That is a different puzzle piece. But all this sounds really good. I *think* it sounds good. We end the call with new plans to meet.

Chapter Eighteen
With a Little Help from My Friends

Instead of taking the bus, my dad drops me back at school, finally. I have a little time before my first-period art class. Being absent from school can be fixed. Being tardy is one thing you don't want to do. They are usually very strict. Hey, we're run by the military. What can I expect? Our teachers aren't members of the military, but boy, do they enforce the rules. If tardy, you have to stay after for 'detention' work at some point. Not fun. So, I am mindful of not adding late to absent. I look for some of my friends. I know I can get by with a little help from my gang. I get handed my first note.

Dear Danger 9b,

You're back! Hope you're feeling well. Oh, I am so honored to know your secret! I had no idea. Fortuna told me all about it. How can I help? As far as your feelings for Fortuna, she gets it. Run to her! She is full of life and mystery. You two are such a match. I will help where I can. You are the best boy I have ever known.

Athena

Wait a minute. Who is Athena? And why does she know my secret? I start learning some things I missed. In the hall, I find Jill and Marie.

"Who is this Athena?" They look like two Cheshire cats beaming. As if one goddess isn't enough, there is now Marie. She's usually there, thank goodness, to keep Fortuna in check. Jill, being the international citizen that she is, just naturally gravitates to Marie, as exotic as she is, in a totally opposite way. With her Jamaican accent and her black skin, Marie <u>is</u> exotic. But she is Marie, so nice. What's Jill doing?

"I changed her code name. Now that we're all junior agents, 'Lily' was not going to work for Marie."

"Junior agents? What? Jill, Lily is a perfect name for Marie – no teacher is going to connect her to that."

"It's so gentle," Marie agrees.

"Be bold, Marie! Be bold!" Jill uses it as an excuse. Jill takes her art ruler in hand. "By the power of all that is vested in me, basking in the region of the gods," she taps Marie on each shoulder and declares, "I bow before your grace and dub thee, Athena, O mighty Athena, Goddess of War!"

"Yeah. Yeah. We've been through this," Marie says.

"Not in public. Now, it's official. I have a witness and the counsel from Roman philosopher Musonius Rufus, way back in Roman times." Jill declares.

"Oh. Now, this Rufus enters the picture. Who is this guy?" I ask. "He

taught that women should be as educated and bold as men and study philosophy to better themselves. He was so ahead of his time."

"Oh. Bold. Philosophical. Ah, okay," is the mild and timid response from Marie, "was there ever a black goddess?"

"There should have been. Anyway, there is now," Jill adds.

So, Athena, it is. Fierce, fiery, bold, and daring as they come as a character.

"Oh, okay, if you say so," says Marie.

She is as mild as unbuttered white bread, or dark rye bread in her case, and sort of mom-like as they come. With her tight curls, her hair tucks under just below the ears, parted in the middle, with slim-rimmed glasses and a really lovely, round face. Fortuna and Athena forces to be reckoned with.

Now Dave pulls me aside.

"Delighted to be of service, Danger 9b. It probably will end very badly but I am now junior agent, Mr. Mustang."

"Junior Agent? Mr. Mustang?" I turn and look at Jill, who gives me a bigger smile.

"Really? Dave, have you changed your name again? All the teachers know you are obsessed with cars. Your last name is a car. How obvious is that?"

"Yeah. You're probably right. I'll get busted and inexorably humiliated. Those American Mustangs are so cool! Have you seenone?"

"You keep the model on your desk."

And on it goes. The first mistake is to tell Jill to keep it a secret. Did I forget the real first part of the puzzle? *Girls love secrets*. They just don't love keeping them.

"Jill, what were you thinking? This is supposed to be *our* secret."

"You told me not to tell any adults. So, I didn't. Just Marie. OK, then I told Tom. Well, then I told Dave and Will and Mitch."

"MITCH? MITCH? What? Why him?"

"Oh, he's really good at observation. He gets people. Ricky, you are going to need all the help you can get."

She calls me Ricky. How can I go on and protest anymore? "Okay, but no more." Tell a girl a secret, and you may as well hire a skywriter to spell it out in the atmosphere.

Tom corners me and pulls me under the stairwell.

"So, who are you now?" I ask.

"Spitball."

"What?"

"Did you know that Ed Walsh dominated the American League from 1906 to 1912, mostly on the strength of his spitball? He still has the record for the lowest earned run average."

"Have you all gone *deli* on me? All the teachers know you are a pitcher and I am a catcher. It's not going to work."

"Well, Princess loves it."

"Princess?"

"Shhh. Keep your voice down. Karin is now 'Princess'."

"Oh yeah, your girlfriend with figurines of Snow White, Sleeping Beauty, and Cinderella hanging on her purse. That makes sense. No Teacher will guess that. Wait a minute, she knows?"

"No. But since some of us are changing, she doesn't want to be called 'Downer' anymore. I like it. But that's not the issue. Buddy, whatare you thinking? You told her you were a spy? Come on. That's fartherthan far-out. I know better."

"You can't tell anyone. I mean, *you can't tell anyone*."

"My lips are sealed even if my mind isn't. I think you're taking way too big a bite out of this story. You're like that mad dog in a wrecking yard that's chomped down on an intruder, and he can't let go. How are you going to pull this off?"

"Tom, you gotta promise. I'm working on it."

"It's safe with me, OK? I'll help you sell this. Actually, it sounds fun."

"What sounds fun? And what are you two hiding from?" a passing Jill asks.

"Who are you now?" I ask her.

"Don't worry. I'm still Fortuna, and Mitch is keeping Diablo."

"Well, that's a relief. Once a devil, always a devil."

"Rick, be nice."

It was all OK. I have the upper hand now. Jill and I are… something. Not sure what, but a whole lot better than it was. I don't know what to do next. The problem is Mitch is going to up his game somehow. Diablowill be on duty. I can feel it, probably with a dumb poem. Go ahead – try. He doesn't know our folks have put us together. Take that! The bellrings for first period. We beat feet to art class.

Chapter Nineteen
I Wanna Hold Your Hand

"Miss MacGregor, I need to hold your hand to grade your hand. Your hand cast was to be here, not home. I'll tell you something I think you'll understand. You get a zero on this assignment." Mrs. Finney, our art teacher, chides Jill.

"Wait. When did we get this assignment? Where was I?" I quickly ask.

"I don't know, Mr. Foster. Where were you? Oh, that's right, out." Miss Finney replies.

"I can't seem to find mine. Can I make another cast?" Jill asks.

"That's terrible. Where could it have gone?" Nora says out loud. "We all know Mrs. Finney was grading them today and doing boondoggle designs."

I squirm a little and retrieve my cast from the art closet.

"Miss MacGregor, double up with someone today."

"Mrs. Finney, Jill can share mine," Marie says. With that, Nora walks by and 'bumps' Marie's desk while 'tying' her shoe. Marie's plaster hand shatters on the floor.

"Oh, dear. I'm sorry, Marie. That was so clumsy of me. Maybe you should have kept it in your box like you were supposed to."

"Marie, here, you take mine. I don't feel so well." As if drunk, I stagger up to Miss Finney's desk. "I gave Marie mine, Mrs. Finney. I don't…" I let loose, emptying my bucket into her garbage can.

"Ahhh. Get away!" Mrs. Finney screams.

I can't tell if I'm really good at this spontaneous stuff or if I'm really sick. Carrying the garbage can, I head to the nurse's office. I know the school health code requires it.

While making a quick recovery in the health room, I re-examine my note from Athena. There is something more to worry about. She calls me 'the best boy she's ever known'? This is a lot to live up to. I don't know how to read between the lines. Is there something else there I don't see? All I focused on was 'run to her'. I think this is the lyrics or title of some song. I don't know it. I should have known I could not control this. When the bell rings, Jill tracks me down to make sure I'm okay and hands me a note.

Note from Fortuna to Danger 9b:

I hope you're OK? That came on suddenly. I think Athena is hoping you will dance with her at our cultural night. Please! Do this for me? You know, you should really pay her some attention, and while you're at it, can you tell Spitball next period that Princess feels he has been ignoring her? She did NOT get a note last period from him.

So is the nature of our notes. Let me review it. The girl that I really like, who I think I have won over for a time, wants me to spend time with her best friend? Not that it would be bad, but this is not my plan. Danger! Danger 9b! I see trouble ahead. Before the late bell rings for second period, Will stops me in the hall.

"Hey, boss. Welcome back. I hear you don't like our new names."

"Not you, too?"

"So, what would you pick for me?"

"Something not Texan and not Canadian. Like 'Poopsie'. That would throw them off. Marie and Aisha would love that."

"Poopsie? Yeah. That's hacked, man. Try 'Sarge'."

"Oh no. Good grief."

"And Dave's love, Aisha is now 'Jane'."

"See, there you go. They will think, naturally, she's a girl. It makes it too easy. You too. Your dad is a Sergeant. And you read comic books that feature that character's name. Are you all gone *deli*? You don't care if the teacher corps captures your notes and easily deciphers them?"

"Ok. What's your next suggestion?"

"Oh, I don't know. How about 'Pookums'? Athena will love that. They will never catch on."

"Yeah, that won't catch on because I'm kissing it off. Are you twelve? Pookums? Uhgg. And I ask you for love advice?"

Will, or now, 'Sarge', really likes Athena. I think I am the only one he has told this to. So, I try to think up things that will put them together. I didn't tell him that Jill had asked me to dance with her. So, I pipe up.

"Will, look for her at Cultural Night. Just show up at her side. And don't tell her about the latest Superman episode. OK?"

"What do I talk to her about? I only know about comic books."

"You're asking me for romance advise? I can say this much. I doubt she wants to hear about Batman, either. Maybe she likes 'Archie and Veronica' stories?" They are two characters in comics about girls and boys in high school.

"I don't read that stuff."

"Well, you better now."

Our second period's gone when I spot Tom.

"Hey. Did you write Princess yet?"

"No. I flaked out." Tom is shorter and squatter than I and sports a crew-cut hairstyle. He is all muscle. He has this goofy sense about him for facts no one cares about. I don't know where he learns this stuff. His low, gruff, scratchy voice has a comic element to it like he was a

character on some cartoon show. Oh, does that add to his charm with the ladies. But he is only interested in one, Princess. She is one pretty girl. Yeah, I noticed, but Jill is my focus. So, I don't argue with him. Spitball (Tom) and Princess (Karin) it is.

"I'm just saying, don't ignore Princess. But you know, I've got the only androgynous name of you all – neither male nor female. No teacher will know my gender."

"Oh yeah, they will. Easy."

"Danger? What's wrong with that?"

"I'm not talking about Danger, but no girl would pick that. It's the 9b. No girl wants to be associated with any size labeled 9b for anything. That would be humiliating. Hey, did you know people first used to answer the phone by saying 'ahoy' instead of 'hello'? And off he goes to our third period.

So, to keep it all straight, I make mental notes because it will be fatal to write them down. Consider these my mental notes:

TOM = Spitball

KARIN = Princess

DAVE = Mr. Mustang

WILL = Sarge

MARIE = Athena

MITCH = Diablo

RICK = Danger 9b

BILLY B. = BILLY B. (So clever)

JILL = Fortuna

Then I jerk back to reality when I hear a loud BANG off to my right.

"Hey, dork head, he's in the one labeled 'food only'," my brother Steve calls out as he lumbers down the hall with his chortling friends.

I go and fetch Billy B. out of the garbage can. He is often confused with a seventh grader. It takes some effort to extricate him. The late bell then rings.

"Thanks, Rick. I think it may have been your brother."

"Yeah. I figured that out." And off we go to face the late music of our third period class.

Our military-run school goes from seventh grade to twelfth gradeall in one building. Wicked witches and powerful wizards occupy the same land as poor seventh-grade Munchkins. You know who wins that contest.

So, I have this older brother, Steve, three years older and probably the top wizard in the twelfth grade. At least, he thinks he is. Yeah. Do the math. He is old for high school. What does that hint calculate to? Okay, I'll be nice for a second. Everyone knows him. He is in a band called 'The Suedes'. He plays the lead guitar. Having an older brotherin the same place is supposed to insulate me from the older guys messin'with me. One would think. The trouble is, he's not the great and benevolent OZ protector, far from it. Billy B. gets the worst of it. My brother is doing plenty of the messin' with me all by himself. I will get even.

After our third period, I pass this note to Fortuna:

Ahoy Fortuna!

Spitball got held up after class by Dirty Water. I'm doing beter, fiin, fine, ok ... I think it was Mrs. Finney's perfuum.

I am covering here for Tom and me. He forgot to write Princess. Oh, 'Dirty Water' is our name for Mr. Tollet, our science teacher. It willmake sense later.

He didn't have time to find Princess. He was so upset.

I am covering for him again here. Tom hates to write notes.

Can't you ask Sarge to dance with Athena? I have important misons, new plans, to discuss with you!

Danger 9b

I know what you're thinking. It's not a secret. Everyone knows I hate to open the dictionary. Who needs spelling when it's clear what I mean? I memorize everyone's code names to keep them straight. After a while, it's easy.

Then, there is Aisha Venkataramanujam. Is that a cool name, or what? I can spell that one. Why do I have such time with my papers? Never mind. Yeah. Remember her? Billy B. still has a Snickers bar crush on her. But she is the love interest for Dave, Mr. Mustang. Not hard to beat out Billy B.

She chooses something sensible, 'Jane'. We have no Jane in our group, or anywhere we know. So, it works. I put in my two cents worth and suggest a masculine name, 'Bilbo'. But Jane, it is. Mr. Mustang is madly in love with her. But she plays it cool. Dave is not the overly manly type. He does have a mop top – like the Beatles, almost. His and Will's dad are diplomats. Dave's dad at the British embassy, and Will's at the Canadian embassy. Will is Canadian? Yeah. His mom is from Texas. Guess what genes have won out there? He has quite a drawl. So, they don't have to worry about a dad insisting they have a more military (short) hairstyle or be clean-shaven. Will is glad about that. He sports a pretty good goatee and sideburns.

That's the gang. Some of them consider themselves 'junior agents' now. This is getting harder.

Chapter Twenty
Don't Let Me Down

A few days go by. Mitch is really bummed out with me. He looks like he's had a bad wipeout. I have taken 'his' girl. He pretends to hangout with Nora, but he barely knows what hit him. Bang. Danger 9b has pulled his best caper. Stealing Jill from Diablo. It's a grand victory, for now. Fate and Fortune are on my side. O Fortuna!

Then more worry sets in. I'm up. Please don't let me come down. But Jill is like a butterfly, fluttering among the poppy fields of Oz. Poppies! Poppies! Yeah. They put Dorothy to sleep. Who knows what direction Jill will flap in next? I must figure out how to be the final flower to land on. I am not sure of the next step.

Mitch confronts me when I next see him. "What kind of training did they give you to be in espionage?"

"Shh. Keep it down. Oh. All kinds of stuff at the academy." I know my dad was sent to Washington, D.C., for specialized training. "Yeah. A technical spy school for families. I don't get to do the cool stuff, like shoot stuff. My dad does that. Don't you remember how crummy I was at marksmanship at scout camp?"

"Yeah. You couldn't close your aiming eye. But what kind of cool stuff are you talking about?"

I have to reach into my Hardy Boys knowledge. "Well, all the regular stuff, you know, tailing, we look for other spies. We stake out places and people, looking for, you know, suspicious crap, not the glamorous stuff. And they… they… oh yeah… they teach us… how… how to look for bugs."

"Bugs? What kind of insects?"

"Not that kind, Einstein. Listening devices. Yeah. We look forthose." I need to distract him. He sounds too suspicious.

"Hey Mitch, what does <u>your</u> dad do again?"

"You mean my stepdad or my real dad?"

"You never talk about your stepdad." I know a little of his story.

"For good reason." He seems suddenly nervous. "My real dad owns a restaurant back in the States."

"Oh. That's right. I remember. Cool. Free food." I try to lighten his mood.

"Sure, if I ever saw him."

I'm in desperate need of a caper. This time it will need to be a joint operation. I don't have to think for long. On the bus to school the next day, Jill sits on my lap. Probably against transportation authority rules, but I like it.

"I got our next assignment," she tells me.

"Oh, good. From where?"

"I don't have to sit around waiting for opportunities – *carpe diem* – seize the day."

"OK." And I grab her.

"Alright, lover boy, don't get all souped up yet." I release my hold, and she slides off onto the seat. "You know that new high-rise they are building for the Airmen to stay in?"

"Yeah, their new billet until the base is finished."

"Yeah. And about 30 stories high," Spitball butts in. He stands in the aisle of our bus and practices his yo-yo tricks.

"Watch this. I can 'walk-the-dog'. I spin it down, it stays down, and I let it roll down the aisle, and then, whoop, up I bring it back to my hand."

"No *hunde,* no dogs allowed on bus, *schwein,*" Nora shouts out.

That's one rule I did not know. But I did know you weren't supposed to stand while the bus was moving.

"I'm working on 'the boomerang'. The idea is to throw it out, then swing it up and jerk it back." Bang. He bonks himself in the head in the middle of a boomerang with his fancy YoYo, a Coca-Cola Russel. "Oww." rubbing his head.

"Sit down back there!" shouts the bus driver. Tom quickly puts his rear in its normal place next to Princess.

"That was twitchin'. You OK?" Karin asks, rubbing his head for him.

"Hey, did you know the Greeks had YoYos way back in 500 BC? They used them as weapons."

"Athena should have that in her war arsenal," says Jill, giving Marie a quick smile.

"Ha! Good one. I'll have to teach you some tricks." Tom chuckles.

We pass the Airman's building under construction.

"Look at the size of that thing. It's grown as tall as the Pyramids," Spitball observes, careful not to let his YoYo stray too far. "Last time we visited, it was only a few floors high. Hey, did you know thePyramids were not built by slaves? They were all paid labor," and he goes right on, "I suppose the workers on this building are paid too, butI know they don't work on Fridays or Saturdays. Maybe we could explore someday."

Mitch, sitting alone a few rows away, finally pitches in.

"And what would be the point of that?"

At this stage, it's just an all-cement frame, the full height of the building. There are no walls, no wood, and no metal. It probably has some steel, but all you see is cement.

"That would be cool. Spelunkers above ground," Tom says.

"What's that?" Mitch asks.

"Spelunkers, cave explorers." He looks at me and quietly adds, "Could be a great mission." Then he turns to the others. "I just read a book about some famous caves in Turkey. The early Christians hid in caves to escape the Romans trying to kill them."

"Yeah. It does sort of remind me of caves," Jill says.

"Those Romans. They were brutal soldiers," I add.

"Again, I ask, what's the point?" Mitch asks. Jill rolls her eyes and tells us,

"It's pretty obvious. Airmen know secrets, and they might get to talking in their own living quarters. You see where I'm going with this?"

"Ha. That's right, bugs," Tom says.

"Listening devices?" Mitch is so proud to remember.

"Right on. Isn't that how you say it?" says Jill.

"Right on, skirt," Tom agrees.

I sit in amazement and relief. This time the butterfly flew right to my lap. The next mission is set without me needing to do anything. It seems a little silly to me, and trespassing to boot, but everyone is buying into it. I can't refuse.

Despite my hesitation about this new mission, it doesn't scare Spitball. He is ready to go 'spelunking', and somehow 'Romans' got

mixed up in there. I think he may be overselling this. But I need all the help I can get.

"I think you're going to need some muscle. I'm in," says Will, knowing Marie is going.

Taking both his hands away from rubbing his face, Dave adds, "Okay, it's probably a mistake on my part. But I'm in, too."

The adventure is on, and so is, unfortunately, Diablo.

"OK, team. We have a baseball game on Friday, so we go in on Saturday. There will be no workers on site." I tell them.

"Yeah, but there will be a guard," Spitball adds. "We saw him. He's an old guy that wears those baggy pants."

Jill declares.

"Oh. The *kapaci*. I know all about them. Enforcer of the rules," Tom says as Princess pats his head.

"Is it really worth the risks?" Princess asks.

"She's right. Very risky. Probably not a good idea," says Dave.

"You just said you wanted in," Will chides him.

"Well. If you all insist, Aisha won't like it, but I'll go."

"My guess is that the *kapaci* will be asleep or listening to that awful stuff on the radio. He should not be a problem. It's agreed then. Nine in the morning," I tell them. Jill nudges me and quietly adds,

"There's something more there," and leaves it at that.

Chapter Twenty-One
All Together Now

I pick up Jill at her home with our favorite taxi driver, Bullet Head, and make our way to our meeting place. At the outer fence, we make our final observations. This new multi-story structure is one, two, three, four, oh try some thirty floors or more. It was only five, six, or seven when we were here last. I love it.

"OK, team. It's all clear. There are stairs going up to each floor that look like they're just ramps," I say, "we can now do this all together and have some fun. Look at me. See, I'm smiling."

"I'm trying to," Dave adds.

"There is a stair landing halfway between each floor," Tom adds.

"Yeah. That's the way they build them, pea brain. They have another ramp going up the opposite direction to the next floor," Mitch so nicely informs us.

The ramps go all the way up. There are no steps yet, no guard rails, and no walls other than cement – all hardened, rough cement that has not been finished particularly well.

"Why are you carrying a purse?" Mitch asks me.

"It's a rucksack. It's stuff we might need today." I want to keep up appearances and look the part. I put all kinds of stuff inside, just in case, and it has some weight to it.

"Well, he doesn't have that cool comm set device the Russians took from him," Jill tells everyone.

"Yeah, you two. That story was outta sight," Will pipes in.

"I wager the Russians are using it to spy on us," Dave mumbles.

Marie's eyes go wide, "Right now?"

"You have to expect the worst," Dave replies.

"Just let them try any funny business. I'll bust a few heads," Will says as he strokes his short goatee. Our present Adonis is the only oneof us that can grow any respectable hair there.

"You should have seen the Russian guard. He was more like one of Tolkien's Orcs. You know how scary that is," Jill assures them and winks at me.

"Well, thankfully, our guard here is not as onerous as an Orc but not as harmless as a Hobbit, either. I am prepared for a *kapaci*." Tom says. He then dawns a replica battle helmet on this head. Now, this is typical Tom.

"What's that for?" Mitch laughs.

"Hey, this is Karin's idea. Since she couldn't make it, she doesn't want me to get whacked."

"Who are you going to kiss?" Jill whispers and nudges him.

"All right. I can make this fun, can't I? Yeah, it will be good protection for my vulnerable head. Isn't this cool? It's my Roman centurion helmet," he says as he clanks on its side a few times, "one-piece molded aluminum."

"As long as I don't have to wear that silly thing," Mitch grunts.

Jill jumps in, "No. Really. I like it. It's a distraction, a deflection. It throws off any suspicion with confusion – a great spy tactic."

"And oh, guys, did you know that there were Romans who earned their living plucking hair off people's armpits?" Tom adds and runs off to be the first to enter the site.

"Good to know," says a smiling Marie, "I bet it was a smelly profession."

The place is surrounded by a crudely built wire fence. It's easy to manipulate and create an opening. The guard shack is on the other side of the building from where we are entering, which is near one flight of the cement ramps.

Past the fence, we climb to an opening in the outer wall and make our way to the ramp 'stairs'. We look like creeping cats, carefully placing our feet between the crackly rubble strewn all around. The only other sound comes from the girls, who want to stick together and gigglemost of the time. Up to the first floor, we go and spread out.

"What are we looking for?" asks Athena.

"Wires and stuff," came my reply.

"This is stupid. There are no wires here," Mitch complains.

"Well, then that's good. You can just quit if you want," I say.

He mumbles.

Jill glares at us both. "Would you two stop? We have a lot of ground to cover."

I can only guess what's going through her mind. Here are her two 'boys', one 'interesting' and the other a 'puzzle'.

"Okay. Jill. You can stop staring now. We'll be good," I tell her. Mitch just grunts.

I know the laying of the phone and electrical cables in the structure will be done much later. So, I don't think we will find anything to make it seem legitimate, but we press on.

"Owww!" Mitch yells out, "My foot!" He's kicked a loose brick stacked by the stairs.

"You know, Musonius Rufus, the Roman philosopher, said,"

"That guy again?" Marie interrupts Jill.

"Roman?" Tom perks up. "Watch out for those Romans. I wonder if he was an armpit picker?"

Jill continues calmly, "Rufus argues that since we get all good things by pain, the person who refuses to endure pain all but condemns himself of not being worthy of anything good."

"What good is good when you're hurting?" Mitch mumbles, almost poetically.

"Oh, you're on one today," I add.

"Ha! Another boy puzzle piece in place. You are all *whimps* for pain. I bet you'd be in bed a week for a sliver in your pinky." Jill pipes in.

"Oww. That would hurt considerably," Dave confesses, "oh, you said 'pinky'. That would hurt, too."

Mitch and the others wander off, leaving Jill and me alone for a few moments.

"Rick, after what we've been through, I know you are one person I can trust. With all this searching, I get distracted because I'm on a different kind of search."

"For what?"

"I've hinted that my grandfather was a peculiar man. Very peculiar. I loved him dearly."

"Your mom told me he adored you. But what's he got to do with your search?"

"He was very well off. You might have guessed. He was quite a collector of things with a passion for history."

"Yeah. That library was stoked with some pretty heavy stuff."

"Our library is only a thin slice of his collections. With him now gone, some things are missing. Very important items my mother knows nothing about."

"Well, you know I love a good secret. Can I help?"

"I'm not the only one searching for them."

Just then, Marie and Will come back with Tom.

"Nothing here. Let's keep moving," he says.

I look at Jill and mouth, 'later'.

We search a few more floors until they are tired. There is building stuff strewn all about on each floor, as Mitch found out. Knowing that I am in Jill's favor at this point, Mitch seems more like a loyal puppy following her around as he proclaims another original poem, his specialty,

Step by step by step we go

Look at all the mess

If we make it to the top

Will be anybody's guess

Jill giggles and pulls me up the next ramp, followed by Marie and Mitch, expecting a pat on his puppy dog head, churning to come up with another dumb poem. We don't worry about that because Tom speaks up,

"Hey guys, you know my family has a ranch and farm in Wyoming. So, I have to ask, what do you get if you add 50 deers with 50 sows?"

"You mean pigs?" Marie asks, falling into his trap.

"We call them sows, and they are worth a lot of money now."

"I'm sure you'll tell us," Mitch says.

"50 deer and 50 sows add up to a hundred 'sows and bucks'."

It doesn't take long, and Jill adds a glorious Jillian laugh. It reverberates through the building. The cement walls almost shake. It's one of her classics I'd gladly give a hundred sows and bucks for. The others laugh just to hear her, along with the ones that get the joke.

The ramps are a little slippery, being roughly unfinished cement. It becomes sort of a race to get to the top floor. Mr. Mustang, Sarge, and Spitball go to a second flight of stair ramps to beat the rest of us to the top. So, Tom yells out,

"Hey guys, did you know Basneji dogs are the only breed that doesn't bark?"

Dave changes pace to a tiptoe, "And maybe our breed is barking a little too loud on the way up." At any rate, we make it to the top floor, and all collapse from exhaustion.

On this top floor, there is a smaller cement structure, probably going to be a penthouse, about the size of a large apartment.

"Let's check the very top out," Jill suggests, then stops when she sees the only way up.

"What would Rufus say about this?" Marie mutters. Yeah. She is referring to a primitive wooden ladder, set up against the wall of the small structure that goes to its roof.

"Gentlemen, I don't like the look of this," Dave observes. "The bottom of the ladder is perched on the very edge of the skyscraper. It looks like a fast ticket to ride down thirty floors."

"Hmmm. Rufus encouraged a commitment to live on the edge, live for virtue, not pleasure, since virtue saves us from the mistakes that ruin a life," Jill quotes.

"Well," states the sage Marie, "this ladder is a mistake and could ruin my life. I'm staying put here." She is the only one to really have

any sense about her – even though she is the Goddess of War. Not Jill. Something is driving her to the top.

"Last one up smells like baggy pants," she yells as she scrambles up the shaky ladder.

"That would be me. I'm not touching that thing," Marie states, "are you sure you all want to go up there?"

Not to be outdone, Diablo is next up.

"Hey, this thing is pretty rickety," he says. He is followed by Sarge and Mr. Mustang.

"We got this," they chime in.

I was next, leaving Spitball and Athena below.

"I'll hold it steady," Mitch assures me. About halfway up, the rucksack I had on shifts on me. The ladder pivots on one leg and comes away from the wall. With Mitch holding, it was supposed to stay leaning on the wall but now is heading in the wrong direction – out.

"It got away from me!" Diablo yells.

Athena screams. And when the Goddess of War screams – it's a call heard throughout the land.

I suddenly am tossed sideways, forcing one of my hands to come free and touch the wall. I look up and see a cable coming out the end of the ladder at the top, catching and temporarily holding me and the ladder perfectly perpendicular. One nudge more, and I'm off the edge.

As it pulls away from the wall, Mitch grabs the exposed cable, holding it the best he can. "It's slipping!"

"I'll get it!" Spitball yells. He reaches out as the ladder teeters in the vertical, with me halfway up, and pulls the ladder back to lean on the wall again.

"Good catch, pitch!" I sputter out.

I continue up and thank Tom again when he arrives. I give Mitch the stink eye, "I thought you were holding it."

"Sorry. It got away from me," he says as Jill stands staring at him.

'That was really stupid, Rick.' I am thinking to myself.

It is an even better view of the city from up here. It provides quite a thrill. I take out my binoculars from my rucksack. They are like high-powered telescopes for your eyes.

"These are cool." Sarge observes.

"Yeah. My Dad keeps these in our apartment to check things out from our building roof if needed.   We live only a couple blocks from the American embassy. He has communication with them somehow from up there."

That sounds pretty authentic. It is the truth, finally. At least the binocs make me look legit.

"Look," I said. "You can see the Soviet compound from here."

The others are interested, but that is ancient history for Jill. Everyone takes a turn finding stuff. Jill pulls me over and whispers,

"That's what I was seeing," she points to the pole on the far side of the roof, where a Turkish half-crescent moon and star flag is flying. "I heard my dad comment how strange it was."

"Okay, a flagpole. Yea for Turkey."

"No. Turks don't put flags on uncompleted buildings. Now, follow the cable."

I didn't see it before, but that same cable that held my ladder from falling runs alongside the building and over to the flagpole.

"I bet that's an antenna. Not a flagpole," she says anxiously.

"This is boring," calls out Mitch.

"You guys having a good time up there?" Marie yells, "come down."

The others are done, too.

"You guys go on down. We'll come right after you," I tell them.

As the others descend, Jill and I move over to the flagpole.

"You're right. The flag looks like an afterthought. It is barely tied on with string."

"And the pole is metal, painted to look like wood. See, there's a connection down here at the base to the cable."

We follow it to a black box at the corner of the penthouse roof.

"This is Russian Cyrillic printing on this box and cable," Jill says excitedly.

"You can read this?"

"No, silly. But the symbols match the stuff we saw at the embassy."

We hear Marie yell out, "You coming? I hear voices down below."

"Yeah, on our way," I call back.

"Let's tear this down," she says.

"No. Then they would know we know. Let me report this and leave it alone. Maybe someone can tap into it?" I surprise myself with how logical this sounds. Jill stares that stare into my eyes again, but his time like she's surprised. Then adds,

"Good thinking. Let's go."

We turn to go back down. There is the ladder. Not risking too much, I throw my rucksack down to Marie, who is there to greet us on the top floor.

"I'm hearing noises way down in the building," she tells us, "maybe they heard me scream?"

This is not good news. There is some kind of commotion on the lower floors. We make our way back to the set of stairs we came up.

"It's the guard! He's yelling something. The *kapici* on his way up!" Tom blasts out, "he's about halfway down. He's found us."

We quickly move over to the other set of ramps.

"Holy Roman Emperor," mutters Tom, "there are two of them, police."

"Two blokes in suits? They are not constables, worse, they're haberdashery salesmen," Dave adds.

These stairs are our only way down. We can see this since the building is still just a shell. Marie is standing stock still. Her eyes aren't blinking.

"Oh, Dear! Oh, Dear!"

"This is it as I predicted. All is lost," says Dave.

"I just want to bust somebody," Sarge adds.

"Cool it, Will. We'll figure something out," I say.

"Let me just pound these guys."

Jill doesn't say anything. The rest of us guys are quiet as well, pondering our next move. Tom peers down the stairs.

"The old guy has got a stick, team. A big stick."

"What's that for?" Marie asks.

"The lot of us," states Dave.

Striking a pose with his hands on his hips, Will says, "He thinks he's going to beat us? Ha. Just try."

"Or maybe it's a walking stick. Those steps are steep for an old man," I say.

"It's undoubtedly an electric disintegrating probe," Dave moans.

"Anyway, he can't move very fast with those baggy pants on. The other two suits have stopped for some reason. We have time," Tom replies as Will steps over to calm Marie. He takes her hand and reassures her, "I'll make sure they get you last." Marie starts to cry.

'Oh great, Will. That helps,' I mutter to myself, then to the others, "we'll figure something out."

"Well, it better be quick. This was your mission, Mr. Danger 9b. What are we going to do?" Mitch turns on me.

"Tell them you have a bomb in your knapsack!" Tom blurts out.

"A bomb?" I ask.

"What is Turkish for 'bomb'?" Tom asks.

"I think it is *böcek,*" Mitch guesses.

"No, that's the word for flying insects," I tell them.

"Well, that does it. We're saved," Dave announces, "'*We're going to release this ladybug on you.*' will certainly shock his baggy knickers off of him."

"Then let them say *merhaba* hello to one of these," Will says, holding up his fists. While we argue, Jill has already formed a plan.

"Ok, guys, here's what we'll do. We'll let the *kapici* climb to us. We'd rather face one old guy than two police. Get him good and tired. Let's even look over the edge and encourage him, '*merhaba effendi*'," she yells down to him.

That was a polite way to say, 'Hello, Sir'. We all take up that chant, but his return words are not so polite. Our Turkish vocabulary does not

include the harsh Turkish coming up at us. This doesn't exactly calm us down, especially Marie. We say nothing about ladybugs.

"Marie, you keep that up, *merhaba effendi*," as Jill turns to the others.

"*Merhaba effendi*," she weakly calls.

"Marie! Be bold! Athena's voice," Jill demands.

"Okay," she meekly says. Then '***Merhaba effendi***' comes out more like a grunt.

""What do you want us to do, dodge his stick, distract him while you run for it?" Diablo asks her.

'Oh. That's big of you,' comes to my mind. That sounds a little like he is trying to be a hero.

"It's not going to end well if we try to confront him. Someone's bound to get hurt," I say, glancing at a defiant Will.

"Tom, did you bring your YoYos?" Jill asks.

"Yeah, my two Duncans."

"That will really impress this guy. 'Hey, watch me 'walk-the-dog'," Mitch says.

"What did <u>you</u> bring, Mr. Sarcasm? Don't you know they were originally weapons? Maybe I can scare him off," Tom counters.

"Let me introduce them to <u>my</u> two Duncans, double and trouble," Will insists, flexing both arms and fists this time.

"Wait. Tom, can you do that double boomerang thing?" I ask.

"Ooo. A double. That's tricky." Then Jill pipes in,

"That's it! Rick, that's a great idea. Tom, be ready to follow me. Be ready for the boomerang," Jill tells him, and he beams.

OK, this is the situation. We are not supposed to be here in the first place. It's dangerous, contrary to what our dads were thinking for us, and we are trespassing. Not sure what the penalty is, but we don't want to find out. Jill continues.

"Tom, when he gets to the ramp just below us, walk down the ramp towards him with those YoYos going. It will confuse him. Oh yeah. Put on your helmet."

"Right, more confusion."

"Then, you all follow me."

It's happening so quickly that we don't even question her. The *kapici* gets to the half-floor platform just below us, leaning on his big stick and panting heavily. Jill sends Tom towards him.

"Merhaba effendi. You like the boomerang?" Tom bravely teases as he walks down, Roman helmet on his head, and starts one YoYo going. Then he starts both going, one in each hand. "Boom. Try this one, too. Impressed?"

Now, I'm not sure if this was to confuse or amuse the guy, but the look on his face was not one of amusement, so my bet is on confuse and maybe turning us into refuse. Jill is following right behind Tom, gingerly walking down the ramp towards the guy.

"Jill! What are you doing?" I yell.

"Follow me," she says.

Along with his confused face, the *kapaci* starts cursing up a storm. He starts swinging his stick, still too far away to do any damage. Maybe the YoYos look menacing? Then, as Jill and Tom get halfway down the ramp, YoYos flashing, she turns and jumps to the ramp just below the *kapaci*, avoiding him altogether.

"Brilliant," I thought.

"Come on, he's too tired to chase you!" she yells.

Will is pulling Marie into position.

"I'll catch you, Marie," then turns to the guy and flexes, "Feel lucky you didn't meet these guys," and jumps. "Come on, Marie. You can do it," holding out his arms.

Without hesitating, she leaps down into his outstretched hands as he cushions her landing. That earns him a well-received hug.

"Please convey my goodbyes to Aisha for me as I leap to my death," Dave blurts out and jumps. He doesn't die. The rest of us follow in quick succession. It's a little tougher for me, but Will is there to help me land. This leaves only Tom, double boomerang still going strong.

The *kapici* takes a step forward up the ramp and swings his big stick, and catches Tom's helmet right in the feathers as he is the last to jump. It goes flying several floors down as Tom lands on the ramp just below the guy and follows the rest of us down.

"Merhaba, effendi!" we yell.

Now, this feat isn't as simple as it sounds. There are no edges or railings to the stairs yet, so anyone of us could have tumbled some distance if we had misjudged. Jumping from an incline ramp to an opposite inclined ramp makes us quite the acrobats. We scramble the rest of the way down the numerous flights of stairs and make our escape, laughing with excitement most of the way.

"Who were those guys in suits? They were not police uniforms. Where did they go?" Mitch is the first to ask.

"Romans," Tom flatly states.

Jill seems strangely calm by the whole thing, but I detect a tiny smile that peaks out. I think she really liked the adventure. These are good points for me, I think.

Dave hunches over double, disheveled, and panting loudly, "What did I just do?"

Jill then casually says, "You know what I really need right now, Danger 9b?"

I am all ears at this point.

"I really need a peanut butter sandwich, a real PBJ."

She noticed all the vendors on the streets like the *Ekmek* (bread) guy with his *Simiit* bread rolls on a rack carried on his head. Now, let it be known. I hate peanut butter. Yuck. But she wants a PBJ? Huh? I'm thinking. Well, okay. After that excursion and energy-burning scramble, it tends to make one hungry. However, there is no peanut butter to be found in our military commissary (grocery store). She knows this. And the Turkish people certainly do not eat that stuff. It willchoke them. Jill has not had any for some time.

"What have you got in that knapsack of yours? Any snacks?" she asks, digging into the contents.

"I'll give you a big sloppy kiss if you have peanut butter in here," she whispers to me.

Now, a good Boy Scout, which we boys all were, has the motto 'Be Prepared'. Well, I am not. It isn't my fault. There is no peanut butter in all of Turkey. She pokes her head into my rucksack.

"This stuff weighs a ton. You carried this all the way up?" And starts pulling things out.

The binocs are on top, then a coil of rope (I know a few tricks), a rubber mallet (never know when you need to pound something), a paperback copy of "The Great Conquerors of the World" (might get a break in the action), a can of Spam, a winch for the rope, (every good rope needs a winch) a...

"A can of Spam? I hate Spam!" Jill says.

"Me too," adds Mitch, quickly agreeing. Thinking fast, I add,

"I brought it for an emergency, just in case someone needs quick energy," I explain. Spam is a sort of canned meat product that my mom occasionally uses on sandwiches. It was invented way back in the 1930s. So – it is known as a cheap, long-lasting food. I am not about to admit that now. It was popular with the military troops in wartime.

"What else is in here?"

She blindly reaches in and pulls out a pair of underwear.

"Arrrgghhh!" Jill staggers back. "Why is <u>this</u> in here?

"Are you a Billy B.?" Mitch quickly follows up.

"No! No!"

Billy B. had this sort of nighttime and sometimes daytime (sixth grade) leaking problem.

She holds them up for all to see. Yeah. That brought a real turkey dinner feast of laughter – with all the trimmings, dressing, and fixings that one would expect. It is giving me time to think up a response. At least they were clean. 'No, don't say this,' I'm thinking. I had been to the community pool the day before and forgot they were in there.

"Well… a… aa… that's for a… a… emergencies. I mean… just in case… a… a… a… They were left in there… by my dumb brother!" I quickly come up with it. Jill throws them back in.

"Yuck! I'm not looking anymore, but my offer still stands."

Whew. I am thinking. This could have been worse.

Now, what am I supposed to do? In this silly and spontaneous caper of exploring a dangerous construction site, we actually *found* something odd. Who was I going to report it to? Certainly not dad. He'd blow his top. I'll just tell Jill I did, and all will be well.

But for some reason, having to do with the promise of a big wet kiss, I HAD to find something else odd - peanut butter in Turkey. Another puzzle piece in place – *girls have obsessions.*

THE RIVALRY BOX SCORE:

The game was now at full intensity. Diablo vs. Agent Danger 9b. So, I figured the score was something like this: One and one-half points for Danger 9b for the adventure. Maybe a half- point for Diablo for participation and a dumb poem. Oh. He losta full point for suspicion of homicide with the ladder. OK.Maybe I lost a half-point for the underwear. Well, maybe a full point. I was about to name that stair hopping, acrobatic procedure the Jillian Maneuver, but that designation really was more suited to what came next involving my Arkadaşlar, (friends)

Episode Three

The Jillian Maneuver

Chapter Twenty-Two
Don't B(r)other Me

In all fairness, the underwear? Not my fault! I blame my brother, Steve. Just go away and don't bother me, brother. Leave me alone. But it is not to be. Mitch set me up. He tried to link me to Billy B.'s problem. Not cool. I am hoping Jill does not fall for this.

But anyway, I am in charge of my own laundry. That means I have to wash my own clothes. This is not as easy (but just as unreasonable) as it seems. Mom is a working mom. She only has one leg due to an automobile accident before I was born. Those are reasons enough. Maybe not so unreasonable, I guess.

Things in Turkey are more primitive. It's just a fact. The washing 'machine,' or should I call it 'apparatus,' is two fifty-gallon barrels strapped together – like you might see attached to wagons in the old western movies. I am instructed to agitate my clothes by rotating the hand crank for 50 turns.

"Really? You're going to give a lesson in washing clothes?" (The Jill in my head pops in here.)

"I am making a point."

"You? Fifty times? Ha!"

"OK. Maybe I can do ten. I can, at least, count to fifty, don't doubt me."

Then, I take the clothes out, one at a time, and put them between two rolling pins to fall into the rinse tub. Again – 50 hand cranks.

"Be Honest!"

This one, I usually get to twenty turns.

"Questionable engineering. They should have consulted me," you know who suggests.

Then I send them through the rollers one more time and hang them on a rope to dry. It stretches the length of our balcony on the side of our apartment. I was using my brother's rucksack, and *he* took his underwear from the line and threw it into the rucksack before we wentto the pool. *His* fault, Jill, not mine. But now, this excuse is too late. It will follow me to my grave, or at least to school.

Chapter Twenty-Three
I'm Happy Just to Dance with You

"Make circle now, students, big circle, all of you," yells out Miss Beydol, our Turkish culture teacher. "Take a hand to person next to you."

I delightfully obey since it is Jill on my left. There is nothin' else I'd rather do. Happy again, just to dance with her. However, to my right, it's Billy B.

"Can't you trade places with a girl, Billy B.?" I whisper.

"They keep moving away, and I ended up here." The music starts up.

"Everyone, stay in circle and take three steps to right."

Billy B. starts out to his left, but I set him right before he crashes into us.

"*Çok Güzel,* everyone. Now, everyone, raise hands at next step, then put down on next."

That almost requires me to lift Billy B. off the floor. Jill smiles at me. Maybe I can gain a point by being nice to him. On we go learning this Turkish folk dance.

"Now repeat. To the right, one, two, three. Hands up. Hands down. To the left, *bir, iki, üç.*"

The whole Sophomore class is here. Most of the girls are dressed up in colorful native dresses. I am not about to wear the traditional folk baggy pants. It isn't expected of the boys. But Billy B. thinks it's cool. He looks like he's wearing an open, multi-colored parachute from the waist down. A puff of air and he would be whisked away to Oz.

I have not forgotten that Jill expects me to dance with Marie at some point. Why? I don't know. The music stops to give us a break, and

Jill goes off to the girl's room. I quickly move away from Billy B. to the stage. To mix things up, they have hired my brother's band, 'The Suedes,' to play some numbers in between so we don't have to be completely immersed in folk dance. My brother's guitar, a Fender 'Stratocaster,' sits on a stand a few feet from my reach.

"Don't even think about it," my brother's voice booms at me from off-stage. "No touchee, no playee, my baby."

"Just looking."

"No, lookee, either."

"Hey. Play something slow for me tonight, will you?"

"Oh, you with your honey, Jill, tonight? Then, I got something special for you. I'll even dedicate it to you."

Oh, now I regret even paying him any attention at all. Mitch then pulls up to my side.

"Wow. What did you think of my partner?"

"Yeah. I saw you drooling."

"I thought only belly dancers wore that stuff."

"You weren't so much admiring Nora's belly, I noticed."

"Yeah, she fills out a costume pretty nicely. Wasn't like that two years ago."

"We're not supposed to talk about stuff like that."

"Oh, come on, you noticed as much as I did."

"Yeah, I notice, but I try not to dwell on it."

"Too bad Jill isn't so endowed."

"Oh Mitch, let's not drag her into this. She looks great."

"Look. You haven't gotten any further with her than I have. Let me guess – no smooching. Have I got that right?"

"You haven't…?"

He shakes his head. "I'll make you a bet, a deal you can't refuse. I got a bunch of guys in a contest. You participate, and I'll leave Jill alone for a while."

"I smell something nefarious."

"No. Nora thinks it's fun."

"Nora? What's she got to do with it?"

"We get to guess her measurements."

"What?"

"Yeah. Three numbers, top, middle, and bottom."

"Yeah, I know what measurements are. Why?"

"Bragging rights. But for you, safety. We all have to change the combination on our lockers to match our guesses. That's it."

"And you'll walk away?"

"Well, for a time. Two weeks. Look out, choir boy. You just might have to 'dwell' on it and live a little on the edge. You up for a challenge, Danger 9b?" Jill finds us in conversation.

"Well, if it isn't my two boys, all chummy again. What challenge?" I turn to Mitch.

"You're on."

The music starts back up again, but this time it's the Suedes. They vamp for a few measures while my brother takes the mic and announces to the crowd,

"I'd like to dedicate this first number to the grooviest guy I know, my little brother, Dorkus, I mean, Rick, and his hot new crush... Nora Schulte.

Chapter Twenty-Four
She's So Heavy

Danger 9b,

Well, well. That was a night. Besides some fun folk dances, I learned something else. Brothers talk to each other. What is it that I don't know? "A hot new crush," really? Diablo and I had fun. You didn't dance with Athena. Will did once. He couldn't stop talking about some people named 'Archie and Veronica.' Who are they? Athena didn't know. AND You had Billy B. dance with Athena for you? He was, at least, thankful about it. Do we need to talk?

Fortuna.

She doesn't say a word, but that's what I get handed to me on the bus the next day. I should have just come out and said, 'I want you, yeah, so bad.' She's hanging so heavy on my mind. So, during our first period, I pound out the best reply I can.

Deer Fortuna,

Yes. Yes. You are still deer to me. After all that, I really wanted to burn ruber and split, but where could I go? I was set up. The Vulture just grabed me out to the floor, and then her flock sort of swarmed us for the rest of the dance. I've complaned about my brother before. Remember? I couldn't mess with Sarge and Athena. I had nothing to do with Billy B. Wasn't I nice to him, bagy pants and all? Yes. Let's talk. I always love that.

A sorry Danger 9b

I saw Mitch in the hall after history class.

"When are these two weeks going to start? You didn't waste any time last night with Jill."

"Yeah. Wasn't that interesting? I think I like your brother now. You flaked out on her, so I was there to take up the slack. I'll start as soon as Nora checks your locker com numbers."

Princess walks by and shoves a note into my hand.

DEAR Danger 9b,

Yes, dear. I have no tail. It is d-e-a-r. NOT d-e-e-r. All is forgiven. Musonias Rufus had a big heart, so I will, too. You better keep your distance from Lolita. By the way, I say again, you dance a terrible Twist. I got a new way to teach you – it's called a 'hula-hoop.' Standby. Hey, I got some great ideas about a new mission. And maybe we can talk about the help you offered me.

The fab and forgiving,

Fortuna

Girl puzzle piece number, whatever, solved. If you can fake a good enough confession and apology, *you can be forgiven.* Oh yeah, and the vulture is really called 'Lolita,' her code name. Something tells me she's circling for a kill.

Chapter Twenty-Five
I Call Your Name

While waiting for the bus after school, Jill and I sit alone on the steps.

"Hula-Hoop? Is that what you called it? Was I really that bad? Don't you know I can't take it? Just call me a name, lame brain, or something."

"Just wait. This device will put a little 'danger' in your 9b moves. By the way, I'd like to hear how you picked Danger 9b. I mean, after your secret, it makes a whole lot more sense now. How do you say it, 'What's your bag'?"

"You're catching on fast to the lingo. But you did call me a square, remember? You weren't the first one. So, before you, I had to come up with something a little outside my normal me."

"Well," she nudges me, "you are kinda square, in a good way. Hey, did you report our antennae discovery?"

"Oh yeah… sure." I quickly go on. "I got another 'danger' theory. Back in London or Paris or Bern, did you ever get to see American movies?"

"Some."

"I really like one called, 'The Invasion of the Body Snatchers.' If the characters went to sleep in this picture, an alien plant pod would grow in the shape of their body form and just take over. The real person never woke up."

"Well, that sounds 'dangerous.' I get it. That's so creepy. Sometimes, being a girl, I feel like I am possessed by some alien creature."

"I've noticed." She turns and gives me a stare. "Oh, not you." I cross my fingers behind my back. "You know, girl stuff – part of your thousand puzzle pieces."

"Boys. You don't know a thing about it. But that title is interesting. You really do feel like your body is being 'snatched.'"

"That's what I mean. These movies have this aura of 'danger.' Get it? Anyway, there was another one called 'Plan 9 from Outer Space.' Maybe this is where I got the '9'. I thought the title was 'Plan 9B from Outer Space.'

"Now it all makes a little more sense. What was that one about?" "It

had something to do with kidnapping women from Earth to re-populate some other planet. It was really cheesy and so awful it was good."

"Kidnapping. That's serious business."

"It was just a movie, Jill. So, no teacher is going to trace me to Danger 9b. Wait. You're serious about the kidnapping?"

"You don't get it. Despite my dad's job as base commander, we have a lot of money. I mean – a lot. Grandfather Fontaine, you remember? It's really my mom's money. Dad has his pride. He doesn't want to give up his career. Anyway, that potentially puts a target on me, on the family. That's why my father took this job, to get far away – out to these boondocks of the earth."

The bus horn honks and ends our time just when it is getting important. We couldn't really talk about it on the bus.

"Rick, I think I may be in danger. Call me tonight."

Chapter Twenty-Six
Drive My Car

With all the science fiction outer space movies I have seen, getting around the universe seems easy. Hop in your spaceship, and off you go. Moving around Ankara as a teen is a bit trickier. If I were famous, a star on the silver screen, we could do something else between – like maybe you could drive a new car? Just dreaming. Driving as a teen in a foreign land is out of the question. We don't have bikes - too dangerous. Yeah, there is a bus system. A lot of what we do is all within a reasonable walking distance. That's mainly what you do – walk - or, as my grandfather would say, 'ride shank's pony.'

Jill decided if you are an American kid or any of our other friends from other countries growing up in Turkey, there are certain things you have to do. You HAVE to do them, at least among your friends, to stay in good graces. Her good graces. She calls these things a 'rite.'

"A rite is an action, ceremony, or duty that one must perform to move ahead with life or within your group," Jill tells us. For us in Ankara, it is 'the ride.'

The 'ride' is a little dangerous, so, being the root of my code name, I am on solid ground.

"It isn't so dangerous." Jill always tells me.

Jill is the main instigator, the inventor, of this daring and off-beat rite.

"Thank you very much for the credit. Much deserved," she also tells me.

She is the creator, at least the Western brains, behind the 'Jillian Maneuver.' What goes on in that pretty little head of yours? It was far out.

The phone rings.

"It's for you, dear," my mother calls out, "Jill."

Jill: You were supposed to call me.

Me: Your line was always busy. How could I?

Jill: Never mind. I can't really get into what we were talking about. Too many ears.

Me: Yeah. Here, too. But danger? Really? You worry me.

Jill: Yes. I've got some good ideas for another mission where we can talk.

I am waiting for this. Who is supposed to be getting the assignments here? This is encroaching on my credibility, so I quickly add,

Me: They already gave me one.

Jill: Oh great. What?

Me: You know 50 Yil Park?

Jill: Oh yeah. 50-Year Park – just up from my house. What do we do?

Me: They think it's a drop zone.

Thanks, Hardy Boys book number two – 'The Secret Panel.'

Jill: Oh. Yeah. That's where they hand off secret messages.

Me: Right. I'll gather the posse.

Jill: Oh. One distressing piece of news.

Me: Tom got whacked again for PDA?

Jill: Worse. Nora wants in.

Chapter Twenty-Seven
Day Tripper

Nora? Really? Jill would consider Nora? Apparently so. Didn't she know Nora only plays one-night stands? You couldn't please her if you tried. On second thought, if Nora is around, Mitch has to behave. Score! But I have two free weeks coming soon. Hmmm. I have changed my locker combination. Just waiting. Jill has something in mind for Nora, and I think it has to do with what we call the 'Jillian Maneuver.'

You see, Ankara is built on a number of hills. In America, the richer you are, in most places, you build your home higher up the hill or mountain. In Ankara, the poorer you are, the higher up you live in the hills.

So, we are pretty much traveling in the flats and low hills in our living area. If anyone in our family needs to go somewhere far, we havea Taxi stand on the corner of our street, just a few buildings away. The main driver, if not the only one, is a huge man with a completely bald head. Yes, 'Bullet Head.' I think his name is '*Bey Efendi*' or Mr. Bay. I asked him one time,

"*Bey, Effendi*. What are those strings of beads behind your back?"

"*Aanlamıyorum*. No understand."

"*Onlar ne?* What are those?" I point to his beads.

"Oh. Little Foster. These prayer beads. Americans like to say 'worry beads.'"

"Are you worried?" I ask. He laughs.

"*Hayir*. No, I religious man. I use beads to count prayers."

So, prayerful Bullet Head was my go-to guy when I needed to pick up Jill if I didn't walk. But our favorite way to get around is the source of our somewhat dangerous rite.

"There you go again, but I will accept 'somewhat' dangerous,' the Jill in my mind repeats.

She must have seen the local kids do it. I don't know.

"Yeah, well, they did it wrong."

Why we didn't think of it before, I don't know. "I know why. You were not fun," Jill tells me often.

And I would add a lack of courage and nerve to the 'not fun' part. Even though this is her first year in Turkey, once the donkey was out ahead of the cart, as the saying sort of goes, she had to promote it.

"OK, gang. Only a one-way ticket, yeah, is needed for this ride, a little daring. It's just a little day trip for fun. No stops to look for, no routes to memorize, no street numbers to know," she says as we are corralled for our first lesson.

Along with cars and a few trucks, the street is mostly traversed by wooden wheeled carts pulled by donkeys or horses. The Turkish word for donkey is *eşek*, or ashak, pronounced 'a-shack.' This is the primary way goods are hauled around the town. This is stuff like water jugs, vegetables, bread, construction materials, furniture, garbage, material to be reused, and on and on. The walls on the cart are generally low all the way around. The driver sits up front on a bench with a whip in hand to convince the ashak to move or turn, stop, or go faster.

"I will assume I am the first to show you the 'Jillian Maneuver,' and I expect you all to adopt the practice," she pronounces. I had a preview of this lesson, so I say,

"I dub you the chief shenanigan inventor. I think 'Shenanigan' is really your last name. It's an Irish word, right? It should be, don't you think?"

"You mean to say I am 'up to no good,' doing dumb stuff, not intended to be hurtful? Maybe, but I will keep my Scottish MacGregor all the same."

When any of our group gets together, we attempt to travel by ashak for as far as we can, using the 'Jillian Maneuver.' It is expected of us – by each other.

There is an art to this, as Jill teaches it.

"First of all, be on the lookout for the ashak coming your way. Now this is important. As it approaches *don't* look at it."

"Why not?" Spitball asks.

"You need the element of surprise. Just keep walking on the sidewalk, looking forward, until the cart passes you. Got it?"

We all nod.

"Second step. The ashak is your friend. Say it."

"The ashak is our friend," we repeat.

"Hee-haw how? He makes so much noise with his hoofs on the pavement that no one will hear you dart into the street and run up to the cart from behind. *From behind.* Got it?"

"The ashak's behind. The ass's ass. He is our friend. We got it." Tom repeats.

"Don't get too close to that 'behind,'" Will adds.

"I am not optimistic about the outcome of this maneuver," Dave says.

"Will, come here. Jump up on this wall and hang on to the fence," she commands. He dutifully obeys. "Now scrunch down like you were… ah… just scrunch down."

"Got the image, boss. Clear the air space," Will quips.

"This is the attachment technique. Hold on to that rear cart wall, with your feet on the axle and duck down below the edge," Jill instructs.

"Am I not risking my precious stern here riding inches from the ground?" Dave asks. "My feet will probably be smashed by the turning axle."

"No, Mr. Mustang. Your bum is not in danger. The turning axle is inside a housing – like a car."

"Ahh. Got it. But me bum might 'crack', you know. Just a little British humor."

"Ducking down is the key. Only your hands will show. Da ta ta da." Jill bows, "This is your 'Jillian Maneuver.'" There is lite applause.

Another brilliant part of the Jillian Maneuver, option one, is to hide behind a parked car, then apply the same tactic once the cart has passed. I like this one the best. It works better, most of the time. So yes, I got up the courage to learn the maneuver and mastered it. One step closer to pleasing Jill. You have to do this at least once or feel the wrath of your friends relentlessly, forever – or a long time – maybe a few hours.

"So, team, the cart drivers are unaware of unauthorized passengers, but the drag on his c art soon becomes apparent. He will turn his head and see our hands hanging on the back wall, and out comes his whip. Be prepared for bad words to come out."

"*Kapılı p...*" (Off! You... a bad word about our birth) is one. I hear.

"Your dismount is the most important. Otherwise, you're going to faceplant on the street. When you want or have to get off, you only have a few moments to get your feet going at the same speed as the cart and then let go. If you are lucky, the whip misses your fingers. Otherwise, it will sting for a while."

The dismount is going to be trickier for me. But I make it work. Much depends on the speed of the cart. Most of the time, it's not a problem. Jill, being who she is, always calls out to the driver,

"*Çok teşekkürler ederum*, thank you very much." We eventually shortened that to '*Çok tek*' – pronounced: "choke tek." Not sure that communicates what we want, but it is easier to say.

On the appointed mission day, we all gathered outside my apartment. Mitch starts up,

"Do we have to go on another stupid adventure? This place only has a one-hole W.C."

"Oh, Mitch. Don't be such a stick in the mud. Rufus says we must practice. Practice, not just <u>talk</u> about stuff," Jill scolds him.

"Oh, Rufus again?"

'Oh, Please, be a stick in the mud, Mitch.' I think to myself. I don't want him along. He's not supposed to be here. When are my two weeks going to start?

I sent Bullet Head to pick up Jill. When he drops her off, Mitch pipes up.

"Chrome dome! Good to see you, *effendi*."

"What mean this chrome dome?" Bullet Head asks.

I try to be honest, "Nice man with… ah… shiny, ah… *parlak* head."

"Oh. *Çok guzell.* I chrome dome. I shall tell my wife this," he says with a happy smile, "she calls me chrome dome *bey* now," and he takes off.

Jill just glares at Mitch and even more when guess who arrives just then? Yeah, the Vulture.

"Nora! You made it," Mitch beams.

Jill steps in the middle of us, "Gather up, now, team. Oh, Marie! Love the shoes," Jill gushes, "Sooo Athenian."

"Oh, thanks. Mom picked them up in Greece on her trip," Marie admits. Nora just huffs and adjusts her tight-fitting top. Yes. We all notice. Jill just stares.

Then Mitch pipes in with a mocking,

"Oh, Rick! Love your socks. So stylish." Ok, so they didn't match. Then Tom jumps in with his crackly voice in a high pitch,

"Hey fellas. How do you like my Shishi shirt? I got it at the bazaar last week." We guys bust up.

"You all look really dorky. You know that, don't you?" Jill adds. We all snicker some more. I pull Mitch off to the side.

"What's the deal with inviting Nora? And what about our deal?"

"You're the one who called this shindig together."

"You could have said you were busy."

"Yeah, but Nora makes it all the more interesting, and I can keep clear of Jill with her. Besides, our timer hasn't started yet. She hasn't been to your locker yet, right?"

What could I do? Now that we are all at my apartment building, Jill commands, "Enough. Okay, Mitch, take this one *lira* coin and smear this air-plane glue on one side."

"Huh?"

"Just do it. I guarantee something fun."

"Jill, not this again," Marie whispers.

"Now, Tom, put it on the sidewalk down at the start of the fence with the glue face down."

"But it has glue on it."

"Yeah. That's the point."

"Ohhh."

"All of you, stand back over here. Just watch."

Nora smirks, "Aren't you the wicked one."

One *lira* is worth far more than a silver US dollar coin. It can buy a lot of stuff for the Turks. For them, it would be like finding a week's worth of groceries on the ground. A few people walk by before the first victim, a baggy pant man, notices. I admit, we all laugh from some distance away. He bends down. Unsuccessful, he bends down again and pops up when his grip slips. He circles around the coin. Other passers-by must move around him, puzzled as he hides the coin with his shoe. He tries it again. Kicks at it. Then stops, rubs his head, and hurries off like he has another idea.

This repeats with a few others until John, my upstairs neighbor, comes down the sidewalk and sees the coin, then us. He was not part of our circle of friends. Just mine. He bends down and tries until I call him over.

"Hey, what's up, you guys?"

"Just watch," I tell him. Nora leans over to me with unusual interest.

"Who is he?"

"John, my neighbor. He just moved in."

Jill whispers to me, "This is that John? Your John?"

I smile at her, "Yes."

"I love the hair," Nora says and smiles at John. Yes. He notices.

Yeah. John looked like he could have been a junior John Lennon of the Beatles. His mom wanted him to fit in, so she copied Lennon's clothing style and made him wear it, keeping his hair long and shabby. I didn't tell anyone he was only in eighth grade.

By this time, an elderly, poorly clothed woman approaches, clearly a beggar. She has a blue-painted walking stick that clicks as she walks, worry beads in the other hand. She walks towards us. Beggars sometimes roam the streets and knock at your doors. She sees the coin and bends down excitedly on all haunches to examine it. She tries her best to dislodge the coin. She looks distressed. Jill can't help but notice.Mitch just snickers.

"Maybe it's not so funny," I say to him, but I know Jill hears me.

"Ah. It's just for laughs," he replies.

"Okay. Everyone. Let's go," Jill quickly commands us and turns away.

That's how John is with us this day. He isn't part of our gang, but he is a convenient friend who lives upstairs from me. Now, I didn't wanthim to hang out with us.

"Who is this John guy, and why is he hanging with us? He's such a weirdo," Mitch corners me and demands. Maybe he is jiggered by the fact that Nora is taking notice.

I should ask Mitch why Mitch is with us and why he is such a… okay, Rick, be nice. This is supposed to be another assigned time with Jill. AND I was ahead of Mitch in the scoring. But here are weirdos John, Mitch, and Nora I have to deal with. You are raining on my parade. Jill is my attention today. But John – he needs some explanation.

Chapter Twenty-Eight
I've Got a Feeling

Struck by the Jillian effect, deep down inside, I got a feeling I could apply some whacky fun that I couldn't hide. So, I shared with Jill my recent history with John.

John is annoying, but he is a guy I can easily spend time with since he lives in my building. We even connected our rooms by wire. His is directly above mine. That made it easy, with the right gear, to connect with each other through a pair of wired, toy 'walkie-talkies.' My mom works for the American military procuring all kinds of things. That means – she arranges to get stuff, buy materials, and distribute things. Often it was stuff other folks could not get. This was a surprise for my birthday. They are similar to military field phones, but it has to be connected by wires. I had them just sitting around and decided to link us up. John lowered my end of the walkie-talkie out his window, and I grabbed it and pulled it into my window. We could talk anytime we wanted.

(BEEP)

Calling Rick. Calling Rick Come in, Rick. This is John.

Who else would it be?

Do you read me?

(BEEP)

Gotcha, John. I read you loud and clear. What's happening?

(BEEP)

Wanna play "Spy Detector" tonight? Over.

Spy Detector is the big game of the year, where you try and discover 'who done it.' The other game that is just a year or two old at that time

is 'Risk.' It is the game of world conquest, with a roll of the dice as weapons.

(BEEP)

We need to finish our Risk game first. Remember? I, Alexander the Great, will take your Anatolia with ease tonight.

(BEEP)

My Persians are ready. Attack tonight! Crap yeah.

This is John's signature phrase. Don't know where he got it, but my mom would never let me get away with using it. But for John, it was 'Crap yeah' all the time.

Since John lives in my building, he got to know through me, sort of the *kapici's* kids, the Chobanians. They are the caretakers of the building. They live all the way downstairs, underground, in the basement. John is not good at language. He doesn't even try. He has notlived overseas before. I guess he expects everyone to speak English.

Strange, but Turkish isn't even offered at our school, only in your senior year. My Turkish is getting better and better, in large part because I am friends with the *kapaci's* kids, Salpi and Koko. TheChobanians are Armenian, now that I think of it, not Turks. But they speak Turkish.

Wow, Armenians in Turkey. That's a long history and very sad. Turkey still denies this, but most historians say as many as one million Armenians were killed in the early part of the 1900s by Ottoman Turkish soldiers. They call this the Armenian genocide. It is still a sore subject of contention today.

If you see someone's name that ends in 'ian,' that is a sure clue that they are of Armenian descent. I have known other Armenians. Some are American citizens with last names like Ouzunian, Bedrosian, and Sassounian.

Anyway, John got to know the *kapici's* kids, the Chobanians, through me.

"At least learn to say your name in Turkish," I advise him.

He perks up, "How do I do that?"

I must confess here. Jill has infected my mind. So, I concoct a little fun.

"The first words to learn are *'benim ismim'*. That means 'my name is.'"

"Ok. Ben –IM Iz – meen." He slaughters it, but that's OK.

"Close enough. Then you say, *banyo*. That is 'John' in Turkish". So, he repeats, "*Ben-em izmeen, banyo.*"

"You didn't. Tell me you didn't," laughs Jill in my re-telling of the story. "You devil."

Technically speaking, it is correct. Banyo is the name for a 'John,' yeah, that kind of a 'John.' Like, 'I gotta use the John.' Crap, yeah.

One day, as it often is for me, he also gets invited to share a meal with the *kapici* family in their basement apartment. I am totally into their custom of eating from a common tray – very different foods. John is not.

First of all, as one should, you wash your hands with a common jug of water. Okay. John gets that. Then you sit cross-legged, surrounding a large brass tray where all the food is arranged, elevated off the floorby a few inches. John is not used to this. He wants to lie with his feet to the table. That is considered rude. I correct him. So, he stretches out with his feet away from the table. Okay, strange, but it made the family laugh.

"What did I say?" he whispers to me.

What should I tell him? I am thinking. I finally say, "They think you're funny."

"Crap, yeah!" he smiles at everyone. "Benim ismim, Banyo."

They laugh again, big time. John just smiles, so happy for the attention. I smile, too.

"*Hoş geldin, Banyo efendi!*" The kids say altogether. ("Welcome, Mr. Toilet") Yeah. I did this.

"How do you drink around here? There are no glasses," he whispers to me.

One more of the peculiar things here is how to drink.

There are no glasses. They have an unusual glass bottle or pitcher. It has an opening at the top. The jug also has a spigot, and an open tube, sticking out the side. One learns to pour the water into one's mouth without the spigot touching the mouth. If your mouth touches it, it is considered unclean since everyone uses the same bottle. There is an art to swallowing and breathing at the same time. John has no such aesthetic. There was a lot of choking on my part when I first started. I do not want John to even try and end up in disaster, so I tell him.

"Oh. We better not drink the water; besides, they don't drink at dinner. Do you think you can do that?"

"Crap, yeah," came the reply. This seems to satisfy him

Salpi, the oldest daughter, maybe 14 years old, repeats,

"*Carap yah? O nedir?*" she asks me. (What is that?)

"*Iyi degil,*" I reply, meaning, 'NOT GOOD.' That is the literal translation. I keep it simple. My vocabulary is also not good. I want her to understand that the words are not good, you know, not nice words to use. I don't know how to say that. I am hoping she will understand that it did *not* mean exactly 'not good,' like 'not pleasing.' I didn't want to

literally translate 'crap.' That really would be 'not good.' I am not sure what she understands.

"*O. Carap yah*," Salpi repeats, nodding her head. And Koko, her little brother, chimes in louder, now getting it cleaner,

"*Crap yeah*? Mr. Rick, you talk Turkish *crap, yeah*!" pointing at me, Koko rubs it in. With their Armenian accents, it's even funnier. Now I know Koko does not get it. But learning American slang was really a thing. I think Salpi and Koko are hooked for good (or not good)on this now. Thanks, John.

So, we get into eating. There are no spoons, forks, or knives. You are given a little plate. John is looking around, very confused. I tell him,

"Just do what they do."

They take the bread and tear it into pieces and use it to scoop out various sauces, creams or vegetables, and other unknown food dishes. Then move it to one's mouth. They do the same using lettuce leaves.

Now, there are certain delicacies or special foods that are sometimes brought out for guests or special occasions. Some *look* absolutely irresistible. John digs into one of these eagerly *with his hands* (not good). Before I can say anything, he shoves it into his mouth. He does not swallow. Now, I've seen contortionists on television twist their bodies in all sorts of pretzel shapes. I now know John has that same talent with his face. I think he says something which I interpret as,

"What is this?"

I lie and tell him, "Goat guts."

As if he is in some horror movie, I swear his head spins completely around in a circle, looking for some kind of solution to his plight.

"Ahhh! Ahhh!" he sputters, pointing to his mouth. Then, he spits it out all over his shirt and the floor!

NOT COOL.

The Chobonians all run to get a cloth or something to help him. Salpi questions him.

"Crap yeah?"

Now, from what I said before, can you figure out what she meant by that? Not good? Then John adds,

"CRAP!" He spits again. "YEAH!"

I did not invite John to any more meals with the *kapaci*, the Chobanian family. I'm sure they were grateful for that. Crap yeah.

Chapter Twenty-Nine
In Spite of All the Danger

With John in tow, we leave the poor desperate woman, picking at the *lira* coin, to fend for herself. Off we go towards 50 Year Park. Nora hangs back to walk with John, much to Mitch's disappointment, no doubt to make a new recruit for her flock. John is not supposed to be with us, but here he is. In spite of any danger we might face, yeah, right, we are off to observe any suspicious behavior and 'detect' any drop locations.

"Sorry about John taggin' with us," I whisper to Jill.

"Sort of sorry about Nora, too?"

"You don't seem particularly worried."

"Oh, I'm not. Actually, it's perfect. I think I have another puzzle piece in place."

"What would that be?"

"*Boys like girls* – especially Nora girls."

"Big shocker there, Sherlock. But don't lump us all together in the same pile. Some of us are pretty decent guys. What I don't get is why you're not more bummed out about Nora."

She gives me that devious little smile, and I know something is up. I am much more bothered by Mitch hanging with us. At least there is Tom and Will to keep him company. Will is so glad Marie is with us, too. His flame for Marie is burning bright.

"Shenanigans are afoot!" Jill whispers to me, borrowing from the Sherlock Holmes character, as we walk ahead of the group. "I think the 'Body Snatchers' might just be invading Nora and John."

"Why is that? Giant Pods around?"

"Maybe something just as alien."

Donkey carts are passing us now and again. Jill is looking up and down the street like she is expecting something. Suddenly, she turns and calls back to John and Nora.

"Hey, you two. Have you experience with the ashak 'Jillian Maneuver'?"

They both get a funny look on their faces as John says, "I don't drink that stuff."

"No, silly," she says. "You want to hitch a ride on a donkey cart?" He lights up. Nora looks a bit more alarmed.

"Oh! Really? Crap yeah!" Yeah. There it is again. He is so delighted to be with us.

She points to a cart some distance down the road coming our way. Now, being the experienced *ashak* rider that I am, there is one particular two-wheeled, one-axle cart I know not to bother. And Jill knows it very well. It is usually covered by some sort of canvas. John nor Nora, I suspect, know this, and Jill will not tell him. I look down the street and see it.

"No, you're not. Really?" I whisper.

Jill just smiles.

The wind must have been blowing in a particular direction. Nora and John are walking now right behind us. Marie and Sarge are just behind them, followed by Tom and Mitch. Mr. Mustang, Dave, is not with us, attending an Aisha dance recital to impress her.

"She'll probably trip because I'm watching, blame me, and ignore me forever," he told us.

In typical Tom fashion, "Hey Mitch, do you know what B.O. stands for?"

"Not this again," Mitch protests. Marie just smiles.

"It's not what you think. Bromhidrosis Osmidrosis," Tom flatly states.

"That is not what I am thinking. What is it, Turkish?"

"Not Turkish and not body odor either. And do you know, sweat itself does not smell bad," Tom adds.

"Well, something around here does," Mitch says, as I feel his stare piercing through me like a word-laden crossbow arrow.

"That sweet aroma is just the normal stuff," Tom adds. Then off Mitch goes on a poem, out loud,

> *The Jillian Maneuver is so divine*
> *Like riding a windstorm*
> *Or a bucking bovine.*
> *Take a little hop, blow Jill a little kiss,*
> *She's the instigator,*
> *A really fine Swiss miss.*

Jill giggles. I groan. I'm just glad he doesn't have his guitar.

There are a couple of carts closer to us, so Jill tells Mitch and Tom to 'take a little hop.' Marie declines. She knows the drill and hangs with Sarge.

"Watch closely, you two," she calls back to Nora and John.

Now, Mitch and Tom are pros at the Jillian Maneuver. Mitch defiantly sort of skips boldly alongside the cart (not officially sanctioned or recommended by Jill) while Tom sneaks up, as to protocol, from behind.

"Mitch, what are you doing?" Jill yells. He turns, blows her a kiss, and just shrugs as he skips alongside the cart.

"He's going to ruin the whole thing," she whispers and sternly gestures to him to get behind the cart. Mitch finally joins Tom at the back of the cart, and they perform the approved maneuver flawlessly. Up the street, they go. Easy peasy.

"Hmmm," I'm thinking, "what's got into Mitch? Ha. Is it I? Yes!"

"Here is your chance, John and Nora." She points to the approaching two-wheeled cart with the canvas cover. She quickly gives them a verbal crash course on the maneuver. John is all into it.

"You saw what Tom did. Ignore Mitch."

Nora shakes her head, "*Ja,* I ignore Mitch, but dis 'ting so *gefährlich*, much danger."

"Oh Nora, you know you want to, you wild thing," I tell her

"*Da Stimpt. Ja.* I am, as you say, on *das 'vild'* side."

"You got to be stealthy now," Jill adds.

"What's that mean?" John questions.

"Quiet, secret, and careful."

"Oh, OK. Crap yeah. Stealthy, good. Watch this," he whispers as the cart comes up to us. He must think the body snatcher pods are after him 'cause he is off like a shot.

"Come on, 'vild ting.' We got this," he calls after her, and she follows.

We watch as he darts to the street and attempts the proper maneuver, with Nora right behind. Mitch has not been a good role model for the practice. But John finally gets to the back of the cart. However, his feet do not plant on the single axle quite the way Jill has taught. Nora is right there with him, far more agile than John. This particular kind of cart is trickier than others. After all, it is John's first time. So, holding on to the back wooden wall, his feet are dragging behind him. Nora has

already locked in. The cart driver's whip does not come out soonenough to save them. Not too many seconds pass when the back wall snaps off, and the cart tips backward. Down comes the contents of the cart, spilling all over John and Nora as the cart drags to a stop.

This *ashak* driver is responsible for shoveling up the substantial horse and donkey dung off the street. Even though it gives the driver some satisfaction to see his two stowaways mostly buried in their own evil deeds, he is not happy about shoveling up the contents again. Morebad words in Turkish are expressed as John pulls Nora up to run off as best they can before the driver can get his whip on them. Their rite of passage is now complete.

Will speaks up, "I think they both have caught a bad case of Bromhidrosis Osmidrosis." Marie busts up. Good for Will. He needed some points.

"I think I have a new name for your creation," I say as we watch John and Nora run down the street, chased by a very upset *ashak* driver.

"What would that be?" an innocent voice asks me.

"The 'Jillian Manure,' Crap, yeah."

That gets me my stratospheric prize for the day. It takes Jill a while to recover when she says,

"They're still there,"

"Who?"

"I'd swear that car has been following us for blocks."

"What do you mean?"

A new *ashak* cart has just passed us.

"Come on." Off she goes on her Jillian maneuver. I quickly follow. I feel my legs tighten a little as we come up from behind. I have to dodge a copper pot hanging on the back of the cart as it swings and bangs back

and forth. The streets right now are just Antville. I mean, they are as busy as I have ever seen them. Our cart starts to pick up speed as we attach ourselves with a crack of the driver's whip over the *ashak's* head.It's too loud and too risky to ask any more questions. But I give it a shot.

"What's this all about?"

"Keep watching," Jill shouts back. This is a pretty rough ride. The pot, bouncing all over the place, keeps whacking me in the head. The cart continues to speed up, that poor donkey, and takes us for a couple of fast blocks. When my head is knocked around by the pot, I can't help but notice the black sedan behind us.

"That's it," Jill yells, "the same car." Cars usually zoom around the slower-moving *ashak* carts that tend to hug the curb when they can. This sedan is hanging back the whole time. Whack! The pot hits me again, and my hands slip off the cart.

"Rick!" Jill screams.

My feet hit the ground running, but it's just too much for me. I fall and roll further into the street, right in front of the approaching sedan. It screeches to a stop just as I stand and slap the hood, staring right into the window. The passenger ducks down but not before I notice a good part of his nose is missing. The car slowly creeps around me when the passenger reappears at the open window wearing a *kufiyah*, an Arab headdress, covering his face.

"You, little man Foster, no help girl, or we make much trouble for you and big man Foster."

They speed off down the street, following Jill on the cart. I turn around just long enough to see Jill and the cart turn at an intersection and disappear behind the buildings a block up the street. The black sedan follows.

By the time I get myself together and hobble up and street, it takes me at least five minutes. When I turn the corner, I see Jill running towards me with Mitch and Tom.

Tom's face is flushed as he asks, "Jill said you fell off the cart. Are you all right? We got a game tomorrow."

"A few scratches. Maybe it will help my batting?" Jill is right behind him, passes him, and gives me a big hug.

"You're here. I'm so relieved."

"What happened to you?" I quickly add.

"You should have seen her, Rick. It was amazing!" Tom blurts out.

"The cart was going too fast to jump off, so I hung on," Jill tells me.

"Which is what you were supposed to do, sharpshooter," Mitch quips.

"Hey. I was whacked by a copper pot. Give me a break. And this black sedan about does me in." I look down the street and see the cart upended, contents strewn all over the pavement.

"Whoa. What happened, Jill?"

Tom perks up, "Was there a guy in it with half a nose?"

"How did you know?"

"When my cart slowed down, I jumped off, and the sedan drove right into the side, spilling all the cargo. It all happened so fast," Jill explains.

"We didn't see it, but by the time we got there, Jill was poking and thrusting and jabbing." He is really animated, re-enacting the scene. "Pow and move and jab and move."

"At what and with what?"

"These two guys. Mr. No nose was huge! They were trying to get to Jill," Mitch adds. "Two policemen were across the street and ran to help, but the guys took off. Then we came up."

"What happened to the cart driver?"

"He's fine. Probably as dazed as I am," Jill says somberly.

"And the *ashak?*"

"He was eating the apples from the spilled baskets last I saw," Tom adds as he takes a big bite out of a particularly luscious Red Delicious.

RIVALRY BOX SCORE:

Mitch may have lost a point for not following the Jillian Maneuver as prescribed. Don't know what got into him. She was very particular about those things. But then, there is the poem. Ahhhh. Worth anything? Not in my book, but he got a smile out of Jill. Nuts. I, on the other hand, gained maybe two points. One for bringing John along. And two, for NOT warning him about a certain ashak cart. Then, maybe I lost a point as well for bringingJohn along. I may have got some sympathy points for the spectacular fall. I, at least, got a hug for it. Either way, I was staying ahead of Mitch. Maybe, for now.

Episode Four

A Bad Combination

Chapter Thirty
If You've Got Trouble

(BEEP. BEEP.BEEP.)

Calling Rick. Calling Rick Come in, Rick. This is John.

Who else would it be?

Do you read me?

(BEEP)

Yeah, John. I'm up now.

(BEEP)

Man, we had real troubles. Why did you guys leave me yesterday?

(BEEP)

I don't have to think hard about this one.

Well, you weren't exactly ready to join the human race at that point. And we didn't want the cart driver to turn on us. So, we skedaddled.

(BEEP)

Well, I wanted to come, but that crap went down my shirt and pants! And you should have seen Nora. It went down her shirt as well. Watching her shake that out wasn't so bad.

(BEEP)

Trying not to laugh again.

You devil.

(BEEP)

It was all good until she asked why she had no class with me. Is eighth grade so bad? She screamed and ran away. I still was thinking you guys would at least help me. I didn't know what to do.

(BEEP)

The only thing I could think of was;

Well. You do now! You've got less trouble than I do.

(BEEP)

Do you know that old lady picking at the coin? She was still there when I got home, working on that thing. I gave her my mom's kitchen knife, and she finally pried it up. She didn't seem to mind my smell. I told her my name as you taught me. She just looked at me funny. Probably my accent. Just thought you should know. Over and out.

(BEEP)

Chapter Thirty-One
Ob-La-Di, Ob-La-Da

"Jill. Who were those guys? Do you have any idea?"

It was game day. Yeah, Danger 9b was also a baseball player. Diablo – was not. Jill and I sat in the empty bleachers well before my game. Score one more half-point for me.

"I told you I was a target."

"Good golly, Miss Molly, were they trying to take you? Tom said they were grabbing at your purse."

"Oh… yeah, to get to me. That's it. That's… what I think. Don't worry. Life goes on."

"Of course, I'm worried. What was that stuff Tom was telling me, jabbing, poking, and all?"

"You saw my fencing trophies. I was trying to protect myself, so I grabbed the *ashak* driver's cane. It kept Mr. No Nose away."

"He almost ran over me. I have to tell you; they don't seem to want me around you."

"How do you figure that?"

"Well, for one thing, they seem to know my name and my dad's, too. Just like the Russians."

"That doesn't make sense."

"I know. I'm trying to piece that together. Did you tell your parents?"

"Ahh. No. It's best they don't know."

"Okay. Yeah. I hope you're right. I've already gotten you into enough scrapes as it is."

"I'm trying to forget about it as much as possible."

The bruises and scratches on my arms won't let me forget. So, I drop it for now.

I'm not sure Jill likes baseball. Ah oh. Maybe that takes me down a point? We play our games at our school fields on the unfinished airbase. A carnival celebration or fund-raiser is going on today as well. This day there are dumb rides on donkeys, dunking, and other game booths, including a kissing booth – but Jill was not involved in that one.Nuts. I thought she could have earned a fortune for charity, at least fromme.

"You are nice to think so, Rick. But no one would pick me."

Was she kidding? I didn't want to push the point.

"Hey, there are camel rides."

"That I will do, but this is my first time with your sport. I don't get baseball."

"Well, when you're fifteen or sixteen and overseas, you play Little League Senior baseball. It's an international organization. We play a bunch of games, and at the end of the season, an all-star team is selected to compete for the European Little League Championship to be held in Germany."

Where in Germany?"

"The airbase in Wiesbaden."

"Oh. My dad was stationed there for a time."

"The winner will fly to the United States to compete in the World Series Little-League playoffs. To be an all-star, you must be the best of the best. Flying back to the States to play in the World Series would be more fab than the fab four."

"You wouldn't have a problem leaving me here with Mitch?" She smiles.

"Oh. A big problem, for sure."

"OK. So, explain this game."

"I am a catcher. He is the guy who crouches behind the batter and receives the pitches, the thrown balls that get past the batter."

"These people you are talking about seem like a violent sort or a little crazy."

"What are you talking about?"

"Well, your 'batter' sounds scary, like he is after people to whack them down, and there's this other guy who is throwing balls at him, and someone else, you, I guess, is crouching and hiding to catch the batter. Please, someone, help my catcher to stop that wild man batter! Or is he after the pitcher?"

"No, that's not it. You know Tom, he is a pitcher. A good one."

"There are bad pitchers?"

"Sure. You see, the pitcher is trying to strike out the batter who is trying to get a hit."

"Even worse. It sounds like war! Don't let the guy strike anyone or let the other guy hit anyone. Sick the catcher on them both!"

Ahhhhrrrggg, girls, and sports.

"You are reminding me of the greatest comedy sketch of all time."

"I am that funny?"

"You are."

"There are these two guys, Bud and Lou, talking about baseball. Lou is like you, hardly knows a thing – about baseball."

"Who is Lou?"

"You."

"Oh, good."

"But Bud describes a very unusual team. Bud, me, names the first few players.

'Who' is playing on first base? 'What' is on second base. And 'I Don't know' is on third. After naming these first three players…"

"Wait a minute," Jill interrupts me. "Who is 'playing' on first base and why?"

"That's right. Who is – 'why' hasn't entered the game yet."

"What is this guy playing on first base, the Tuba?"

"No. What is not playing on first base or a Tuba? This is baseball."

She is starting to turn a bit red. "Who did you say was playing on first base?"

"That's right."

"Who?"

"Yes."

"What is his name?"

"No, he is on second."

"Who is?"

"No. He's on first. What is on second!"

"What are you asking me for? I don't know."

"Oh, he's on third". She then hits me over the head with my ball cap.

"Stop! I can't take it anymore. Give me a breather."

I almost regret trying to explain it to her. But it is fun. It lets you understand what comes next. Tom (Spitball) is my best friend in Turkey. Nothing can ruin the friendship between Spitball and me. Nothing. We will always be friends. He can call me names,

"Hey, Dumbo ears. Flap and cool me off, will ya?" and we will still be friends. I can call him goofy.

"Hey, Goofball, your underwear is on backward," and we'd remain friends. If he does not pick me on his team (foolish mistake) for dodgeball, that is OK. I really have great upper body strength. That's why I am a catcher.

"Ahh. I'll pick Mitch," says Tom. (That's OK, too. He is lousy at dodgeball.)

He can even start liking Jill, and I am fine with that. (Princess would clobber him.) He can even make me some...

"Hey, have some of my **peanut butter** cookies."

No...that will do it! That will end the friendship. I hate them.

"Hey Rick, did you know that Spadefoot Toads smell like peanut butter?" Tom tells me.

I hate toads, too.

"Hey, did you also know that arachibutyrophobia is the fear of peanut butter stuck on the roof of your mouth?"

I just know I have arachibutyrophobia. I think I also have a fear of spelling that word.

Besides that, there is one other thing that did try our friendship. We do not play on the same team. He is on the 'Indians,' and I am on the 'Dodgers.' Jill then tells me,

"I guess I am a girl who probably, definitely, most assuredly does not like baseball."

"How is that possible? Everyone likes baseball."

"Who is everyone?"

"No, who plays first base? 'Everyone' is in left field. Ha Ha. Don't want to be boring."

She then takes my catcher's glove and whacks me over the head again.

Chapter Thirty-Two
The Sheik of Araby

The carnival is going on. All the games and booths are up and going. We walk over to take a look. I've got my Dodger uniform on, and she gets around to asking,

"What does it mean to be a 'dodger'?" She asks, "You trying to avoid me?"

"Ah contraire, my Swiss miss. Why don't we just mosey on down to the kissing booth?"

"Now that I will dodge. In your dreams, buckaroo."

"Okay then. How about a camel ride as a consolation prize?"

"That sounds fun."

"What sounds fun?" A voice from behind perks up. It's Mitch.

"What are you doing here?" I quiz him.

"It's not for the baseball," he assures me. "I think Nora is manning or womaning the kissing booth. See ya later."

While in line for the camel ride, Colonel MacGregor strides by in his striking Air Force blue uniform.

"Hello,   you   two."

"Colonel MacGregor!"

"Hey Dad!" The camel tender spins around when we say this. I think this is a bit strange, but okay. The man is wearing an Arabheaddress that covers most of his face. Usually, this is to keep the dustout.

"Take good care of these two. They haven't a clue how to ride this," he says to the camel tender.

"Yes, *Efendi.*"

We load on the camel to take our spin around the prepared track. After some quick instructions, the camel lurches forward, then backward to rise. This causes Jill, sitting behind me, to grab hold aroundmy waist. I just might buy myself a camel.

"Hi O Silver, away! I'm the Sheik of Arabia," I say as we head out.

"You know, you are much more of a goofball than I thought. Another part of your puzzle piece is coming into focus."

"What about the other pieces?"

"I'm working on those. But you're in the wrong genre with Westerns and quoting the 'The Lone Ranger.'"

"Okay. I'm not wearing a mask or on horseback, but I'm in the ballpark. Get it? Besides, it's your fault I'm growing a mane."

"What?"

"Being a bit more daring. I feel like 'Lawrence of Arabia.'"

"Now you're in the right genre. I did see that movie. That Lawrence actor, Peter O'Toole, has the dreamiest blue eyes. If you're going to talk to camels like he did, you should be saying, hut, hut."

With that vocal command, the camel lurches into a quicker pace, and I lurch forward suddenly. Riding a camel is a tedious sport. You are constantly thrown up and down, then sometimes forward and backward. Although I love the close contact and the hug, I'm glad it's a short track.

"Ahhh. Wow. You did see that movie. I just thought that was a made-up dialog for that O'Toole guy. Hey, my eyes are blue, too."

"Not even close, *efendi*. I must say, I am much more comfortable as an equestrian."

"Equestrian. Is that an eating disorder?"

158

"Horses, silly. I had equestrian training in Switzerland. I have horses back in Bern. Grandfather saw to that. He called me 'Buce' for short."

"Buce? What for?"

"Short for *Bucephalus*, the war horse of Alexander the Great. My Grandfather had this obsession about that ancient conqueror."

"*Bucephalus*. That's right. Now it makes sense. Bucephalus supposedly had one blue eye! That's so cool."

She gives me an extra squeeze.

"But Buce or '*Bous*' is Classical Greek for "Ox." What does *phalus* mean?

"Greek for 'head.'"

"Hmm. Ox head. Not really flattering. OK, Buce it is. But, you know, it was said Alexander's horse was so stubborn he couldn't be tamed. That fits, Miss Buce." I get pinched in the stomach. "Yeoww"

"Couldn't be broke, except by a King's son named Alexander, *Ricky*," she says with some emphasis, "so says the legend."

"Don't worry. I won't even try. Hey. Did you know my middle name is Alex?"

She pinches me again.

"Nice try."

"What was all that stuff about being the daughter of Alexander in another life?"

"Wishful thinking, I guess. But that guy you picked, Diogenes? He was a nut case, you know. I hope you're not related.'

"Oh. I thought he was a philosopher that knew Alexander."

"Diogenes lived naked in a barrel in Athens, a cut-out wooden crate and defecated in public. Enough said?"

But this time, our camel arrives back at the start. Just as he stops, the camel tender reaches out, and our camel bolts. He lunges to stop the animal but only grabs a corner of Jill's purse. As his hands slide off, he almost pulls Jill down. Our camel is now into a full gallop. I can't reach the reins. We are jostled so violently that we won't last long on top. Out of the corner of my eye, I see Mitch looking like a cheetah cutting diagonally across the track to us. I clamp my legs down harder and hold the saddle horn tighter to keep us on. Mitch catches us in maybe 20 seconds. He moves in front of the charging camel with his hands up just as I finally reach and pull the reins. From both actions, the camel stumbles to a stop. The camel tender arrives, out of breath.

"My apologies, *effendi*," is all he says, and he commands the camel down for us to hop off.

Colonel MacGregor is right behind him. "I think you better retire this beast for today," he commands.

"Yes, *effendi*. Yes. This I do."

The Colonel thanks Mitch, and so do I, reluctantly.

"You never run like that in our football games, Mitch. That was some sprint."

"They don't call me Mitch the Meteor for nothing," winking at Jill.

I had never heard that, so it is nothing to me.

"We might have been killed or badly injured," Jill gushes. "Mitch is my hero today," she says as she wraps her arms around him tight. Nuts.

"You going to come to Rick's game? Tom, Dave, and Will are playing, too," Jill asks.

"I guess. It's free, isn't it? I spent all my money at the kissing booth."

"You poor thing. You'll have to sit with me and recover. You know how much we both <u>love</u> baseball."

Mitch gives me an annoying shrug. "She asked me," he whispers.

Chapter Thirty-Three
I'm a Loser

Tom and I played our game, his 'Indians' against my 'Dodgers.' It was a tight score all game long, with Jill yelling rude things from the stands, cued by Mitch, I'm sure. The coach and my teammates are really good to me. I know I am a special case. They know my weakness is running. I can get good wood on the ball, but it's going to have to be a solid hit. All I must do is get to first base, and the rules say they can then substitute someone to run in my place. The catching part is the bestpart of my game. I'm really pretty good. It didn't help this day. At the last part of our game, Tom slides into my home plate for the final winning run, and I reach out to tag him 'out.' I have him 'out,' but I drop the ball when I hear my thumb go 'snap.' I jerk off my glove. If I use that thumb to hitchhike a ride, the driver will think I want to take a sharp left turn. I get a nice cast put on. Yeah, I lost.

Jill is shocked and sympathetic. She calls me on the phone when I get home that night.

"I'm so sorry. Are you and Tom still friends?"

"All is good."

"I told you this sounded like a violent sport. Good thing you already have a hand cast from art. Now it has a companion."

Tom also calls me that night but not so much to talk about our accident. I know he is very sorry. Not really his fault – only bad if Peanut Butter is involved.

"Didn't Jill tell you? Mitch told me he saw the camel driver loading up that beast when his face covering fell off. He was missing a good part of his nose."

"The same guy you saw at the cart?"

"It could have been. I guess it was a pretty quick look, but who else would be missing a snozzle and be that huge?"

"There are plenty of beggars around here that are missing all sorts of body parts. He could be wrong, or it just might be a coincidence?"

"Well, maybe. I wasn't going to say anything. As you say, maybe it's a misjudgment. But when Mitch and I saw Jill from a distance at the crashed cart, she was talking to those two guys, particularly mister missing snozzle."

"I thought you said she was sword-fighting them?"

"Not at first. Maybe they were arguing. I don't know. We were too far away to tell."

Since I can't really talk to her on the bus, I corner Jill in the courtyard outside the school. A cast is on my wrist, and I wing it around for all to see. I am really hoping for some sympathy points from Jill. Mitch and Nora pass us with a quick glance and move on.

"Jill, I'm really confused. You didn't tell me about the missing nose guy at the carnival."

"I didn't see him. Well, I mean, I didn't know it. Mitch told me."

"Let me be straight with you. Is it the same guy you were talking to at the crashed cart?"

She looks down for a bit.

"Yeah. I think it is. I'm sorry. I haven't been completely honest with you. His name is Tigran."

"You *know* him?"

"When he's not in disguise."

"Jill. What's going on?"

"He was on my grandfather's staff in Paris. He took care of my grandfather's correspondence. He kept him informed of what was needed and drafted replies."

"So why is he after you?"

"He knows things. And he is looking for the same things I am."

"And what is that?"

She doesn't answer. She just stares at me. Finally, she ventures, "I don't have much time left. I don't think he is trying to harm me."

"Are you blind, Bucephalus? He seems quite intent on violence. And it may not be just against you. And what do you mean you don't have much time left?"

"It might all just… go away… all be lost."

"What's going to be lost? Hey. This is not going away. *I am* not going away."

The bell rings. She seems relieved.

"Let's pick this up after school," and off she goes.

We're in the same first-period class, so I trudge off behind her. Later, between first and second period, Jane (Aisha) passes this to me in the hall;

To the most auspicious Danger 9b,

It's time. Lolita (This is her 'official' code name. I still call her 'The Vulture') *is calling in all contestants. I hope you're ready. I'm trying to keep my part of the bargain. Mostly. Not my fault Fortuna keeps calling for me. Lolita says she will find us all at our lockers today sometime.*

Diablo

I'm not well versed on these things, but I know what a tape measure is. I've done my part and changed my combination to the required estimate. It seems a bit slimy, but it's done all in good fun and, for me, room for a more competitive advantage.

I need to pick up my history book. I head to my locker. Jill is standing there.

"Oh. Hi! I can walk with you to Mr. T's class now."

She is like a stone pillar – with stone-cold staring eyes.

"What?" I ask.

She is wearing a turtleneck sweater. Yeah. She leans against the locker and folds her arms, still staring. She says nothing at first. I feel the trickle of water increase, flowing out of my cast. Then the stone pillar turns into a pillar of fire. "Don't lump me in the same pile as otherboys, you say? OK. Open it, buddy. You like contests? Just don't be shocked at the prize."

I look around. Isn't it going to be the Vulture meeting me?

"You've been talking to Mitch? This is just for fun."

"I didn't have to, Nora told me. You – fun? Ha. Do the numbers – out loud."

Why do I feel a twelve-member, all-girl jury is standing over me? My hands are now quite clammy. It makes it hard to spin the dial.

"Ahh. Okay. The top num… I mean… the first… 48."

She cracks a slight, steely smile.

"42"

Her eyes narrow. She almost laughs.

"46"

She stops smiling. "Really?"

I guess these are not good numbers. The locker opens. There is a rumble of noise at the bottom, and a certain ceramic hand tumbles outto the hallway and breaks apart. A lone finger goes spinning out to the center of the floor. It might have been her middle finger.

Jill stares down at the spread of pieces. Her mouth drops open. Her eyes flare up at me. I think the all-girl jury has reached a decision.

"You? That's where it went? It was you all along?"

"I can explain."

That pillar of fire can't evaporate the water welling up in her eyes. "I trusted you. And I've been blaming Nora all this time? What possessed you to… never mind."

"There is a good reason. I…"

She storms off. Without turning around, she says over her shoulder, "Doesn't matter, klepto. By the way, you lose the bet. Those aren't even in your ballpark for my numbers."

I freeze.

"Your numbers?" I call out in a panic, "Wait. You got it wrong. It's not you."

"You better believe it's not me. You got more than that wrong – big time. You know, you aren't who you appear to be," is the last I hear as she rounds the corner.

"I'm not a kleptomaniac," I call after her, then quietly, "just a stupid loser."

I arrive late to History class, but Mr. Tenney doesn't notice, thank goodness. He's started his lecture.

Mr. Tenney: *It's 334 B.C. People. What's happening here? In this very land?*

Aisha: *Help! We're being invaded.*

Mr. Tenney: Exactly. A young Macedonian King, after conquering Greece, decides to take on Darius and the Persian Empire. That kingdom extended from India to the very western shores of our land here called what in the day?

Tom: Oo. Oo. I know. Turkey Major.

Mr. Tenney: You mean Asia Minor. But that's not what they called it yet.

Marie: Cappadocia.

Mr. Tenney: I'll accept that. Thank you, Miss Hairston. And who is this incredibly young warrior/king?

Jill: Twenty-year-old Alexander the Third, Alexander the Great, succeeding when his father is assassinated in front of him

Jill offers casually.

Mr. Tenney: Nice bit of detail there.

He goes on, and she seems to check out then, knowing she won't be called on again. She gives me a quick glance. I see note paper come out. I have no excuses. I think I might make things worse if I try. I get the note a minute later.

Rick

(Now I know I'm in trouble. Codename out the window.)

I can't even speak to you right now. I'm so mad. No not mad, really disappointed in you. First of all, I got the only B grade of my life not having the hand cast. But far worse, you think so little of me to belittle my very being. Have fun playing baseball.

Who are you?

And he is NOT on first.

She doesn't even sign it. That's when I know I have hit rock bottom. I spend some time trying to explain in a note, but when she gets it, she crumples it up without even looking at it and deftly scores a basket in the trash.

Chapter Thirty-Four
Misery

I feel the whole world is treating me badly. I've lost her now. I'm pretty sure. Jill does a good job avoiding me. She takes a different bus or rides to school with her dad. I finally corner Mitch, who also is avoiding me.

"You set me up, you fink."

"Don't blame me. I had little to do with this. It was all Nora."

"Well, the Vulture is feeding well off your sorry carcass."

"Well, she is still plenty bummed out about the manure pile Jill put her in."

"Purely accidental." I feel bad lying, so how can I blame Mitch?

"By the way, I won," he says.

"What's the prize?"

Mitch just walks away, smiling. "Enjoy your time with the boys and your misery. It's sure gonna be a drag."

What he is referring to is that Tom and I have been selected for the Ankara All-Star team. Somehow, it doesn't seem as joyful to me under the circumstances. I learn how to play and bat with my cast. Tom is our all-star pitcher, and I am the all-star catcher. My cast is buried in my catcher's glove, so it doesn't affect my grip and throwing.

We first have to beat the all-star team that plays in the city of Izmir. These boys are from the U.S. Air Force Base located near that city, which is on the west coast of Turkey. This means we must be gone from Ankara for a time. This will leave Mitch alone with Jill.

I'm stuck. Marie won't talk with me either. Since Will has the hots for Marie, I get bits and pieces from him, who hears shards of info from Marie. Who knows how accurate it is?

"Don't believe all I tell you. If you feel like smacking someone, I can take it. Or maybe if I give you a good shiner, they might feel sorry for you?" Will tells me.

"What has Marie told you?"

"Well, Mitch was speaking Spanish to Jill, something about Jill, *mi Corazon*. I think that means 'my heartthrob' and something about wanting to go do something fun while we're gone."

"Oooo. That rat fink. He said he'd stay away."

"Mitch complained this place is like a desert island, with nothing to do."

"Oh. Poor Mitch."

"Then she pretends to do a Tom and asks him, 'Hey Mitch, did you know that Musonius Rufus was banished to a desolate, barren island between here and Greece by the Roman Emperor, Nero?'"

"Oh boy. Rufus again? At least it's aimed at Mitch. But Nero? Bad actor."

"Then she tells Mitch to be more like this Rufus guy and do something like 'embrace' the difficult stuff of life. Yeah. Do you want me to make it difficult for him?" He pounds his fist into his open hand, "want me to, huh?"

"Just go on. I can take it."

"Anyway, Mitch asks her... hold on now, don't lose it on me... he asks, 'Can I embrace *you*?'"

"What? Are you sure, Will?"

"Don't hit me. I'm just the messenger. Yeah. You are losin' out big time here."

"Then what?"

"Oh, she gives him some more advise, and he thinks he is getting banished by Nero Jill."

"Oh. That sounds better."

"Well, this won't. He tells her he wants her back. I think Marie said, 'Like the old days' when it was just the two of them. Now don't hit me. That cast will hurt."

"Go on."

"He tells her he has doubts about your 'you know what' special training. But Marie tells him her dad says there are all kinds of CIA people that work at the embassy. She's on your side. And we're having so much fun helping."

"That's it? What happened after that?"

"Doom, depression, ruthless backstabbing, knudeling, heartless falsification, I don't know. I'll do some bone-cracking if you want. You do the spying!"

Chapter Thirty-Five
Rain

I have the feeling of running and hiding my head or more like I am dead. Even so, I haven't forgotten the promise I made to Jill to look for Peanut Butter. Maybe the base in *Izmir* has some. I'll be gone a week, maybe two, if we win in *Izmir*. All I get from her is a terse reply.

"OK, your loss by your win."

Strangely, that makes sense. My hope is to hold her to her promise if I find peanut butter. But that seems an impossibility right now. She has not tasted any for many months. Now remember, my mom is in procurement as a job. She gets stuff for people. I plead with her.

"Please, please, please, Mom! Can you procure some peanut butter? Pretty please? It would be very good for me. I <u>need</u> it."

"Ricky, you hate peanut butter. Why the need?"

"Chemistry class. I need to do… an… experiment with it." It may or may not have convinced her. Time would tell.

It is an agonizing two weeks. Because we win in Izmir, we fly off to Germany in a military cargo plane. I am wary about being away for another week. Being with my team is so fun, but I have the feeling there are more important things to do at home, things I am missing.

"Rick, what are you talking about 'more important'?" Tom corners me when I mention it to him.

"What could be more important than baseball?"

It isn't just Jill. I mean, it is, but there is more going on with her than just us. It's bothering me. I just am not on my game.

We win the consolation bracket at *Wiesbaden*. OK, we win the loser's bracket. I think the coach secretly blames me. I hear a few grumblings from my teammates about my play. Tom is eerily silent. I just didn't play well. Maybe, unconsciously, I did it on purpose. It's notall my fault. It takes a team to win. But that gives us third place in the European Championship. This is something to be proud of. No trip to the States. I don't complain much. The problem is, I return with no peanut butter.

"So. What did you do while we were gone?" Will innocently asks Marie on our return. I'm right there, snooping on their conversation.

"I took Jill and Mitch to a Turkish salon," she proudly proclaims.

"A what?"

"It's a place where you get pampered – nails done, make-up, hair fancied up, and a massage."

Will's face says it all, "You took Mitch? Did he get his nails done?"

"No silly. They give boys haircuts and, OK, they trim toenails, no painting, but they give a massage."

Oh, this is a choice! I can really get him on this one. But wait. Don't do it. Jill thinks this is fun, and he was willing! While the cat is away, devil mice will play and play and play. I should have known.

"Oh," she tells Will, "Jill gave Mitch some of my zit creams. He insisted Jill show him how to use it."

What? Why is she telling him (and me) this? This is gross in my book. Finding underwear is one thing, but applying zit cream?

I guess being a macho, manly baseball player and an all-star catcher with a cast on my broken thumb is not all that impressive or worth some sympathy.

"They went all kinds of places. Nice restaurants and walks in the park. Jill liked that he showed his vulnerable side. Mitch left her with another poem. I can show you," she seems to say in delight.

Hands so good
Hands so warm
Zits mock manhood
Jill's touch reforms

Why am I reading this? When the rain comes, it pours. I was gone too long. I have all this back schoolwork to catch up on. I feel like two camels are sitting on my chest, lazily chewing gum, probably Juicy Fruit flavor, and casually glancing around at the grim desolate scenery of my life. My teammates hate me. My coach hates me. Jill hates me even worse. I have no one to talk to about it. I get no letters, no notes, and nothing waiting for me when I get back.

'Who' is not on first base now. Mitch is.

I hate baseball.

UPDATE RIVALRY BOX SCORE:

Danger 9b – Probably a minus one for introducing her to baseball. I did hang on to the camel. So, I'm back to 0. Then I really blew it with the contest and hand cast. I'm well below 0 now. Diablo – Two points for being Meteor Mitch. Two Points for hanging around and being so 'vulnerable.' He got a half-point for the poem. (I would have docked him one point) Oh. Maybe I lost another point because I did not come back with peanut butter. I'm well into the minus number zone.

Episode Five

Scouting Out the Enemy

Chapter Thirty-Six
Thank You, Girl

Ring, ring. I hear our phone, located on our kitchen wall down the hall from my room. It's morning. I'm still groggy from all the travel and play and worry.

"Hey Toto brain, it's for you," my brother yells, then cackles, "I'll get you my pretty and your little dog, too."

"Ricky?" I hear through the earpiece. My heart stops, sort of.

"Jill?"

I pull the phone cord out of the kitchen and into a closet. It's quiet on the other end.

Finally, I hear, *"I'm sorry."*

"Is it really you?"

"Don't make me say it again."

"No. No. It's good. It's all good. Thank you. That's all you gotta do."

"Nora told me everything. The contest wasn't about me."

"No. It was still stupid of me, but..."

"I know. I pulled your note out of the trash and finally read it. I'm furious with Mitch. If he wants to fool around with Nora, she can have him, the little rat."

"He promised me he would leave us alone."

"I know. But that was never going to happen. Now, about my ceramic hand, oh, how is your thumb? Did you get the cast-off?"

"Tomorrow. I wanted to surprise you. I..."

177

"Let's talk later. I do want to know —but I forgive you. I need you now more than ever."

Chapter Thirty-Seven
Carry That Weight

There are no rollercoasters in Turkey until now. I am on one of the wildest. I was at the bottom and probably stuck there for some time and nowhere in sight to get off. I was going to have to carry that heavy baggage, that massive weight, for a long time. I had no idea my car was then going to click, clank and climb to the top. Do I have to go down? Man, how many points is that worth? I feel like things are better than ever. Poor Mitch. No, not poor Mitch. He stepped right into this. The Vulture wanted him back all the time and this may have worked.

Along with my rivalry with Mitch, there is an even longer rivalry with my brother. Lucky for me, he is not an athlete and not interestedin baseball. Good thing, I may fare worse if he had sported any muscles at all, brain or otherwise. Let me explain.

My first obstacle and survival challenge was and is my brother, Steve. He is three, almost four years older. I think I get picked on more than I should. Here is what I mean, this is the major start of our brotherlyrivalry.

During my short stay in the United States, our mother sent us to swimming lessons that were about a mile away. At that time, I was a small seven-year-old, and he was a big eleven or twelve-year-old. We had to walk along a busy road to get to the pool. As it still is, smoking cigarettes was a very common thing and people would toss their empty cigarette packages out their car windows as if they were radioactive debris. And they sort of are. Not flattering actions on both counts – smoking and littering. My brother seized upon the moment and invented a new game.

"Rick. Do you see all these cigarette packages?" Steve pointed out. "Look at the names. Hmmm, this one says, 'Lucky Strike.' Here is a 'Kool,' a 'Winston,' a 'Marlboro,' a 'Camel.' What is this? A 'Pall

Mall'? That's a weird one. Oh, what's this, a cool green one that says, 'Salem.'?"

Then he found a brand called 'Pyramid.'

These were just a few of the many in the United States. As we walked along the road, Steve found one of these empty packages and used it as an excuse to perform some kind of torture on me. I am afforded the same option if I find a package. As supreme ruler of the universe, even the Great Oz, he set the rules.

"If I find a 'Lucky Strike,' I get to deliver one punch to your arm."

Of course, I was the victim most of the time.

"Now, if I find a package of 'Salem,' I perform a 'Salem Slam'!" Picture that one for a moment. It got worse from there. He was the first to find a 'Camel' package. "I will perform a 'Camel clobber' with this one."

Then there was a 'Pyramid Pounce.' Imagine this one and think three years older and probably one-hundred pounds heavier.

Now, when you're three years younger, what kind of damage could be delivered in reverse when I found a package? This was on purpose. Upon inflicting my pathetic damage on him, he turned into a Hyena without the biting. Of course, he sold the game as totally fair. How could I oppose the supreme leader? He declared it 'fair.' Whatever I found, I could deliver.

"I'm going to give you a 'Marlboro mauling'!" I gleefully yell after finding this empty package under some bushes. After delivering some ineffective blows (a mauling), he mocked me,

"Oh Stop! Stop! You're killing me!" then, out came the Hyena again.

The two worst ones to find are (or best ones, depending on your point of view) a 'Winston' or a 'Pall Mall' package.

"If I find a 'Winston,' well, that one is the best. I will deliver a 'Winston Workout.'" It's as if he was conjuring up the worst Roman emperor's form of punishment.

A 'Winston Workout,' which is just shy of impalement, entails spinning your opponent and delivering multiple punches as they twirl around.

"But if I find the rare 'Pall Mall,' well, that one is worthy of the 'Pall Mall Pummel'!"

That was the hated one. You can deliver several well-placed punches anywhere at any strength. This was the one that put an end to the emperor's brutal reign of terror. But the title, supreme ruler, probably is still in effect.

After finding the rare 'Pall Mall' package in a gutter, on our way back from swimming, he delivers a punch to my forehead that rises into a 'goose egg' bump right in the middle. As I am stumbling about, he sees the wound and runs off. I am in such distress a policeman notices me while driving by and delivers me home. Yeah. The real supreme ruler delivers quick justice.

It is usually best to avoid Steve. By the time we get to Turkey, he is more interested in other things (girls and music) than me. This is working out just fine, but he is on my 'radar.'

Chapter Thirty-Eight
If I Fell

This day I have a date with Jill. She is waiting for me in her garden. In her hand is a large, round, circle thingy tube.

"Do you trust me?"

"I don't know, with what?"

"Don't run and hide on me."

"Why would I do that?"

"Behold, the hula hoop!" She holds it over her head and then moves it down to her waist. It's hard to describe what happens next. It toys too much with my biology. She flings that hoop around her waist and starts gyrating her hips. That thing flies around her middle and keeps going, round and round, to the rhythm of her rotating body.

"Ta Da," she talks while she hoops. "What do you think?"

"You might not want to know. But is that supposed to help my dancing?"

"It takes some getting used to." She stops and it falls to her feet.

"Makes my side ache a little," as she rubs her right abdomen. "No matter. Now your turn." She slides it over my head and holds it at my waist. "I'll give it a shove, and you rotate those lovely hips of yours."

"Must I?"

"Do it, Elvis." She throws the hoop around me, and I start to move. It goes around twice and falls to the ground.

"I'm not much of an Elvis the pelvis," I call up images of Elvis Presley, famous for his gyrating motions while he sings.

"I wasn't expecting much. It took me a while."

"Did you know the Soviets call those things the 'symbol of the emptiness of American culture'?" A familiar voice calls out as Karin giggles at my second try of hooping.

Tom and Karin are joining our bowling excursion. They both try the hoop.

Jill whispers to me, "I thought we would be alone?"

"Sorry. I didn't tell you. We will later, at the tennis courts."

"I have to see Tigran again,"

"What? You can't be serious."

"Before it's too late." She leaves it there and off we go. The bowling alley is not too far away. It's a beautiful afternoon but a little crisp. We don't walk far when Jill spots something not so rare here.

"Oh look! A man is leading a bear by a rope. What is he, the dog catcher, animal guy?" We pour across the street.

"*Para için dans edecek,*" says the man. They all look at me.

"I think he said he would make the bear dance for a price."

"Oh, I gotta see this," Jill digs out a few *lira* from her purse. That purse – the special leather purse. Tom said her attackers were grabbing for it. I look around cautiously. I wish she would just leave the purse at home.

"*Yukari!*" the man says and the bear rears up on his back legs. The man pulls out a recorder. It looks like a flute. He starts to play. Yeah. The bear dances.

"I think I know this one," Jill shouts out and starts to prance around to the music with the bear. She moves like a Scottish highland dancer. She knows that routine.

"Jill, you can't do that!" I yell.

"What? There's a law against dancing with a bear on the street? Lighten up, party pooper."

"I think the law is you can't dance bare on the street," Tom states with a smile. "I like your style, though, and so does he."

The bear sees her and gyrates a little crazier. These images of her goofy dance with this brown bear on his hind legs will stay with me for a long time. Especially when her braided hair whaps the bear in the face and he hip butts her, sending her flying.

"He's got better moves than you," I say as I pick her up off the sidewalk, a little scuffed up. "Let's see if you bowl as well as you bleed."

I don't know why we picked bowling. There wasn't going to be any place to talk here, but we did have a date at the tennis courts later that afternoon. I am so blessed.

At the bowling alley, I remind myself what I have practiced. I repeat in my mind. 'Stand at the dots, toes on the two far-right dots. Take four steps forward and swing your arm with the ball back as you walk. Release the ball smoothly, close to the wood (no bouncing) and overthe foul line. Be careful not to let my toes go over the line. Lift your hand up to put a spin on the ball and roll it over the painted targets ten feet down the wooden planks. Ok, now throw your right leg back behindto the left.'

Picture that. I am the image of bowling ballet perfection and grace and beauty.

"I like your style. You should try dancing with a bear." Jill teases. I never look at the pins until the end. I often watch that ball roll over those marks, make a short little arc as it rolls down the alley, and hitthat head pin just right.

Have you ever seen how pins just scatter and sound when you score a strike, knocking all ten pins down in an earth-shattering thunderclap?

Well, that rarely happens, but sometimes it does. Does this make me less boring? I don't know. We are learning to bowl. I am actually fairly good. And Jill? She is not. Ah oh.

This creates a little bit of a conundrum. My best thinking says, with all the lessons I take, it might impress Jill with my prowess on the alley. Don't think too hard when girls are involved.

"Jill, pick the pink ball. It's just 8 pounds – perfect for you."

"Yes. Pink. Pink, Pink, I stink – at bowling." She has her hair braided in two long strands of ethereal rope – a ladder to heaven in my book.

"Oh, don't be so hard on yourself. I'm helping here. You hold the ball with these fingers."

I take her hand, finger by finger. Oh, am I sneaky? Then I put my arms around her waist to help her know how to cradle the ball. Even better!

"Hmmm. This is a nice lesson. Will it help me?" She wants to know.

It probably would not, but boy, I would work this for all I could.

"So now, you stand here, then walk four steps forward." I push her legs forward. "While at the same time, you swing the ball back."

WHAP

"Owww!"

She gets me a good one.

"Oh my gosh. I'm so sorry!"

"Where did you learn to do a 'Lucky Strike?'" I ask her. She knew all about my brother.

"Here. I'll give you a Winston Workout," she quickly adds and spins me around, hugging me as she goes.

185

I like bowling.

When it comes down to it, she just doesn't have the patience for it, but I love the teaching. Then there is Tom.

"Hey, guys, did you know the ancient Egyptian peasants wore a bag of mouse bones around their necks to prevent bed-wetting?" He casually states. He would tell me this one over and over ever since we went to scout camp together years ago. So, I go along for the benefit of the others.

"Wait a minute," I ask. "Why mouse bones?"

"I don't know. Maybe they were easier to find and wear than elephant bones." Then he goes on, "Oh, for my style of bowling, you don't need all that fancy pants stuff," he says to Jill and Karin.

Like some kind of gorilla or early-man Neanderthal, he grabs an over-weight ball like a bomb, runs up to the line with his short but massive legs, and heaves the load down the alley. It crashes on to the wood and hurtles down the lane to the pins.

BAM! A thunder clap. He knocks them all down.

"That's how it's done – ka-boom," in that gravelly voice of his.

Oh no! Do I have another rival to contend with? Of course not. Tom is heavy on Karen.

The bowling was great. I win in more ways than one. We saygoodbye to Tom and Karin, and Bullet Head meets us to drive to the tennis courts.

"Let's see if your backhand is as good as your 'bear' hands," I tease.

Jill belongs to a private tennis club. Yes, tennis. My Mom is trying to expose me to every worthwhile thing she can.

"I want you to be well rounded, Ricky," my mom tells me often, "balanced."

I think this is a big factor in wanting to know something about everything. Jill just gives it a bigger boost. But tennis? Yes. So glad I have taken lessons for a while. Why? Jill loves tennis.

In Turkey, the tennis court surfaces are made of clay—very fancy ones that professional players use. The ball bounces differently on a surface made of clay as opposed to a surface made of cement. I am learning how to play and score.

'Serving' the ball is the hardest. You have to throw the ball up high above your head, then bring your tennis racket around fast. You are to meet the ball with your racket coming down at the exact angle to send it just over the top of the net, strung across the court. Again, I am pretty good. I even won a trophy – not just a 'participation' trophy.

But do you know who is really good at tennis? Yes, Jill. Mitch does not play, thank goodness. She had started younger in England. I love playing tennis with her, of course.

At her classy private tennis club, you are required to wear white while playing. Jill has on this fabulous outfit with a short, white pleated skirt. I had seen those extraordinary legs in dresses, but this was something new. We had a word for it – gams. And these were great gams. Wow.

On my way to the court from my dressing room, I hear two attendants talking.

"Did you see that red head with the outfit?" He then proceeds to walk around like he is a pigeon with bowed legs, "Squawk, squawk, squawk."

"Yeah. Poor thing."

I am about to go and smack them with my racket. I don't understand it. Some people have no taste and are just rude.

Now, scoring tennis is done a little differently. In scoring, when you start at 'zero,' it is called 'love.' Yeah. Love is zero in tennis. Right

where I started with Jill. She and I are starting our game, and whap, she serves a good one on me, and I smash it up into the bleachers.

"Home run!" she snickers. "This is tennis, not your baseball." I smile – sort of.

"15 - Love," I call out. She's ahead. But, after hitting my return shot way afoul, my eyes are drawn to two guys sitting way up in the shadows at the top of the bleachers. They're wearing suits. Now, most men wear suits. I get it. Maybe they are watching other players. I don't know. They just look out of place here. I don't let on that I notice them, and I don't say anything to Jill. They are behind her.

When she gets another point, the score goes to 30 and me at love (zero).

"30 – love," I call out.

Then I get daring. I hit my return into the net, giving her the next point (her third on me), which puts her score at 45 and me still at love.

I softly call out, "45 – love, love."

"What was that?" she yells.

"Aaa… a… you're 45, and I'm in love. I mean… aaa… I am in love, still," I quickly respond.

"I heard you," she says softly, "oh Ricky, you are getting less boring."

I like tennis.

We finish our match before I tell her about the two guys. As we leave the court, I see, out of the corner of my eye, that they get up and move through the upper doors to the inside. I stop Jill.

"I saw them," she admits. There isn't much time to talk. "So, here's the plan. Just before I go into the women's locker room, we wait around the corner at that drinking fountain by those bleacher double doors.

When they exit, I'll deliver a 'Lucky Strike' with my racket, and you start the 'Pall Mall Pummel.' Or, at least, a 'Camel clobber.' Got it?"

It sounds good to me. It doesn't occur to either of us to ask for help. So goes the adrenalin of the moment. We wait on either side of the door. It opens and she swings her ladies' wooden racket and smacks my head with the strings, which bounce off. It's gone right over our would-be attacker's head and back to her head.

"Oww," she screams. I start to administer the pummel when we both look down to see a wide-eyed Billy B. ducking and covering his head and yelling out,

"Help! Stop!"

"Billy B.?!" We both blurt out.

"What are you doing here?" I yell.

"He's a member," Jill admits.

"What are you two up to? I expected to get in a game of love, not get a licking."

Maybe we are getting a little too paranoid, but I must admit, it was exhilarating. Maybe not for Billy B.

"Sorry," we both say. I'm surprised he didn't wet his pants. We don't find the two in suits. All is good.

We find a quiet spot in the bleachers as Billy B. plays with his sister far below us. Staring straight out at nothing, Jill says, "I have to see Tigran again."

"That does not make any sense. Why in the world do you need to find this Tigran again? Jill, he's a dangerous man."

"Let's back up. Let me tell you about grandfather first."

"OK. But you are freakin' me out."

"I told you grandfather was 'odd.' He just had unusual tastes and he had the money to indulge in them, as you saw in the library."

"You said that was just a small part."

"Yes. Mom and I need to go back to Paris and finalize his estate. He left me a special gift - a shadow inheritance."

"Yeah, a golden tennis racket."

"Don't be too hard on yourself, loser."

"I let you win."

"Oh, you liar. You were trying your heart out."

"I don't mind being in love most of the time. I hope it translates." She bumps me with her shoulder as she likes to do. "So, this special inheritance. What's that got to do with this Tigran guy?"

"I'm not sure exactly what the inheritance is. By design, my folks don't know about it. Let me just say that Tigran holds an important key, and it could disappear at any time – along with any hope of knowing what grandfather wanted me to have and to do. We have to get it from him. And he wants something from me."

"Is that what all the jabbing and poking with him were about?

"Mostly."

"Again, this doesn't make sense. I assume this may be a lot of money?"

"It's not money. I mean. I guess it may be worth a lot of money. But grandfather told me not to tell my folks about it. It might put them in more jeopardy. Now I am telling you. I hope it doesn't do the same to you. I said he was unusual."

"So, how do you know about it?"

"A conversation and a strange written note. Grandfather said he had three clues for me to solve. He did so, he said, to keep me and the items safe."

"Safe from whom?"

"Well, you're starting to see what he meant. He also wanted to make this an adventure for me and hard for anyone else."

"Jill, shouldn't we be getting someone official aware of what's going on?"

"I can't and I told you, they aren't after me."

"Of course they are. If it's what you have, that means you."

"Rick, you have to promise. It must be just us for now. You may not like it."

"Ridiculous. If I can be with you, help you. What could be better?"

"I have not shared anything with Mitch."

"Oh," I pause for that one. "I don't get it, but OK. Just us. You're saying there are 'item-s'. Is that plural?"

"Yes. I guess that could mean more than one."

A tennis ball bounces behind us and rattles between the seats next to us.

"Sorry." comes the tiny voice from the court. It's not Bill B., but his sister's.

"That used to be how Bill B. sounded."

"You've known him how long?"

"Let's see, since eighth grade. Now, what about these clues?" She looks away for a beat, then looks back.

"Let's leave it at that for now."

"You're torturing me and leaving me with a million questions."

"Aren't I a devil? Let's talk theatre!"

I have distracted her from asking about her broken hand cast in my locker. So, it isn't too bad to move on.

"In eighth grade, I was cast in the musical, 'The Wizard of Oz.' I got a prime part."

"Wait a minute. I can guess, 'The Cowardly Lion'?"

"Oh, yeah. You've seen my magnificence."

"My party is coming into focus. Come on, spill it."

"I did keep the program, Rick Foster as the 'Cowardly Lion.'"

And I sing my own version,

My paws are cold, you know it, missy

Please don't say that I'm a sissy

Cause I like to munch hors d'oeuvre

Oh, am I a brave little fella

'cause I sing this A 'Capella

And show I have the nerve.

She claps like a wind-up monkey.

"That's it. Type casting. You fit the part!" "Hey.

Won't you agree, I'm just a little better?"

"You are making progress, Cowardly Lion. RaArrrrhh," she roars and paws at me. "I like this story far better than your baseball stuff. Blah, blah, blah, Crap, yeah."

"Wait. I'm getting to the good stuff. First, let me complain. You know when the Lion and Dorothy and the rest of the crew meet the Wizard for the first time? It's supposed to be all scary with fire and booming noise and all. And the guy playing the Wizard…?"

"No. Don't tell me."

I point down to the court.

"Billy B.'s sister?"

"You are impossible. Yes, none other than Billy B. At the time, he was still the tiniest person in the whole school with the tiniest little voice. I was shocked that he could even talk. He was so small. Yeah. Bladder man Billy B., the famed Aisha poet of which you have heard."

"I think it was genius casting if you ask me."

"Hmmm. Maybe you're right. I think someone else was his voice over microphone for the big Wizard scene. But it was funny to have him revealed at the end as this little guy."

"I am great and powerful… Oz," she declares in as much character as the part demands.

I look at her with fresh eyes. In her skimpy white tennis outfit, she is just a shimmering light and laughing that unbelievable lilt. She is a goddess sitting on her thrown with her golden orb of a tennis racket or her fencing sword. What were those attendants even thinking? Stupid men.

"Hmmm. I believe, Richard, the lion-hearted, you are getting less boring all the time."

"Now you can only see the movie once a year on TV, Thanksgiving night."

"Only if you live stateside. They bring the film around to theaters once every seven or so years. I saw in at a large cinema in London a few years back."

"We are so underprivileged," I sigh, "sitting in your exclusive, run-down Tennis club sipping mint juleps."

She bounces her racket strings off my head.

New female puzzle pieces are now in place. I tend to notice the difficult stuff first, but, you know, girls can be *fascinating, fun friends.* I didn't want to stress the 'friend' part. And I realize all girls are *beautiful* in their own way. Where do those fit? Somewhere with all the other pieces.

If I can make this afternoon last forever, it will be heaven to me. I am getting more and more nerve in my ability to romance Jill. Take that, Mitch – I can sing and dance (sort of) and bowl and play tennis and baseball, and now I'm a spy to boot. Yeah. I know that's a problem. Those other things are real. What happens if she finds out that…? Oh, I can't think about that now. Match that, Mitch! But I shouldn't be too harsh on him or gloat. Tomorrow, anything can happen.

Forget about tomorrow. I should talk a bit about yesterday – or my past with Mitch and the others BJE – 'Before the Jillian Era.'

Chapter Thirty-Nine
I Me Mine

I admit. It is me. It is all mine. I have a problem with the 'Scout Law.' I need to back up a little in my history. I was around twelve whenI joined the Scouts in Turkey. Mom got me and my brother, Steve, involved in the local Boy Scouts of America, as we had been back in the States. We were organized into 'patrols' that were mostly by age group. My brother, Steve, was a troop leader over a number of patrols
– including mine.

Noooo! But there he was. It was like asking a Red-tail hawk to look over a chicken roost with free access.

Who else was in the troop? Or course – Tom, Will, Dave, and yes, Mitch and a few other classmates, oh, including Billy B. They mixed the British and Canadian systems with ours. It really wasn't Mitch's thing - but he was there. I really don't think he wanted to be.

"My mom pays me to come and Gary insures I do in other ways," he told me.

"Who is Gary?"

"My mom's husband." This was prior to the Jillian era, long before we were rivals.

So here is part of my present problem. The scout oath begins with 'On my honor I will…' and then lists the things you're supposed to do as part of your honor. Also, the scouts have a twelve-point list they call 'The Scout Law,' which we recited every week, and you had to memorize for advancement in rank. You were supposed to follow these principles in your life. Well, right now, it doesn't look good for me rightoff the bat. Consider the twelve points of 'The Scout Law':

A Scout is Trustworthy. Ok. I was sort of fine back then. But now? Oh boy. With my whopper going strong, a stolen and broken artifact, a

stupid and questionable contest, and trespassing on private property, this is a problem.

A Scout is loyal. I was loyal to Jill, maybe not to Banyo John.

A scout is helpful. I take out the trash for mom.

A scout is friendly. Merhaba, hello, is my favorite phrase, crap yeah.

A scout is courteous. I blow my nose in a tissue most of the time.

A scout is kind. Except for John, I'm OK here. Oh, except for my brother, too.

A scout is obedient. Hmmm, mostly?

A scout is cheerful. I am a real cut-up when I want to be. Got this.

A scout is thrifty. I think this has to do with money. I don't have any. All good.

A scout is brave. Well. I was brave enough to be the Cowardly Lion. I had the nerve.

A scout is clean. Hey. I do my own wash. Maybe not 50 turns of the handle.

A scout is reverent. Sunday School – every week. Does that count?

So, it's looking pretty good excerpt for the trustworthy thing. I don't know what to do about that yet. Oh, yeah, the kind of thing? Well. I might have to work on that, too.

I had a feeling that Mitch was dealing with harder things than the rest of us. He was Latino and maybe that tan skin made people treat him differently at times in his life. Even in his own family. So that was strange. But it sure attracted the girls, even then.

"Yeah. Gary wants his privacy," he would tell me. We were twelve. What did we know about adult stuff? It didn't matter to us what color someone was or where they were from, or what they believed. I was

taught to be very careful to treat all people that way. Mom would often quote me something from the guy who penned 'Peter Pan.' He wrote,

'Always be a little kinder than is necessary.'

Got to work on that one. I think Mitch was not always treated fairly. Maybe sometimes by us.

You were supposed to work on moving up the ranks in scouting by doing certain actions, earning badges, completing tasks and knowledge questions. Scout camp was the best opportunity to earn a bunch of badges and move up in a short amount of time. So – we went.

Chapter Forty
Mother Nature's Son

Mitch was not a lover of Mother Nature. He'd rather be sitting and singing songs for anyone. It was our first time at a scout camp. It was supposed to be two weeks of fun and adventure. It sounded more like going to an amusement park for fourteen days without the amusement. This was our second year in Scouts and the rivalry had still not begun. Why Mitch was still in scouts beats me. But here he was. The camp was a full day of travel to the mountains of south-east Turkey, a place called *Egridir*.

I shared a tent with Tom and Will. Poor Mitch was in another tent with Billy B. Yes – little Billy, my Wizard of Oz, was there as well. We all got along pretty well. But two weeks is a long time to be away from home for the first when you are twelve.

We all started off working on the marksmanship badge. It required learning about firearms, safety, and skills for shooting at targets. Steve, as our leader, was the assistant instructor.

"Ok, you morons, try not to shoot your eye out or your toes off. To aim your rifle, close one eye and look down the barrel at the little bump at the end. Line the bump up with the target, the middle circle of the four concentric circles printed on the paper."

Billy B. is squinting as hard as he can at the circles, "It looks like the targets are in New Jersey."

"I'll give you bus fare to get there if you leave now," Mitch tells him.

For some reason, I could not even hit the paper. I was really struggling. But Billy B. sitting on the ground, feet straight out and resting the rifle between his toes, was rippin' it up.

"Take that, Hoboken."

The next day was my final day to get the scores I needed to pass. Mitch noticed me at the range and how awkward I looked.

"Something is wrong here," he tells me.

"Don't rub it in. I just am bad at this."

"I can't figure out why your head is crooked when you look down the barrel."

"Crooked? I'm just trying to eye up the target."

"Wait a minute, what eye are you using?"

"My left eye."

"But you're shooting right-handed. You have to use your right eye."

"I can only close my right eye. I can't close my left and keep the right open."

"You silly owl. That's it. Look, take my bandana and wrap it over your left eye, then look down the barrel."

Bingo – that was it. I was using the wrong eye.

"Ahoy, Captain Blackbeard," Billy B. called out as he passed me, marksmanship badge in hand. I did feel like a pirate. All I needed was a peg leg to rest my rifle on, but I hit the paper for the first time. I then worked on getting the scores I needed. This is Mitch. He was helping me. This was early in the camp. More was to come. I eventually learnedto shoot with both eyes open.

"Attention, you toad heads," Steve announces, "canoeing is your next adventure. The first thing we're going to do is to sink your canoe, then bail the water out and paddle back to shore. If I'm lucky, most of your sorry rears will drown and I can cancel the rest."

Yeah, my brother was the only instructor. We had both taken swim lessons together back in the States, remember? That was the start of the 'Winston Workouts' and all the rest. There were no cigarette packages here. I thought I would be safe. But there he was. The counselor. He was always harder on me than anyone else.

"Which one of you goof balls is going to help my fart-face little brother goof ball learn to paddle?" he would yell out. That and a lot of other unpleasant things about my lack of abilities.

Of course, you had to know how to swim first. You were supposed to have earned the swimming badge before starting on this one. Much to my brother's dismay, we all had to wear a life preserver just to be safe. Mitch sat on the ground with his arms folded and head down. He was the last to plod down the path to the lake, prodded by my brother.

When we all had to split up in pairs as partners in a canoe, it was no surprise no one picked the sulker, Mitch. My brother purposefully had me pick last. So, when I had to pick, the choices were either the wizard, Billy B., or Mitch. Ahhhh. Okay.

"Hey Mitch, let's do this." I was trying to be positive. I guess Billy B. would have to watch from the shore. He would have lasted ten seconds in the water. He had no fat. A goldfish could have swallowed him and still feel hungry.

With only me paddling out with our canoe, Mitch asked, "Why are we doing this?"

"Hey, you gonna help me or what?" I complained.

"Why should I? You seem to know what you're doing. You don't need me."

"It's twice as hard to get where we need to be. At least pretend, or my brother will taunt us endlessly."

"At least you have one."

"Really? You lucky enough not to have a brother? What about a sister?"

"No. I'm alone."

"How great is that?"

"Yeah, great."

When it came time to swamp our canoe, you know, tip it over to fill with water, Mitch protested.

"I don't want to do this."

"What do you mean? This is what my brother put us out here to do. Don't make me look bad."

"I don't want to do this."

"Yeah. I heard you. Why not?"

"I don't know how to swim."

I stop paddling. "You've got to be kidding me!"

"No. I'm not."

"Even Billy B. knows how to swim. He's just afraid of the fish. How did you pass the swimming course?"

"I stole the badge."

"Well, you've got a life preserver on. That should help."

"I panic even with this thing on."

"Oh, great," I mutter. From the shore, my brother is taunting us.

"What are you guys doin' out there? Throwing a prayer meeting? Come on, Foster, swamp the sucker."

I had to think fast. The water was sort of clear, good enough to see a few feet down. There, not ten feet from us was an underwater island, maybe three feet under the surface of the water.

"Quick, Mitch, let's paddle over there." We made it to the underwater island. "Ok, you see what I see?"

"Yeah, trouble. Maybe it will work."

So, we follow what everyone else is doing. We tipped over our canoe and fell out.

"Don't stand up," I whispered, "just start bailing."

We do our best to look like we were floating and started to get water out of the canoe using the two milk jugs that were cut in half and attached to the canoe seats. Then we hauled ourselves back into theboat.

"Try not to make it look so easy," I told him.

"How is this possible? You losers are killin' it," yells Steve from shore. "How did you losers do that?"

"A great teacher!" I lied through my teeth, knowing that would score me some points. (Maybe not the 'trustworthy 'thing to do, but certainly the 'brave' thing to do.)

We paddled back, long before the others, with a great look of satisfaction. Billy B. was being attended to by the camp nurse.

"What happened?" I asked him.

"I was dangling my feet in the water and a trout bit my toe."

He was lucky the fish didn't drag him under.

That was how Mitch and I sort of became friends, to a degree. Mitch and I were on our way back to our tents from our triumphal experience on the water when he tripped on a tree branch, fell, and pushed his arm through a hole in the ground among the roots. This was how we

discovered the 'Hairy Mongers,' the coolest spiders I ever saw. I didn't think hair could stand straight up, but I swear, that's what Mitch was doing. He was up doing a dance a whole lot better than he did at Jill's party years later.

"Did it bite me? Am I bleeding? Am I going to die?"

I wasn't exactly breathing normally, either. After we recovered and saw we were still alive, I thought, "Hmmm, if this freaks out Mitch this much, what might it do to someone else I know?"

Now to understand this next event, one would need to know about my brother's fear of spiders. It would also be better to disregard the scout law of 'be kind' for a moment. After all, this was my brother. The formal terminology is 'arachnophobia.' 'Arachnids' is the science classification for eight-legged crawlers, and 'phobia' is a Greek term for fear. It perfectly describes my brother's relationship with the creatures. If they jumped, it was even worse.

"I officially dub thee 'Hairy Mongers,'" Tom declares. He was not afraid of much. "Hey, did you know jumping spiders can leap over 40 times their body length?"

Oh please, let these be the jumping kind. Steve couldn't stand even baby daddy's long-legged spiders. Even they would creep him out, no matter how small. I was supposed to keep his condition a secret. But I don't have a great track record in that department.

"This one appears to be dead," says Tom connivingly. "You thinking what I'm thinking?"

So, Tom fished him out and we put it at the feet of my brother's sleeping bag one evening. The shenanigans were afoot with only Tom and I as the instigators. We waited behind another tent. Before the lantern in Steve's tent went out, we could see he crawled into his bag.

"Okay, any minute now," I say, anticipating the result like a dog staring at his empty meal dish at dinner time. But nothing. Come on!

The moment his feet would feel that big hairy thing, he would fly through the end of the tent. Right? But nothing.

We just had to wait a while because our little hairy friend must have warmed up, woken up, and crawled up the bag and under his pillow before Steve retired. All it took was for my brother to nestle into his pillow, slide his hands under the pillow, as we all sometimes do, and bingo! Out he flew. He didn't bother opening the zippered door. The sight was a bit like putting a cat (don't do it) in a sack and tying the opening shut. The cat eventually finds a way out, but the sack is confettiafterward. Steve tried to smash right through the tent wall, which only upended the tent with him still inside. I thought he might roll down to the lake in the thing. I had visions of our hairy friend tumbling and jumping all over the tent.

It was all delicious. Tom and I could hardly keep it in and hoped he hadn't heard us. How could he? He was grunting with the struggle, trying to muffle his screams. Somehow, he got out, found the spider somewhere, and smashed it with his flashlight and pillow, all casualties of the affair. Our hairy friend performed a noble sacrifice for a worthy cause that night. The Hairy Monger will be a name forever hallowed in our hearts.

From that night on, Steve conducted a thorough search of his stuff (without the benefit of a flashlight and pillow) in a tent thoroughly taped up with duct tape and so secure that even a federal prison would be proud of it. I'm sure sleep on our remaining nights did not come easy for him.

Chapter Forty-One
I'm Down

My brother suspected something. He was asking all over camp about the spiders. He didn't think his encounter was an accident. Camp leaders told him they were discovered by Mitch the day before. This was good for me – not good for Mitch. He was really down.

"Your brother thinks I put the spider in his tent."

"Spiders?" My vibrating shoulders give my mirth away.

"How can you laugh when I'm down?"

"What spiders? Oh. Your spiders."

(Sorry about the 'a scout is loyal' thing.)

"They are not my spiders! Steve is not happy. He says he is withdrawing my invitation to join the order."

He meant the 'Order of the Arrow.' This was a unique privileged group of special scouts given a high honor within Scouting. It had some peculiar requirements. But no self-respecting member of the order would dare pull a stunt on a fellow order member like I had. So, if I could join, Steve would never suspect me. But he thought it was Mitch, so no invitation was given to him.

"You don't get it. All Gary said to me before I left, besides good riddance, was to make sure I came back with the 'Order of the Arrow' patch. I guess it's a big deal to him."

"Didn't you tell my brother you had nothing to do with it?"

"You think he would believe me? I told him spiders were all over this place. Why did he think it was me?" He said in a desperate voice.

"You have a good point."

"Can't you talk to him? It's only going to be worse at home if I can't do this."

If certain things were admitted, it was going to be worse for me at home, too. Mitch was good cover. Should I sacrifice Mitch for my own skin? It was tempting. I was home free if I said nothing, but then Mitch takes it on the chin at home, maybe literally? (Here goes the 'trustworthy' thing again. Not doing very well in this department either.) If I admitted the source of Hairy Monger intrusion, then I wouldtake the heat and probably an unauthorized 'Pyramid Pounce.'

"Ok. I'll see what I can do," I told him, delaying any decision in my head.

"That would be great, thanks."

I knew I had to do something.

All in all, Mitch was having a hard time. It was obvious. There were physical signs. I just didn't put it all together yet. Billy B, on the other hand, should have been having a hard time. He was just so thrilled to have the courage to sleep in a tent overnight. He was beaming all the time once his toe healed from the fish bite. However, he did have one peculiar problem at nighttime – yes – luckily, there was a camp laundry to wash his sleeping bag. Otherwise, Mitch's misery would have been doubled.

I had a problem to solve. So, I did what I was good at.

"Steve! Someone said you had the same problem we did the other night – huge spiders?"

"What?"

"Yeah. There were several all over our tent and the tent next door where Mitch is. Didn't anyone warn you?" I was very convincing. I knew he did not want anyone to know about his 'incident' if he could help it.

"Mitch? He had spiders on his tent?"

"Yeah, great big hairy mongers."

"Do they jump?" He was quite earnest.

"Oh yeah. 40 times their length." Thanks, Tom.

I let this sink in, hoping it would make my brother reconsider his vote to not invite Mitch for the consideration of the Order. Did it work? Yeah. But somehow, I thought this did not get me out of my brother's suspicious mind.

So, the invite to the Order was back on for Mitch.

"Wait a minute. It was you who put the spiders on his tent?" Mitch whines after my confession. Maybe I was back on track with 'a scout is loyal'.

"Technically, it was one spider *in* the tent. So, yes."

"You were going to let me take the blame?"

"I didn't know it would come back to you, so I lied a bit. No big deal. Look what it got you." I was trying to justify my actions and thinking this was more 'trustworthy' of me.

"You seem to be good at it, *muy bueno en eso.*"

With Mitch as an only child, I found that curious. I had always been surrounded by a sister and a brother and extended family galore. He just wasn't used to this. I think he was really conflicted. Home did not seem to be a comfortable place, and neither was this camp. We were young, so give us a break. I had a brother with me. Home was not far away. I couldn't get away from it.

Mitch was more emotionally delicate, but he sure gave the appearance of ruggedness. He was one good-looking kid, despite my continually saying otherwise. I think he was fragile on the inside. This

was his strength that eventually would attract Jill and other girls. He was vulnerable but, according to her, "so gorgeous."

I was not, apparently. OK, fine. I have other good qualities, right? I'm getting a little more adventurous and courageous, even before Jill. And I was getting better.

"Okay, Order of the Arrow candidates, tonight is your first task. You will take a blanket, a flashlight, and a canteen of water and hike to our designated spots far from camp. Then spend the night alone. Got it? Alone." This was the instruction from our adult Scoutmaster.

"No food?" I asked.

"Alone?" Mitch added.

"Yes and yes," he said.

For Mitch, it had been almost two weeks gone and it was certain to break him. He was not in a happy place. I didn't realize this at the time. Thanks to my brilliant strategic lie, we were both invited to try the ordeal. It was a must if you were going to be able to join this elite group. And he had the extra pressure that his stepdad was demanding it for some reason. This was something you could only do here at camp.

We were both given directions on where to go. Hey, for me, this was perfect. To be away from the critical gaze of my brother was great. By this time, he was starting to question if the Hairy Mongers were really an accident. I had to lay low.

I could tell that Mitch was worried when he started out. He got this twitch in his hands when he was stressed. I saw it first on our canoeing outing. Here it was again. I was quite conflicted as well. I was glad to go away from my brother, happy as a turkey about that, to explore the wild outdoors of Turkey, but the unknowns out here had me worried as well. Hey, I had been introduced to Hairy Mongers. What else could be lurking out here? Would there be an 'Order of the Arrow' awaiting me on my triumphal return?

I assumed that the adults were supposed to know where we were camped, but we had no idea if we were in the right place or not. It was a breezy night. There were sounds that I had not heard when we were in our tent. And it was cave dark. The main scout camp had these occasional powered lights overhead. They were nowhere to be seen. We were way out in the boonies. There was no moon. It was overcast, as I remember. That made everything far more eerie and sinister since you did not know what creatures were out here. As much as I knew about Hairy Mongers, I did not want them crawling on me, or anything else for that matter. Lions and tigers and bears, oh my. There definitely were bears, but I wasn't too worried about the lions and tigers. So, I adapted some cowardly Lion verses to fit my situation that I sang softly.

I'm afraid there's something out there

I pray it's not a black bear

And so I will conserve.

Oh, I could find some gadgets

That might scare off any rabbits

And show I have some nerve.

I was pretty sure the rabbits were not going to be the problem. The cave darkness fell quickly once I found my spot. I made an impromptu cushion out of leaves, checking for any hidden creatures first. I then spread out my blanket. Time passed. I just sat, staring into the blackness. I was conjuring up all kinds of stuff when I heard a wild rustling in the bushes to my right. A weird light was shimmering off the leaves and branches in the distance. I was sure – it was an alien landing craft looking for me. Then it got closer, pointing now directly at me. I quickly turned off my light to not attract attention.

Suddenly, a flashlight beam lights shine up on a face. Aliens! So spooky. I jumped.

"Rick?" A voice called out softly. Okay. Not aliens. Maybe leaders were checking up on me, or my brother was trying to pull a fast one.

"Is that you, Rick?" the voice queries. "It's me, Mitch."

My body collapses in a heap. "Whoa, it's just you. You okay?"

His hands were twitching like a quaking aspen leaf. I'm sure he didn't want to really say what was going on in his head. He had his stuff with him.

"Yeah. I guess. I'm not used to… to… all this."

"It's okay. Come on over."

Now, according to the official Order of the Arrow rules, you were supposed to be alone all night. It supposedly forces you to think about what is important in your life. All I think it accomplishes is to scare the ever-living bejeebies out of you. None of us needed that at our age.

"I'm glad you found me," I admit.

"Thanks," he says quietly. "I knew what direction you were headed, so I was hoping I could find you. I think I would rather wander all night than stay in my camp alone."

Now, this was coming from a guy who was used to being alone. I thought being an only child would be just great. Not so much for him. Somehow, we eventually got to laughing. It may have been when I broke into my Cowardly Lion and sang 'If I only had the nerve.'

The night was so much better to have someone to say, 'What was that?' to besides worrying by ourselves. We didn't sleep much. Mitch knew the next night he would be back safely in his own tent with his tent-mate, Billy B. As he left my camp in the early morning, he turned to me, jumped, clicked his heels together, and said, "I'm off to see the WIZZER," and dramatically skipped off.

"Tom and I will look for mouse bones," I call after him.

Mitch made sure he was back at his camp not too long after sunrise when the adults came to fetch us. No one ever suspected anything different. We fulfilled all the other requirements. We were officially ushered into the 'Order of the Arrow.' So, Mitch and I had a strange relationship that got more complicated as we got older. Keeping score only developed later.

A scout is friendly. A scout is kind. A scout is loyal. (Ignore trustworthy for now)

And we were friends.

Episode Six

I'm Being Tailed!

Chapter Forty-Two
She Came in through the Bathroom Window

Sunday, she's on the phone to me.

Rick: What about Mitch?

Jill: I'm inviting him on our next mission.

Rick: After all he put you through?

Jill: Nora used him to get back at me.

Rick: Jill, she's protected by and was born with a silver spoon in her mouth. She has means. She will always sneak through anything to get to Mitch, any window he leaves open.

Jill: Didn't anybody tell her? It may be easy to steal a heart, awfully hard to rob. Silver spoons are very rarely the answer. I should know.

Rick: Nora has loved Mitch from day one two years ago. This is just a new chapter. Maybe she is good for him.

Jill: Maybe. But he needs us.

I am hoping she doesn't mean she needs him. Here we go again. I am going to spend Thanksgiving on a trip with my family, but I need to get on a mission before we leave. If this is going to work while I'm gone, I need to keep Mitch on his heels, so to speak. I'm swimming in an ocean of anxiety with no land in sight. Not as much about Mitch as much as me.

I don't know what to think of the warning the men in the car gave me, this Tigran guy. On top of that, what happens if Jill finds out it's all a big scam on my part? She trusts me now. It would blow us apart.

But why are these guys threatening the Fosters? Have I put my dad in danger by all this foolishness? Stuff is going on in Jill's life that I'm so confused about. I think she needs me, but at what cost? I think I'd

rather be a loser than to lose her. I'm sure I'm like those Polar Bears in the zoo that just go round and round on the same path all day as if in some captivation stupor. I've just pried open a bear trap and put my leg in willingly. If she only likes me because I am getting more adventurousand have this supposed 'daring' assignment, then what happens when it all disintegrates? When she discovers, I'm not cool anymore in her eyes, what I have got left? Then all there is just the real me. Not sure that will ever be enough.

Mitch is on my tail and is doing all he can to cause her to doubt. I figure the only way I can go is forward. The time I have with Jill, even stolen and risky, is so precious. So, I keep it going.

"Ok, gang. We need to perfect the art of 'tailing.'"

I had seen this in some spy movies – following someone for a reason. That might mean more hand-holding and whatever else comes with that.

Tom is right there with support, "Ha. That will be fun. Can I pick what tail I am going to follow?"

Princess whacks him on the arm.

"I meant you, sweetie. Of course." He knew she couldn't come. "Just having fun."

"I have the assignments and the suspects. Standby."

I get old Bullet Head to help me with this. His English is good enough.

"*Bay effendi, yardiminiza itiyachim var*, I need your help."

"Yes, little Foster bay. I help."

"I want to follow someone in the market for fun. Have him stop and do stuff. You know, have him eat, buy things, talk to people, and not notice me and my girlfriend."

"Ha, little Foster bay likes this girl? *Çok Güzel*, very good. But it will cost ten *lira.*"

Ten *lira* to them is really good money for an hour. I can get that from my mom, calling it to pay for doing my wash or whatever. It works, and Bullet Head sets it up. We are going on a Saturday. Bullet Head and I pick up Jill that morning and the others meet us at the *Pazar*,the large outdoor market. This is a place where they sell all kinds of stuff. One area is food – like an outdoor grocery with fruit and vegetables and a meat market. Some other areas have clothes, jewelry, art, and other house stuff. It's big and it's crowded. It's a mixture of tents and more permanent structures.

Not everyone can come. No matter. Jill has her own ideas.

"OK, guys, let's do this first. Mitch, you and Tom stand over there at the entrance and just look up into the sky. I want you to point it up occasionally. Mostly look up and then pepper it with some pointing."

"What are we peppering?" asks Tom.

"A flying saucer, a meteor, doesn't matter. Just be earnest about it."

"My name is Earnest for you today," Mitch is all in.

"I don't know about this. Could get us in trouble," I warn.

Jill gives me a look and I go quiet. We stand back to watch. Tom and Mitch go over to where people are streaming into the *Pazar* and start the routine. It isn't long before a large group of people is gathered, all looking up at the sky and asking one another,

"*ne?ne?*" What? What? "*Ne görüyorsunuz?*" What are you all seeing?

We can see Tom and Mitch snicker as Jill gestures for them to come back. It creates quite a stir and keeps growing until a vendor with a fruit basket on his head, walking around the crowd, is forced into the street and is grazed by a motorcycle passing by. The fruit flies everywhere. Passing traffic smashes much of the fruit as the vendor desperately, mostly in vain, tries to rescue what he can. Mitch is in hysterics with laughter. Doesn't seem right, but I don't say anything to Jill.

Jill lets a deep breath out, "Oops. Didn't see that coming. Time to move on."

I turn to Mitch and point across the street.

"OK, Mitch, I want you to sit here and watch that guy. Take notes. If they are good, you get another day at the solon." This is brilliant on my part, a good dig at him and spatial separation.

"He's a shoeshine boy. What is that going to accomplish?"

I think to myself in reply, 'A lot.' But I tell him. "Just watch for suspicious behavior. My contacts tell me he is tricky."

"You can get your shoes looking better too. That keeps a close eye on him," Tom adds. This seems to satisfy him.

"Tom, you and Will take the clothing area. Look for a man in baggy pants."

"They all wear baggy pants," Will states.

"This guy keeps his secret papers in his blue pants. His drop point is somewhere in there. He wears a red turban and has a glass eye."

"So, we're to watch for a guy that can't see straight and looks funny," Will quips.

"Glass eye? Cool." Tom says. "Hey guys, did you know Ben Franklin invented the first glasses with two lenses – one for close-upand one for seeing far?"

"Well, just keep an eye out for this guy," I tell them.

"This guy must really be able to keep an 'eye out,'" Will chuckles.

"Good one!" Tom's crusty, croaky laugh is always good for our spirits, and off they go.

Marie is not with us, which leaves just Jill and me.

"OK, Agent Fortuna reporting for duty," she salutes me. I take her hand, and off we go. I am sure Mitch is watching, so I make it very obvious by swinging our hands as we head off. Then I stop.

"Oops." I let go of her hand. "Sorry, PDA. I might get whacked."

"Not the rule breaker today? Your loss."

"Our guy is wearing a grey sweater with squiggle designs around his middle. Don't know why, but that's what I am told."

On cue, I see our guy get off at the bus stop.

"There he is." He walks off into the market with us, not far behind.

"Take notes and don't follow too closely. Act casual."

"Gotcha boss. He has taken forty steps."

"Not that detailed."

I think asking her to take notes is not good. Makes her think too hard and she has to use both hands. Nuts. Well, I really take a chance if I want to hold hands.

"Maybe we should just take mental notes. There is so much."

"I don't know. You might miss something."

"I already have," and I take her hand.

"Ahh. Gotcha boss. Good idea." And she holds on to me with both hands. Double yes. Just then, a very little girl runs into my leg, falls, and starts to cry. I kneel to console her.

"Ohh. *Küçük hanim, iyi misin?"* (Little girl, are you OK?) I ask earnestly. I hold her shoulders and she looks at me with eyes as big as Jill's.

"Well, she almost has your eyes," I glance up at Jill. The little girl turns around to face her.

"Ahhh!" Jill gasps and staggers back a few paces, turning away.

I guess I am used to these things in Turkey. Jill hasn't been here long enough.

"It's okay, Jill. She won't bite."

The girl's teeth haven't all come in yet and her hair is starkly patchy, what there is of it, very scraggly. The hardest thing is she has anuntreated lip deformity. And I know why Jill is so affected.

The little girl points to Jill's freckled and patchy spots on her arms. I take her closer.

"*Hasta misin*?" she asks quizzically, touching Jill's arms.

Jill slowly turns to face her, still visibly shaken.

"*Hasta, Hasta,*" I repeat. "Oh, sick. She wants to know if you are sick?"

There are no redheads in Turkey and so they have never seen the white and freckled skin that redheads mostly have. At least Jill's arms. Not so much on her face.

"*Hayir*, no, it's just me," Jill says politely.

"*Iyi misin?*" I ask again. Are you hurt? She raises her chin and makes a clicking noise with her tongue between her teeth. It's a Turkishnon-verbal way to say 'no.'

"*Anned nerede*?" (where is your mother) I ask. She points down the aisle, and I let her down. She runs to her.

After a few moments, Jill seems to calm down.

"I'm sorry. I didn't mean to react so strongly." She pauses for a moment, then, in earnest, she asks, "Rick, do you really find me… pretty?"

It's an easy answer, but I know where she is going with this. In this alley, between the frantic pace of people and shops, it's an odd place to start this conversation. I take her hands and pull her off to the side between two flower vendors. The pink hydrangea and sunflowers form a picture-perfect frame around her. I finally reach out and stroke that exquisite hair at last. It's like the golden fleece. Her eyes and cheeks are wet. I reach over and slide my finger over one tear.

"I didn't know how I felt at first. When I got to know you, nothing else mattered. Yeah. That first day, I heard all the comments about you. But there you were, my Swiss miss, boldly announcing to the world, here I am."

"I have no need for pretty. As much as I like pranking, pretty is a trick girls use, a crutch. It holds power over them. I got very used to the ridicule growing up with what I was. I didn't know how to handle it then. You take a school ground of third graders playing with the only odd and redhead among them. If something went wrong, it was just too easy to point at the weird one and blame her. It really limited my life of crime," she winks.

"Yeah? Well, you've made up for it since then," I give a hopeful grin. She looks away, then back to me.

"But it gets to me. My worth is not tied up in the way I look – pretty or not pretty. Take that as a puzzle piece. I try to ignore it. Those past days still hurt. They hold me hostage. This is why I don't let you…"

"I know. It's okay. Maybe when the time is right for you."

"I was so shocked when you and Mitch paid me any attention at all."

"Look, Mitch is in this for the conquest. I'm in this to be blessed."

Once that sinks in, her eyes well up again. "Don't be so hard on Mitch. He's trying."

"Yeah, very trying."

She starts to look around. "Hey, where's our guy?"

He has stopped for a cup of *chi*, Turkish tea. We move nearby and share a cheese-filled *ekmek simitt* (round bread stick).

"You're the baby of your family, aren't you?" Jill asks me.

"So are you."

"Yeah, but you clearly have been around kids," she adds.

"A little. I conduct singing time for the children on Sundays at church. They seem to like me, but I have to work at it. My mom is a good teacher," I assure her. I don't mention that the little girl has just picked my pocket, a few *lira*, no big loss.

"Rick, sing me one of your kid songs."

"What? Oh, you mean what I teach at church. Really? Here?"

"Yeah. Teach me."

"OK."

I pick up my round *ekmek* bread stick, tear it into a straight line and hold it out in front of her. I turn the ends down. And I sing.

"If you chance to meet a frown, make it go away."

I flip it over to make a 'U' shape,

"Promptly turn it upside down and smile that frown away."

I then push the corners of her mouth down and sing with a low, exaggerated voice. *"You don't want a frowny face."*

Then I push the corners of her mouth up and change the tenor of my voice to something more positive.

"Turn it to a smile. Make today a bright bouquet by smiling all the while."

She claps and giggles. Oh yeah. I'll sing anything to get that giggle.

"Jill, tell me something," I ask seriously.

"Something."

"I mean, I feel like we've been riding a big wave of wonder together. It's been grand."

"I agree, boss. Many ups and downs." And she stuffs a piece of ekmek in my mouth. "We need to clean up one bit of business in our ups and downs. That would be the matter of my ceramic hand cast?"

I knew that would hit someday. With a mouth full of the bread, I swallow hard and mutter, "Oh, that. OK. Well, you see. I am going to Istanbul soon. The shops there are famous for the Turkish friendship rings or puzzle rings."

"Yes, the ones that are several rings interconnected. They are also called 'Harem rings.' So, what about them?"

"I wanted to… to…"

"Oh! I get it. Size me up for your harem."

"Harem?"

"Yeah. That's what they call the collection of the Sultan's wives."

"No. I mean. I thought they were called 'friendship rings.' I wanted to make it a surprise after all we've been through."

"Well, I hope you didn't note my ring size from that broken middle finger?" Now it's my turn to laugh.

"So, I'm forgiven?"

"I give you full absolution, my son," she says with a mock genuflection.

"Back to what I was going to ask you. Help me with your puzzle."

"I'll find a corner piece for you. Fire away."

"What's important to girls, I mean, to you in a boy?" I am surprised at my own boldness.

"Now you're getting heavy. Ooo. So brave, Ricky. Let's see. Excitement. Humor. Communication. Mystery." She ticks them off quickly.

I figure I'm holding up pretty well in those departments so far. Need to work on humor. Then she says

"But you've already shown me the best, and that's honesty."

My flashing signals go off. Danger, Danger 9b! My train of trouble is approaching my body, stuck on the tracks at my crossing. Then she adds,

"Honesty in emotions, feelings."

Oh. Here we go. I know this puzzle piece; *they never say what they really mean.* "Jill, what does that mean?"

"Oh – he's on the move again!" She pulls me away and off we go before I get an answer.

"He's stopping at the bookstore. He's getting a book from the shopkeeper. This is it. There is a paper sticking out of it!" She pulls me closer to the transaction and pretends to look at some books.

"The paper is in Russian!" she whispers. She should know.

The man suddenly turns to go and knocks me to the ground.

Jill lets out a "Hey!"

"*Affedersin,*" he says, meaning, excuse me and walks away. Jill kneels on the ground to help me up. I am a little dazed. In confusion, Jill pulled the bookmark paper out of the man's book.

"Wow. I think he meant it. Good distraction because look what I got," Jill whispers and holds up her prize.

"I think we got a little too close," I conclude. Then I see her paper. Wow, that is some authentic, not-planned action. "Which way did he go?"

Just then, Tom and Will run up to us, quite excited and arguing.

"I didn't see it," Sarge contends.

"Well, I did," Spitball insists. He pulls me off to the side, out of earshot of Jill, leaving her alone.

"That guy with half a nose. I'm telling you – he and another guy are here. They were watching you - only - they are girls!" Tom blurts out.

"Girls?" I ask, very confused.

"Women," Sarge corrects him. "Two guys were *dressed* as women he thinks."

"Yeah. They were wearing their head coverings over their faces and watching you," Tom continues.

"Tom, they weren't guys. OK. Some of the women around here look like guys, I admit. But who would do that? That's just silly," Will insists.

"I saw what I saw." This goes on, back and forth for a couple of minutes. And while we all argue, we look around and realize Jill has wandered off. We don't see her anymore. We scout the area, and she is nowhere to be seen.

"We better split up and find her," I quickly make assignments. "Tom – you head to the meat market. Will, take the vegetable market, and I'll head to clothing. Meet back here in fifteen minutes."

Why I choose the clothing and textile market is only a guess. I am quickly running through the aisles and aisles of vendors with all their colorful offerings. Rugs, blankets, clothes of all kinds, scarves, and dresses all hanging up for display, softly billowing in the slow-moving breezes, like dancers in a cultural pageant.

She may be anywhere. And there are women everywhere, most with head scarves. Can there be these two guys on her tail again – blending in so cleverly? I stand out like the only weed in a manicured flower patch. Too much time has passed. My worry meter has notched up a bunch of ticks.

In the mix of textiles, I run a few shops I can only describe as hobby vendors or collection vendors. There is a miniature toy shop, a toy train shop, a coin shop, then a vendor for stamp collectors. As I pass by this tiny stamp shop, a very strong hand reaches out and yanks me inside. At first, I see an odd-looking, very large woman. Quickly, I can tell who it is with little problem. Mister No-nose!

"Tigran!" I say. It takes him back.

"La petite fille t'a parlé."

"I don't speak French."

He stares me down, then menacingly adds, "So, little girl talk to you?"

"What have you done with her?" I go to strike him, but he is a huge man and just crushes my arm in a tight grip.

"You tiny boy. No hit, Tigran. No want girl." He releases my arm. "I want what *Professeure* Fontaine gives her."

"He's probably given her lots of things," I say with gritted teeth, nursing my arm.

"No. Something in the purse. I do not stop 'til I get."

"There's only girl stuff in that purse. Besides, she doesn't have that today."

"Tigran knows this. Oh, little man. You know nothing. You tell girl, I have one clue, one piece. I need more, or I will tell."

"What are you talking about? Tell what? You don't have her?"

"You talk her or Tigran tells," thumping his chest. He then covers up and runs out.

It all happened so fast. I couldn't think straight. What am I telling her? At least I know he doesn't have her. I quickly keep moving through the textile area. Then I hear it. You can't mistake it, the otherworldly lilt that only my Fortuna can make. I can feel my heart pumping. I turn into a silk vendor's booth, and all I see are the backs of two women in head scarves. Then I move around them, and there is Jill, flaunting a full-length, flowery-patterned silk dress, sauntering back and forth.

"Ricky!" she says in surprise, "I forgot all about you guys." I look at the two women with her. They sort of look like men in dresses.

"Oh. This girl. So *güzel*," one says.

Once I get over the shock, I add, "*Evet. Onun adi, Jameela.*" They both laugh.

"Okay, smarty pants. What did you say?"

"That you were very naughty and that you shouldn't have wandered away from me and that I was so worried sick that I might lose you and never see you again and that your name is Jameela, the beautiful one. Was that emotionally honest?"

I guess I'm getting good at making her cry. "That's so sweet. I'm sorry I should have told you. These two followed me because they loved my shoes, and they took me to this dress shop."

Because of the cultural taboo on public affection, I missed out on a great opportunity. But I was so relieved. I was going to tell her about being accosted by Tigran when Tom and Will find us again. We start back where we left Mitch at the shoeshine stands. There is a crowd gathered around, and no Mitch is in sight. From behind the crowd of people, we hear the strumming of a guitar and singing,

Yo soy un hombre sincero

De donde crece la palma Y

antes de morirme quiero

Echar mis versos del alma

We pass through the crowd. And yeah, it's Mitch. Jill just sways back and forth in her new silk dress, eating it up.

Guantanamera, guajira Guantanamera

Guantanamera, guajira Guantanamera

"It's a classic Cuban poem - a love song about long-lost love," she breathlessly sighs.

"What was that? So cool. What does it mean? Where did you get the guitar?" Tom asks Mitch excitedly.

And Mitch goes right into it,

"I am a truthful man

From where the palm tree grows

And before dying, I want

To let out the verses of my soul."

"There is a music shop just over there. They let me borrow this when they realized I could play."

Oh great. Just what I need. Back in the presence of Diablo again, just when things are getting good.

"I thought you were supposed to be surveilling the guy at this stand. Now you're serenading him with 'one ton potata'.

"Pretty sneaky, wouldn't you say? And it's Guan-tan-a mera. I'm not singing about an ethnobotanical spud.

"Mitch, you wouldn't believe it. This guy attacked Rick, well, sort of. Knocked him over." Jill tells him.

"Really?" He turns to me.

"Yeah. Pretty intense," I admit.

"What did you have me stay here for? I could have taken the guy out."

"You?" Will says, "Ha." Then I jump in,

"How? Croon him to death? Jill handled it just fine." Then he gets into my face.

Will chimes in, "No, he needed to eat my knuckle sandwich."

"You put her in danger," Mitch angrily tells me.

"Danger? Oh, come on you two. Knock it off. It was great," Jill shouts out. "We lifted this secret note."

"Looks like a bookmark to me," Mitch comments as he looks it over.

"Well, anyway. Before we saw the ladies tailing you, look what we found!" Tom interrupts our confrontation. Out comes a collection of

what looks like glass eyes. "Check these marbles out. The guy calls them glass eyes!"

"We never did see your Turban, guy," Sarge tells us. By then, my man has disappeared and has earned his ten *lira*.

"I'll take the paper, Jill, and get it analyzed. Good work, Agent Fortuna!" She grabs my hand,

"Rick, your arm is bleeding."

Chapter Forty-Three
Tomorrow Never Knows

"Of course, I know it was him. I didn't turn off my mind and float somewhere. He jumped when I called him by name. He makes for one ugly woman." Our taxi makes a sudden turn that throws Jill into me and my arm against the door.

"Oww. *Yavaşla lütfen* (slow down please)

"So, just a scratch, huh?"

"I'll be fine. I'm not dying." I didn't want to confess he easily handled me.

"He was dressed as a woman? I guess that is an easier way to hide your face."

"Jill, he said you have something about your purse he wants. That's weird. Why would he want that?"

"I'm not sure," she hesitates, "what else did he say?"

"That he has a piece of some clue. He said he wouldn't stop until he getse the others. I guess he means the clues that you talked about?"

"Probably. They could be connected to the grandfather's diverse artifact collection. Perhaps the clues are among them. I have a lot to find out."

"He said he would 'tell' if you don't give it to him. Jill, what's going on? We have to be in this together." She looks away at the city as it streams by our windows, looking like blurred photos on a long exposure. For some reason, this is hard for her. She takes my hand.

"Do you trust me? I trust you."

"Jill, this is wild. Of course, I do. But it's getting far too serious to avoid."

"I know. And I will tell you what I can. But…"

"Yeah?"

"It's complicated. I can tell you this much…" The taxi then arrives at her home. She pays him, and we sit in her front garden.

"You know we're heading out of town for the holidays. This can't wait," I plead with her. She takes a deep breath.

"I got to reading one of grandfather's history books about the Crusades in our library. He put a strange entry in the side notes. He mentions that he thought some of the Crusader castles might still contain buried treasure – gold coins."

"Now, that sounds like an adventure he would want you to have."

"He writes that sometimes the Crusaders were under attack or under siege and had to bury their treasure to not lose it to their enemies. Particularly if they had to abandon the castle quickly with the intention of re-taking it later. In some cases, they never came back."

"What's that got to do with any of this?'

"Grandfather was quite clever about these clues – to keep them secret and separated. The first clue he gave me was verbal. Just before he passed, he specifically named *Kiz Kalisi* as one of my clues to inheritance. The other came to me on a note a week later."

"*Kiz Kalisi*? Where is that?"

"Right here in Turkey. It's a crusader castle."

"Is that what Tigran is talking about, a piece of the clues?"

"I'm pretty sure he wants to know what I know. That's the problem. Since we are studying the Crusades, I talked with Mr.Tenney. I didn't say anything about my grandfather, but I said I have an interest in the castle, and I am sure our classmates will also. I suggested we take a field

trip. I tell him mother will pay for the buses and food. And he is going for it!"

"You are something! When?"

"Not sure. Sometime after the Thanksgiving holiday."

"What was on the note about *Kiz Kalisi*?"

"He wrote, 'Look to the tower.' That's it."

"Tower? At the castle?"

"I assume so."

I sort of raise my voice in irritation, "But I still don't understand what Tigran meant about 'telling' something. You're leaving information out. I don't get it. You want me to… "

She slams her hand down on the garden table and rises, "Rick! I can't tell you!" She storms through her garden gate and up the walk. Yelling back at me, "Will you trust me on this? *C'est la cata.* You can be so annoying." Before she slams the front door, she yells, "I'll call you a taxi."

"Don't bother. I'll walk," I yell back. I bend over, my arm in agony.

Chapter Forty-Four
Why Don't We Do it in the Road?

I feel a bit better in the morning, my arm, that is. Where did this other fight come from? No one was watching us, so how am I to know? I am just trying to understand and help. This girl puzzle is not coming together well, but here is another piece; *girls are unpredictable*. Not sure where it fits.

It is a little tense at school the next day. My family is doing the road, heading out for the Thanksgiving vacation the following day. For Danger 9b, it's not a holiday but a mission to Istanbul, that famous city that bridges Europe with the Middle East. Long ago, it had a different name, given by its Greek founders, Byzantium.

"I foresee a geography and history lesson coming. Wake me when it's over," I hear the calm and pleasant version of Jill echo in my mind.

"Jill, you know full well we studied this last quarter, and you loved it," I remind her. I talk to myself often, more results of the Jillian effect.

"Oh, that's right. It must be the peanut butter deprivation that has settled on me. I've been so long without it. OK, carry on, professor."

"Good idea. Let me quote Mr. Tenney, our history teacher," I suggest.

"Oh. Can you talk funny like he does? I think they call it a 'lisp'? That will be worth it."

Mr. Tenney never avoids words with 's.' That makes his lisp even more noticeable. It doesn't bother him, but for us, it is hysterical. One can count the words with 's' and compare which day is the funniest. Yea for the 'Ss'! So, this day in history class, it is:

Mr. Tenney: Byzantium was conquered by the Christian crusaders, and the city re-named? Quickly students. Quickly.

Tom: Bizarreo Land!

Mr. Tenney: No. Mr. H. Yes, Jill?

He calls the boys by their last name initials – not the girls. Tom is Mr. H. He always gets picked on. Tom is Tom. He knows lots of facts but somehow can't put the right answer together at the right time.

Jill: That would be Constantinople in honor of the Roman emperor, Constantine.

"Show off," I tell her.

"I can't help it."

Mr. Tenney: That lasted, yes, over a thousand years as a sun- soaked city until the suspicious Ottoman Turks surrounded and subjugated the city. Its name was silenced as it changed or somehow transformed into Istanbul – meaning "the city."

Now, count the *S*'s and even the same sounding *C*'s in this one! My sides are aching, almost putting me on the floor. A new record.

If you look at a map, Istanbul sits next to a waterway called the Bosporus Straits.

"Oh, Please. Mr. Tenney, say 'BoSporuS StraitS' for us!".

Yes. Jill would ask that.

The Bosporus Straits is the only way into the Black Sea by water – an essential passageway for Russian ships. Sounded like I could use this somehow. I have to tiptoe around Jill just a bit, so I tell her.

"I'll check in with you as often as I can."

"How? You'll be 275 miles away."

"I'll phone you." I had to leave it at that. But then she adds.

"Make sure you do. Be safe. Happy Thanksgiving."

That sounds good. The problem is, leaving Mitch alone with Jill again. I think I've given him a way back in. I hope not. He is getting far too suspicious. But, with all that is happening, I kinda hope he keeps a close watch on her. This sounds a little conflicted. Oh boy, I think the steam whistle is blowing wildly on my pressure cooker. They will not just sit home while I'm gone. Nothing I can do about that. They will probably have a holiday get-together. Yes, a party. This will be fun, no doubt. Right now, it's torture to think about.

I am helpless. It's a long drive to Istanbul. The roads are narrow, one lane in each direction, and will get even narrower and crooked as we pass through a bunch of small villages. It could snow. You can't drive very fast. So, it's going to be a long day before we get there.

Driving in Turkey, one needs to be on guard. I have no experience of driving. But it seems crazy to me. Dad seems to just go with the flow. At busy city street intersections, there are no traffic lights.

"You see the guy on the wooden platform there?" Dad asks.

There is a policeman standing in the middle of the intersection in a little round, elevated box.

"If his shoulders and body are turned in the direction you want to go, I can drive through. So, what do you see?" Dad asks me.

"He is facing us."

"And that would mean?" He is giving me my first driving lesson.

"Stop?"

"You got it. Just in case you ever drive here."

"Don't even think about it," Mom adds.

My sister, Brenda, is not traveling with us on this trip to Istanbul. So – I have more room in the back seat. My brother, Steve, occupies one back window, and me at the other. The windows are our only form of air-conditioning if we need it. After all, it is November. Dad calls it 250 air conditioning – two windows down at fifty miles per hour.

When we reach the small villages, the road bends around littlehomes and shops. There is no need for traffic cops here. Dad just needs to be alert. I'm sort of dozing, gazing out the side window, when I heara wild screech. We all lurch forward when there is a loud thump and bang. I snap my head to look out the front window.

Two boys' faces and a red substance smash all along our front window.

The red stuff is all over the place, and the boys slide off the hood to the ground. The windshield is not broken, but it looks awful and serious. Dad charges out of the car, but the boys run off! All that remains is a crumpled bicycle and what is left of a smashed watermelon.

Yeah. It was two little boys sharing the same bike, one steering and the other on the handlebars, apparently trying to balance the large melon on his head. Crowds of villagers form around the car. They are all talking and some yelling. These folks don't seem to be hostile. The problem was – no one spoke English.

Steve is yelling at me,

"Get out and talk to them, you know, in Turkish!"

"I hardly know squat at the speeds they're talking. Why don't you get out your Stratocaster and play for them for all the good it will do?"

We cleared it all up with the local judge. They dragged the two boys into his court, and he buffed them about their heads. Dad had to pay a little *buckshish*, bribe money, and we were on our way.

Chapter Forty-Five
You're Gonna Lose That Girl

We finally make it to Istanbul. Wow. What a site. It is built on multiple hills. The architecture is much older than the more modern Ankara, where we live. There are Islamic mosques, equivalent to Christian churches, almost on every block of streets. Minarets, the tall towers that stick up at mosques, seem more numerous than chimneys in England.

I want to tell Jill about the place in the one phone call Dad lets me make to her. Most of us only have one phone in a house or apartment, she has at least three and it sounds like it's the one downstairs in the parlor. I get her on the phone.

Rick: *Jill! Merhaba, hello from your sultan in Istanbul!*

Jill: *My what?*

Rick: *I was in the palace of the Sultans.*

There is a lot of noise going on in the background at her house. I can't hear her well. I think her parents have friends over.

Jill: *Oh! Hi Rick! What's up with the Sultans?*

She sounds herself. She's not yelling at me. Good sign.

Rick: *Yeah. The guys that were rulers had these palaces where they kept their harem and other cool stuff.*

Jill: *Oh, yeah, the Topkapi palace. Did you see all the jeweled daggers?*

Rick: *And the thrones and swords. What's all the noise?*

Jill: *(a little muffled) Hey, everyone. Rick is on the line. Cool your jets. Pipe down!*

Then, it does quiet down, and I hear her very clearly.

Jill: Mitch is here with all the gang. It's just a little get-together. You know me. We miss you!

Then I distinctly hear The Beatle's new recently released hit record start-up in the background entitled. *You're gonna lose that girl.* The Beatles are a massive hit around the world. Two, named Paul McCartney and John Lennon will not let me quote their lyrics. So, I willparaphrase. That means I will approximate their meanings as close as I can without using the actual words. This is for a reason. I am allowed to quote a title of a song legally. So, think about them singing the title two times.

You're gonna lose that girl.

You're gonna lose that girl.

Then, in the background of the song, the boys in the band agree, two times, using a word that starts with 'y' and rhymes with 'mess' and means 'we agree,' then they quote the title again.

'We agree, we agree,' you're gonna lose that girl

Then the lyrics suggest that I better pay attention to my girl tonight, or she will have a change of that gray matter in her head. That word starts with an 'm' and rhymes with 'kind' and sort of goes like this:

You better pay attention to that girl, or she will change her (the word that rhymes with 'kind')

The background singers then agree, two times, again using a word that starts with 'y' and rhymes with 'mess' and quoting the title again.

'We agree, we agree,' you're gonna lose that girl.

It also loses something in my translation. It's a great song now playing at the wrong time. The point is Mitch is behind the playing of this, at this precise time, on purpose. I just know it. It's sabotage to the worst degree. He's placed explosives on my love train. I'm three

hundred miles away, and I can't do a thing about it. Wait! Unless I can come up with something clever on the phone. I have to keep my point totals up against Mitch. So, I think fast and continuously.

Rick: Well, I just wanted to say hi. And tell you, we had to waste a couple of foreign agents who were tailing us the other day.

Jill: Waste? What??? Quiet everyone!

I stay cool, calm, and collected. I let the words sink in, trying to let the song finish unnoticed in the background. Nice and slow, I go on.

Rick: Yeah. Yeah. Dad had to mow them down with the car. There was red stuff all over the place.

OK, so I twist the action just a little. No big deal. There was red stuff, so it isn't all a lie. 'A scout is trustworthy' is still in the ballpark. What can I lose at this point? Oh, yeah, the girl.

Jill: That sounds awful! Hey guys! Rick's dad had to shoot his way out of an ambush!

This sounds even better. I do not correct her. I can hear them all crowd around the phone. I hear various voices.

"No way! Wow. Is he OK? Cool!"

Rick: I had to clean up the car so we could make a getaway. We had to pay some buckshish to keep it all quiet. So, you won't read about it anywhere.

Jill: Are you alright?

Rick: Oh Yeah. I helped translate a few things. Önemli değil. No big deal.

This Turkish phrase, *Önemli değil,* 'no big deal' in Turkish, probably translates closer to "not a large transaction or sale," but it was working.

Jill: Goodness, Rick. Do you think it was those guys we've been dealing with?

This has not occurred to me. This is getting better.

Rick: No, these guys were a little... smaller.

Jill: Please come back to us alive.

We end the call not long after that, at about the place where the song ends. Nice timing, Rick. She doesn't have to think about that Beatle title message. Diablo is living up to his name. I am in agony.

Chapter Forty-Six
The Long and Winding Road

I am not sure why I get to go on this next adventure. I have no idea whose door this will lead to, but it's a real mission. It's our last day. While my mother and brother, who are sent to accompany her, go to thefamous international bazaar, the *suq* or market in Istanbul, I get to go on an 'outing' with my dad. His plan is wild, long, and winding, that is for sure. He is quite insistent I go. This bums out my brother. He wantsto go. Mom wants a brass table and some Turkish rugs. You just can't let her be alone. My dad is after something more. Maybe I am a really good cover. I don't know. Maybe it's because I can speak and read someTurkish – only some. Whatever his reasons, this is the real thing.

There is an Armenian family he says he needs to visit far into the countryside outside Istanbul. I don't know what it is about. The image of the Armenian situation in Turkey is vivid in my mind, thanks to my friendship with the Chobanians, the *kapaci* family downstairs. Their history is complicated, but many of them still live in Turkey and have for generations. There is an ancient country along Turkey's far eastern border called Armenia. Many went there after being pushed out of Turkey, but Armenia has been around for a long time, long before present-day Turkey. The Armenians were the first entire nation to convert to Christianity. That is part of the conflict. Armenians are Christians and the Ottomans (the empire before Turkey was formed) were Muslims. It is still an issue today.

What fascinates me this day is the effort it will take to get to our destination. From our hotel, we take a '*dolmuce*.' It's a car, like a Taxi, only it goes on a certain route, and you only pay for your seat. You get out anywhere along the route. Perhaps Dad doesn't want anyone to follow. I don't know. He seems to know what to do.

We flag down a *dolmuce*.

"Ask him if he goes to the Subway station."

"Metro istasyonu? "

"Evet" is the reply. It is a Mercedes Benz that takes us to a subway station. We don't need to do that, but we do. We ride it out for one-stop, switch subways and ride it down to the waterway on the Bosporus straits. We get purposely lost in the crowd. I'm just following hisinstructions. Dart here. Go in this door. Wait. Go out the far door. Go downstairs. Wait. Then we put on sweaters and hats he gets from a locker, along with small bags. So cool. We finally make our way to a passenger ferry and jump on at the very last moment. This boat takes usinto the Sea of Marmara and to another port. We get out at the port and get on a train out to a certain city. I help Dad read the signs.

From there, we are met by a man who leads us to an ashak cart, modified to legitimately take passengers. (I don't need to use the Jillian Maneuver to ride. I would need to train my dad.)

Along the way, I notice a few trashed cigarette packages. They are all Turkish brands, except one, a 'Lucky Strike.' I dash off and pick it up. That entitles me to a lucky strike, right? My dad hardly notices. He is lost in thought. I decide to save it up for the right person.

That donkey cart carries us way out into the countryside. We get out, and my dad's contact walks us along a country road, a long and winding pathway for about a mile. We stop at a little house surrounded by planted crops and fenced-off pastures for sheep. I can't see that anyone is following. We can see for miles, or should I say, many kilometers. We are in the area known anciently as the 'Hellespont,' nearthe legendary city of Troy.

So, it takes a car, a subway, a boat, a train, a donkey cart, and now we ride 'Shank's pony.' That was what my grandfather called 'walking.' All of this we experience in one part of a day! Where elsecan you do that? We need a plane ride in there somewhere to complete the circle. I think this is really cool.

Dad goes inside the small home. He tells me to stay outside with some other kids around the house close to my age. They think I talk funny. I suppose I do. They teach me some Armenian words. 'How are you?'

Ինչպես ես

Yeah. I stare at the scratches on the scrap paper. The kids tell me it is pronounced inch–pes-es. (How are you?) To say 'Thank you' is, in letters, I can read *shnorhakalut'yun*. I think Turkish is much easier. I can at least read those letters. The Armenian alphabet is like it came from 'Plan B from Outer Space.' It sounds and looks like a far-out language.

Dad does not tell me what the meeting is all about. That doesn't bother me. It is such a cool adventure. I have my dad to thank for his understanding and love of different cultures, people, and world history. He is not boring. I am his son. Therefore, I cannot be boring. Take that, Mitch, the Diablo!

When we see my mom and brother again, they report on their adventures. Their stuff is going to be shipped to our place in Ankara. I tease my brother carefully.

"You enjoy your little shopping spree?"

"I was a bodyguard, little brother," he insists.

"Oh, right. Protecting Mom from the big bad shopkeepers? Most of them are little kids."

"OK, smarty pants. What did you do?" he says, trying to change the subject.

I give him a lucky strike to the arm and show him the trashed package.

"That all you got, wise guy?"

"Oh, yeah. I was a little wise. I just learned Armenian today. I had my smarty pants on."

Ինչպես ես?" I ask him.

When you are almost sixteen , you can really be annoying when you want. Just ask Jill. He just turns around and huffs off.

My mind quickly turns to what I am missing at home. I really want to call again, but I am not allowed to. Calls are not free. The score has to be tightening. Mitch has been spending more time with Jill than I can count. I can't even keep track anymore.

RIVALRY BOX SCORE:

I don't even know what it is. Am I ahead? I'm sure of it. But by how much? My desk is getting full of box scores. Songs, poems, action, confessions, adventure. How does it all add up? All I couldthink of was, 'You're Gonna Lose that Girl.'

Episode Seven

Crusade to the Castle in the Sea

Chapter Forty-Seven
Act Naturally

Really? I don't know what the score is right now. Jill and I are sort of wavering, while Mitch is hovering, still in the picture. Why? I don't know. I feel like I'm a star in my own movie, playing a bad guy all alone and hurting.

"Just act yourself!" the director yells at me through his megaphone. Not hard to do.

Jill's been with me, but I go away far too often. Cleverly played Jill, keeping us both on our toes, always guessing. Watch out guys. The puzzle gets harder. Here is another piece. *Girls are very tricky.*

I do get that paper translated Jill pulled from our guy in the market. Dad has a friend that can read Russian. I tell him it is for a school project. Not that I am expecting anything. It turns out it is a bookmark with a picture of Ataturk's tomb, right here in Ankara. It is explaininga brief history of modern Turkey. Kemal Ataturk led the country from the old Ottoman Empire to a more westernized country in the 1920s. He modernized the language, moving it from Arabic based writing to a Western alphabet, and many other changes. He is well loved here and admired. It explains the belief that many Turks think he will come back, reincarnated as a cat with green eyes. So – that is partly why there are so many cats in Turkey. They are respected. So, I send a note to Jill.

I did have a certain document, obtayned in the market, xamined by our experts. Good work. It could have been coded for Russian agents here in Ankara. They are studing for any clues. You just might have a future in this business! Meet at lunch.

Danger 9b

We find a private table in the cafeteria and break out our lunch boxes. Mine has a picture of Bert Lehr as 'the Cowardly Lion' from the 'Wizard of Oz'. She has a picture of the actor, Peter O'Toole from the movie, 'Lawrence of Arabia' on hers. Yeah. His eyes are so much bluerthan mine.

"Are we cool?" I ask sweetly.

"Yes. Why wouldn't we be?"

I could give her any number of reasons, but I don't. Another example of the complexity of the puzzle – *girls keep you totally off- balance.* I guess that counts as my earlier 'unpredictable' piece?

"Just wanted to be sure."

"Da da da dat ta da," she announces with a fake mouth trumpet. "Attention all you budding archeologists. Our trip is on."

"For real? To the castle? When?"

"Tenny called last night. In two weeks, before vacation break and it gets too cold on the coast. The information goes out to parents today."

The bell rings and stops the conversation, only to promise to talk again.

"The game is afoot!"

This is so Jill. There it is again. Having lived in England, the "afoot" line was something out of Sherlock Holmes mystery novels. This is about as big an adventure as my spy operations, which are declining in

some ways. I think they may be tired of them. I haven't had any assignments to offer since the market. 'Out of sight, out of mind' is the saying. This castle search seems to overshadow anything I can come up with. What a pair we make.

So, the class field trip is on to the castle, *Kiz Kalisi,* on the south coast of Turkey, near a city called *Salifki.* We are living right here in the crossroads of history, the land of the Crusaders, so it is quite exciting.

Unfortunately, I am not the only one invited. The whole class is in on it. OK, the more the merrier? However, we keep the buried and forgotten treasure information secret and only known to our gang. The 'look to the tower' clue? That's just between Jill and me. Both factors really elevate the excitement about our trip.

Mr. Tenney, our history teacher, is getting us all prepared.

Mr. Tenney: *Before our field trip, I have a pop quiz you all need to take.*

We all groan.

Mr. Tenney: *Please describe for me the beginnings of the Crusades and its causes. That means, Mr. H, which you will need to write your answer down with words. Essay style.*

Essentially, what he is looking for is something like this: In the year 1095 A.D. the leader of the Catholic Church, Pope Urban II, convinced a lot of his followers to form an army to liberate Jerusalem from its Muslim occupiers. That started a bunch of military campaigns, called Crusades. Some of the battles were fought here in Turkey on the Crusader's way to the Holy Land – Jerusalem - and the land surrounding that city. There were principally eight major Crusades which were

spread over two hundred or so years. Turkey, or Anatolia, as it was called, was a perilous part of the journey.

Mr. Tenney: *We are fortunate that Mrs. MacGregor is sponsoring our trip to real Crusader castles, two of many that are found all over Turkey. They are national treasures here.*

Castles – very cool – right? We were excited, especially about Jill's quest to find treasure. That was even outta sight.

Chapter Forty-Eight
*Everybody's Got Something to Hide
(Except Me and My Monkey)*

Before we head out on this school adventure, I know I need to beef up the rivalry scoreboard a little. I think maybe I am a little low on the 'humor' part of what Jill likes in boys, and supposedly the "emotionally honest" might not be so high either. How do I know?

"Hear ye. Hear ye. All agents are invited to a night of mystery and entertainment!" I declare to the gang.

"Is there food involved?" Tom asks.

"Yes! Most definitely." I invite my close gang to my apartment for a magic show. Magic? I wish I can conjure up a permanent magic love spell on Jill. Mom gets me a boxed magic kit. She pushes me into so many things, always wanting me to work toward her motto: 'be well-rounded in life'. Jill is another motivator, in a different kind of way, to stretch my horizons and thinking. The tricks in the magic box kit are okay, but I am going to do some of my own tricks, one with a special surprise. So, we gather this night.

"Mitch! Take it easy. Take it easy. Come on. Put me down!" Jill giggles in delight.

"But this is such a joy," Mitch cackles behind her, his arms around her middle and lifting her off the ground.

"There will be no levitation tricks tonight!" I say with some annoyance at the start of my show.

"Down I say!" she commands. He drops her. "Oww!" she yelps, rubbing her side.

Why is he goofing around with Jill in my living room in front of me? Ooo, it irks me. I shake it off.

"Behold! I will now astound and amaze you."

I repeat the words printed on the magic box script.

"What's the goofy wizard hat for?" Tom asks.

"You ask this? Mr. Centurion helmet man?"

"I acquiesce, oh great one, to your omniscient powers," Tom bows.

Yes. I have on this goofy wizard hat. I have draped a make-shift stage with sheets and my favorite blanket.

"Yea, bravo. Cheers," calls out my loyal group of friends, Marie, Aisha, Karin along with Will, Tom, Dave, Jill and, of course, Mitch. I approach Marie.

"Young lady, will you hold this little bag for me with a big surprise inside? Don't open it. What is this, ladies and gentlemen and young lady?" I ask of Jill. I show them what appears to be a little wooden ball. "It's a little wooden ball," I say. "Just like this young man's head." I clunk it against Mitch's head.

I hear Jill whisper to Marie, "Looks like a big seed to me." I go on.

"Yes. My baseball fans, this is a little ball."

I take out a magician's cloth and let them inspect it. I put the ball inside and fold it up the corners. I let go of the sides and the ball disappears.

"*Voila*! Gone!" I say just as I hear Mitch mumble,

"Everyone's got something to hide."

Not a bad trick. It got pulled up into my sleeve. There is much applause. Good start.

"Now, I will use my magic wand to perform a colossal transformation."

"I hope it's a colossal lot of food," Tom says. I approach Marie and tap the bag.

"Now young lady, open the bag. Could it be?"

Marie opens the bag. "It is an Avocado," she states.

"An Avocado?" Tom repeats. "That's colossal? I hate that stuff." I ignore him and continue.

"How could this be? But wait, what is inside?" I cut it open.

"*Voilà!* Our little wooden ball."

"Wow! How did you do that?" Tom blurts out.

Jill claps like a wild lady. They all join in. If you haven't cut open an Avocado, trust me, there is a little wooden ball inside. Pretty goofy. It only sets the stage.

The next trick is all my own doing. I previously got a Cheerios cereal box and took everything out, flaps and all. It was now just a hollow box, but I had glued a hold down flap inside. I show them a crumpled paper ball.

"Yes folks. What you see here is a hollow box, Cheerios, the breakfast of champions!"

Will intercedes. "Ah. No. That's Wheaties. Cheerios are for babies."

"Okay, babes, these are for you." I wink at the girls. "I have here another ball, baseball fans." I know this will please Tom. I show the crumpled paper ball.

"Yes. Another ball for all you first place consolation bracket European all-star champions. I will now perform the magic."

I hold the box up now and hover the ball over the opening. I let it go and it falls straight through into my other hand, below the box.

"What's the magic in that?" Mitch asks.

"What? No magic? Says the ill-informed young man in the back." I show the hollow box again for them to see inside.

"It's just a hollow box. But if I say the magic words along with a breath from a beautiful princess, magic will happen."

I hold it close to Aisha, and she blows on it.

"Venkataramanujam!" I pronounce.

Aisha agrees. I drop the ball but it does not fall through.

"Magic, my adoring fans." They all clap.

"Venkataramanujam!" I shake the box and the ball falls through. My brother, who has just walked in, calls out.

"Lame!" then walks away.

"No. It was good!" the others proclaim. I think it is pretty good, being my own creation. After that, I do perform a few more truly lame tricks. Then the finale.

"And now, for my final offering. Don't we all seek for the one true treasure?"

I wink at Jill.

"Something so valued as to be worthy of a great reward? I shall make a true treasure appear out of thin air."

What could I have up my sleeve besides a stinky avocado pit?

"I will need the help of a beautiful assistant!"

Tom jumps up.

"Oh. Pick me! Pick Me!"

"Yeah! Make him disappear," Mitch pleads.

"I shall ask the beautiful goddess, Fortuna." Jill takes a bow and steps forward.

I know she really likes theatrics, so I lay it on thick. Yea forhumorous me.

"Now, my able assistant. Please show the crowd this simple tablecloth." She takes it from me and begins to flow it over everyone's head, singing The Beatles, 'Please, Mr. Postman'. Not sure why she picks this. It is a song about love letters.

"Please Miss Postman lady, place the tablecloth over the mystical portal. It has magical powers having now been touched by the great goddess of Fortune." I point to my main table. She spreads it over in dramatic fashion.

"Please join with me in the mystical chant, 'O Fortuna, O Fortuna'." They all join me in the chant as Jill sways back and forth. I move my foot to a hidden lever I designed that pushes up an object in the middle of the table which pushes up a lump in the tablecloth.

"Behold! The greatest treasure of Fortune! Remove the covering!" Jill does so. And there, in the middle of the table, is a beautiful jar of:

Skippy Peanut Butter

It glows in my lamplight. Mom has pulled through for me 'procuring' right in the nick of time. Jill screams and grabs the jar and starts dancing around.

I go get a spoon from our tiny kitchen and Jill follows me in. I feel a little self-conscious as she eyes the miniscule space. A few things line the walls.

"Nice jugs," she quips and winks at me. Alone with me, she digs the spoon into the thick, light brown, nutty cream. "Hmmmm. Ahhhh," comes from her delighted expression.

"Do you still remember your offer?" I ask with a sly, expectant grin.

"My what?"

"Your promise. The reward for getting you this most valuable treasure."

"Oh, yeah," she bows and says, "Many thanks, O my Sultan."

"That is not it!" Does she really not remember? Another puzzle piece in place, *promises are long forgotten,* along with the previous, *inability to keep secrets.* "A big wet one you said."

"Oh, that? That was a long time ago, but yes. You really want that <u>now</u>? Here in your kitchen? With peanut butter breath and all?"

"Well," I do pause about this one, "Yeah, double the pleasure," I lie. I hate peanut butter. I think I may have mentioned that a few times. She goes to our water jug that stores our fresh drinking water, wets her hand, and then rubs it on my cheek.

"Big wet one, coming up," and then follows it with a quick peck – on the cheek.

Really? I wait all this time, conjuring up the promise in my mind she has made for months. All the anticipation, work, and effort with sweet visions of ecstasy, like the prince finding his long-lost royalmaiden in the forest, offering the most passionate kiss ever and this isit?

"I owe you one, buddy," she says as she walks away, still dipping into the jar and sighing from the sweet taste of peanut butter. She turns to see our family pictures hanging in the hall.

"Oh Ricky! This is you? In knickers?"

"Give me a break. I was three, living in London."

"You were so cute. Blond curly hair? What happened?" Then she pauses and gets quiet. "Never mind. Not a nice question."

With all the extra supply of peanut butter, my mom pops in to serve peanut butter cookies. What? Why didn't she ask me?

"Hey guys, did you know it's possible to turn peanut butter into diamonds with enough pressure?" Tom flatly states, downing three cookies at a time.

I personally do not want peanut butter <u>anywhere.</u> Not with diamonds, not on bread, not on crackers, not on celery sticks, not with chocolate and certainly <u>not</u> in cookies. I'm a little anxious about offering Jill more peanut butter.

"I love these!" Jill exclaims. "My future man better like these too and know how to make them!"

I grab a couple of the poison cookies off the plate and openly wolf them down. Crap Yeah. I try not to croak.

"Oh, yeah. Mom and I just whipped these out. I thought you might like them."

Ka-ching! I'll take that out of your cash box, Mitch! Did I move up?

Chapter Forty-Nine
Golden Slumbers

After my triumphant debut as a budding magician, the next day is Saturday and I'm reading "The Novices Guide to the Crusades" in my room, feet kicked up on my bed rail, when our telephone rings. My mom calls me to the phone. It's Marie, but I'm having a hard time recognizing the voice in between sobs.

"Rick, Jill is in the hospital – I'm at the emergency room, alone, can you come?"

Mom lets me run down to Bullet Head who gets me to the military hospital. I run into the waiting area and find Marie, who envelopes me like a Venus flytrap.

"Her parents are in with her. No one is saying anything. I'm so worried."

Who comes running in behind? Mitch.

"How long has she been here?' I stammer.

"Since last night. They performed emergency surgery."

Just then, Jill's mom comes out to greet us. The long lines on her face and sunken shoulders indicate a long night.

"The three of you are her closest confidants. I think she would like you there."

The walk to her room seems like a pioneer trek across the plains. Not that it is far. Hospitals are where bad things happen with hidden terrors around every bend. My nose tells me they are trying to cover up something wafting through the halls. The only sounds are our feet clicking on the polished floors, the whirr of menacing medical devices, hushed voices and moans creeping out from the rooms we pass.

Three worried and somber friends quietly enter her room. She lays still, asleep, or unconscious, we don't know. The sheet is pulled up to her chin. The pink of her flawless skin is gone. She looks so very pale, even for a redhead. Mitch moves gingerly to one side of the bed, and I move to the other. Marie stands at the foot, holding so tightly to the endbed frame even her knuckles look white. Her fear vibrates the whole bed. We all glance at each other, not knowing what to say or do. Mitch and I are almost nose to nose, staring at each other across the still form below us. Is she breathing?

"She was holding her side after your play time wrestle last night, Mitch. What did you do?" I whisper accusingly.

"What do you mean, me? You're the one who filled her with peanut butter to the gills after your silly magic show."

"Come on, she hardly had more than a couple of spoonfuls. Okay, and some cookies. It isn't my fault. It has to be you!" His eyes are glaring and his hands twitching.

"Me? You were the one who… "

"SURPRISE!"

Guess who opens her eyes wide and giggles? Yes, that giggle.

"Ooo, that hurts. Now, would you two just stop. I've had my appendix out. No one is to blame."

"She is going to be just fine," Mrs. MacGregor says, with Colonel MacGregor sitting quietly in the corner, smiling. Apparently, her mom has the same bizarre sense of humor as her daughter. "Jill just loves to surprise people, so I went along with her little game here."

Marie moves forward and gives Jill a cautions hug. "I'm so relieved!"

Mitch and I leave the room so Jill can show Marie her new tattoo, as she calls her forming scar.

"What's an appendix?" I quietly ask out loud when Mitch and I are alone.

"Beats me. Some kind of female stuff, I guess. I was afraid to ask."

We coolly stare at each other, comforted. It could have been worse.

Chapter Fifty
Here Comes the Sun

After two weeks of lessons on the conquerors of Asia Minor, the Byzantines, the Persians, Alexander the Great, the Romans, the Crusaders, and Ottomans, our trip is finally at our doorstep. Jill is back for the first time since her surgery and cleared for take-off. It's alright, she's alright. We all say, come on sun, we want some fun on the beach.

I have to get to my locker before first period and our bus is late. I can't afford another tardy mark. I charge off the bus to the school doors and burst through. Jill is still sitting with Marie on the bus.

As I open the final inner door, I am hit with a horrid sight. I freeze. A wave of nausea comes over me, and I barely keep it in. The assault has swarmed through the whole school. I grasp at the picture and pull it off the wall, the first one to greet me at the door.

I frantically start to rip more down, one at a time, of maybe hundreds scattered throughout the hall. It is fruitless as I go tearing down the corridor, jumping up high to get the ones I can. I look back up the hall and see Jill come through the door. She can't miss the carnage and walks over to a nearby picture I missed. She lifts it off the wall, stares at it, then looks up at me, staring at her from down the corridor. Dozens of crumpled prints float to the floor from my hand.

"Who would do such a thing?" she mumbles. "I even forgot where this was."

Marie finally pulls the picture out of Jill's hands. I don't know if she is going to scream, faint, flail or swear.

Jill walks slowly to me, expressionless. All is quiet except the sound of her heels clicking inevitably toward me. I fumble about and a few more ruffled pictures swoop down from my hands. She picks one up, stares at it, looks at me.

"Jill, I… I…"

She walks over to the wall and slaps it back up. Stepping back to me, she gives me a huge hug. Then steps back and yells, circling the hall with hands up,

"I'M FREE!"

I'm going to count this as the world's eighth wonder, bursting over my head like the morning thunder. If not the eighth wonder, then surely part of the creator's great mysteries – girls.   Before I could even begin to defend myself, I end up being some kind of unwitting hero. Yea for me! What did I do?

I thought I was the only one who knew about this picture but having never seen it. All evidence was pointing at me. How did I even escape her everlasting punishment? Grace is real.

"Jill, it wasn't me who plastered these all over."

"I know. I forgive you."

And there you have it, again. The great girl puzzlement. Now I am forgiven for something I did not do – grace from a heavenly goddess, freely given, and totally undeserved. Just stop Rick. Don't say anything. This is not in the rulebook.

"This has been hanging over my head for years. This is before my first operation. I don't care anymore. Who didn't look disastrous growing up? Not this dreadful, I admit. Nora now has no power over me."

"Nora?"

"Of course. Who else would do this?"

"If so, she spent a lot of money on prints and a great deal of energy on placement. I'll grant her that," Marie says. "I keep my family pictures under lock and key."

260

"Well, Nefertiti, the symbol of ancient beauty, did not do a good job of guarding this one," I admit.

"My Nefertiti? What's she got to do with it? "

"That's where it was, behind her statue. Your mom found it because of me. And again, she did not show it to me."

"No. No. It was in a picture book in my mom's closet."

"That's not where it was that night. Nora must have done a lot of snooping."

"That's creepy," Marie says.

"I wonder what else she took," Jill muses.

Nora enters the doors and sees the commotion. She walks over to a picture and takes it down. Her hand moves violently up to cover her open mouth. Her hands and shoulders droop down as her eyes move up from the picture to Jill.

"It's not Nora. It is my mother.

Chapter Fifty-One
While My Guitar Gently Weeps

I look at them all, see the class load on busses two days later with our teacher, Mr. Tenney and parent chaperones. I don't know why nobody told me how quickly girls heal. Jill looks great and is as feistyas ever. With every mistake I make with her, I'm surely learning, just let it be.

We will only have time for two castles if we all split up. One is in the town of Salifki and the other is the castle built in the sea. That oneis located near the ancient city of Korykos, about fifteen miles south of Salifki. This is the castle of *Kiz Kalisi* – Turkish for "Maiden's Castle". It wasn't built by the Crusaders. It was probably built by Alexios – the emperor of the Byzantine Empire that controlled this land. But the Crusaders and others used it and built it up over the centuries.

When we arrive on the beach, there is the castle looming up about 500 yards offshore in the Mediterranean Sea.

"That's better than any of your magic tricks," Tom observes.

"It looks like an Arabian desert fortress surrounded by a mirage of ocean, just stuck out there in the water," Jill tells us. "How did they do it?" We have a little time to play in the water, but it's too late to mount up our crusade to explore the castle. We start to set up camp here on the beach.

Just down from us, maybe 300 yards, is an area that is roped off. A Turkish film production company is making a movie. We learn that two of Turkey's biggest stars are making some kind of romance picture.That sounds pretty good to Jill and off she goes to see. One of our dads sneaks some good pictures.

I am thinking that Turkey, with its Islamic foundation, might frown upon such a thing as a movie industry – especially a romance. We learned that modern Turkey was founded in the 1920s by Kemal

Ataturk. He saw more of a secular nation – that is – a government not centered on religion as a base, but still respectful of the teachings. There developed a movie industry along with other practices influenced by the culture of the West – Europe and America. By the 1960s, here is a thriving movie industry churning out Turkish movies.

I and some of the others follow Jill down to as close as we can get. Somehow, Nora joins our group of on-lookers. It's a beach scene with the two stars and a co-star in their bathing suits. There is a camera ona tripod and a few shiny boards around them and crew members with their gear. The shiny boards, essentially wood with aluminum foil gluedto them, are used in the movie industry to reflect sunlight into a scene when they don't have electric lights.

Jill looks and coos from the wings at this scene they are staging, "Whoa, he's handsome!"

I don't know about that, but he is not where my attention is. "I'd say she was pretty fair looking, too."

"Oh, she hasn't got much." Nora declares. Then whispering so only I can hear, "Like someone else I know."

"Oh, she's okay," Jill murmurs, then gets this far-off look and mumbles so I can barely hear.

"Ahh. A romance movie. Just the two of us, stretched out on the beach. The breeze off the sea caressing us both as he takes me in his arms. The waves crash, echoing our thunderous emotions. Ahhh. Wait! Who would I want as my leading man?"

"*C'est Moi,*" I whisper. Meaning 'me', the only French I know other than yes, yes,'*oui, oui*'.

"You? In your dreams. I think I'll go with… Peter O'Toole."

We didn't stay long at the scene, it gets boring, but it starts Jill to thinking.

"Tonight, we will stage the legend of *Kız Kalesi*!" she loudly proclaims.

We all give her puzzled looks but know better than to suggest otherwise. She then goes about giving assignments and casting parts for the production she has in mind. Of course, with my grand theatrical experience, I gladly help.

It is going to be a cool night – temperature wise. We build a nice campfire on the beach between the tents that house the girls on one side of the fire and the tents on the side that house the boys. The sun has gone down, so there is a great fire-lit scene there on the beach with the castle in the sea, *Kız Kalisi*, as our backdrop. After a hot dog and beans dinner, the fun continues.

"OK, to begin tonight's festivities, we will have a little song by our own Mitch," announces Mr. Tenney.

While this is a surprise to most, it is not for me. I have a little surprise of my own. With just a few twists and turns of some knobs on Mitch's guitar, my plan is all set.

"I would like to play a little Spanish love song for you all," he gloats. (My interpretation) and winks at Jill. She is just beaming. Mitch strums his first chord. It is precious. Everyone's face was trying their best not to crack up, like trying to quench a natural reaction to a big fat fart that was launched in their midst. I think his guitar is weeping, not so gently.

"Oh! I'm sorry," Mitch stammers as he fumbles about.

I snicker. I think Jill knows 'who done it' because she just glares at me. Mitch is so flustered that Mr. Tenney intervenes.

"Well, we'll get back to that later. Places everyone. It's time for the legend of *Kiz Kalisi*. Take it away, Jill." She recovers quickly from her icy stare at me. It's showtime.

"OK, background music – begin!" Jill yells out.

The prearranged group of kids start humming some obscure, rhythmic nonsense and banging on some cooking pots with their hands.

"Ooom Pa Pa. Ding Dang. Ooom Pa Pa Ding Dang." And so on.

Then I emerge, not as the Cowardly Lion, but a Lion-Hearted King wearing a t-shirt around my head and a sheet flailing behind, making a kingly march towards the fire. I am followed by Nora who is twisting and dancing with a tablecloth that whirls out as she twirls. This was supposed to be Karin (Spitball's princess), but she had stepped on a bee earlier. So, I recruited and trained Nora to replace her. It is sheer providence. Dancing and bouncing around her as she twirls is the court jester, Billy B. He has somehow balanced someone's sandals on his ears.

"Clear the way. Clear the way. King Alexios and the Princess Kiz approach," Billy B. squeals.

He sticks his thumb on his nose and wiggles his fingers at us all. Jill must have cast him at the last moment. Wasn't my idea.

Jill narrates:

"The King of Celicia proudly but secretly walks to the hut of the famed fortune teller. His daughter, the princess Kiz, follows behind unaware of her coming fate. The court jester lightens the somber mood with his foolishness."

"A pox upon you all if your head is higher than our King," the jester announces.

I proudly, and with an air of dignity, sit down next to Marie, who is draped in a long black scarf around her and her head. Nora, the princess,

sits, swaying back and forth, not far away. The jester is gone. One of our big metal cooking pans, filled with water, sits in front of Marie, the fortune teller. It is her 'crystal ball'. Marie rocks back and forth.

"Hmmm. Hmmm. Ooooo," she wails, waving her arms over the pot and looking into the water.

"I see, I see, a cooking pot. I mean, I see doom, doooom!"

"What is it? O oracle of the future. What doom?" I ask earnestly as the King.

"Danger for Princess Kiz," she wails again.

"Danger, for my only daughter? What manner of dark proportions do you see, oh wise one? What ominous scenes swirl around in the shadowy mists of your pot, I mean, your ball?"

There are a few snickers in the audience. I am making it up as I go and having fun. Jill was beaming. The fortune teller continues.

"I see slithering. I see a treacherous fork-ed tongue. I see a slimy scaly thing."

"Oh, what apparitions of horror and distress accompany your ill-omened visions? Oh, seer of the future."

Marie starts to laugh, out of character, and continues out of character with her own voice.

"OK. I see a snake." Now she gets back into character voice, "a dangerous poisonous reptile."

"Oh no. A snake. I hate snakes. What do we do?"

"You must protect the Princess from this venomous adversary," Marie declares, voicing the lines written with pride by Jill.

"But how? Should I build a tall tower?" the King asks. "No, father, no. I hate heights," Nora, the Princess, exclaims. (My

written line) She is not great at this, so I keep her words to a minimum. But she looks great.

"A castle in the sea you shall build. There are no snakes on islands!" wails the fortune teller.

"Ah. Ha. This shall I do to protect my precious Kiz," I proudly announce with my finger stabbing the air.

Then the narrator, Jill, kicks in. "So, King Alexios begins the task to build his fortress on an island. Strong, firm, and wide with the strict decree – no snakes allowed! The Princess proudly occupies her kingdom in the sea welcoming all suitors." Then Jill adds in her own voice, "That means her boyfriends, ladies."

The girls giggle. Then off in the distance, four of our female friends surround a figure crawling in the sand. I am particularly proud of suggesting this portrayal. Who would make the best snake? Mitch, of course. He may still be reeling from his weeping guitar, but I tell him he has to crawl through the sand the entire way, apt punishment for a nemesis and him none the wiser.

Jill continues her narration,

"But, as fate would have it, hiding in a bunch of grapes delivered from the mainland, a venomous ('but cute', she adds in her own voice, an aside <u>not</u> written by me) snake lies hidden in the bundle."

I direct Mitch to pop up now and again above the heads of the surrounding grapes, the four girls, and slither his tongue in and out. It is delicious. So, type casting works.

The snake finally makes his way to the Princess. He rises and bites her… on the neck several times. Jill looks at me. I figure this might irk Jill a little to have him be so friendly with, as it turns out scrumptiously, Nora. It's just a slight divergence from the script by my secret direction. Jill goes right on,

"Finally, fate takes her course, and the Princess is bitten *on the foot* (staring at Mitch) by the dreadful, poisonous creature and dies," delivered with great drama.

I had her die *in* the snake's arms with great flourish and movement. It took a long time to die (my direction) while Mitch was holding her oh so gently and fondly. (And so willingly) It was nice to know Jill noticed this, too, along with the bites on the neck.

"So, the castle fell to ruins until the mighty Crusaders re-built the edifice to its previous glory. But beware, are there still snakes on an island? The end." Jill adds in a great crescendo.

Yeah – I think my re-direction gets to Jill. It does not occur to me that it could backfire.

That legend is used in several other stories of castles in Turkey, so who knows what the truth is. It makes for a memorable evening. I watch as Marie and Jill head off down the beach, deep in conversation. Mitch doesn't get the chance to play his song. I'm so sad.

I find Jill down by the water's edge later that evening before our 'curfew' lights-out time. I sit down quietly beside her on the sand. I pat her hand.

"Bravo! Author, author! A new star among us." She pulls her hand away slowly and sort of smiles. The stars are as bright and full as I have ever seen them. They give us just enough glow to make us seemethereal. There are no city lights to dim our view of the expanse covering us. She seems kind of solemn, given our triumphal performances.

"Can you believe what we can see?" Jill says in awe. This is starting to look very good for me. Then you know who strolls down and sits on the other side of Jill.

"Hola amigos, funny meeting you all here. Oh. See that formation right there? That's Cassiopeia – queen of Ethiopia right above thecastle," Mitch says.

"Hi Mitch. Wow. What's that one there?" She tests him.

"Easy – Ursa Major – the big dipper. Tom isn't the only one with a few facts up his sleeve."

Not be outdone, I must come up with something.

"You know, there should be one out there named 'Fortuna'. Oh! There she is – the one with the two beautiful eyes."

"Oh, stop," Jill probably blushes in the dark.

"Sorry, no Fortuna constellation," Mitch pipes in.

"Well, there should be. If the queen of Ethiopia gets one, the goddess of fortune should too. But hey, you see the thick band of stars that go from our horizon clear over our heads to the other horizon? Thatis our view of the stars only in our Milky Way galaxy."

"The ancient Egyptians thought it was the gods' river in the heavens," Jill adds, 'you sure can't see that in Ankara."

"Fortuna should be right in there," I say.

Mitch picks up some sand and lets it sift through his hands. "Do you think he is out there, somewhere, among the stars?"

"Who?" Jill asks.

"God. The astronomers tell us, there are as many stars in the visible universe as grains of sand on all the seashores on the earth." He quotes almost like a poem.

"That hurts my head. I can't imagine that." Jill wets her finger and dips it into the sand, then separates all the grains until there is only one. "Here we are. Our sun and us even smaller. Just one grain in all this ocean of light."

"Kinda makes you feel worthless," Mitch adds, his voice almost quivering.

"On the other hand, it should make us feel grand. We are part of all this, and we will go on." I quietly say.

Quickly looking up at me, Mitch asks, "You believe that?"

"I do. Life is eternal."

"Now my head really hurts. You both are too much for this little brain. But you're wasting your time trying to convert me. I've lived in Paris. *Je sais déjà qu'il y a un Dieu au ciel.*"

French is so sexy. She's doubly caught our attention, and she interprets, "I already know there is a God in heaven. I've tasted his *éclairs.*" Jill gets up and heads back to camp. "Good night, my boys, sweet dreams."

Mitch and I just stare at each other. Probably good timing, we've already exhausted all we know about the universe.

The parents are patrolling this night like German shepherds at a POW camp. We don't want to mess with that crowd so no shenanigans are attempted over the night as you might otherwise guess. That doesn'tstop the conversations that go on in the various tents this night.

"Who likes who? Who thinks soda pop is gross? Do the Yankees have a chance this year? Who doesn't like who? Will Batman accept a Batgirl. Who has changed their mind about who likes who?" and so on.

Should we have tried to snoop on the conversations in the girls' tents? Too risky. But Marie tells me it was more of the same,

"Who likes who, who better not like who, who thinks make-up is evil, who would like to like who, who is cute and who is not so cute."

This seems more interesting, except the make-up stuff. She does not provide any answers to those tough questions. It is still very confusing. Who will be the 'who' that who likes? So maddening, but enticing.

Chapter Fifty-Two
Good Day Sunshine

Jill does need to laugh. And with the glorious sun out, it's going to be unusually warm and she's got plenty she can laugh about. It's her release but this day is not without its tension. Most of our class is going to the bigger *Salifke* castle. Mr. Tenney seems to have reserved *Kiz Kalisi* for Jill and our group. I don't know how Jill connived thisarrangement. She did put up the money for it. Nora has finagled her wayto join our group excursion. I know why but I don't know how.

I don't think the others going to *Salifke* are water-worthy, so they have no problem going to the larger castle on the hill above the town. Maybe the thought of cold Sea temperatures scared them off. The rest of us are prepared for water. We brought some floaty inner tubes, and blow-up cushions to use as boats to make the 500-yard trip to the castle, the length of five football fields. Nora did not. I guess she is not afraid of the distance. The adults assume we all can swim.

Does that raise a question about you-know-who, who cannot swim? Why doesn't Mitch and his twitch choose to go to the other castle? I know why. That's what love (or conquest) does to you – makes you takerisks you would not otherwise take. Don't I know that? None of us wearlife preservers.

Mitch brought a little dingy – a small blow-up boat with an oar that only one can sit in safely. The rest of us sort of use our floats to keep us above the water and use our arms as paddles. Jill gives Mitch two shovels to carry in his dingy. Oh, would I love to poke a small little holein a certain tiny boat. He'd flutter all over the Mediterranean like a spent balloon that finally collapses, and in this case, sinks in the ancient sea. I know. That would be homicidal – not part of the scout law, last I checked. It would probably backfire, and Jill would rescue him with mouth-to-mouth resuscitation!

Mr. Tenney has decided to be our chaperone and sort of guide, I guess. He has hired a local guide for the other group going to *Salifke* along with our chaperones. We dutifully blow up our float devices whileNora helps Mitch prepare and launch his dingy.

It's a bit on the nippy side in the Mediterranean this time of year but we're lucky it's such a warm day. It might make us paddle faster. It's not too bad. Let's see, we are going to be out on the water in full sun. Then at the castle in the sun for hours. Would you think that would require some kind of pre-caution? There is nothing on the market that prevents the burning rays of the sun to do its damage. Maybe someday there will be. I will let that sink in for a minute. *Da,Da,da,da, hum, humm hum and a pa rum pa pum pum.*

Was that a minute? We are going to be on our stomachs, paddling maybe 45 minutes out to an island in full sun. There is stuff like suntan lotion, but that doesn't protect most people. Jill already has a routine. She <u>has</u> to cover up with that delicate skin. She puts on some leggings,a long-sleeved t-shirt and has this crazy straw hat for protection. Marie, even with her dark skin, has to take precautions too, which she does. Mitch? Remember, he was of Latin origin and is already pretty tan as well. But he isn't dumb. Me? Oh, I'll hide in the shade. Right.

The sun was sparkling off a still Mediterranean, as calm as a mountain lake. You could see clear to the bottom of the sea floor. Tenney tells us at one time there was a causeway – a land bridge out to the castle. There goes that legend. The snake crawled out there on land.I think that is why the seabed was not as deep where we put in.

We paddle away. Nora decides to swim alongside Mitch and his dingy. Using his oars, and her free swimming, they move faster through the water than we can. They get away quicker and advance some distance from us. As only I know, he doesn't want anyone to see his natural reaction to water or stress. Nora is too pre-occupied to notice. As the group was paddling away, as usual, something comes to Tom.

"Hey guys, did you know they used hay as toilet paper in castles? And the toilet was called a garderobe. Did anyone bring any hay? Just asking?"

"No, that's because there is no garderobe on the island," Tenney tells us.

No one thought about this issue. Oh, well. No one wants to hear about that anyway.

"Hey! Did you also know that knights would hang their laundry in the latrine so the uric acid and ammonium would kill the lice in their clothes?"

"Good way to kill off your enemies, too." Will says an aside.

Every castle's royal court has to have a jester. We are glad to have Tom, and not Billy B.

Exotic adventure with your best friends, what can be better? There is Tom and Karin, Aisha and Dave, Will and Marie, Jill, me, Nora and Mitch – plus good ol' Mr. Tenney.

But then, we have another visitor. Mitch is the first one to see it.

It's a fin coming straight at his dingy.

"Shark!" Mitch yells. Nora starts flailing in the water with unknown German words flowing free and fast in between deafening screams of terror. Mitch picks up one of the shovels.

"*Hilfe!* Help me Mitch, pull me up, *hoch*!"

"You're gonna tip me over. Stop!" I thought Mitch might whack her with the shovel. Nora looked like a Wolverine wildly digging its way to its trapped prey, kicking and clawing her way unsuccessfully into the dingy.

Like a wildfire raging sideways from us and ravaging the trees in the distance, there is nothing we can do but watch the catastrophe

unfold. The rest of us all huddle together. With Nora's furious splashing, the water fanning up like a screen, it's hard to see clearly. The fin is getting closer on a direct course for the little boat. I've seen pictures of giant white sharks leaping out of the water with a seal in its mouth. I didn't want Nora to go that way. Okay, not Mitch either. Suddenly, the fin disappears below the surface. Oh no. Then the creature leaps out of the water right in front of Mitch and over Nora's flailing legs and dives down into the water again.

"Ha!" Tom yells, "just as I thought, *stenella coeruleoalba*, a striped dolphin! Come back here little fella!"

"How do you know these things?" Jill asks. Karin replies,

"He's been reading all the way on the bus about sea life in the Mediterranean."

"She is the most prevalent dolphin in the Mediterranean. I was hoping we would see one," Tom says in delight.

Mitch is twitching like a forest of aspen now. Only I see it. Nora is still in panic mode.

"My legs! He hit my legs!" She pulls them up. They are both still attached.

"It's just a dolphin having fun," Tom yells, "relax." He circles and jumps again just ahead of the dingy.

"I could have beat him off with my fists," Will brags, "come get me, baby."

"They're harmless and a protected species," I tell him, "it's against international maritime law to harm them."

"Well then, I would have ridden him. Wahoo."

"You wouldn't want to do that. He might have a Mediterranean disease," says Dave.

Marie giggles more out of relief than anything else. We all start paddling again.

"Frankly, I am more concerned about sea snakes," Dave adds.

"You need not concern your moppy little head about that. There are no sea snakes in the Mediterranean," Tom assures us.

"You were so brave!" Jill calls out to Mitch. He raises a shaky shovel in victory. Nora calms down and begins to swim again.

We all beach at the castle's edge. It's not a huge place, maybe three football fields. It kind of has a triangle shape with the walls going almost right to the edge of the island.

"So, students. The Byzantine King, as Miss MacGregor depicted last night, built this castle after the first Crusade. The square towers are from that era. The Armenians, much later, re-built the north and west sides of the castle with their distinctive rusticated ashlar masonry and round towers."

"Towers," Jill whispers to me.

"I see six of them," I whisper back.

He goes on, blah, blah, blah as Jill assigns the search parties, pairing us all up. We have two shovels for ten of us, we sort of keep hidden from Tenney.

We are six or seven hundred years after they first built the main structure, and it has been rebuilt a few times over the centuries. This place, I'm sure. Has been well picked-over and explored many times. We are likely not to find a thing. No matter. We are in a real and old castle.

It's an adventure and gives us something even more exciting than exploring what is left of the run-down fortress. What are we looking for? We tell them gold coins. And who does Jill pick to pair up with? Mitch. When I complain, she tells me,

"Rick, we can cover more ground that way. Don't you worry your devious little head about it." Uh, oh. I know I'm in trouble.

OK. Maybe I overplayed my hand last night with the guitar shenanigans, and a little creative direction. I didn't know. It is driving me crazy. Nora looks a little bummed out, too. Jill pairs me up with her best friend, Marie, our previous night's fortune teller. Was this planned? Will just stares at Jill, then looks at me with a 'What's her bag?' look on his face. He wanted to be with Marie. I just shrug. Instead, he gets Nora. That has its limited rewards. No one argues with Fortuna. Marie should be with Will, but Jill sends him off with Nora.

Fortuna and Diablo take off in another direction. Spitball and his favorite, Princess, her bee sting much better, are off in the opposite direction. Dave and Aisha go their own way.

Mr. Tenney sits to stare at the castle. He calls out to us all,

"Behave yourselves. Don't get hurt. You've got two hours."

"Okay, time to use your magic power, fortune lady," I tease Marie.

"I foresee, I foresee, dirt!" she divines, swooning like her play character.

I'm looking over my shoulder to see Mitch and Jill scramble through an opening in the wall and disappear.

We head through what must have been the main gate, facing the beach. The opening isn't very big. I imagine wooden doors would have been mounted behind it.

The walls are still very much intact, maybe twenty feet high in places. You can still climb around. Boy does this place need repairs. There are three round turret towers and three square towers. The castle takes up the entire island. Inside, there are archways down a long corridor.

"This place is in shambles. Wow. But if I were a Crusader and my fortress was about to be overrun, where would I place my treasure?" I wonder out loud.

"How could you escape this place if it were under siege?" Marie asks as we make our way into the interior.

"Boats. Had to be boats to the open sea. But wait, didn't Tenney say it was connected to the mainland at one time? So, if I am a Crusaderand I am thinking I am in the service of God, where might I place my treasure, and have it protected?"

"A church," we both say.

"Did they have a chapel or something here?" Marie asks.

"They always did."

Off we go to the first round tower. We don't think the chapel would be in one of the square towers.

"Look! Look!" Marie points to the wall. "A Crusader's cross!".

On an inset stone, mid-way up the wall, there is etched the unmistakable mark.

"This may have been their chapel," I call out. The dirt floors are either lined with stone or are hard-packed. We don't have one of the shovels. All we can do is kick around. The stones would need a jack hammer. Maybe a shovel might move one. It would still have a hard time in the packed ground.

"Dirt," I exclaim, "we found dirt, fortune lady!"

I bow down in mock reverence. Then I think, 'look to the tower'. I see nothing but the cross here.

"I wonder if they performed any marriages here?" Marie wonders.

"Marriages? They didn't take any women on crusades, did they?"

"Sure they did. There was often a mix of a bunch of cultures and languages, too. There was even a so-called children's crusade. There were all sorts of women that accompanied the crusaders, even women soldiers," she continues without a breath. "Rick, do you believe in marriage?"

"Me?" The question is so bizarre I am stalled for words. "Ah… a… of course. Why?"

"Do you ever wonder who it will be?"

"Well. I hope I have some time to decide," I stumble on the words.

"Do you think anyone would ever choose me?"

Whoa. I did not see this coming. I am not one with quick answers. But I say, "Marie. You are stunning. Why wouldn't anyone choose you? Sarge sure will."

She seems genuinely surprised at this.

"What about you? We've known each other since eighth grade."

Now I know I am in trouble. My girlfriend's best friend has just proposed marriage to me, sort of.

"Ahh, well," I am really stumbling now. "I… I… I'm almost sixteen, but I can't say I am ready for marriage."

"Oh, I'm sorry. Stupid Marie, Jill is always telling me to be bold and live up to Athena. Not marriage, just, you know, be a couple."

Wait a minute. Has Jill given Marie the 'all clear' to go after me? Was that what they talked about on their stroll last night? Just then, we hear Tom and Karin yelling from across the courtyard. That saves me from answering a very tricky question, and we leave it hanging as we scurry over to one of the round towers, where they are pointing to some strange inscriptions high up on the wall.

"Well. It isn't Arabic," Tom says.

"It isn't Greek or Turkish either," Karin adds.

"They're not like any European alphabet I've seen," Marie says, "they are really strange, like some alien graffiti."

"Wait a minute! I've seen that alphabet before. It's Armenian," I proudly announce. Tenney then shows up.

"That's right, Armenians re-built and put in round towers in the 1400s in their own style." Tenney takes a picture of the wall andwritings and scribbles something in his notebook.

Nora then appears around a wall. She is smiling broadly, leans on the wall with one arm up, looking dazzling, like a swimsuit model in her yellow bikini.

"What's up, team?"

Will then appears around the same wall, red-faced and somewhat dazed-looking, with a slight smile.

"Yeah. Ahh. What are you all up to?"

We look at them questioningly but are more puzzled about what we see on the wall when we hear Mitch yell from another tower.

"We hit something," Mitch yells.

Tenney stays behind, scribbling notes as we all scramble over to the sound. Mitch is poking his shovel into the ground and hitting what sounds like metal. We take some turns trying to penetrate the hard- packed dirt around it. Finally, Tom unearths the object, and it flies out, banging high up on the wall and crashing down.

"That's worth at least a double, slugger," I exclaim.

Marie is the first to retrieve it. It's covered with dust and hard- packed dirt. She takes her t-shirt tails and starts to rub off all the debris.

"I see letters!" Jill takes the object from her and continues cleaning with her own shirt. "It's a European alphabet. The first is the letter, 'S, '"

she pronounces. Then she rubs a little more off, "*P*," and then the rest becomes clear as she says, "*A-M*."

"Congratulations!" Dave yells out, "You've unearthed an ancient can of SPAM!"

Jill is not pleased.

"It does look a little old. I heard soldiers were camped here in WWII," Tom tells us.

"Well then, good guess it's not Crusader Spam. Who knows what camper left it here? Could have been last year," Mitch adds.

About this time, my legs were starting to really hurt. Marie inspects and says,

"Well, you're not a white man anymore. You just turned red from the thighs down."

Yeah. It really hurt, and I had a trip back over the water still to do. We eventually explored the whole castle and towers. I look at Jill. She whispers,

"Anything?"

"Yea, maybe."

The back of my legs is starting to blister it is so bad. Who steps to the rescue? Mitch. He volunteers his dingy where I can sit with my legs down. It is still painful to have my legs touch anything, but that is a lifesaver for me not to expose my legs to the sun again.

Tenney gives me a towel to put over the top of my legs on the way back. So, what is Mitch going to do now? He and Jill double upinflatables and paddle back together, laughing, splashing, and talkingthe entire way with each other. Mitch's hands were as calm as a sleepingbaby's.

We ten amateur archeologists are reluctant to report our stupendous find to our fellow students. But Nora takes care of that bit of news for us. It is a story too good to bury. But now I am buried with a bigger problem.

RIVALRY BOX SCORE:

It is definitely headed in the wrong direction.

Episode Eight

Skating Around the Issue

Chapter Fifty-Three
Maxwell's Silver Hammer

Bang. Bang. Buzz. Buzz. A thousand bees are let loose on the back of my legs. They aren't collecting pollen. I think the whole hive is moving into roller-skate on my femur. And yes, we do have a roller-skating rink. My head feels like a silver hammer is pounding out a honey of a morbid melody.

Our skating rink is in the old gym behind our first American high school, built in the middle of Ankara. It's a great gathering place for us. We usually meet there on a couple of Fridays a month. That's when the Sophomores can use the rink alone. My sunburn is so bad I stay out of school all week. By Friday, the blisters had mostly popped, and the skin was starting to flake. I am a little better. Jill calls me up Fridayafternoon.

Jill: Hey! We are missing you. Did you get my present?

Me: The chocolate? So tasty, but I was hoping for your can of Spam.

That did just want I wanted. There was that precious giggle that went on longer than I expected.

Me: Now that is what I really needed.

Jill: You are getting funny there, Mr. Cowardly Lion.

Yeah. Movin' on up the 'humor' scale.

Jill: Is it any better?

Me: Thank goodness. The worst is over.

Jill: Feel like skating tonight?

Given the situation, I don't, but you can't say no to a goddess.

Me: You bet. I'll see you there. It was good of you to call. Oh, did you get the pictures from Mr. Tenney?

Jill: Yeah. Do you think those writings could be it?

Me: That's our only hope. See you soon.

I get a ride with my brother to the rink.

"Don't sit by my guitar case. Your sun-bleached body heat may melt it. It holds a Stratocaster, you know."

He reminds me of that every day, it seems. The 'Suedes' are going to play on and off at the roller rink tonight. They do this once a month. This time it's for the Sophomores. The whole gang is here. Everyone is still talking about the trip as we skate around the floor. It's an 'all skate' time, so everyone is rolling around the floor. You can only go in one direction, but Marie and I are like opposite magnet poles. No matter how close I get, she gets further away. That is both good and bad. I do not want her to feel embarrassed. She really is a neat person and lovely in her own right. But she isn't Jill. And when you set your mind on something, it's hard to change. But I change my polarity and catch up with her. We both are a little unsteady in more ways than one.

"*Merhaba* hello. I had a lot of time to think this week, more time than usual since it wasn't fun trying to sleep," I try and say cheerfully above the din.

"Yeah. It looked bad. You were miserable on the bus home."

"Did Tenney show everyone the picture of the Crusaders' cross?"

"Finally got it back yesterday. Everyone was jealous they didn't see it for real."

We skate on without a word. The Beatles play overhead through multiple tinny-sounding speakers, '*You're gonna lose that girl.*' Great, thanks, management.

"Yeah. About that. I…" a wild skater then blasts between us, barreling his way through and around the rink. It's Billy B.

"Sorry!" he shouts back. Then the lights flicker, which is a sign the time has come for a rink change.

"Couples only," comes the voice over the loudspeaker just as Jill skates up to me.

"Ready for this?" She takes my hand, and off we go. I look back at Marie and shrug. Now, neither one of us are great skaters, but it is pure joy to hold hands and skate side by side. After all my shenanigans, I really don't know where I stand.

"Did Marie say anything to you about our trip?"

"About what?"

"Oh. Maybe how she was feeling?"

"She's feeling fine. What are you talking about?"

Can this be another puzzle piece, a short memory? No, *definitely* not. Girls do not have a short memory. *They hang on to things forever*. This is a solid part of their puzzle, for sure.

Clearly, Marie has said nothing to Jill, I surmise. The lights flicker. "Couples change," says the voice over the loudspeaker. That's when the boy skates to the girl ahead of him, and the guy behind takes your girl. And who would that be? No. It's Billy B. He pushes me off to Marie, who is now in front of me, and I skate up to her.

"Hi again," I take her hand. That wasn't always necessary in a 'couple's skate'. She looks down at our hands and starts to cry. Oh no. Nothing more terrifying than a crying girl.

"I'm so sorry," she says as softly as she can and still be heard over the blaring music and the rumbling of skates on wood floors.

"Marie, there is nothing to be sorry about. I meant every word. I just didn't get a chance to think about it."

The lights flicker again, and the voice says, "Couples change." It was not usually that quick, but the management keeps things moving. I don't want to change, but when Mitch shows up, who has moved behindme, trying to get to Jill, I have to move on. It's Nora in front of me.

"Oh, *Herr* Foster. *Ja. Sehr* good to seeing you. You shtill have the *schwarzen brot beine*?

"*Beine?* Oh, legs. Yeah. I think you mean my toasted little legs?"

I glance back at Mitch. He's with Marie, who is still crying.

"*Ja.* Your tiny tree legs still *Schmerzen?"*

"All the way up the trunk."

Nora and I make one loop of the rink when the lights flicker, and the voice says, "Boys skate." All the girls have to leave the floor, and it becomes like roller derby madness. No girl wants to stay, especially when Bill B. is on his terror ride through the boys. It's his way of feeling equal to us. He can really bullet. Someone crashes into me. I assume it's Billy B again.

"You called her a name?" I spin around and fall to the floor and look up to see a fully flushed face Mitch.

"What are you talking about?"

"Marie is crying because of you, and all I can get out of her is that you called her something." He is really in my zone and pushing.

"Mitch, you need to stay out of this one." I painfully rise and skate off. My gang assembles around Mitch. I can see them all talking and pointing at me. I then look around to see Marie off in one corner, surrounded by her girlfriends. Jill is right next to her. The lights flicker and the speaker blares, "girls skate". I skate over to the side at an empty corner and see Jill and others pull Marie out on the rink as they pass my group of accusing friends. Jill and company skate around until they come to my corner and all of them stop. There is no escape, they've laidsiege to my castle.

"You called her that? Really?" Jill says as she rolls over to me then tenderly kisses me on the cheek. Followed by Karin, Aisha, Debbie (another friend), and finally, Marie rolls up next to me and does the same.

"Stunning. He called me stunning. No one has ever said such a nicer thing to me."

I sit there on the rink wall, surrounded by astounding beauty. And I am stunned. What just happened?

The Suedes start up playing. It's their cover of 'Pipeline' the song by the recording pop group called, 'The Ventures'. My brother is playing the famous guitar rift in the song, sliding his hands down his Stratocaster neck to duplicate the sound. We all move to the floor by the stage to groove out. Jill skates over to my side.

BANG! An object crashes through an upper window and thuds to the floor and purges smoke into the rink. It's rancid smell spreads panic.

Just outside erupts a flurry of what sounds and feels like cherry bombs. These are legal big-ticket fireworks with explosive energy. The odor is distinctive and permeates through the open windows. Then all the lights go out in the rink. The band's amplifiers shut off and the music stops. It's pitch black but for the light show through the upper windows that reflect off the growing smoke bomb filling the building.

This is followed by all kinds of streaking, flaring and more exploding rockets – all just beyond the exit doors. It's like a massive fireworks display has been aimed at our rink. The flashes on the ceiling pouring through the upper windows look like a colored lighting storm. They keep going, BANG. BANG. BANG.

It's like a ground-based fourth of July outside. What in the world is happening? The exterior doors, closest to us, burst open and two large intruders with flashlights barrel their way through the growing haze. Their fast-moving silhouettes glow by the deafening, exploding array of pyrotechnics behind them.

The girls all scream, and everyone scatters as these figures blast right through the fleeing crowd, pushing and shoving this way and that, and come right at us. They grab Jill's purse and swing her around on her skates, smashing into me as we both are flung to the floor. I see a knife glimmer in the beams of their flashlights.

The figure heads straight for Jill.

I fling myself on top of Jill trying to protect her as the blade slices through its target. I feel her scream vibrate through my body. I hear another loud <u>smash</u> and a 'Ooof'. I think it comes from an attacker. The two intruders stumble and escape out the same doors and into the commotion outside.

Eyes wide open, my head is buried on the floor next to Jill, our faces cheek to cheek, my arms still around her. She is lying still. One emergency light in a far corner flickers on. I jerk up and turn her over. She groans.

"Jill! Jill! Are you hurt?"

"I don't think so." She opens her eyes and looks around. "Just scared. I saw the weapon and hit the floor hard. I thought… I thought they would…"

"Thank God. I know. They didn't."

Two more figures burst through the doors on the opposite side of the rink and tear across the floor and run through the same doors the first two just exited. The fireworks are still rocketing outside. The rink screams continue. Everything is in chaos and dark. Only the flashes of

colored light blink through the few rink windows, casting bizarre shadows of the fleeing crowd against the walls.

"They only took my purse."

Like a sudden microburst of wind, it only hit the two of us and no one else knows what just happened to Jill and me, it was so fast and so dark.

I help her sit up. Everyone else continues to crowd the entrance, flinging off their skates, still in a state of mass noise, inside and outside, mixed with confusion. We remain, sitting up, where we fell. She takes my face between her soft, cold hands.

"You… you risked the knife… for me?"

I can't say anything. I just stare into those unearthly dual-colored eyes when she delivers on her forgotten promise. Like the gentle press of a tulip on my skin, it is tender, warm, and sweet. The aroma of her touch caresses all my senses. I can feel different textures as her lips gently press against mine. It's luscious. She lingers there, but not long enough.

"Buce's still in debt. That's just a deposit."

I then see Steve, a little way off. The emergency light is still dim, but I can see he is holding his Stratocaster, now in two pieces.

"I got him good, little brother. I'm surprised the guy could even walk."

Chapter Fifty-Four
Girl

Well, I was exonerated. They listened to my story, and I think my girl just might stay around. But all that was forgotten. It was the next day, Saturday, and some of the gang had gathered at Jill's just to talk things through. No one knew they attacked just us or that her purse, a guitar and probably one of the attackers meeting a flying Stratocaster were the only casualties. Jill and I didn't know who to tell.

"It was two guys. I saw that," Tom tells us. "I hear your brother really wasted one of them? This is all getting very weird. You two had to have seen them – they knocked you to the floor?"

"It was all too fast," I tell them, "we don't know." Jill and I look at each other nervously. Everyone sort of couples up to talk, leaving Jill and I alone.

"What of so great a value would they risk so much to get from your purse? Your peanut butter jar?"

That has the right effect, but the giggles are quite contained. She seems very hesitant.

"Think. Why your purse?"

"I'm sure it must have been Tigran getting more desperate. I don't know what he thinks is or was in my purse."

"It might not have been Tigran. Maybe guys he hired?"

Tom and the gang finally converge on us again.

"What's for lunch?" Tom eagerly asks.

"You sure you don't want to tell your dad?" I whisper.

"I don't know." I left it at that.

Diablo had tried his best to thwart me at the rink. Poor guy. Wait a minute. No! Not a poor guy. That was downright dastardly. He thought he really had one on me. But I had nothing to do with how it all turned out. A scout is trustworthy.

Maybe there was hope for me yet?

Chapter Fifty- Five
Two of Us

"My father is being blackmailed," Jill confesses to me, "and he doesn't even know it."

"Blackmail? Is that like *buckshish*?" I ask.

"It's when someone demands money or, in this case, information because they think they know something about you that can do you harm or great embarrassment."

"What have they got on him?"

She says nothing. It's just the two of us, walking nowhere. But really, we're on our way home to her place. Jill and I are back on ourold walk, roaming the streets to be alone. It could have been another romantic stroll, but it's the middle of the day, it's cold and the circumstances are now quite different. We behave ourselves.

"Can't you tell someone? I mean, why me and why now?"

"Rick, you know this. Everything is getting complicated. We're two of a kind, and I trust you. I couldn't tell you before."

Her red cheeks and elevated breath, fogging up our walk, lets me know her condition.

"It's okay. I'm with you – all the way."

"I've always known that, even if I haven't shown it. Do you know what Philatelic people do or what a numismatologist is?"

"No, but they sound like more violent characters." Normally, that would have got my laugh out of her. Not this time.

"The first one collects stamps – rare postage stamps."

"Well, OK, not violent, but they can still lick you," I wink at her.

"Will you stop? I'm trying to explain."

"And I am trying to help calm you. So tell me about these ah... Philadel – Philharmonic... a... a... stamp people and the numisma... whatever."

"Rare coin experts. My grandfather was a collector, rather, an investor in both, among his other curious interests."

"He is getting more interesting all the time."

"This must be about something in his collections, coins, books, weapons, statues."

"Statues?"

"In his vault in Paris is one of the greatest recent finds in Archeology, a marble statue of Alexander the Great – not found where grandfather thinks his long-lost tomb may be."

"Well, I'm going to guess they don't think _that_ was in your purse. Maybe coins or stamps? I mean, they're an inch square on paper. How valuable can they be?"

"I don't know for sure, but I read some can be worth millions."

I stop walking.

"For a piece of sticky paper? Do you think he had any that valuable?"

The question hangs in the air, for just then, in the distance above us, we hear the roar of some strange mechanical source, like a manic metal hawk. It beats down on us closer and louder. Suddenly, fighter jets burst through the clouds and scream low overhead. They barely clear the houses.

Their machine guns open fire at some close-by target, ripping up the ground just past us.

I pull Jill down against a stone wall. We realize it's the wall of the Russian embassy. Two more planes follow, coming in more in line with our street and the embassy. They open fire on the buildings just aboveus in the complex. We can hear them hit and tear into the brick facades of the buildings on the compound. Stone and tree fragments rain down on us. Jill screams out,

"We gotta move!"

Her house is closer than mine and we beat feet for it as the jets circle around, presumably to make another pass.

"I sure remember this spot a little differently. Good grief. They've called out the military on us," I yell out, trying to keep up with her.

"Sounds like bullets are hitting the Russian and probably the American embassy," she yells back.

By the time we get to her house, her mom has just got off the phone with Colonel MacGregor.

"Thank goodness you're here. The Turkish military is mounting a coup. They're firing on our embassy and other Turkish government buildings. Dad says to stay indoors."

"Yeah. And they got the reds in their sights, too," I add.

"Mom, what's a coup?" Jill asks nervously.

"A coup…," she pronounces it 'coo', "is when a military tries to take over the elected government or tries to wrest power from a dictatorby force. Rick, you're our guest tonight. You better try and phone home," Mrs. MacGregor advises me.

Pow, pow, pow, pow.

We hear the machine guns fire off more rounds in the distance. After getting off the phone, I tell them my brother is the only one home. He's watching from our balcony. Dumb brother.

"They're firing on the American embassy two blocks from our apartment. Steve tells me dad is trying to sneak over to the embassy to report on the attack." It sounds dangerous but there is nothing we can do. I can't say I am disappointed at the arrangements. Jill and I need more time to work things out.

So, a coup is going on. What can we do about it? Just wait it out. We don't know if troops will be hitting the street or bombs or what. Mrs. Macgregor seems rather calm and optimistic about the situation. I guess she has been through this kind of thing before.

We need to pass the time and the MacGregors have this gorgeous grand piano in their music room. So, Jill sits down on the bench, pats the open spot, and calls me over.

"Ok. Maestro. Time for us to hit it. You still take lessons?"

"Yeah. From my Turkish music teacher, Mrs. Duruaki."

"You like her?"

"Well, sort of. She whaps my fingers with her ruler when I don't have the right form or don't count."

"Artists always have a ruler, and I know how to use it."

"Yikes, OK. What's it going to be, Schumann, Chopin, Liszt, Beethoven, or Mozart?"

"Show off. How about 'chop sticks'?"

"Oh, you mean, the only one you know?"

"Don't rub it in. As always, I'm on the top hand. Then you can play me that 'Clair de Lune' I love."

"Oh, the Debussy piece? I don't know. That may be too romantic."

"If you're lucky."

So, off we go playing 'chop sticks' or "The Celebrated Chop Waltz" to be precise in the middle of a coup. Then she starts to make up and sing some lyrics to the tune.

We are in Turkey. This coup is so stinky

If you weren't so risky, I'd give you some whiskey

I see by your face that you are giving me smirky

I'd love it so much now if you weren't so quirky!

"Whoa. Not bad, Fortuna. Hey, we make a pretty good duet. Can we keep this up?" I plead. I then plow into my meager ability at lyrics as we play together.

Oh, my Jill rides a donkey. She hates playing hockey

She'd be pretty good if she wasn't so flaky

Her friends call her kooky, but I say she's goofy

If I keep on playing, I just might get lucky!

"Ha. It got *shaky* there at the end. If you would stop messin' up the bottom hand, we could be better."

I hip-bump her and catch her before she falls off the bench.

"I'm *quirky*, huh? Okay, time for something less *squeaky*."

I begin to play Debussy's 'Clair de Lune'. In the past when I played, I got so nervous my foot on the sustain peddle would bounce my leg as fast as a constant double dribble. Now, it's like I'm floating on a calm musical stream, a positive outcome of the *Jillian effect*. It's Jill's favorite piece. She starts to sway and dance around the room as I get to the middle of the piece. She then sits on the bench with me as I end.

"Something happens to me when you play that song, Ricky. Don't ever stop."

"Am I getting lucky?"

"We'll see."

Finally, I have something as romantic as Mitch's poetry. It certainly isn't in my poetry. Where is Mitch now? Ha Ha.

We walk around her spacious downstairs. Hanging on her parlor wall is a curious instrument of some kind with wooden pipes sticking out of an animal hide.

"My grandfather gave us those – MacGregor heirloom bagpipes. Apparently, we were the first Scottish family to take up the pipes – back in the day."

"You know how to play those?"

"Yeah, a bit. And dance the highland dances."

"That I have seen from the bus. And I am reminded that our dancing bear did not appreciate your Scottish heritage."

"Oh? I 'barely' noticed. Listen, I've got to help Mom with dinner. You be okay by yourself for a while?"

"I'll try not to get lost."

I get poking around the living room, somehow with Mitch on my mind. I'm thinking,

I got you now, buddy, sports, theatre, magic, music, and a spy to boot! What did he have besides a beautiful Spanish accent and great looks, his guitar, and his poetry and . . . oh, his poetry.

Just then, something catches my eye sticking out of Jill's book pack. Dare I? I pull it out. It's one of Diablo's latest poems to Jill. And yes, it's written on a heart.

Oh, my sweet little Coco bird,

Your song is so tasty, like a sweet curd.

Dance and sing for me, my little chickadee.

Oh, please! Really? Come on. Does she fall for this? 'Sweet Curd?' Give me a break. English was not a second language for him. Really, 'thick honey'? What is the score after this? Billy B., where are you and your poetic genius? Come back! I have to be ahead after all that has happened, but who knew? Nothing is making any sense with this contest. 'Thick honey'? Oh please.

After dinner, Jill's mom has made a fire in their 'conversation pit,' a cozy little sunken nook with a nice fireplace. Cushioned benches, built in a half-circle, put everyone equidistant from the warmth. Mrs. MacGregor is as lovely as her daughter. I can tell where Jill gets her classy looks and dress.

"Rick, Jill tells me your mom had an accident the other day. How is she doing?"

My mother has a full-time job in Turkey. "Thanks for asking, Mrs. MacGregor. She is doing better. She takes the military bus to work most days. She slipped near the bus stop last week as the bus approached. The driver got out to help her in, but no one got up to give her a seat."

"I'm sorry to hear that."

"She got on that bus not knowing she had a broken wrist, hobbling with her wooden leg. I still get mad when I think about how no one got up."

"Your mom walks with a prosthesis?"

"Yes, Mam. She lost her leg in a car accident before I was born."

"That's so sad. We all have things we have to deal with in life."

She looks over at Jill and smiles.

"Well, it's not too bad for my mom," I say.

"How is that?" Mrs. MacGregor asks.

"She gets a half price discount for a pedicure."

Mrs. M stares at me for just a second, then I discover a genetic inheritance. The two of them join together in a most delightful operatic duet of stratospheric cackles. The Metropolitan Opera of comedy cannot compete with their performance. As they come back to earth, Mrs. M. gets her composure and continues.

"Well, I think she has a son that keeps her smiling. That's something. Good for her. I just don't understand some people. Not giving her a seat. I'm sorry. I don't know her well, but she sounds likea remarkable lady," Mrs. MacGregor says so sweetly.

We all talk for a while until her mom says,

"Well. I'm tired. I'm heading upstairs. Rick, I've made up the bed in the guest room downstairs and towels in the adjoining bathroomwhen you're ready."

"Mom, can Rick and I stay up a little longer and talk?"

"Sure. I don't think your dad is coming home tonight."

I couldn't have planned out a more tempting situation if I could have even dreamed of it in my not-fun, humorless (getting better at that, I think) sneaky little brain. I just may write a thank-you to the Turkish military, but I supposed there would be casualties with all the fuss. So, I'll skip writing that note. They would not appreciate my spelling.

In the flickering firelight, Jill's face just glows, and her eyes look more alluring than ever. But there is business to discuss.

"So, where do we pick up?" I whisper.

She snuggles up closer. I guess to keep the conversation private. I don't mind it a bit, but I know her glorious scent just might render me useless. I take in a deep breath of her, then gladly settle in.

"I can tell you this much, Grandfather left something specifically for me, not part of his will, without saying what it was. Whatever it is, it's hidden. It has been just under a year since he died."

"I'm so sorry."

"I suppose it could be anything, sure. But there may be some strings attached, you know, obligations he has put on it. He had his hands on so many things. He only left me the clues to follow."

"Boy. That's a strange way to treat his heirs."

"I think he was trying to protect me and whatever it is."

"From what? Do you know?"

"Well, besides the obvious. I have a half-brother who is not happy with the inheritance arrangements. He's contesting the will. Let's leave it at that. Grandfather was peculiar and stubborn."

"So that's where you get it."

She punches me.

"Oww. OK. I deserve that."

"He loved history and archeology. Those were his passions – especially during the time period of Alexander the Great. Oh, let me show you something."

She goes to the library and brings back a little velvet case. She opens it, revealing a small, roughly minted silver coin sporting an image of a man with a wreath on his head. "King Phillip of Macedonia had this silver coin minted to celebrate his horse's victory at the Olympic gameson the same day of the birth of his first son, who he named Alexander – after his brother. That was in the year 356 B.C."

"This coin is over 2,000 years old? Whose head is that?"

"That's an image of Zeus, and the back is the victorious horse. Alexander was touted to be a son of Zeus as well."

"Well, Buce, did you have competition back then? An Olympic champion?"

"This was minted at least twelve years before Bucephalus shows up."

"So, how much is this one worth?"

"Oh, maybe $50,000."

"What? Why do you keep it here?"

"No one knows we have it. And Mother loves to look at it. But that's nothing. In our bank vault in Bern, we keep grandfather's 'Athens *Dekadrachm.*'"

"Another coin?"

"It's the rarest of ancient Greek coins. Worth close to one million."

"No way."

"Yes. I'm just telling you this to know my grandfather was serious about his history and his passion for collection, and he had the wealth to do it."

"So, maybe he has other coins he is giving you?

"Maybe, but I doubt it."

"And your folks don't know about it?"

"As grandfather insisted."

"What about your brother?"

"He knows nothing, as far as I know. But he is largely left out of the will. He doesn't have the greatest of relationship with us anymore. It's sad."

A crackling log spits out a fiery ember on the mantle. I take a pair of tongs and pick up the glowing coal.

"So, the burning fact is Tigran has a clue we know nothing about. He thinks you have a clue in your purse he knows nothing about. We have a possible tower clue that we know he knows nothing about."

I toss the ember back into the fire and snuggle in again.

"Rick, maybe it's not what he thinks is in the purse. Maybe it is something he thinks is on the purse. I can't believe I didn't think of this before."

She goes over to a drawer in a cabinet and pulls out a cloth wrapped around something.

"Here is part of the leather piece that didn't get made into the purse. I thought this part of the leather was marred, so I just had them cut this off."

We lay it out flat and see the imprints burned into the texture.

"Looks like a bunch of shapes," I admit.

"Hold it. Turn it around. Now what does it look like?"

"I don't know. Why is a star there? It's the only thing other than lines."

"Rick, whoa, look, it's a map of the western edge of the Mediterranean. There is the island of Cyprus."

"Yeah. Yeah. So – the star – it's in Lebanon. It's Beirut, the capital."

"What could be in Beirut? He did live there for a short time."

"It was a French colony after WWI. So, being French, he probably got around pretty easily. They speak French and Arabic there."

"It's just such a simple map. I mean. Why not tell me. 'Hey, Buce, in Beirut is a treasure'?"

"This is what they were after. They just didn't know."

"I hope they like my lipstick. They really need it."

I bust up. "Who's the comedian now? You funny, Buce." She pecks me on the cheek and then gives me the gift of her laugh.

"Well, I'll let you know soon about what's in Beirut. We'll be there twice. Going to and coming from the Holy Land for the Christmas season. Seems right. If you find out more, maybe I can help in our short stay there."

"Me going to Paris and you in Beirut. Where is all this leading?"

"This is getting stranger by the minute. Jill, what have they got on your dad that he doesn't know about? That must be what Tigran warned me that he would 'tell.'" She is quiet for a moment.

"Rick. I just… I just can't share that with you. Please understand."

"I don't, but you saying you can't is good enough for me."

"You need to look at this."

She takes out a folded note from her pocket and shows it to me. The writing is pasted down with cut-out letters from magazines, Turkish magazines. The alphabet is a little different.

Ü haf ve vant. Ve nö

Ve kan mak Ü papa in large tröble

Ü müss çall numbr here we mak meet

Ü hav not lot time – i tell bg sicret

"You can tell they're not English majors. They spell as bad as I do," I confess.

There was a date, time, and number scratched at the bottom of the note.

"They put their phone number on this? These guys aren't too bright, are they? I think if this is the guy with half a nose, he now has half a brain to go with it."

Jill doesn't react.

"Wait a minute. You called them?"

"It was to a pay phone at a specific hour."

"Oh Jill, that was so risky."

"I had to call. I bought us some time. I played a dumb kid and admitted my parents were taking me out of the country for a few weeks. I couldn't do what they asked that soon. So, as bright as they are, they say okay. But add, 'We will be watching.'"

"Do you have guards on the house?"

"You would be surprised and have a great alarm system. So, don't wander outside tonight. Even Chuk sets it off some nights, so we sometimes leave it off."

"What were they asking?"

"We are to meet at *Gölbaşı* Park, at the Ferris wheel, whenever we decide."

"We?"

"I told them I had to bring a translator. This is all in our favor. We can make a trade. Their clue for our clue. They don't know we have anything more. We can do this."

"I'm not going to be much help as a translator."

"That was just an excuse to bring you along."

"Which clue are you talking about?"

"It will have to be the leather map. They know the purse has something to do with this."

"This big secret. I mean, the blackmail stuff. How bad is it?"

"It could mean the life of my father – so – bad."

Chuk is now purring and rubbing against my legs. Her green eyes glow eerily in the firelight, then wanders away. My Hardy Boys' mystery mind is humming. It's quiet just for a moment. Each crackling of the flaming logs seems to evoke even more questions. We spend some time discussing a preliminary plan of 'attack.'

"Enough! I can't do it anymore. It's enough for now. These are good ideas." She leans back on the cushions and sighs. "Do you ever think that all this is a little too much for mere young mortals like us to handle?" She clutches my hand tighter. I swivel and face her, taking both her hands.

"Mere mortals? Are you kidding? You are Fortuna – the goddess of fortune and good luck, and I? I am Danger 9b. Danger! I'll tell you. Two fearsome adversaries for anyone. We laugh in the face of Danger. Ha Ha Ha."

I let out my best mock evil laugh, and then there was that exquisite ethereal giggle. And now, my Cowardly Lion character has come out. And in my best theater accent, I stand up and pronounce,

"We'll face those hoodlums! I'll go in there for Dorothy, I mean Jill. Knives or no knives. Wicked witch I don't know or nose less witchI 'knows.' Spam or no spam. Lipstick on or lipstick off. I'll fight 'em with one paw tied behind my back and my whapping tail. I may not make it out alive, but I'll do it. I'll do it for Jill. There's only one thingI want you to do!"

Giggling, Jill asks, "What's that?"

"Talk me out of it."

"Not a chance, bub. I'll just provide the motivation."

In the fading light of a dying fire, she pulls me down and adds another sweet, long deposit on her promise, and bids me goodnight.

RIVALRY BOX SCORE:

It was as if I had no rival this night.

Life was good, but . . . there was the poem in her book pack.

Episode Nine

International Escapades

Chapter Fifty-Six
She Loves You

"No way! You had a sleep-over at Jill's? Whoa. That's more than Mitch ever got." Spitball needles me. "I guess PDA can also stand for 'Private Display of Affection' and legal."

It was a night never to be forgotten. The coup attempt was winding down in failure. Things were sort of back to normal for us. Jill and I had an audacious plan – but we needed backup.

"Oh, come-on. It's not like that. The coup had started. I couldn't go home."

"I should play that Beatle song, she just may love you, yeah, yeah, yeah. Whoa, that can't be bad. You have turned into quite the Don Juan."

"Somehow, I don't think he was a very nice person. Don't lump me with him. But I have gained a notch or two on Mitch. That is for sure."

"I have real doubts about this plan of yours. It doesn't even count as one of your missions. You're 'off to see' a whole different kind of wizard. OK, you can't tell me the why. Alright. But these two guys that keep entering your lives sound serious."

"Yeah. That's why I need you. You've always been one for adventure, and somehow, now I am too."

"You know who you need is Will. He always wants to pound on somebody."

"Don't I know, but we really can't."

"Don't worry about me. I'm all in. I'll be ready. We got a whole two weeks for us to work it out on our trip."

Chapter Fifty-Seven
Any Time at All

Tom and his family are going with us on this vacation. We are off to places I have only heard of in my Sunday School classes. Places in the Old and New Testament from the Jewish and Christian bible. They will now come to life for me. Of course, Turkey was around in those olden days too, but it was not known as Turkey. It was sometimes referred to as 'Anatolia' or 'Capridocia' then later, 'Asia Minor'. The 'Turkey' came much later.

At lunch, I tell Tom, "At least we don't need to pretend to be doing something devious, but Jill has this mystery going on. It reaches all the way to Beirut. Maybe we can help."

This is the adventure for the new year of 1965 to the ancient city of Jerusalem. Beirut, Lebanon, is a major stop for us, going to and coming back. The city of Jerusalem is divided between the country of Jordan and Israel.

"There is a 'no man's land' down the middle of Jerusalem."

"I know. It's a strip of land used as a buffer, a sort of shock cushion between two enemy countries," Tom says.

"No one is allowed to enter this area or, possibly, you could be shot at – yes – with guns."

"Cool."

Jill hears this last conversation.

"Why not a no-women's land? Would they not shoot at a girl? I need a grand adventure, any time at all. You're getting so much more interesting. Take me along! All you need to do is call. I'll be there."

"But you're heading to Paris. Fru Fru land. Tom and I are looking forward to some action."

"So am I. My mom and I have work to do to finalize my grandfather's estate. With all of us gone, I guess that's good timing?"

Anyway, with that information, does Jerusalem sound like a nice place to visit? It seems a bit odd to think about a divided city. This is holy land to three major religions, Islam, Christianity, and Judaism. Berlin, in Germany, is still divided between the USSR and the West. So, I guess this is not so unusual.

As the bell rings to end lunch, Jill leaves me a note to read later.

Ricky,

I am hoping to get a few more answers from my grandfather's estate while I'm in Paris. It will be fun but kind of lonely. Let's write to each other. Let me know where to send my letters before you leave.

Jill

She leaves me her address in Paris. Oh. This is a personal note, and I am now 'Ricky'. Okay, I'll go with that. There will only be time for maybe one letter each. I get an address from dad where she can write. So, I know where she is going to be, and I know where I am going to be. The bigger question is, where will Mitch be? Ha. We are leaving him behind.

Chapter Fifty-Eight
Dizzy Miss Lizzy

The morning we are leaving our phone rings. Jill is on the line. Her voice is anxious. I pull the flexible phone cord out into the stairwell for privacy.

Jill: I got a letter from my grandfather.

Rick: How is that possible?

Jill: It was sent by his executor, the person in charge of his estate. She is only following his wishes. The instructions said when to send it and I got it this morning.

Rick: What did he say? That's a little eerie.

Jill: "Turn the Whirling Dervish"

There is a pause. I'm expecting more.

Rick: And? That's it?

Jill: I'm afraid so.

Rick: Far out. Really weird.

Jill: Don't you remember Tenney's lesson? It was only a couple of weeks ago.

Rick: Enough to pass the test and to tell mom about it. So, what's weird is, she convinced dad that we need to see this Whirling Dervish for my education. That is where we're headed first on our way south —a city called Konya.

Jill: That's really out of sight! So boss!

Rick: *You're sounding more American all the time. We're rubbing off on you.*

Jill: *Just in case I move back, I won't sound so foreign.*

Rick: *Well, Buce, my Swiss miss, I'll see what 'turns' up. You be safe. 'Turn the Whirling Dervish'. Got it.*

My head was spinning. I am never one to like puzzles. They seem like a waste of time. Not the girl puzzle. That is for a great cause, and so is this. So, I add this new clue to our known pieces. The car honks,

"Rick! Get in the car!" I hear dad yell. I run for my history notebook and bound down the stairs to the street.

Our families drive south, out of Ankara. We move in our brown, 1960 Plymouth sedan, all five of us and Tom and his family in a station-wagon. Mom and dad are sitting in front. My older sister, Brenda, and my older brother, Steve are in the back with window seat positions. Then there is me, stuck in the middle of the back seat between them. This is probably good for mom and dad. It seems my brother and sister always have irritations between them. Now, it's me.

"Your legs are too sweaty! Can you not touch me?" my sister whines.

"You want to strap me on top of the roof?"

"Oh Please, dad, can we do that?" my brother pleads.

"I can't move any further away."

"I'll move you. Don't tempt me," my brother adds.

I take out my history notebook before we get to the city of Konya. It is a couple of hours on the road south of Ankara. We timed it so we can experience the 'Whirling Dervish'. Since we are in Turkey, our

studies include a lot of what is around us. I am recounting the lesson. Please count the *S*'s and tell me if this was not another priceless day.

Mr. Tenney: *OK class. We are going to talk about a certain group of believers in Islam, a sect that practices the mystic rites of the Sufi dervish– the "Whirling Dervish". What's up with these folks?*

Is it a new record? We lost count.

Tom: *They Whirl!*

Mr. Tenney: *Thank you for that brilliant insight, Mr. H. Anyone else?*

Aisha: *They put themselves in a sort of trance by performing a dance, twirling round and round and...*

Yeah, and I will add, round and around and around in circles, endlessly, to a live music band, not rock and roll.

Mr. Tenney: *And why do they do this?*

Dave: *To impress their women folk.*

Mr. Tenney: *No.*

Will: *To get exercise.*

Mr. Tenney: *No*

Tom: *To hurl.*

Mr. Tenney: *NO! Girls. Please help them out.*

Jill: *It's a form of worship, meditating through dance, clearing one's mind to communicate with the heavens.*

Tom: *Whirl 'til you hurl. That's what I think.*

They do not hurl. But I thought Tom would. But no, this is an interesting cultural experience my dad insists we watch. There are a lot of spectators sitting in the stands that surround the floor.

What should I be watching? What does 'turn' mean in the clue?

"Ok Tom. Count how many times they turn for Jill."

"What are you, blitzed or something? That's way gnarly. I'd lose it quick."

"I guess you're right. So, let's just guess. How many spins per minute then see how long they dance."

"Hey. Math is your bag."

"Just keep track of the time."

The dancers are all men – I count about 20 of them. Maybe that is an important clue? They fill the dance floor in this building. This is serious business for them. The Dervish wear white, skirt-like attire that swoosh out as they twirl. They have white pants on under their skirts. They also wear gold-colored turbans with a twirly thingy on top. The band is on a covered stage and have instruments that sound like nose whistles, some kind of flutes, bongo drums, funny looking guitars calledlutes and maybe a violin or two.

It is pretty interesting for the first five minutes, but we are supposed to be here for an hour. Twirling for an hour? Tom wasn't far off. You better have a bucket handy. Not them. But I know Jill will ask,

"Ok. Admit it. You tried it – just for the adventure. Admit it."

Tom and I went behind the spectators. It was a contest. Who can be the master whirler or hurler? Five minutes twirling, if that long, is an eternity.

"I can't do it anymore," Tom gives up. He looks almost purple. I smash into the back wall and slide down. I am looking for a bucket. But we both hold it together. So goes this portion of our cultural experience. We stagger back to our seats, on the floor rugs in front of the stands, with our families.

"Okay. They do about 30 turns a minute."

"And they are still going, 40 minutes so far."

I guess this form of worship is like praying, standing up. You just let your mind go into a trance – another world. Well, it isn't long into it, and I want my mind _and_ body to go someplace else, too.

On my trip to Istanbul, I created a practice of a mild and more acceptable form of portable graffiti. It continues here. Hey, I already get a lot of practice writing our notes in school on little scraps of paper. This wasn't too far off.

I write my name with great flourish, then add where I am from and the date. I then stick this under a rug or somewhere hidden for future posterity. I do this in mosques, churches, museums, restaurants, boats, and on and on. It's non-destructive yet personal. Tom notes,

"Hey Rick, did you know that some lady writer called Edith slept in a coffin to get her in the mood before she would start her day of writing mysteries?"

We both probably felt we were in a mood for dying too, but it did pass the time.

"Yeah. You might have Kilroy's disease," Tom tosses out.

"Kilroy? What is that?"

"Kilroy was some funny little cartoon character the soldiers in WW Two would draw everywhere with just a nose and eyes sticking over a wall with the words, 'Kilroy was here'."

"Well, now, it is me." Richard was here. *Konya*, 1965.

Chapter Fifty-Nine
You Really Got a Hold on Me

I start to write pieces of my letter to Jill. I'm not sure I want to, but I need to. I'd rather see her. She's got that tight of hold on me. I begin,

I'm always thinking of you, it seems.

Then I keep it focused on our trip for now although my head was still whirling with questions.

We stop overnight in a place called Iskenderun. Mean anything? Yeah. It means Alexander, and it's one of the many cities the great conqorer founded where he named it after himself, or something close. It's on the coast of the Medit... Sea, still in Turkey. Has a nice beach

Tom and I have not done much. We did twirl and not hurl. We estamate guess the turns. 30 turns per minute for 45 minutes times 20 dancers. You do the math. Maybe that will make sense at some point?

So, Jill, I got to tell you of a quick stop, (there was more than one) we had to make along our way. We had to have gas – I had plenty to spare – ha, ha. But the car needed it, too. And we had to take care of busyness, if you know what I mean. "Banyo nerede?" Crap Yeah!

Anyway. Whoa. Let me tell you what I saw as I opened the banyo door! All I see is a big hole in the floor and two footprints to step on. Wow. That's it. Nothing to sit on and NO toilet paper, just a pitcher of water. Work that one out. It wasn't for drinking.

The next day, we drive a short distance to the border of Turkey and Syria. We had to show that our passports are stamped with their visa, our permission to enter. That's what embassies are for in all countries. They approve who can come into their country in advance.

My passport is getting a lot of cool stamps in it. We finally get back on the two-lane road. One lane goes south, and one lane goes north. To our right is nothing but sand and sand dunes. To our left is also nothing but sand and dunes. You have to admire the people who make this their home, they must be strong. Occasionally, we pass through a little village with mostly mud huts, some made out of cinder block. I continue my letter.

A dust storm kicks up and dad has to slow our car to even see the road. Then he slams on the breaks. A whole heard, hurd, herd of camels are crossing the road. Dad steps out of the car to take a picture and one of the herdsmen comes charging up to the car on his camel, full speed. He looks like he knows how to ride as opposed to someone else you may know. He starts yelling, "La, La, La." He's not singing. That's Arabic for 'no'. I guess he didn't want his picture taken. Dad tells us they think it captures their soul. (Can I take your picture?) Anyway, the camel gets right up to the car when dad takes out a pocket full of coins. A little buckshish goes a long way. The Syrian guy was so happy I thought he might escort us all the way to Beirut!

Chapter Sixty
Ticket to Ride

The road takes us to the outskirts of Damascus, the capital of Syria. Then the road turns west. We are heading to Beirut, Lebanon. Coming to the border between Syria and Lebanon, is a new experience. First of all, the border stop is quick. We have our visas to enter Lebanon. But the valley we enter, the Bekaa valley, is so beautiful! It is so green. It's the farming and pasture area of Lebanon.

We pass by the ancient ruins of Baalbek. These are huge Roman era structures, a temple to Jupiter and so much more. Some of the buildings are partially restored and recognized as a world cultural site. They put on many music concerts here with the huge Roman columns as a backdrop. You can't believe the size of these babies. They could do thisway back then?

There is a stone quarry here, a mine where the Romans could get granite rock for their building projects all over the area. One almost perfectly rectangular block of stone granite is still here. It is mostly carved out. It is as long as a semi-truck from engine to the end of the trailer. That big.

"Well," observes Tom on top of the stone, "by the size of this thing, I guess those Romans employed a lot more people than the ones pulling armpit hairs."

"They do call this quarry a 'pit' so maybe some had two jobs?" I add. "Can you please tell Jill how funny I am?"

"Funny looking, I will admit."

I could not imagine how they could even begin to move stones this size. It is still attached to the hillside but that is the size they were cutting

and moving. But now, this is my first sight of probably my favorite country in the world. It is time to remember history class again.

Mr. Tenney: Lebanon! The Switzerland of the Middle East. Why is that? Not you, Mr. H.

Aisha: Because of its' banking system, snowy mountains and a wider mix of people and religions.

Mr. Tenney: Someone has done their homework, Mr. H.

Tom: Yeah. Well, she's a girl.

Mr. Tenney: Many of the other countries in the region are or have been ruled by military leaders or by a King or by a religious Islamic leader. What is different about Lebanon? Mr. F?

Dave: They have Lebanese people?

Mr. Tenney: Brilliant. Girls? Help them.

Nara: Ja. Day hav system where day share behörde, ah, power by religious population.

Mr. Tenney: Yes. The President must be a Maronite Catholic and the Prime Minister, another top leader who shares power, must be a Sunni Muslim. All the offices below them are determined by the population of different religious beliefs.

Enough on politics!

As the 'Switzerland' of the Middle East, in Lebanon you can go snow skiing in winter months in the morning up in the mountains then you can be swimming in the warm Mediterranean Sea in the afternoon. Lebanon is so diverse in geography – unlike the deserts that surroundall their neighbors. Beirut, the capital, has very modern buildings and

full services of electricity, and underground sewers and running water and an established transportation system.

We pull our cars up to this fabulous hotel, called 'The Phoenicia'. It is time for a bit of luxury.

"This place is so . . . alive. Look, the sea is right next to our hotel." Tom exuberantly comments. "And Ice Cream malts!"

"TV," I say. Yeah, a choice of three channels. Okay, all in Arabic.

"Real hamburgers!"

Correct, there are no hamburger joints in Turkey? Not one. Ahrggggg. But here we are, we can sit by the pool on the edge of Mediterranean Sea and order a hamburger and fries. Luxury for us.

Jill, you wouldn't believe it. Tom and I went swimmin in the pool and doov dove down to the deep end. There were windows in the pool walls and people were watching us swim! It was the hotel bar below the pool. Maybe they thought I was Tom's Mediteranian dolphan we sawor something. They were probably a little drunk so it didn't matter. I suppose we look like fish in a fishbowl for their entertainment.

I send my letter first class to Jill's hotel in Paris. Because of direct flights, she will get it in only two days. Beirut is such a vacation spot. We are staying several days before going to Jerusalem and several days coming back. It's the swimming in the pool and the Sea and drinking malts that are the best for Tom and me.

The U.S. Embassy is just down the street. It works to help hold the peace in the area. Dad tells me the Middle East is and will be for some time, a very unstable place. But what do we know about that as kids? The whole area has had a troubled past for centuries. We are here at a time of relative peace. But my peace is soon troubled. I get a telegram, like an instant letter from Jill, delivered right to my room in Beirut.

Oh, you adventurous Richard! I got your letter and had to get something quick right back to you. Send my best to Tom. I am enjoying the food in Paris. I hope you are sitting down. I ate frog's legs and snails! Crap yeah!

I could just imagine her giggling here – my ears tingle with the thought.

It isn't so bad if you don't think about what you are eating. Guess what I can see from my hotel? It's big and tall! Our pool in the Paris hotel does not have windows. That would be fun, but it does have a high diving board. I wasn't going to dive off, just jump, but Mitch pushed me!

Wait a minute. Did I just read that right? MITCH? Diablo is in Paris? I panic.

"Tom, Mitch is in Paris, with Jill!"

How did this happen? 'Dad, I want to fly to Paris!' Should I demand this? Totally impractical. How could this be true? He is gaining on me fast. The scoreboard is not going to be kind to me.

Tom takes the telegram from me. "Hey, relax, read on, oh ye of little faith."

Yes. He pushed me off the high dive. I was furious at him. My swimsuit did not stay on as I hit the water. Luckily, I could adjust myself before I came up. Could you imagine if there had been windows in the deep end like you have?

This is not an image I wanted to admit to visualizing. But the news was very encouraging.

Needless to say. I said goodbye to Mitch right then. He was heading to London with his mom, so it was all for the best.

Yes! Yes! Score one big one for Danger 9b and surely a minus one for the devil. Could it be true? Someone is looking out after me.

We met with the executor of grandfather's estate today. I was given a second letter from his vault addressed to me. Mother is not quite sure what all this means, and I have to lie a bit. Terrible of me. But because of what it says, I MUST come to Beirut! Dad seems to understand. He will talk to your dad and make the arrangements. I'll be there when you return to Beirut from Jerusalem.

Jill, coming to Beirut? I couldn't believe it.   I thought I was going to be sad. But it's not today. She's got her ticket to fly. It had to be something important. Of course, the cost was nothing to her. For some reason, our dads are so accommodating. What's up with that? Doesn't matter. I am so stoked! It's just twitchin' fab. It's still a week away, but so much to look forward to.

We say goodbye to Beirut and all its comforts and head back to Syria and turn south to the country of Jordan.

Chapter Sixty-One
Get Back

I can't think of much else but getting back to Beirut. My Jameela thought she was a loner, but now she knows that's not gonna last. We spend Christmas day in Jerusalem. So do a lot of other people. Yes, we see Bethlehem, the Church of the Nativity, the birthplace of Jesus. We visit the famous Dome of the Rock, a place sacred to the Muslims, Jews, and Christians. We walk the ramparts of the old city walls, built in 1538 A.D by Suleiman the Magnificent, long after the Romans tore everything down in 70 A.D. I even stuck my toe over the line of 'no- man's' land. I do not get shot. I figure the less I write, the quicker I can get back to where I belong, Lebanon. It can't happen fast enough. The only Christmas present I need is going to be in Beirut.

A very welcome voice calls out across the terrace of the Phoenicia.

"Oh Ricky, Tommy, how about a nice dip?"

We find Jill waving at us, lounging poolside in a green, one-piece, Paris swimsuit looking more like a French fashion runway model. She also is sporting high heels. She's under an umbrella, so covering up is not an issue. Wow. Even Tom has a jaw dropping moment. Then we pull it together and crowd around her.

"Let's order some dinner. It's on me." We do and she dives into the deep end while we wait. I've got my suit on and I quickly follow. She comes up, throws her head back and pulls that luscious red hair back, now straight, which falls so well down her back. I come up in front of her and she throws her arms around me, tightly.

"Ahhh. You're drowning me," I say as we sink below the surface. While down there, she secretly gives me a big kiss. I think I like this mermaid. We surface.

"Still drowning?"

"What a way to go." I'm sure we put on a good show for the people in the bar.

"That's my Christmas present to you."

"I will always love Christmas for more than one reason now."

"We'll always have Paris, in this case, Beirut," she quotes from one of her favorite movies, the 1941 'Casablanca'.

While eating our cheeseburgers, fries and sipping our malts, we bring her up to speed on our adventures.

"This is so unbelievable you're here. But I know it's not just for fun," I say.

"You two have plenty to talk about. Why don't I take a swim and see what drunks in the bar I can scare from the deep end windows," says Tom and off he goes.

"We knew Beirut meant something. I learned grandfather stayed here for months as a base for his research."

"This is making more sense."

"I have more cryptic notes from grandfather. He certainly wanted to make this hard – for a reason."

"Ok, lay it on me."

"It's in Arabic script. But the envelope has his Beirut address. I knew I had to come while you were here."

"Did he own a place here?"

"No. He was renting somewhere in a place called Ras Beirut, along the Cornice it said."

"Well, that's here. The Cornice is the road outside that runs along the coast of the Mediterranean. The wealthier people live here. Come on." I take her by the hand. "We'll go see the concierge." She pulls ona cover-up, and I grab my shirt.

We walk into the lobby. At their desk, near the entrance, is a person whose job it is to help visitors connect with the local population, businesses, and tourist sites.

"Excuse me, Mam. We are wondering if you could translate something for us?"

"At your service." Jill shows her the note.

كنيسة - درج مسعد

"This word", she points to the one on the far right, "says, 'kanisi.' That means 'church.' Arabic is written from right to left, so the next word is 'daraj,' it means 'stairs'"

"Church stairs?" Jill asks.

'Well, there is a dash between, so they may not be connected."

"What about the last word?"

" 'Massad'. It doesn't mean anything but a formal name – maybe the name of the stairs I think."

"Do you know of such a place?"

"One moment, please." She calls over the doorman and says something in Arabic to him that includes the words *daraj massad*. He gets a knowing look and says something back.

"*Shukran*," she says. I know that means thank you. She turns to us.

"He knows the place. It's a stop on the service route – by the port – east of here."

She writes out some instructions on how to get there. We learn that a 'service' (sir-veece) is like a taxi, a car, but it goes on a route like a bus. You pay for the seats you take.

It's already late afternoon, but Jill is so anxious.

"You and Tom meet me down here in 15 minutes. I'll go and change."

The instructions get us to the city center where all the bus lines and service routes converge. There is a juice shop at the top of the square where they grind and squeeze almost any kind of fruit or crop into a drink – lemon – orange –mango - sugar cane – plum – fig. While we're figuring out what to do, I use Jill's cash of Lebanese *lira* to buy us all fresh squeezed orange juice. I'm not too adventurous about the other choices.

"The instructions say to stand at the juice shop street and use this hand gesture," Tom reads and tries to execute the signal.

This is the sign to a driver, which route you want. If it's his route and he has the space, he stops. Tom starts the hand gesture. Several cars honk at him. The guy from the juice shop runs out in a panic.

"*La. La. La* (no, no, no). No do. That hand – bad. Is insult. Where you want to go?"

Apparently, Tom got it wrong and was communicating something offensive. You would not have guessed that by looking at the gesture, but it sure got the reaction.

"Do this," he says and shows Tom the correct hand signal. "This means you want *Bourj Hammoud* car. If driver give different sign, do this." He lifts his chin and does a quick tongue thrust and click between his teeth, which means, 'no'. The Turks do the same. This one we know.

We watch a guy walk in front of a slow-moving car, which stops. He is holding up his hand, all fingers together, pointing up and thrusts this sign at the driver.

"Ah oh. Is that guy in trouble?" I ask.

"La. This means *wa-if*, 'wait' or 'just one moment'," our new friend says. His co-worker asks him a question. He turns, looks at the guy, thrusts his hand out and, simultaneously, rotates his wrist over while shaking his head quickly. He says what sounds like "*shu yanni*". It's another new gesture for us. This hand and head movement with the words mean, 'what do you want' or 'I do not understand'. Language is one thing, but cultural gestures are a whole new language. We are learning fast.

A service finally stops for us. Tom, with another learned hand sign, holds down three fingers, the little one, fourth one and middle, with his thumb and first finger tucked under. His hand is turned backwards with the three fingers pointing down. It means, three, in our case, passengers. To do otherwise could also be taken as bad.

"*iila 'ayn*," asks the driver. This means, 'where to'? I tell him, '*daraj massad,*' and off we go.

"You sister, very *jameela*," says the service driver.

"I thought you were making that up?" Jill whispers to me.

"*Eywa,*" I reply. "*Jameela jdaan. Mish uxti.*" Jill stares at me.

"Okay, I picked up a few things," I whisper back.

'Oh, you speak Arabic? *Ahzeem*! (Excellent) Girl not sister? What her phone number?" the driver teases.

"Aaa… she's taken, buddy," Tom tells him sitting in the front passenger seat.

"Sh*ada*," (what a pity) he replies, "here *daraj massad*." And he pulls the car over quickly to a stop. A car behind us, slams on its brakes and stops almost at our bumper.

"*Shu yanni?*" Our driver yells out the window at the car, flips his wrist and shakes his head. Two guys in the car just sit quietly, looking at a map.

Daraj massad is the name of this typical stairway. It leads up from our stop, maybe one hundred yards, between apartment buildings, to the street above. We are in the depths of the city. It's dusk but no lights are on yet.

"Ok team. Get me to the church on-time," Jill quips, a line from her favorite musical, 'My Fair Lady'.

"Is that what to look for?" Tom asks.

"We guess. We don't know. Something church," I say.

As we learned, Lebanon is a wide mix of religions all in the same place. So, it is not unusual to expect to find a church. Up we go, looking down each alley way and building entrance for any clue. The apartment buildings tower to the sky like imposing fortresses, built on this steep hill with the steps, like a draw bridge, taking us between different entrances.

"These are just apartments, buckaroos," Tom mutters.

We get to the top and stand on the upper street.

"Well, this is a bust," Jill says, with some frustration. I start to walk up the street and I see it.

"There!"

Hanging from a balcony of a building, one floor up from the bottom but at our street level, is a neatly carved wooden sign in three languages, Arabic, Armenian, and English. "The Church of Jesus Christ of Latter-day Saints."

"That's your church," Jill recognizes.

"Well, it's the name but that doesn't look like a chapel to me."

Tom has already walked across the entrance bridge into the building. We follow and stop at the apartment door we think has the balcony sign. The doorbell name plate confirms it. Jill knocks.

"You do the talking, Rick."

Sure enough, the door opens and it's a young man in his early twenties, white shirt, a name tag above his shirt pocket that says, "Elder Wilde". He seems generally surprised.

"Well, hello. Whoa, what are three obvious Americans doing way out here in the city?" he asks.

"We aren't quite sure," is my reply. We get invited in.

"What's an Elder?" Tom whispers.

"Oh, just a title like 'mister' but is an office in the ministry," I tell them.

We pass an office and kitchen. I assume the bath and bedrooms are on the far side, the living quarters for the missionaries, as they are called. It's a very large apartment that looks like it serves as a quasi- meeting house/chapel. I introduce us. Jill and Tom say nothing. I ask the first obvious question.

"Elder, did any of you know a man, a French professor, named *Messieur* Fontaine?"

"You bet we did. Jill? Elders! She's here!" Elder Wilde suddenly calls out. Three other young men come out to meet us.

"Really? This is the granddaughter, Jill?" an Elder Ward asks. "We had many wonderful discussions with Professor Fontaine – ancient American history and writings, rare artifacts, near-eastern history. How is he?"

"I'm sorry to say he passed away about a year ago," Jill quietly answers.

"We're so sorry to hear that. Oh, he was a good and fascinating man. Elders, can you believe this is actually Jill?" says Elder Ward.

This is getting stranger and stranger. Why all the fuss over her?

"He was teaching here at the American University for a semester and doing research." Elder Wilde tells us.

"Yeah, not so much interested in religion," an Elder Wilcox adds. Jill smiles. "Right in the middle of our conversations about his quest forrare objects was his granddaughter, Jill."

"We probably know more about you than you want," Elder Ward laughs. "My word, it's true. Your eyes. Buce is here!"

I could tell Jill was uncomfortable but also so delighted.

"You were so special to him. Hey. Did he ever mount his Alexander expedition?" asks Elder Wilcox.

Jill and I look at each other. There has to be something to this.

"What do you know about this expedition?" Jill asks.

"I guess he felt he could confide in us. He was so excited," Wilcox tells us.

"He was quite sure he knew where the tomb of Alexander the Great was. He didn't tell us specifics on that," says Ward.

"We were taught it was in the city he founded in Egypt, Alexandria," I say.

"Oh, it was. It had been moved from Memphis, his Egyptian capital. He was considered a Pharoah, you know," Ward exclaims.

"The professor taught us even the Roman emperor, Julius Caesar, had visited the tomb 300 or so years after Alexander's death. After that, it became a huge mystery in history." Elder Wilde pipes in.

"He was buried in a solid gold casket, pounded to fit his body shape," Ward adds.

"Your grandfather said it would be the greatest find in Archeology since King Tut's tomb. Only the Jew's Arc of the Covenant might be bigger? Who knows? It was his passion. You didn't know about it?" Wilcox again.

"Aaa, not really," Jill tells them.

"Did he ever find the book?" Ward asks.

"What do you mean?" I ask.

"The first edition copy of the Book of Mormon. That's what he really wanted from us when we first met," Elder Ward says. They chuckle.

"Yeah, like we're going to have a copy of a book worth a half million dollars," Elder Wilcox adds, "but that's what he said to tell you if we ever met. Tell her 'I'm looking.' He was most insistent on this every time we met. He said you would come."

Again, Jill and I look at each other. This is the important part of our many questions. Nothing of more significance is said.

'Tell Jill, 'I'm looking,' runs through our minds.

It is dark outside now. We finish up our conversation quickly and thank them.

"We'd better cut out," Tom says.

"Ah. This isn't the greatest of neighborhoods. Be cautious out there. You should be able to catch a service back into the city center at the main drag down the stairs."

"We can handle ourselves, thanks," Tom assures them.

At the top of the stairs, as we descend to the first landing, Tom asks,

"So. Is that it? I mean. Is that what you are looking for?"

"I think so…" Jill adds. That last word sort of drags out as we look below us to see a gang of five or six local young men lurking in the shadows, like the gathering of a pack of wolves, just circling. A couple of them hold clubs. They wait for us at the next landing. We think about going back up but see a few more figures at the top, behind us.

"Could be nothing," Jill says as we continue our descent. Then it becomes clear as the ones at the top start to come down, and the ones below spread out and start their climb towards us.

"I'm not feeling so well," I admit.

"Well, I have a bad feeling about this, too," Tom says. Then he looks at me. "Oh. That's not what you meant."

"*Qu'est-ce que tu veux?*" Jill yells out. (What do you want?)

They laugh.

"*Vu.*" (You)

Jill holds up five fingers, all grouped together, pointing upwards, and thrusts her hand out to each group. They hesitate, murmur among themselves, and look quickly around.

"*Shu Yanni!*" she yells at the top of her lungs as she thrusts her arm out, twisting her wrist, and shakes her head at them. That really confuses them but they start their slow advance on us.

Four of the boys are just a few steps below us, menacing phantoms on *daraj massad*. The boys above keep coming down. We're stuck between two converging wolf packs like they've practiced how to hunt as a group. My stomach hurts, and my legs just crumble. I fall right onto the gang below us, dragging a few of them down the steps, cushioning my fall. Jill lets out a scream. This is the last thing I remember.

Chapter Sixty-Two
Getting Better

"Despite what the doctor says, I think it may be the ataxic CP acting up again," is the first thing I hear my mom say.

I struggle to get the words out, "No, bad juice."

"You're going to be alright," she says.

"Mrs. Foster, what is CP?" Jill asks.

"He has a form of Cerebral palsy. He caught it with a bout of meningitis when he was younger."

I open my eyes, and I am in my room at the Phoenicia.

"The doctor has been here. You're doing the best that you can. It's getting better. You're going to be okay," I think she was trying to reassure herself. "Rick, you, Jill, and I are flying back to Ankara tomorrow."

"Whaa? What happened?"

"You really wasted those guys on the steps, and you came out without a scratch," Tom tells me admiringly.

"Hi, Tom. How?" I mutter weakly.

"Well, first, just as you collapsed, we called out to two men way at the bottom of the stairs on the street. But they just stood there. I thought they were going to do something."

Jill gives me a quick, concerned glance.

"But then, those missionaries came and scared our would-be attackers off. The two men were gone when I looked next. Good thing those Elders heard Jill."

"Did I hear you yell, '*shu yanni*' at them?" I ask her.

"Better believe I did, Crap Yeah."

"And that worked?"

"It delayed them."

"You're full of surprises."

She leans down to me and whispers, "Well, I have some more surprises for you. Exciting new games to try out, I learned in Paris. There just might be some kissing involved."

"Yes, I think I'm getting better since you've been mine." I smile.

RIVALRY BOX SCORE:

Better update the box score. But oh boy, did I like the kissing news. That is my kind of medicine. I was going to have to wait and find out. It seemed very exciting. The scoreboard was looking good. I scored my own coup with Jill coming to Beirut.

Episode Ten

Ankara Home Games

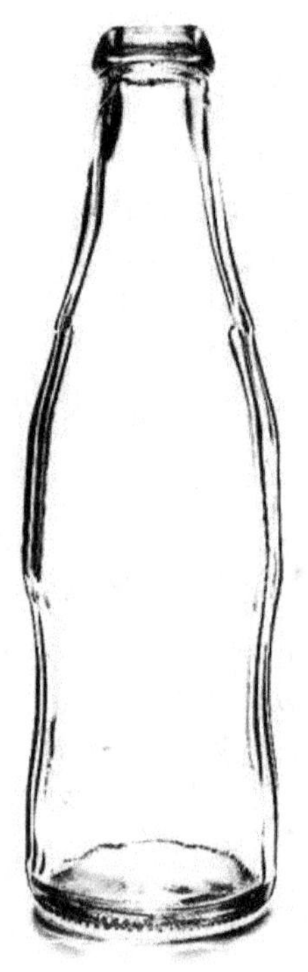

Chapter Sixty-Three
Honey Pie

I get checked out at the military hospital. I'm perfectly fine. Well, not perfect. I've had to deal with this since I was nine, when I first got sick. It pops up now and again. I just can't run as fast as others in between these bouts.

After a few days, I need the exercise to get my legs back, so I walk the mile to Jill's house. Bullet Head is not on duty, and I didn't have any credit with the other drivers. Jill is sitting on the wall outside her house when I approach.

"I did it," she yells out to me, pointing to the corner of her street. I am passing where she is pointing and there is a five *lira* coin at my feet on the sidewalk. It's like finding gold. I know better than to try and pick it up.

"Ooo," I utter. It's so shiny, it gleams like a goddess. Here we go again. "This again? Jill, what's up with this? That's a pretty big prize, it's a honey pie. Gonna drive somebody crazy and I'm just too lazy to try."

"Ah, don't be such a… downer, isn't that the word? It's for fun."

The first to come along are two young boys. Maybe around the age of eight or so. One is a little darker-skinned than the other.

"Look, it's you and Mitch," she says.

I chuckle, then watch. These two are so shocked to see the coin. They freeze, then look around. We are some distance away, trying notto notice. One dives down for the try with no success. The other joins him. Together, they try to pull up the treasure. It's not going to work. Then one boy shoves the other. Responding, the other hits back, and soon, there is a mini brawl on the corner. At that moment, Jill's mom

calls us in for lunch. Jill just stares at the feuding boys as we retreat into the house. As we walk inside, I admit,

"Five *lira*? I'd be tempted to throw a few punches for that treasure."

"Well, back to our real world," she says.

"What did you find?"

"I flipped through the whole book, carefully. I know it's a first edition and valuable but there was nothing special. There isn't anything to indicate something out of the ordinary."

"Well, I know the book and I wouldn't say it was 'nothing special', but I know what you mean. I'm surprised you didn't find another note or something."

"*Bir şey değil*, not a thing."

"Oh, very good Turkey girl, along with your French, German, the little Spanish and oh, your two words of Russian."

"Good times. *Da, Spasibo*."

She pulls me into her conversation pit to be a bit more private. Funny, but I see Mitch's poem laying under a book on the fireplace mantle – you know – 'thick honey'. Can I ever get rid of this guy?

"Ok. It's finally on. The meeting. *Gölbaşı* Park this Saturday night – Ferris Wheel."

"Whoa. You called them already? OK. We'll be ready. Tom knows his part." We know the plan and don't really want to dwell on it and the anxiety. So, we snuggle in. I love this part of her house, for good reason.

"I think I have some more of your boy puzzle pieces worked out."

"Oh yeah? Well, if so, you are way ahead of me on your puzzle."

"I know."

"Ok. Lay it on me."

"One big piece is food. *Boys are motivated and driven by their stomachs.*"

"Point taken. Agreed. What's for lunch?"

"Next new piece, sleep. *Guys sleep longer and deeper than a hibernating bear if left alone.*"

"Do we dance as good as that bear?"

"Only in your hibernating dreams."

"Okay. You're on a roll. What's next?"

"Sports. *Boys can't talk about anything else, in any kind of depth.*"

"Hey. I can get pretty deep. Not fair. But I do love baseball… and bowling… maybe football, oh and basketball and golf… and tennis! And…"

"Yeah. I get it."

"Did you know that Roger Marris broke the all-time home run record for a season at 61 in 1961, beating Babe Ruth's…"

"Enough already!"

"Just rubbing it in. Ok, keep going. What's next?"

"Sex."

It suddenly gets quiet. I look around for her mom. It remains quiet. I get quieter.

"Ahh. I don't know what to say. I suppose you're right. Not been there."

"Neither have I. Not ready for that."

"That's really a marriage thing for me."

"Not ready for that, either."

"So, we're good on that count?" I pause, then continue, "But, do you want to marry? I mean, sometime in the future? I mean… ah… not necessarily me, I mean…"

"Relax. Yes".

"Even if you can't have kids?"

"What are you talking about?"

"Well, you know. Your operation. You won't be able to have kids."

"What?"

"Your appendix was removed."

She just stares at me. She stares at me longer. What comes next is not just stratospheric, it's to the moon and back.

I must have nailed the humor thing. Not sure how.

Chapter Sixty-Four
Glass Onion

Coach blows his whistle.

"Line 'em up, teams. Foster, are you sure you still want to play?" Coach asks.

"Yes, Sir. I'll be fine." It is Thursday. Flag football day for P.E. We play next to some strawberry fields, and the girls are watching. Yeah, they are for real. The weekend is approaching fast. With 'thick honey' still on my mind, Mitch and I are on opposite teams, as always, it seems. He snarls,

"You really think you can guard me, Foster?"

"Don't get too cocky. It's a tool of the devil,"

We both play one of the 'end' positions, opposite each other. Flag football requires us to wear little strips of cloth, tucked in on both sides of our waist at the belt line. These are our 'flags'. If you have the ball, all someone must do to make you stop is pull one of your flags and holdit up. You cannot tackle them as in regular football. This is good thatJill is not commenting on this sport. We would never get through this. But she and Marie and the girl gang are playing field hockey in the nextarea over from us. They watch us even when they shouldn't. We can hear their coach, Miss Taylor yell at them.

"MacGregor! Keep your head in the game!" This is the sport; hockey, which, by the way, Jill stinks at.

Our flags are supposed to be tucked loosely in our pants so they can be easily pulled out. Well, guess who does not follow that instruction? No, not me. Mitch the 'Meteor.' That is his self-proclaimed title, since he does run pretty fast. He did catch that camel, after all. I prefer to call him, Diablo the Dasher (of hopes and dreams).

To make him harder to stop, he decides to secretly attach the hidden portion of his flags to a loop inside his pants. That makes it very difficult to pull his flag to stop him. This is so very Diablo of him.

So, on this play, Mitch goes out to receive a pass. I am guarding him, and I'm supposed to run alongside him. Well, they all pretty much know it's not a great match up. I know they will throw the ball to him. Yeah. Pick on the cripple. I bump him as the play begins to slow him down. The pass is thrown in his direction, and I am supposed to knock the ball down, but I miss. Mitch has to turn and stop to catch it. This gives me time to stay with him for two steps before he leaves me in the dust. After one step, I dive for his flag with both hands. I grab it and hold on.

Well, Mitch the Meteor spins and keeps on going, without thebenefit of his pants. There he is, in his tighty-whities, streaking off down the field. It's more important for him to score than to figure out what has happened. The commotion turns all the attention to our field. This means all the girls turn to see the results. I proudly hold up his flag, pants attached, and just wait. His other flag is still flapping in the breezetucked in his underwear. Oh. I forgot. Did I say that the flags have been died yellow so we can see them better? Well, I guess the yellow die wiped off on the back of his tighty-whities in a very strategic spot whenI pulled his flag.

I am hoping he will write a poem about this one. Something about thick 'yellow' honey might do. He is not happy with me right now. It's his own fault! It could have been worse. His underpants may have come off.

I think I like flag football. But, somehow, Jill, having observed the whole fiasco, is not happy with me.

Danger 9b,

I must say, I am disappointed in you. How could you be so mean? Diablo is just devastated. He may never recover.

Wait a minute. I think as I read. He scored the winning touchdown (not on that play). I smell something fishy. He is really milking this one. He's probably asking her to feed him grapes and wave a palm branch to cool him off as he reclines on this 'recovery' couch. Oh please. I read on,

I just don't know what to do about the two of you. Can't you be friends? I guess I will see you at my party. BEHAVE!

Fortuna, the disappointed.

I feel hot breath behind me in the locker room. It's Mitch. We are alone, but then I think the echo of his voice is coming through the school's loudspeaker, bouncing around and off all the metal surfaces like a ricocheti   ng bullet. I might have to defend myself physically. He stands over me as I sit to tie my shoes.

"Why?" he demands.

"Hey. Don't blame me for your mistakes."

"I'm not talking about our game, Mr. Snoop man. Infiltrator of nothingness. Man of maniacal magical foolery. You have no regard for her safety."

"Jill? "

"Yeah, Jill. You want to put me down, rub me in the dirt, continually bash what I do, what I am and how I feel. Fine. But you're not the only one who understands how much of a goddess she really is. She gets me. She lifts me. You? We've known each other for three years. You? You never have. Don't risk her life for your stupid games."

The air that permeates my face coming from the open locker door next to me, which he slams shut, is his exclamation point.

Chapter Sixty-Five
Can't Buy Me Love

I am highly anticipating the introduction of the games Jill had told me about. It's Friday night. With our locker room 'conversation' still fresh on my mind from earlier in the day, it puts a big damper on what I think is my triumph over Mitch on the athletic field. Did that not even bother him? Apparently not. What did he know about my activities with Jill? More than I thought.

Anyway, it's the day before our dreaded encounter at *Gölbaşı* Park. I'm not thinking about that now. Jill loves to throw parties. We all love gathering at her place. We are movin' and groovin' to the new Beatles' hit, 'Can't Buy Me Love.' Just when it gets to the part about diamond rings and things that money can't buy, Jill lifts the needle, and the music stops.

"I have a new game for everyone. It's called 'spin-the-bottle.' It's quite mysterious and daring! Don't worry. There is no alcohol involved." This gets a few sighs.

You never know what to expect from her. 'Daring' has me worried. But I know kissing is involved in here somewhere, so I am all ears. I mean lips.

"Now, all of you get in a circle and sit on the floor," she demands.

We dutifully obey, girls and boys. She shows us an empty glass Coca-Cola bottle, holding it high so the overhead chandelier can reflect its curvy lines. Then she proudly proclaims,

"Behold! What secrets this simple glass bottle contains? You think it is empty. Yes? But within its inner chambers lies the secrets of a long-lost love."

She is really in her element now. We all laugh nervously.

"I will now place this love chamber in the middle of us all and be the first to reveal its mysterious powers."

She places it on the floor and gives it a good spin. What is she doing? When the bottle stops spinning, the narrow top points right at Billy B. You remember him? The 'Wizzer' of Oz? Okay, I'll be nice.He is over that problem by now. He has matured since those days, but some things you have a hard time living down. Anyway, Jill marches over and gives him a kiss – on the cheek. I thought Billy B. would melt even smaller from the shock and leave just his empty clothes behind ina heap.

"Now, Mr. Billy B. You now will spin the bottle, revealing the maiden so blessed to receive the object of your affection."

I know I tend to exaggerate, especially when it comes to Billy B. But it's so fun! He may not be the personification of manhood nor the object of any girl's affection, but boy, does he grab hold of this opportunity. His smile is as big as his little head. He spins the bottle. E begins to stroke his goatee. Billy B. goes white as a lily, and laughter erupts. Jill steps forward and explains.

"The magic is now transferred to Will and remains hidden for Mr. B."

He is not required to bestow his kiss on Will. This is part of the rules. Good thing. He would have met one of Sarge's two best friends. Billy B. is much relieved. (I am sure Sarge is, too.) If it stopped on someone your own gender, you lose your turn. If the bottle stops in-between people, you can spin again.

I am hoping (fingers crossed) that Jill will get another turn. Will takes his turn and spins the bottle, and it points at me! Yes! Thanks, buddy. So, I am calculating how I can get it to stop at Jill. Great and careful analyses are involved. I'm thinking hard about the physics at hand, factual hard science. I start calculating with my great brain and steady, well-developed nerve.

'Hmmm. Speed vs. object weight vs. floor friction vs. air resistance vs. gravity angle. Got it.'

I spin. It lands on Mitch.

I hate Physics.

"Great spin there, professor," he says. "I'll take it from here." Ok. Mitch gets to spin. Can you see where this is going? Will it stop on Jill? Ha. Ha. It points to… me again!

O! Fortuna. I love Physics and fate!

So, I spin again, filled with hope. It lands on Karin, Tom's love. I give her a kiss on the cheek. Tom just shrugs. It goes on from there for a while when Jill finally announces a new game, a little more daring. I think she wants more control of the love angle.

It is on to 'Post Office.'

"I love just getting letters. Don't you all? I love 'love' letters. Who doesn't?"

I take note of that statement. Could it be a piece of my girl puzzle? She has most of mine put together by now.

"But the poor Postman gets no attention, no thanks, no fun, but he delivers all the love. We shall now play a game called 'Post Office.' You want to send a love letter? Let the Postman deliver."

Jill has this game more calculated. She has prepared envelopes with our names written on them. She plays the Beatle tune, 'Please, Mr. Postman', then goes about more explanation. "The Postman, that would be me, will now deliver the mail to the males and the fe-mail to the females," Jill continues.

She starts to hand out our envelopes with our names to each of us.

"Could this be a note from a new admirer? An old flame? A start of a new flame? Only the Postman knows."

She lines up the girls on one side and the boys on the other.

"You each can deliver your mail to the person of your choosing. They must then accompany you to the post office and open your mail. Once there, you read its contents together, then follow the instructions."

"Righto. But wait a minute," Dave blurts out. "Before I get this incorrect, let me get this spot-on. We get to choose someone. Got that. Then we accompany them to the Post. Where is that?"

"The Post Office is here," she states, opening the door to a separate room, her dad's study, off the living room. "Quite private. You may stay one minute when I will open the door."

Mrs. MacGregor sees to that.

In each of our envelopes, there is one of three options that Jill has previously chosen.

"Will you be just friends? Will you be something more? Or will love take hold of your heart?" She asks so dramatically.

"What does all this mean?" an excited Billy B. whispers to me.

"Only the Postman knows," Jill adds.

In our personal envelope, there is printed only one of three possibilities,

Friendship. You may shake hands.

Or

I like you. You may kiss me on the cheek.

Or the big one,

You – my love – may kiss me on the lips.

Now, none of us know this until we get into the room with our chosen person. How do I know this? Hey, I've been around Jill a lot lately. I peeked.

We open our own envelope, not the chosen person's envelope. Then, you both read together. What you finally do is a secret between the two of you.

"I see a flaw, or maybe an advantage, in all of this," Bill B. objects.

'Buddy, what have you got to lose?' I am thinking.

"Someone could be chosen to go to the Post Office several times."

"Yes. This is true. However, you can only go once with your choice and letter," Jill explains, "everyone gets a turn – even you Billy B." His eyes get very big. But Jill is very clever to control who gets to do what.

I will assume, for instance, that Billy B., of course, is given a 'shake hands' letter, as will probably several others. It's all a mystery to me. All I will know is my assigned choice when I open my letter.

Tom, of course, choses Karin. This is easy. He gets back and leans over to me,

"I got the big one." Karin, of course, choses Tom. He probably gets the big one again. Lucky boy. This is working pretty well.

Each time the Post Office door opens, there is a big 'ooooo' from all of us, trying to imagine what took place. Billy B. chooses Marie. She is a good sport about it – very kind. Being Jill's best friend, I think she knows she is safe.

Then, it is Mitch's turn. He looks at Nora. He looks at Aisha. He looks at Nora, again. Surprise! He chooses Jill. Nora fumes. They disappear into the room. One-minute passes by, then two. Jill's mom knocks on the door. They emerge. I can't tell anything as everyone lets out a big 'OOOOOOO'. This is not good. Points? No Points? How am I to know?

Dave chooses Aisha. This is to be expected. By this time, she has warmed up to Dave. This is going to be good. I don't know what option Dave has, but he looks pretty happy when he comes out.

On Will's turn, he looks nervous and chooses Marie. Her second trip to the post office. No surprise to me, maybe it is for others. I did say she is stunning, didn't I? They stay the maximum time. Will seems satisfied.

Then, it's Nora's turn. Yeah. Her again, but none of her flock are ever invited. Maybe Jill is feeling guilty still from her Jillian Manure training? Nah, probably not. But remember, Jill is the postman. Only she knows.

Nora moves confidently down the line. She pauses at me. 'Oh please, no' I am thinking. Moving on, (whew) she pauses at Will. They both smile. (What happened on that island?) She then quickly grabs Mitch's hand and pulls him into the study. He does not seem at all surprised and gives me a grin as he passes, being towed by Nora. This was perhaps the shortest visit to the post office in history. Nora comes storming out not 10 seconds after the door closes. Okay, maybe 20 seconds. Ee Mitch follows sheepishly after, looking really disappointed.

Then it is Marie's turn. She chooses me.

Here we go. I haven't had a turn yet, but I have an inkling of how it all works. I give an 'I don't know' shrug to Will as I pass him. He had high hopes. Keep working at it, Sarge. Marie and I disappear into the 'Post Office' study, and the door closes. I look at Marie, and she seems nervous. She opens her mail, and we both read,

"You – my love - may kiss me on the lips."

Wow. I wasn't expecting this. Marie looks a little anxious still, but she is, after all, Athena, Goddess of War, how can I refuse?

"This is good," I reassure her. It was nice. She is a good person even though she is in charge of all wars.

A few others take their turns.

Then, it is my time. Yes, finally.

However, you can see that I have a bit of a dilemma. Marie has chosen me. She is Jill's best friend. She has proposed marriage already. Well, not really. But I am thinking she has the hots for me. Ahhhrrrggg. She knows I <u>more</u> than like Jill. But now Marie likes me? What to do? Jill still hasn't had a turn.   I am not going to let Mitch get the best of me. I choose Jill.

I take her hand (love that) and go to the Post Office to mail my letter. We open my mail. And it says? Now, remember, Jill oversees all of this.

It read:

Friendship – Shake Hands.

'Ahhhrrrgg! Come on! This can't be!' I was thinking this was so unfair when…

"Hello, friend," she says to me as she takes my hand. Then, she pulls me close and gives me a perfectly respectful, wonderful kiss. Nothing to write home about, (not sure why I would do that) but I'm not complaining.

"I'm still paying up. Just remember that," she tells me mysteriously.

She takes my hand again. We emerge. Maybe one and a-half minutes have passed. Not Mitch's record. Hmmm, half- point more forMitch.

Then it is Jill's turn. Oh, boy. Can I strike gold twice? Or is Mitcha better kisser? Yuck. I can't think of that. He and I stand next to each other, shoving and pushing all the while, jockeying for prime position and attention.

She walks over to the boys' line. She walks by Mitch. Yea! She walks by me. Not so yea. Then she takes Billy B. by the hand. What is this?

"OOoooo", goes up from the crowd. They disappear. It is for two full minutes they are gone. Billy B. emerges first. His face is red. We can only guess. What is that all about?

I now confirm, I know nothing about the art or even any science of romance. It's time to just throw all the 1000 puzzle pieces back in the box. It's hopeless.

RIVALRY BOX SCORE:

It is not looking good. Just when I thought I was in the clear – it is suddenly very cloudy. Girls. Ahhhrrrrgggg!

Chapter Sixty-Six
Baby, You're a Rich Man

While somewhat disappointing, so passes another memorable party at Jill's house. Let's do that again. I wonder how she feels about being one of the 'beautiful people', those with no money worries. Doesn't matter because Saturday night is upon us. Jill tells her mom she is at my house, and I tell my folks I am at hers. Tom has complete freedom, so no problem with his excuse. It's just the three of us. Bullet Head acts as our wheels. Jill foots the bill to employ Bullet Head for the whole evening.

The night is cool and overcast. It can snow in Ankara in January. Ominous clouds are in the distance. *Gölbaşı* Park is about a half-hour away in Bullet Head's Mercedes.

"Why you have cat?" Bullet Head asks Jill as she steps into the car.

"For good luck," the goddess of good luck tells him as she snuggles Chuk in one arm and tightly clenches her new purse in the other.

"*iyi şanslar*," Good luck. I repeat to our trusted driver.

"Oh, *Çok Güzel*. Cats good. You know, Ataturk will come back as cat, with green eyes," he says with a smile. We know the legend. Turks have a great reverence for cats – even a fear. Bullet Head then looks over at Tom and does not smile. Tom sits confidently in the passenger front seat with his Roman Centurion helmet firmly attached to his head. The top feathers are bent as it meets the overhead upholstery of Bullet Head's car.

"Him, *çilgin genç*," Bullet Head laughs.

"Yeah, crazy boy," I agree and Tom laughs.

We sit quietly from then on out. Of course, Bullet Head knows nothing of our plans, and he hums some pop Turkish tune from the radio.

"We will be back in *bir saat* one hour," I tell Bullet Head when he parks the car.

"Look at this place! I've never been here," Tom admires. "I didn't expect the crowds."

"Keep on the lookout," I tell him.

"These guys are great. Look! Fire-eaters, kiddie rides, magic shows, and food!"

"And the dreaded Ferris Wheel - way too scary," I admit.

"Yeah. One little rope is supposed to keep you in a rocking seat,"Jill observes. We stroll around the Farris Wheel for a time. Nothing happens.

"Now what?" Tom asks.

"We mingle," Jill replies.

It starts to sprinkle lightly. Even so, a fire-eater brushes past us, blowing a flare of yellow flame before him. Chuk lets out a distressed growl, but Jill calms her with a stroke. Tom fits right in with thecraziness around us. He beams as near-by jugglers throw bowling pins back and forth. We pass an Oud player, belting out some old folk song, with his pear-shaped, fretless Turkish guitar.

"Ooo. Mitch should learn how to play that," Jill gushes.

That's all I need. More reminders of Mitch.

We walk on through the throng when a dancing veiled lady bumps into Jill.

"Oh, I'm sorry." Jill instinctively says.

"*Beni takip et*," the figure whispers and walks off between two carnival tents.

"She wants us to follow her," I anxiously tell Jill, "Tom, come on."

We take the same path until we are behind two colorful tents, the thick woods as a backdrop. Two other ladies in full headscarves that cover their faces emerge from the heavy foliage. By now, the light rain has turned to light snow.

"Those do not look like ladies," Tom whispers to us. Then it dawns on him, they indeed are not ladies. "I think it's them, the ones from the market,"

"*Tu devais venir seul*," the big one says.

"English, not French, Tigran, so my friends understand," Jill tells him.

"Yu to com by self, just one," he says.

"I told you I would not do that," she says. She then whispers to us, "It looks like we are on to plan 'b', boys."

White flakes fall a little harder. Unusual thunder rolls in the distance. The men chatter again with each other in Turkish or maybe Armenian? They keep glancing at Jill. I can't understand anythingexcept, 'kedi' – cat. Yes. It is working.

"Dis kedi – he eyes – *yeşil*," the shorter one says, in a worried tone.

"Yes, green," I tell them. I don't tell them Chuk is a she.

This sparks even more jabber between them. I only catch the word 'Kemal'. This seems to make them more anxious. The legend has great power.

"Who crazy one?" the shorter one says, pointing at Tom.

"Your worst nightmare," Tom grins, tightening his helmet. "They have to know they are the ones that look really silly," he says to us.

"What mean 'silly'?" the shorter one says.

"You know dis," Tigran barks. He takes off his head scarf. It's a bizarre and pathetic sight. He can have pole position at an American Halloween spook alley if he wants. Chuk gives out a light growl. "You give us *Professeure* clues. If not, we tell world about Col. MacGregor – spy for CIA. We have proof. Russians make him die."

I look at Jill. She is staring straight ahead, water dripping off her face, her hair is wet and clings to her coat. "I will make you a deal," shesays.

"What mean this 'deal'?"

"*Tickaret,*" I tell them. I came prepared with more Turkish vocabulary.

"Tigran, my grandfather trusted you. You turned on him."

"*Je suis un honnête homme*! Tigran no turn. *Professuere* promise money to fix face and pay family. He give me clue – *assurance* –how you say? Insurance - to prove his promise. He not do. New Boss will pay us big *lira*."

"New boss? What new boss?" Jill quizzes him.

"No important to you. He find Alexander."

It suddenly becomes much clearer. It's not just money. It's something bigger – a contest for fame and fortune. Chuk is becoming restless in the weather.

"We know 'Whirling Dervish'. We know my clue. We want map, not on purse."

"How in the world did they know about Dervish?" I whisper to Jill.

"I will need your clue," she says.

"You know *Professeure* crazy – he say he make hard clue for bad men no to steal treasure."

"You see, he trusted you!"

"But he now dead. He no deliver promise. Now new boss pay me."

Of course, they don't know about our *daraj massad* information.

"Well then, let's make this fair and square," Jill demands.

"What means this, 'fair and square'?" the short one asks.

They exchange words with each other that come far too fast and too many for me.

"*Peri*," I blurt out, "Fair."

"*Peri*?" They laugh. "Him *peri*!" They point at Tom and laugh even harder.

"Oh, that's the word for fairy, not 'fair'," I admit to Tom.

"Good distraction, 9b," Tom quips out of the side of his mouth.

"*Adil* – Fair," I state firmly.

"You give us map, that *adil*. You already rich man lady," says Tigran coolly.

"No. Here's the deal. You show me your clue. We will give you the map," Jill tells them.

"You have map?"

Jill pulls out her leather piece from her new purse. "*Evet, yes*".

Hmmm. Now I start to worry. Maybe we are making a mistake.

"Here other clue," Tigran's partner pulls out his knife. I've seen this one before.

"This is not *adil*," Jill shouts.

"You give us now, no tattoo," the man says.

"This is not *adil*! You show the tattoo!" Jill shouts again.

"Jill, what's he talking about?"

The man with the knife steps forward when I put plan 'b' into practice. I reach over and pull Chuk's tail, hard.

Now I know why Tom warned me never to pull her tail. Jill holdsa deranged demon in her outstretched arms. All chaos breaks out. Crawling, scratching, churning, screaming - their screaming. Chuk's furious, clawing paws rip at their dresses. Her paws and claws just start tearing at the short man. He dares not harm her, after all, she is a cat with 'green eyes'.

Tom springs into action. Two Duncan YoYos both are flying with his now perfected boomerang barrage, whacking each guy continually. Snowflakes swarm like softly floating, saucer-sized flower petals as thick as a greenhouse jungle. We're soaked. In the confusion,

Jill drops the leather map.

Tigran dives for it and grabs it up. He backs up, holds up the leather map, then gives us a strange smile. A bolt of lightning hits the woods behind us with a tremendous flash. A boom of immediate thunder blasts us with its force of air. Tigran's smile is quickly replaced with a look of agony. With leather in hand, he keels over flat. Wham! He hits the ground hard and doesn't move. His startled partner steps up, looks him over, then grabs the leather map and takes off.

"Rick, quick. Look him over."

"For what?"

"He has a tattoo on him. That's his clue."

"On him? Now you're telling me? He could be dead!"

"Just go. I'll get Chuk."

The ruckus continues to draw the attention of a few people. Dripping wet, I move down to Tigran. I suppose I am going to find a

knife wound in his back or a burn wound from lightning or something, but there's nothing, just a lifeless, breathless, wet corpse, I assume.

"Do you see anything?" Jill shouts.

"Where do I look for a tattoo? It's not on his face or neck."

"Quick, try his arms." I pull at his ripped-up sleeves but can only get one partially uncovered. Nothing. "I don't see any markings."

"Rick, it's our only chance!"

"Tom, help me look."

Lightning flashes again, Tom and I stumble back into a shallow puddle of water with the accompanying huge clap of simultaneous thunder and shock wave. Some people scatter but others keep coming closer, with the body lying in a pool of water.

"Jill, we have to go now!"

We didn't wait for another thunderbolt.

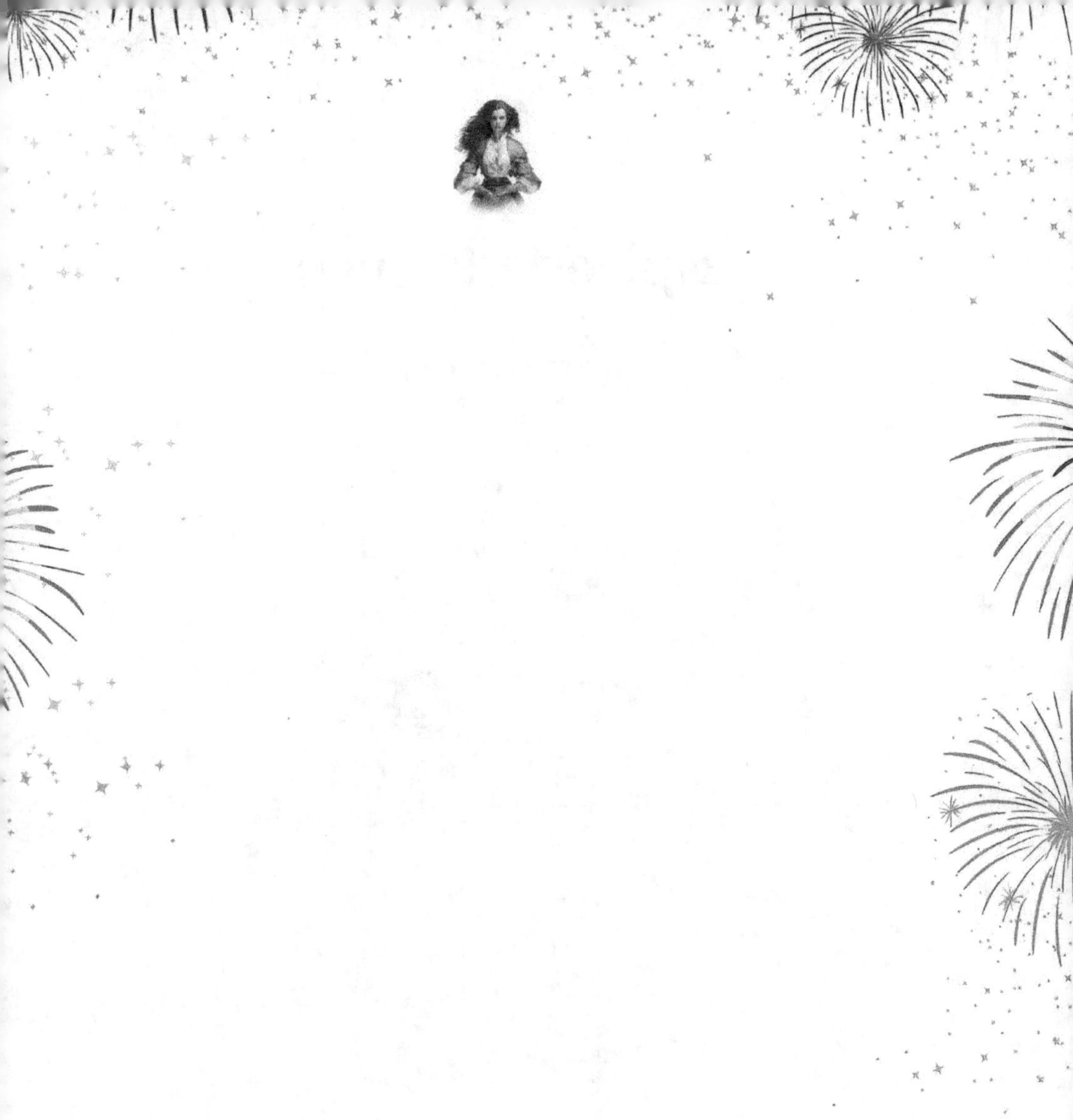

363

Episode Eleven

Resurrection

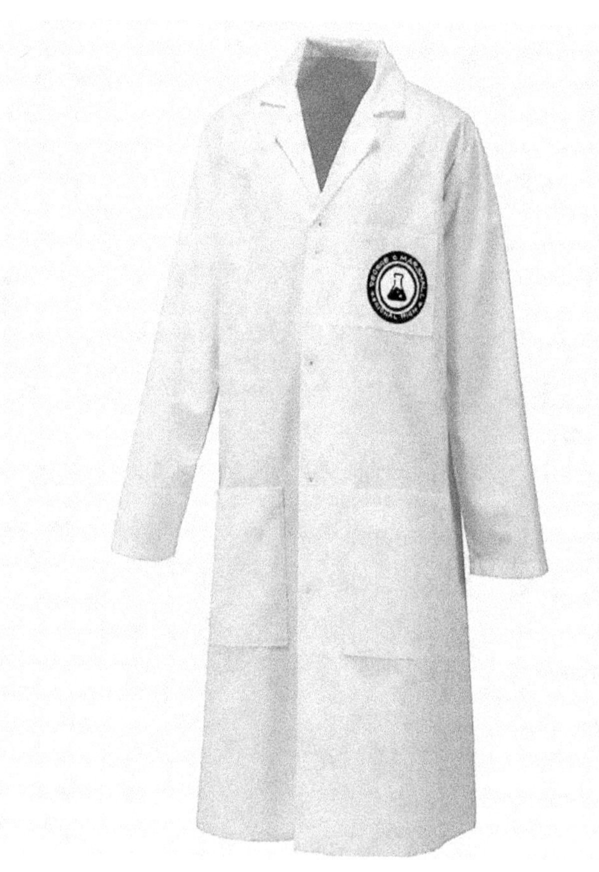

Chapter Sixty-Seven
And Your Bird Can Sing

"You might have warned me." She doesn't look at me. We don't say anything more in the taxi, but we hear sirens as we leave. Unaware of anything, Bullet Head drives us back to Jill's house, dropping Tom off at his place on the way. I can't let this sit, so I go into Jill's houseto decompress. Toweling off, we both plop down, like spent soaked dish rags, in her conversation pit. Chuk disappears into the kitchen. In whispers we talk.

"What just happened? Is your bird broken?"

"My bird?"

"You know, that thing you use to talk and sing. You knew about the tattoo and didn't tell me. We might have done it a little differently, you know? You just don't get me, do you?"

"Rick, you can't say anything to anyone about dad."

"Of course. A map, a tattoo, your dad. What else are you keeping from me? You hiding Nuclear weapons?"

She doesn't answer. Okay, so, I ask, "I wonder if my dad knows?

"My dad doesn't know I know. What does it matter? It's all gone now." She buries her head in her hands. Her body trembles. There are more spies around here per capita than I realized. But that's not the biggest problem right now.

"Jill, it's okay. We may still have a chance. Tigran is not a typical Muslim name, I checked."

"So?" she mumbles through her fingers over her face.

"I think he's Armenian. That means he's Christian. If he is dead, and if he were Muslim, he would be heading for the cemetery tomorrow

or the next day. They don't fool around with mortuaries and embalming." She sits up.

"How do you know this?"

"My piano teacher's father died last month. They mourned him that next day with him laid out in her home, the day after he died. Then off he went to be buried. She didn't even cancel my lesson."

"With him still in the house?"

"Yeah. There he was, in the living room. She should have had me play Beethoven, like 'Moonlight Sonata' or something sad, but there I was playing lite and happy Chopin. I think she needed cheering up."

"That must have been awkward. How does that help us?"

"We may have a short piece of time. Otherwise, your inheritance will be buried with him. That tattoo was not anywhere visible. So, thisis going to get pretty heavy and hairy. Why a tattoo? Your grandfather have a secret admiration of pirates?"

"It's just consistent for him. I guess he wanted Tigran to initially help, or he wouldn't have involved him. He counted him as a trustworthy partner. Besides, grandfather loved adventure and mystery. So, why not?"

"Tigran said something about a family?"

"Yeah, but I don't know them."

"I don't know how we'll ever get close to him, but if he is dead, we have to try. I think I know a way to find out. My dad has contacts."

The next morning, I am clever to explain to dad that I need information about a death at *Gölbaşı* Park the night before. I tell him I need to do a cultural report about Turkish burial customs, quick. He

knows just who to ask on his staff. I have the information when he gets home that afternoon. I phone Jill right away.

Jill: Dead? Really? Did it say how?

Me: They think a blown artery in his head. But they must investigate. It's called an autopsy.

Jill: Ewww. You mean they have to cut him open? That's awful.

Me: That's done by government officials, doctors. So, we have a window of time, especially because they suspect 'foul' play may be the cause.

Jill: Us? Oh dear. I don't suppose it could have been a YoYo burst to his head? That would just kill Tom, so to speak.

Me: I don't think Tom got that close to his head. But the report said three foreign teens were with him at the time of death.

There is silence on the phone for a few beats.

Jill: I think they call it murder in the second degree.

Me: Oh, don't go all **deli** on me. We didn't do it. I hope. We've got to get to him before it's too late. He's at a government morgue in Çankaya.

Jill: What? You're proposing wanted fugitives show up at a government facility?

Me: Maybe we can pose as relatives. You and me. We're family.

Jill: Not yet, we're not.

Me: Wow where did that come from?

Jill: Your wishful thinking. I know what you mean but, I don't exactly look Armenian, and your Turkish isn't good enough.

Me: Well, then Danger 9b will go to my plan b. Can you wiggle two lab coats out of Mr. T's class tomorrow?

Jill: Probably. Whyyy . . . wait. I get it. This is probably harder than saying we're family.

Me: What choice do we have? We're interns, baby. Medical school interns.

Jill: You'll do this for me? It's so risky. I mean, we must be on someone's watch list.

Me: Yeah. There's just one thing I need you to do.

Jill: Anything.

Me: Talk me out of it, will ya?

We had a full schedule of school to endure the next day. It was maddening. I was waiting for the start bell, sitting in Mr. Tollet'sscience class. My mind wanders. I stare at the ring that I got while in Istanbul. Yeah. I did it. I had the measurements for Jill's finger at the time, but I just didn't have the nerve to go ahead with hers. I only got one for me. It's actually four rings in all. They are all looped together.I take it off and it falls apart.

"You know how to put that together?" Tom asks.

"Yeah. Several ways. Beat my brother's record of eighteen seconds by nine seconds."

"Those are Harem rings. You were going to get one for Jill? Aren't you the forward one?"

"What do you mean?"

"Only the Sultan had these for his *harem* wives."

"I thought a *harem* were just dancers?"

"They probably did a lot of that too. If a wife ever wanted to be unfaithful, she would have to take off the ring and it would fall apart. Only the Sultan knew how to put them together. So, he would know she had been unfaithful and, eeeeeeeek." He makes a cutting motion with a

sound effect across his neck. "She doesn't have to 'think' about her status anymore."

"No. It's a puzzle or friendship ring."

"That's just a marketing trick. If you believe it, fine. But she will think if far more formal than you."

"You mean marriage?'

"No dummy but it is like asking to go steady, be exclusive, part of your *harem*. You did have Nora for a time."

"Oh, come on. That thing a year ago didn't count. Please don't say anything to Jill."

"It's not me you have to worry about. Mitch probably already has."

"Well then, good thing I didn't buy her one."

The bell rings, and off we go on some lectures and assignments. At the end of the class, Jill tells me to go distract Mr. T. I ask him a distracting question, 'What's the difference between an aneurism and a heart attack' which is largely on my mind. He takes it for legitimate, and I see her snatch two lab coats and walk out the door. I have to endure the answer.

So, between the second and third periods, Jill taps me on the shoulder and says, "I forgot to show you. Look what I got."

She holds up her finger, and there is a gorgeous gold version of the puzzle ring. Oh no! What is she showing this to me for? Where's Mitch? Has he struck again? This should have been mine!

"Daddy got this for me at the Adana *Carsi*," (sharchi – or bazar).

Daddy? Oh, Colonel MacGregor. Okay, whewww, I am safe.

"Wow, it's like mine – only – curvy. Do you want me to show you how to put it together?"

"I'm not supposed to take it off."

I pause and look at her. Does she know about the legend? Yes. .

"Just kidding, Sultan."

"I set a new record the other day. Nine seconds."

When she takes it off, it falls into, not four, but five connected circles.

"Whoa. I did not expect this. Five gold rings?" I really am puzzled.

"I told you I was not supposed to take it off. Now what?"

I have to show her the slower way to put it together, any excuse to touch. As always, her hands are so delicate. I make sure it takes a longer time to teach her. After we get it back together, I slip it on her fourth finger. Weird. It doesn't fit right. I skip the middle finger and try it on the index finger. Not perfect, but a slightly better fit.

"Hmmm," she says. "That was nice. 15 – love."

And off she goes to fourth period math. I follow and must admit, stare at her the whole class. She occasionally turns around and flashes her ring at me. Now, what am I supposed to think? What does it mean? I am soooo confused. Girls! Ahhhhrrrggg. She is supposed to be all worried about tonight's adventure. What's up with all this ring stuff?

Chapter Sixty-Eight
Here, There, And Everywhere

Marley was dead. There is no doubt about that.

Old Marley was as dead as a doornail.

and

You killed her? Hail Dorothy! The Wicked Witch is dead!

Death was running through my head – thanks to Dickens' 'A Christmas Carol' and Frank Baum's 'Oz' books. Death was all I could think about. But we were after more than the witch's broomstick. Tigran didn't seem fully evil, but there is this issue of a knife. He never held it – just his goon partner did. And he is still out there, somewhere. This is not cool. What is on his body that we desperately need? And why did Professor Fontaine ever think this is a great idea? Whatever it is, it's at this morgue.

Bullet Head waits as I go to get Jill at her door.

"All set?"

"I don't want to talk right now."

"You okay?"

"Just shush. This is hard enough. We don't want Mr. Bey to know anything."

"You got the lab coats?"

"Don't boss me," clutching her stuffed new purse. "What do you think?"

"Man, what's up with you tonight? You're here, there, and everywhere." I put my mouth on pause as I open her door to the taxi. I remain paused and perplexed as I tell Bullet Head where to drop us, only a block away, so as not to raise suspicion.

"This Christian wedding place, *Tebrikler!* How you say, congratulations?"

Jill gives me an icy glare. I shiver it's so arctic.

"You funny man, Bey *effendi*," I tell him. We get out and I mutter, "Don't give me that look. I didn't know. Our target is up the street."

It's around five in the afternoon but at this time of year, it's almost dark. We figure they should still be open.

"Front door, back door, spy man?"

"Always the back door. Get your coat on, almost a doctor."

"Quit bossing me. This is all your idea."

The place is not particularly appealing. It's a grey two-story structure and rather industrial. Maybe it was a warehouse in another life? At the thick metal door, we pause. At this back entrance, a dim overhead light, surrounded by a protective metal frame, beats down on us. It feels like a flashing neon sign saying, 'look at these two fools trying to break into a morgue'. We'd rather be in the dark. A Turkish crescent-moon flag emblem on the door stares at us, emblazoned with Turkish writing. My nose twitches, reminding me of the fragrance ofthe indoor cages at the zoo that haven't been cleaned yet. I look at her. She has covered her hair with a surgeon's cap. She hands me one.

"Got these while I was in the hospital."

"They look goofy."

"Just do it," she snaps.

"Boy, you are really cranky today."

"Why shouldn't I be? I'm a wanted fugitive. Do it. I don't want to be recognized."

"It's working. Who are you and what have you done with Buce?" She glares at me. "Do you have a pin in your purse?"

"Of course. An artist is always prepared." She starts to dig in her purse when her puzzle ring slips off her finger to the ground.

"Crap, it's come apart."

While she is distracted, I carefully try the door. It's unlocked. I say nothing.

"Here you go," she hands me a pen and throws her ring into her purse.

"What am I going to do with this? Write you a poem? A pin not a pen."

Her icy glare has now turned into a freeze ray.

"Ahh. Never mind. You keep it." She lets out an annoyed huff. I pull out my boy scout Swiss army knife, containing a small tool kit. 'Be prepared' is the scout motto. The tool kit has all these gadgets that unfold in it. I pull down a screwdriver and insert it in the lock, then I push open the door. She may as well have put her finger into a power socket. She's that amazed.

"How did you do that, Danger 9b?"

"Well, I do know a bit of magic, remember? And my training," I am quick to add.

"Ok. For that bit of magical surgery, I guess I'll have to call you Dr. Marshall. That's a good name for tonight."

Our coats have the school emblem and name, 'George C. Marshall' as the most prominent words. 'Regional High School' is lower case in a smaller font below the logo.

"Thank you, also Dr. Marshall. We must be Mister and Missus?"

"You have a one-track mind. You know? Besides, aren't you engaged to Athena? It's brother and sister Marshall, thank you." I wave her through the open door.

"After you, sister Dr. Marshall," I whisper. "I am officially disengaged."

She scowls at me again as she enters. How many different faces can she show me?

We actually hold hands, not because she wants to. I can feel her shudder and my legs tremble with each step. This is more or less a cave, minus the bats. Even our voices bounce around the walls. The place drips with dankness and mold. With no windows, the only light is one overhead light shining dimly, way down one end of the hall.

"It really smells awful in here," Jill whispers.

"Yeah. I think we should just follow the smell."

"It's everywhere."

"What do you propose?"

"This way," she says. I've learned not to argue. You won't win and you just annoy. Ha. I solved another puzzle piece, *no use arguing, girls are always right.*

We go up the dark half of the hall. Why not? I like walking where I can't see, the floors are sticky and wet and smells worse than rancid peanut butter. So stimulating. Yeah, right. We shuffle carefully along, side by side. The hallway turns and there is another light, way down the hall. It doesn't help us much.

"Oh, dear," Jill mumbles.

"What?"

"Let's try this door," she tells me.

"No go, it's locked."

"I have to find a bathroom."

"Really? Now? You can't hold it?"

"I have to have a bathroom."

"How am I supposed to find a bathroom in this place? It's not like there is a flashing sign, 'Banyo this way' around here. It would probably be a one holer in the floor anyway."

"Rick. I HAVE to find a bathroom."

"Girls. Arggh. OK."

I try the very next door. It opens. "It's a broom closet."

"That will do."

"What?" And she disappears behind the door.

Is there even a light in there? A slight glow comes from under the door. I don't ask any more questions. Girls' puzzle piece number five or six discovered? *Don't contradict a formed decision.* I'm on a roll.

I slink down to a dry spot on the floor with my back to the wall. While I sit in the gloom, I hear something a few feet across the hall. It doesn't take me long to identify the sound – it's little feet – a rat, to be precise. It scurries right across my feet. I jump up and try not to yell in my disgust. Then a second rat follows right behind. Their curly tails look a lot like long rope nooses making my neck tighten at the thought. The glow from under the broom closet gives me just enough light to seetheir antics. The first rodent turns to the second and squeaks loudly. Strangely, I think I speak mouse. I whisper out loud to the dawdler,

"Don't say anything, buddy. You just got squeaked a piece of the puzzle. 'ladies are always right'. One down for you, nine-hundred and ninety-nine to go."

They scurry on. Do I knock on the door and tell her to hurry? Then I think better of it. It's a broom closet. I don't want to think about what's going on inside. She finally creeks open the door.

"What was that?" I foolishly ask.

"Really? You ask this? Well, it wasn't my appendix pathetic DOCTOR Marshal," is the snarky reply. "And I didn't appreciate you counting."

"I wasn't counting about… " I quickly remember the just acquired rule. "Sorry, I was just consoling a troubled brother."

"What?"

"Never mind. Let's keep going."

We shuffle our way past until we see a faint light coming from a narrow set of stairs going up.

"Voices!" Jill whispers. "Upstairs."

"Quick!"

We panic and blast past, trying to find a hiding spot. We push on the first door we come to and luckily scurry through and close the door, hoping we haven't attracted attention. It's completely dark, it smells like our science room after we dissected our frogs, minus the 'ewwwws' from a lot of mouths. Have we stepped into a freezer? I reach blindly for the wall until I find the light switch.

"Aaaah!" Jill calls out. (At least, it wasn't a 'ewwww'.)

There before us are several metal tables, each draped in a sheet covering bodies.

"Bingo. How fortuitous. Three bodies in cold storage."

"They look so still, so sad."

"Come on, we'll start with the closest one."

As we gingerly step forward, Jill asks,

"Do they do all that Egyptian embalming stuff here?"

"They don't drain the blood or guts here – I think that's done at the mortuary. How do I know?"

"Are they all really naked?"

"Well, I suppose their bare feet sticking out one end gives you the best clue."

"You don't have to be snarky about it. It's gross to think they have to cut people open here to find out what happened." She stops. "I can't do this."

"Jill, we can't back out now. Just, hold your nose."

"What about my eyes?"

There are large glass bottles on the edge of the wall stained with who knows what. Various instruments are arrayed on a separate table. Some things hang on the wall – saws! The stench penetrates to my core.My legs change from a tremor to a wobble.

"You take the first table. I'll check-out the next."

She gets to the first table and slowly, reluctantly, lifts the covering.

"Oh, dear. She's a lady."

"And this is not our guy, either."

"Eye-ther," she corrects me.

There is only one table left. We both move to the table and lift the covering off the head. A guy with no nose. Neither one of us have ever seen a dead body before. It starts to dawn on us what we're doing. I'm surprised neither one of us has tossed our cookies yet. I shakily start to remove the covering.

"Wait. Gross. I don't want to see this."

"How are you going to draw the clue if you don't see it, Miss Artist, sister Dr. Marshall?"

"You look for it first then. I'll turn away."

"Ok. I get it. Here we go. Batter up. I'm pulling down the sheet to his waist. Hmmm. No markings. I'm now pulling the covering back up."

"Really? Do you have to give a baseball play-by-play description, Mr. All-Star?"

"I'm trying to distract my stomach. I've barely rounded first base."

"Well, say hi to 'who' and get on with it."

"I am now approaching second base, pulling cover up from his feet to his thighs."

"I get it. 'What' is on second, anything? "

"Well, that's a bummer."

"You there already?"

"No, I'm still on second and you know 'what' is not on second. I have to take a detour to the pitcher's mound. Unfortunately, I have to look at his private area."

"Oh gross. Hurry up."

I uncover those parts.

"OK."

"What? Don't tell me you found something there?"

"OK. I won't tell you. But something is not what we're looking for. We're heading to I don't know."

"Really? You going to keep this up? Okay, third base. What's on third base?"

"No, what is on…

"Would you stop!"

"You're going to have to help me turn him over."

"Are you nuts? We can't do that! This man is an army tank."

"Just grab his arm on your side. I'll get the other and we'll sit him up then."

"I'm not going to touch him!"

"Then use your coat over your hands. There is no other way."

"Well then, cover him up."

"I'm doing the best I can, sister Doctor Marshall. Now grab his arm and pull."

As we strain to bend him up, she grunts, "I don't think this is what grandfather intended."

"Yeah? Well, tell him that next time you see him."

She grunts some more along with me. "You don't have to be snooty about it."

It's a task, but we fold him up into a sitting position, and I quickly look.

"Ha! There is something! It's on his lower back on your side."

"What do you see?"

"Weird letters. I'll bet they're Armenian letters. You're going to have to draw it."

"Can you keep him steady?"

"Go for it."

Ever hug a giant teddy bear? Correction, a dead hairy not fuzzy-cute teddy bear. Ok, this is sort of like that only this one lives in Polar Regions, is stuffed with rocks, and is not cuddly. While I try to balance the guy to keep him upright, Jill pulls out her pad and pen from her purse and gets to work.

His back is fuzzy and freezing, like tough leather, clammy and stiff. My cheek is sucked into his skin as if I were a fly struggling on a sticky trap. My nose is shmushed up against his hairy back. A detailed aroma/picture of a well-used gym shoe, one worn with no socks, invades my shnoz. And there, right at that nose level, is a soft imprint in his skin. The letters are backwards, but unmistakable, 'Stratocaster'.I hear a faint guitar riff in my mind. My nose starts to drip. It's all I can do to keep from losing it into one of those jars by the wall. I'd have to let go to do this. It would not be pretty.

"Hurry up. I can't hold him much longer."

"Arrrrggg"

It was a distinctive groan.

"I know you're having a hard time, but do you have to groan?" she says.

"I thought it was you."

"Ohhhhhoooo."

Another moan.

The sheet on the first table starts to waver.

"She's moving!" Jill shrieks. I let go my grip. Tigran crashes down on the table. Jill stumbles back against the wall in shock and knocks over a couple of the glass jars that crack, break and scatter across the floor with a tremendous crash.

"Jill! Are you alright?"

She gets up and yells,

"There's stuff leaking all over me."

"We've got to get out of here."

We both crash through the door, and head down the hall. As we pass the stairs, I stop, and she runs into me.

"Wait! We have to tell someone."

I pull her to the stairs.

"Are you crazy?"

"Yes."

We go up the stairs, yelling at the top of our lungs.

"She's alive. Somebody! She's alive."

A man has already come out of an office, and we frantically point downstairs.

"The lady! *Hanim, Hanim.* The lady!"

Another man and a woman appear out of some doors, very confused, and start to yell at us. We crash through the front doors and madly head to the street. We had no arrangements to meet Bullet Head. We're on our own. We duck around and down beside the only parked car on the very narrow street.

"Jill, There's an ashak cart that just passed us."

We rise up from the side of the car and see two surprised men in suits staring at us from the front seat.

"Run for it!" she yells.

We make a dash for the cart. What's good is that it has a covering over the top to hide under. What's bad is that it has a covering over the top for a reason. We don't pause to consider our options. We pull a

perfect dual Jillian maneuver, then haul ourselves up and under the cover. Now, there are only certain ashak carts that are predominant in the early evening after the day's traffic of horses and donkeys. Yes, we got it. We're on it and in it.

"Is anyone following us?"

"Not that I can tell."

Jill pulls herself out of a pile of goo with gobs and goop stuck to her wild red weavings. Her surgeon's cap is stuck in a wet pile.

"You like my new hair-doo?"

"Crap yeah! And I thought the morgue was smelling bad."

I brush what I can from my hands and arms and peek out from under the cover to check the street.

"That sedan is trying to make a U-turn!" Our cart suddenly stops. The driver gets out to shovel. Jill throws back the front cover and scrambles to the driver's seat.

"Hut, Hut" she yells and cracks the whip. This ashak must be related to our camel 'cause he was off like a shot. I hear a lot of Turkish screaming coming from our ditched driver.

"What are you doing?" I yell.

"The car. Is it following us?" Still, under the cover, I lift it up, then throw it off.

"Yes!"

Jill cracks the whip and slaps the reins on one side to turn a corner. We're making a mad dash to a heavily traveled intersection just ahead. I crawl through the muck to behind the driver's seat and peer ahead.

"You have to stop! The traffic officer in the intersection is facing you!"

Yeah. He's a Turkish style 'red stop light'.

"I can't. We can't. Got to plow through."

A few cars slam on their breaks. The traffic officer is going to bust an artery blowing his whistle at us. We blast through as the stopped cars and carts jam up the intersection.

"Where is the Sedan?"

"He's trapped behind the cars."

She quickly turns the cart up the next street and pulls to a stop.

"Run!"

We scramble off. I do my best to keep up with Jill. We collapse into some soft bushes in a small park a couple of blocks up the street. After we catch our breath a little, we start to wipe off what we can.

"What was that?" I ask.

"One murder and one resurrection. Does that make us even?"

"Yeah. And so gnarly. Where did you learn to drive an ashak cart?"

"I told you. I am an equestrian."

"Yeah, but that was on the back of a horse."

"Well, this time I was in back of an ass."

"After all this, did you get it?"

"What do you think? *Da, Spasibo. Evet, Oui, Ja, Si,* Crap Yeah."

Chapter Sixty-Nine
Hello, Goodbye

The phone rings pretty close to bedtime.

Jill: It's me. You okay?

Rick: I don't know. It depends on which Jill is asking.

Jill: It's me.

Rick: Are you the Jill that says high when I say low or the Jill that says goodbye when I say hello?

Jill: Alright. I deserve that one.

Rick: I brushed off as best I could before I got home and started the wash. You know I do my own wash.

Jill: I remember. Did you turn the crank 50 times there, washer woman?

Rick: You know, this time I may have come close. But my brother still smelled something. So, you heard my new name.

Jill: Yeah. My brother Jaque used to call me lots of names.

Rick: What about you?

Jill: Oh, I used the hose in the garden to wash off and threw my clothes in the garbage.

Rick: You walked into the house naked? With your guards around?

Jill: They don't hang around the back garden, silly. Yeah. You missed me, brother Dr. Marshall.

Rick: Probably a good thing. Aaaah... I mean. Not that what you have isn't good. I mean, it would not have been good to see that. I mean, it would have been good – just – not... ahhhh.

She giggles.

Jill: I get it. Relax. Listen. What do we do next?

Rick: Draw me a copy of your art, and I'll see what I can find out.

Chapter Seventy
I'm Looking Through You

It's chemistry week in science class. We don't want to be in school this day, but we have little choice. We are learning about the element chart, valences, atoms, electrons, protons, neutrons, looking through the whole nine beginning yards.

So, this day in class our science/chemistry teacher, *'Dirty Water'* himself (our codename for him), Mr. Tollet, calls on me.

Now, with a name like Tollet, it is only one letter away from something that smelled as bad as a certain *ashak* cart. You don't want to 'mess' around with his name. You have to tread very carefully in class not to raise the snickers and giggles. Mr. Toilet, I mean, Tollet didnot tolerate snickers. So, he calls on me.

"Mr. Foster?"

I stand at the side of my desk and say,

"Yes, Sir, Mr. T." That is a safe reply. This is what you do in a military-run school – some of the time. It's tough to say 'Tollet' and not slip up just a little. Then you are in real trouble, with a capital "T," and that stands for toilet, whoops. Don't giggle. He continues,

"Answer me this. What is the valence and element for the chemical number 16 on the Periodic Table signified by the letter 'S'?"

Oh no. I am not great at on-the-spot stuff like this. I am looking around the room. The periodic table, with maybe the answer, is on a big chart behind me. I don't dare turn around.

"Yes, Sir. This might be . . .

"Might be?" he booms.

"No, Sir. I mean, yes, Sir. 'S'? Oooo. That is stinky Sulphur!" The class giggles. He does not.

"And the valence?" he presses.

"That would be… a…

Jill whispers out to me, "fifteen."

"It's fifteen - love. I mean the valence of Sulphur is…"

Girls, scores, and love mess with your head. The class laughs. Not good.

"Fifteen?" he booms. The largest is eight. Where do you get fifteen?"

Jill has set me up for that one and I went with it. I give her a quizzical look and she just grins that tease face she does so well.

"Yes, Sir. I… I… I… think it… is really two."

"Correct. Thank you. Now – let's talk more about valence. Valence has to do with what chemicals can combine with each other." Mr. Tollet gets on to the subject of how certain chemicals just will not join together, no matter how hard you try. He states,

"Some chemicals are incompatible."

I sure know Sulphur itself is incompatible – with my nose. But, somehow, that day's lecture sticks with Jill in other ways. I do not see where this is heading until too late.

If there is anyway Jill can re-think our relationship, chemistry class does not help. There is a song, first recorded in 1951, by a terrific black

American singer named Nat King Cole called, 'Unforgettable'. It is still popular now, more than ten years later. Jill knows it. The next day she sings it to me as, "In-com-pat-ible, that's what we are."

'What?' I'm thinking. Then she adds,

"Like two beautiful elements, with different valances that just cannot live together, that's what we are."

What? Am I Sulphur now? I smell my armpits. Not too bad. Has the morgue penetrated my skin? I think things are pretty good, but there was her party. After that she has been so back and forth, up and down.Is this just how girls are?

Wait. Is that puzzle piece number six, seven or eight? *Flaky*? Don't say that out loud.

I know, it is the Harem ring thing. This is messing her up, I am thinking. No, maybe it's the flag football game. Maybe she is blaming me for Mitch's embarrassment? But what about our recent adventures? Doesn't that help? And what is the '15-love' all about? I thought it was 15 - love, you know – letting her get ahead again and me in love trying to catch up – playing the good game.

"Rick. You are a good person. But you and I are so different. We still have much to do. We're still friends."

"Is this you, Jill? I thought I knew you. Where did you go? You don't <u>look</u> different."

"Well, I've changed. It's now just someone else. Someone else who 'gets' me. He and I, well, he <u>is</u> 'Un-for-get-able'," she sings again.

She couldn't possibly mean M-i-t-c-h? Nooooo!

"Your Swiss miss will tell you his initials are BB," she says with such a lite air about her.

"BB?" I repeat, then think.

No. No. No. No. NO!! This is impossible. Billy B!!!?? This cannot be Billy B. NO. I refuse to believe it.

"He's so sweet and lovable and non-judgmental and cute. He'sreally come into his own. Yes, he gave me his mom's puzzle ring. Isn't that adorable?"

What? How can this be? Colonel MacGregor did not give her the ring? It's from Billy B.? I mean, his mom? Something is really out of whack. Ahhhhhhh! Oooo. Treachery, sneaky, BB Brutus has stabbed me in the back. I expected something like this from Mitch but from BB?

"You two bore me. I can predict your every move. Billy B.? He's fresh."

Fresh? All this work, toil, adventure, and subterfuge on my part and I am not fresh? She doesn't even know I'm a fake and she still rejects me? How can this happen? How can he be 'un-for-get-able'? The 'Whizzer of All' really zinged one off this time. He pulled a true-blue, new 'Billy-ian Maneuver' on us. Why does Jill tease me with the ring and then turn so badly on me? My head is tumbling and mixing like clothes in a dryer, and we don't even have one.

When I tell Mitch, he just stares at me. Then shrugs.

"Come on. She is just toying with us. Right?" I say.

I'm going to guess at another part of the girl puzzle. I've picked the pieces up from the floor and found one more - girls are completely,

unmistakably *irrational*. If I had not discovered this, it might make me not like her, I reason to myself. Don't be fooled. She is trying to figure out how this boy stuff works as well. She hasn't solved the whole puzzle yet. I don't know how this boy stuff works either, and I am one. Just a dumb teen-ager. I may as well throw all the puzzle pieces up in the air and see where they land. It can't be worse than what I have. I don't judge her too harshly. I try not to be deterred. However, being a teen is not easy – does it get worse as you get older?

I hate chemistry.

RIVALRY BOX SCORE:

All is chaos. I think the periodic tables have turned. Mitch and I are not even on the chart. Girls – Boys that's Valance 15

Episode Twelve

Reassignment

Chapter Seventy-One
Her Majesty

"Her Royal Highness, Jill MacGregor, is a pretty nice girl, but she's got way too much to say. Yeah, she's a nice girl, but she wavers from day to day. I'd like to say that I love her a lot, but all I get is an earful of whine, whine, whine." I chant to Tom.

"Yeah, it's a bummer." He admits.

"This makes no sense, Jill. It's the wrong time to be throwing this at us," I say as I catch her at lunch time. "You're doing this right in the middle of all that's going on? I just don't get it."

"You're free now. Your mind doesn't have to be distracted anymore. You can focus better on our problem. That seems good to me. Besides, I'm a wanted woman, a criminal."

"Oh, give me a break. No one is looking for us."

"Oh? Look at this."

It's the just published local edition of the English-speaking newspaper, 'The Stars and Stripes'. She points to the headlines of an article on the second page.

Mystery Teen Doctors Bring Woman Back from the Dead.

Then right on the next page.

Authorities are looking for three teens believed to be foreigners, involved in a suspicious death.

"Okay, so you are a dangerous fugitive. But look at it this way, the medical profession will take you in with arms wide open for your resurrection skills."

"Yeah? From prison?"

"Maybe they will put us in adjoining cells."

"Well, anyway, you can now go back to Nora."

I pause. "Oh. You know about that. Hey. That was long before you arrived. It wasn't me. She was trying to get to Mitch, and I was overwhelmed uh… at her charms, for <u>one</u> day. She wanted me to be part of her flock."

"So, go. Fly away home to Nora, little birdie. Go sing for her."

"Can we just drop that for now? She's history." She goes quiet, looks away in thought.

"What I'm worried about is that Tigran was not the only one with information about my father. I suspect this new 'boss' is the real culprit. What is he going to do about it? I mean, they could frame us for murder and get my father arrested. He hasn't diplomatic immunity."

As always, the bell rings.

"We can't afford to send any notes about this. I'll catch up with you later," she concludes.

It's now a three-way contest and we have no way to compete with Billy B. I mean, what is there to compete against? Nothing makes sense anymore. I hear some guys mature late in life. I have doubts about Billy B. The butterfly in Jill is really bookin'. She's flitting about in overdrive, or should I say, in frenzied flight.

"All I can say is, you're going to have to come up with another mission or something new to distract her," Tom advises me.

On the way to the bus, I catch up with Jill, and we finally talk again.

"Did you get the translation back yet?" she asks.

"No. They are having a hard time deciphering your art."

"Well, it's not like I had a lot of time or under the best of circumstances."

"Yeah? I was also doing the best I could *directly under* those 'circumstances' and holding tight. I'll let you know when I know."

We are two mountain goats, one head butt, and our horns are locked.

Chapter Seventy-Two
I'll Cry Instead

I've got plenty of reasons to be sad. Billy B. just took the only flame I had. I just have lost my way. Please dad, lock me up today. But he won't, so I'll die instead. Especially when dad sits the family down for a big announcement this night.

"Your mother and I have decided that we're going back home at the end of the school year. We think you all ought to know. I promised her I would retire after this assignment."

"What? We can't do that," I protest. "I just can't, I can't."

I do not want to leave. These are the best days of my whole life. I will stay to the end, but saying goodbye is going to be tough. There is so much to resolve. I feel I have to get in a new assignment.

As far as the missions go, funny, no one has ever questioned me with any kind of doubt except Mitch. That's understandable.

What is there left to do? Time is short. What difference will it make?

COMMUNICATIONS REPORT TO ALL AGENTS: (edited for spelling by Tom)

1) *We have snooped on the Soviet powers by infiltrating the Russian embassy. Almost disaster. Nothing much to report. No bugs planted.*

2) *The high-rise building was cleared of any listening devices. The Airmen could safely move in now. Be nice to the Kapici.*

3) *By my additional report, we have 'wasted' a couple of agents tailing us on our way to Istanbul. Nothing was revealed. Found I liked Turkish watermelon.*

4) *The market was cleared, and suspicious counter agents were tailed. New silk disguises were purchased. Bookmark not revealing. Shoeshine boy now longing for Spanish love poems.*

5) *My cross-border reconnaissance, the infiltration into Syria, Lebanon and Jordon was inconclusive. My toe was not shot off. I will always have Beirut.*

6) *New assignment coming soon. That is all.*

We get to school the next day and Jill runs up to me, breathless. "Rick, this was pinned to my locker. They're getting far too close." She gives me the note to read.

To Jill MacGregor:

Your last chance is fast approaching to produce the real map. The dig is certainly not in Beirut. Strange, but the unsuccessful military coup is looking for a scapegoat. It's so easy to place the CIA's Colonel MacGregor right in the middle of the plot. I think the penalty is a firing squad? And oh, there is the matter of a certain murder. I have a witness. I can conveniently make him disappear. You decide. Here is a pay-phone number to call to make our meeting arrangements. You must call at 5pm today, exactly.

"Here we go again. Jill, you've known all along where the tomb is?"

"No. I know where the secret archeological dig was. There is no guarantee that it is the right place. And it will cost a huge amount of money to start it up again."

"You didn't trust me enough to share this?"

"I didn't feel I needed to burden you or put you in danger by telling you."

"Is there anyone else who could possibly know? Your mom or dad?"

"No one." Then she pauses. "Possibly my brother."

"Jaque?"

"Grandfather never approved of my mom's previous marriage. I think my brother resented our closeness. I told you, he didn't get much inheritance. I guess he suspects I did."

"I thought he was away to a university or something."

"So did I."

The bell rings but we don't care about being late to history. She keeps going.

"Even if we want to go to the authorities, and they had the capability to know where this number is, which I doubt, there is no time. I can't do that."

"This guy is dead serious."

"What choice do we have?"

"It's pretty easy in my book. Let them have whatever it is they want. You think they, whoever it is, has the resources you talk about? Besides, you have all the clues, he does not."

"I have no assurance all this would go away if I did give it up. Do you really think they can frame my father for all that mess?"

"Jill, maybe it's true? Either way, we have to play by their rules."

"Can you get off at my stop today? We can make the call from the pay phone near my place. I can't risk a call from home."

"Sure."

We pile a full ten minutes late into history. We know it will cost us detention later in the week.

Chapter Seventy-Three
You've Got to Hide Your Love Away

I guess she's gone, in one sense. How can I go on? I'm feeling so small. This is maddening. I have to suppress every feeling I have, tuck it way down inside. Just got to hide it away. But she needs me.

It's 3:30 by the time we get to Jill's house. We plop down in the conversation pit, knowing we need to be cautious about what we say out loud.

"Here's what my dad's translators gave me."

Actually, it was Salpi, my downstairs friend, daughter of our *kapaci,* who did the work for me. I show Jill the paper with her drawing and my scribbles, pronouncing what Salpi said to me out loud.

"The symbols say either Ne-pi or Na-fi. That's it."

She didn't correct my 'either', so I know she was nervous.

"What in the world does that mean?"

"What are you two whispering about so carefully?" Mrs. Macgregor breaks in.

"Oh, hi Mrs. MacGregor. Jill is teaching me some French."

"*Excellente.* Here's some *baklava* I made for you. – Greek style, not Turkish." That was my favorite – very flakey and not as sweet or covered in honey.

"You're the best, mom. Rick and I are stepping out for a walk. Be back soon."

We get a block or so away when I ask.

"So. This map. What is it?"

"You know grandfather. This one is also burned onto leather with far more detail. Most scholars think Alexander's tomb is somewhere under his city of Alexandria."

"In Egypt, yeah. But he founded a bunch of cities called Alexandria or some derivation of his name. Any of them could have significance. I wrote you from Iskenderun, remember? Turkish derivation for Alexander."

"Grandfather thought Alexander wanted a more symbolic place. A place dedicated for one who would rule the world."

"And that would be?"

"Let's leave it at that."

"Oh. Ok. I assume you made a copy of this map somewhere?"

"What do you think?"

"OK." I know I have to tread carefully now. "One thing we haven't thought about is how did Tigran know about the 'Whirling Dervish' clue? How is that possible? It was in the note from your executor. That's inside information."

"Tigran didn't exactly say '<u>turn</u> the Whirling Dervish' did he? I don't think he knew. He was toying with us."

We walk a little further. It's 4:45.

"Won't Billy B. wonder where you are today?"

"Oh. Well, maybe he…" She doesn't finish.

Two police cars pull up on either side of us and blare their sirens.

Turkish officers open their doors. We don't give them time to tell us want they want.

"Run!" Jill screams. I follow. "We've got to make the call." She knows this neighborhood and we duck up the alley right behind us.

They shout. One starts to run after us. I see two other figures in suits running well behind the police. I'm not the greatest runner and Jill knows this, so we cut though gates, over hedges down other alley ways,back track, and weave some more. We hide briefly in a shed. It's 4:55.

"There is another payphone just a block away. It's in an enclosed booth. That should help us."

We make our way behind homes and apartment buildings, then come up a back alley to the booth. It's a tight fit, but we both squeezein and shut the glass door. She dials the number. It's 5:00.

"Well, Miss MacGregor. I can see you've come to your senses".

"Just get to the point."

"Ooo. Touchee."

Jill puts her hand over the microphone end and whispers to me,

"It sounds like a 'she' and has good English. She must be American, but her voice sounds fake, put-on, disguised."

Jill's lips are as close to mine as can be. It's torture of the first degree. She stares at me with a blank expression, then talks back intothe phone. I can hear the person's voice but not as clearly.

"Yeah. Very touchy. You could say that. Jaque. is that you?" "Hmm.

An interesting supposition. Just know I will be following you. Don't try to hide. I will know if you have told anyone but your friend. Make sure you always have the map in your possession. I will contact you at the most convenient time for me, maybe not for you. Should you not have it, the consequences may not be to your liking. Comprende? COMPRENDE?"

"Yes."

The line then goes dead. Jill holds the phone receiver for a moment and stares at me again.

"It's done. She or whatever that was sounded strangely familiar. How is it they know so much about me? My brother sometimes teased me in a girl's voice."

Through the frosted glass of the booth, I see two figures quickly approaching. We can't get the door open quick enough as two black suited men confront us.

"Step out you two," one commands.

Police cars then pull up again, sirens wailing.

Chapter Seventy-Four
I Don't Want to Spoil the Party

The room is starkly furnished.

"The Ruskies had a better confinement for us," Jill mutters.

"Do you want to spoil this party and just go?"

"I'd hate our disappointment to show. So yeah, let's go."

"They don't even have the courtesy of a W.C."

We laugh nervously. Luckily, we are still together, all alone.

"Is this a Turkish police or security office or something else?"

"Who knows? Watch out, could be a two-way mirror and microphones as well."

"I prefer the Bolshevik ambience." She makes me smile.

"Why do we keep meeting like this?" Now it is her turn to laugh. I love it, but my leg is bouncing up and down faster than a pogo stick, as if I were giving a piano concert, keeping beat with my anxiety.

"Don't say anything more," putting my finger to my lips.

The door opens and in walks my father, followed by Colonel MacGregor and his booming voice.

"Now where are these two little felons?"

Why was he joking? I stood up and greeted my dad. Jill hugged her father.

"We have some explaining to do," dad tells us.

"And maybe some apologizing," adds the Colonel.

"You have explaining?" Jill says.

Jill and I look at each other. It's a draw whose face is more contorted.

It was a long conversation.

They had their coffee and we had hot milk.

"So, let me get this straight in my head," I say. "There are no charges against us?"

"Not now. With this Tigran fellow officially found to have had a massive heart attack, you were not to blame," the Colonel explains. "We had to do some careful diplomacy there. As to what you were doing at *Gölbaşı* park, well, that's a different matter." He raises his eyebrows at his daughter.

"And these suit guys that seemed to show up at odd times, they were your agents?" I ask, dumbfounded, to my dad.

"Well, it depends on who you saw. After your stunt at the embassy, the Russians really thought you two were on our payroll,' dad explains. "I mean, who would suspect two teens? Of course, we would not officially do that, but they thought we did. They followed you all the way to Beirut. So, we used you. Colonel MacGregor graciously agreed to our little ruse."

"With great reluctance, I might add," the Colonel informs us. "Mr. Foster assured me his agents would be there to handle any danger. Given the importance of ah…ah… his mission, I thought it necessary.".

"There was a lot of chatter, as they say, that we picked up after your embassy break-in. It was an opportunity too good to pass up. They put so much attention on following you, tailing you wherever you went, it left me and my team with the ability to do our work in far more freedom," dad adds. "Let me also say, it was important. You'll never know how much the distraction you provided helped a great cause."

"This is lunacy. Dad, all this time? Putting us together. You weren't worried?" Jill interjects.

"Yes. Maybe it was asking a lot of the two or you," the Colonel replies. "I knew of Rick's reputation, and he didn't disappoint."

"That's the nature of this business and this time we're in. It turned out better than you can imagine," my dad adds.

"You might have told us about it," she grumbles.

"We didn't think that would work. You came up with enough distractions on your own. That antennae on the high-rise building was pure gold. Our two guys figured out what you were up to on the roof. That's all I can say."

That perks Jill up a bit. I had to think quickly and add, "Yeah, thanks for the assignments." It is clear to me, neither one of them know of my own subterfuge.

"But you're free now. They figured it out. You won't have any more tails on you – us or them."

My cover is not blown. I look legit by accident. I'm as shocked as a starving deer who has stumbled into a garden of tulips.

"Father, you have been part of this?" Jill asks in earnest.

"No, my dear. My assignment is… different."

Jill looks at me. By her quivering lip, I can see this does nothing to calm her.

Chapter Seventy-Five
You Can't Do That

Dear Danger 9b,

This is torture. When will she strike and how? Dad doesn't know the danger he is in, or maybe he does? What do I do? We desperately need another mission. I feel more comfortable and safer keeping the team together. I need distraction. Besides, school is getting too boring, but I can't say that about the rest of our lives! Still, I'm restless. I can't stand the thought of you leaving. Sorry for the BB news. It took me by surprise as well. Don't worry, he who has no code name won't be part of our missions. He knows nothing. We need to come up with a name for him so I can talk about it. What do you suggest? I mean – for a mission?

Yours, Fortuna

Under the circumstance, she sounds normal. Jill, you can't do this. I mean, how does she do this? I thought she'd let me down and leave me flat. Wait a minute. I've already placed these two closely aligned puzzle pieces, *irrational* and *flaky*. Nothing new here. We have no choice but to move ahead, and, who knows, maybe there is still a chance for me. I so desperately want to give Billy B. a code name. It's on the tip of my tongue. You can't do that, Rick. I just can't. Jill would think less of me. So – OK, we'll let it whiz by for now.

"She wants another mission?" Tom asks. "Maybe your brief brush with felony and incarceration have dislodged her brain."

"I still need one," I reply.

"Ok. How about bringing down communication lines to critical enemy structures? Does that sound good?"

"Whoa. That actually sounds authentic."

"We might really need to stretch for this one. Remember those wires we thought were power lines?"

"Oh, yeah. The ones that run along the stone walls we played on. That was BJE."

"BJE?"

"I told you, 'Before the Jillian era.' But I remember. We really thought they were electric wires. Dumb. Wasn't that back in eighth grade? It is next to the orchards. They must have been ten feet high."

"We jumped off the wall and just swung."

"I think the wall runs alongside the buildings that got shot up in the coup attempt."

"All the better. Makes them seem like a target."

"But I think it's too much, too risky."

"Hold on. If we make them <u>think</u> the wires are electric, we can make it an adventure, and they'll all bomb out on the dangerous part. We won't have to go through with it."

"Alright, we'll tell them the wires are communication lines the Russians are using to spy on the Turks. Let's take them down. Okay. That might work."

It's dumb, daring, risky, and isolated. No one is in these orchards this time of year. Just what we need.

"We can tell them with all of us together jumping hard. We can get some good swings and crash the poles in."

"Just make it sound natural that these are *electrical* wires. Drive it home so they will object. It will make us look good when we let the others bomb out."

"I like it," Tom agrees, "make it sound natural. Got it."

When we first discovered this activity, being twelve, thinking these were electrical wires, I told Tom, "Just don't let your feet touch the ground while you're hanging. Don't want to bring home Tom and Rick sausages to our moms."

"Ha. We'll be like birds on a wire. They never get zapped. Just don't whiz on them."

"Now, why would I do that?' I remember asking him.

Then he tells me, "my grandpa has a ranch in Wyoming. He keeps his cattle corralled by an electric fence in some places. I got to foolin' around, chasing cows and stuff when I had to relieve myself."

"Got to admit, we men have it easier that way." I'm sure that part of the boy puzzle would not occur to Jill. Then Tom added,

"Yeah. But who wants to turn your hose just on the grass? I was being generous and aimed also at the fence. I'm surprised I still have a hose."

"Oh yeah, the flaming hose story! Wow, Tom, I still can't believe the charge went up your…?

"Better believe it."

"Do you remember what we concluded?" Together we repeat,

"Let's not whiz on these wires."

I now get to thinking about that. This is it. Stupid, daring but safe. I don't have anything else. It will work for what we need. (Not the whizzing part.) It's so close to my leaving. I go for broke.

"Hey guys, I have been assigned another mission." Unfortunately, Mitch and Nora get wind of it.

"We have communication lines to worry about. We must bring down some important communication lines to privent, ... a... a... communication."

I communicated with my team.

I need you to bring flashlights and good, ruber-sold, sturdy shoes – not sandals.

With the Boy Scout motto, 'Be Prepared.' I know that climbing up walls will require good footing. We're pretty sure they will all complain once they think these are power lines. We won't have to jump. I didn't want the girls to get hurt.

We meet at the corner of my street, next to Bullet Head's taxi stand. It's dusk a few nights later. Tom, Will, Marie, and Dave are with us. Mitch shows up in flip-flop-type sandals. But Nora is Nora. She wears a tight-fitting t-shirt and capri pants, and sensible shoes. She knows not to be too provocative in public here.

"Mitch, what are you doing? You're going to slow us all up with those. You can't climb with sandals and keep them on." I protest.

"They are made of rubber. Are we going to be climbing? On what? These are flip-flops, not sandals."

It didn't make any sense to argue.

"Ok. It's your funeral." I proclaim ominously. He stares at me with a lost glare. I can only guess what is going through his head. Sabotage?

"Mitch, Mitch! Are you coming?" Jill's voice shakes him from his thoughts. She looks just fabulous. She has on this black fuzzy hat thing

that comes over her ears but lets her ridiculously gorgeous red hair fall to her shoulders. She wears an alluring black turtleneck sweater. Did I say I love turtleneck sweaters on girls? Another boy puzzle solved –*the allure of the turtleneck*. I got a better handle on 'measurements' now. I think I could win this time.

"*Merhaba, Bay Effendi*," Jill says to old Bullet Head. (Hello, Master Bay. She uses a more formal greeting.) Bay is his last name which actually means 'Mister' in Turkish, so he is really Mister Mister or Mister Master. That's just what it is.

"*İyi aksamlar, küçük hanim,*" good evening to you, little girl," he replies, "and hello to you, little Foster Bay," he calls me in his broken English.

We know him well by this time. I am not thrilled by the label 'little.' I am on an important mission. Don't diminish my reputation, please. Then we march off. It's about a ten-minute walk.

"I love night-time missions," Jill exclaims. "There is just a certain mystique about it."

"Mystique? Oh, good, I thought you said mistake. I hope not," pipes in Dave.

"Yeah, dark gives us good cover. You look fantastic," I try to flatter. "Black is what to wear at night – you blend in," as we both look at Mitch in his white shorts, yellow sweatshirt, and rainbow flip-flops. Nora is right in front of him, in perfect eyeshot. No Billy B. So far, this is going my way.

I lead them through the orchard the long way just to stretch things out. The newly blooming trees look like sparklers against the mostly cloudy and darkening sky. I point out the various government buildings that surround the orchards.

"It's too dark to count the bullet holes blasted by the jets in the coup, but they're still there." We plod along.

"You see that building there? That's the defense ministry building. The Soviets are spying on the Turks through their own communication lines." The wall is just behind. Our target, the 'comm' lines, runs alongside the wall. I lead them on. "Here. This is where we scale the wall."

Jill is right behind me. I reach back to help pull her up. She looks like a cat burglar, whatever that is, a cat on a wall that burgles stuff. Very cute. Mitch pushes Nora up by her rear. I hear no complaints. He then struggles a bit on the way up. The others follow.

"Watch your step up here. It's about thirty yards to the right spot."

We have to carefully make our way along the top of the wall for a short distance before we get to the lines. It's fully dark by this time. Think about this picture - lines of flashlights dancing along a high wall at night with eight kids stealthily tiptoeing along its top – except Mitch. His flip-flops are doing just that – flip-flopping.

"Can you quiet your feet there, *amigo*?" I plead.

We reach the middle of the wires between two poles.

"OK. Stop. This is it, the weakest point."

"Where are your wire cutters, chief?" Mitch asks.

"You all are my wire cutters. I figure, if we all hang on the wires, a little like upside-down birds, and swing long enough, it should beenough to collapse these poles and bring the lines down." As planned, waving his flashlight along the lines, Tom pipes in,

"Whoa, look at that. Are those what I think they are? PzzzzPzzzz. Wait a minute, boss. Aren't these *power* lines?" He says with some weird emphasis. "We can't jump onto *power* lines. We'll all, you know, pzzzzzz, fry." Is he calling this a 'natural' way to scare them?

"Good thinking, Tom," Dave says, "we should just abort and call it a night."

"Hold on," Jill now interrupts, shining her flashlight on the poles. "The black boxes on the lines are signal repeaters. These are phone lines, not electrical."

We're busted. So, I try to cover. "Oh. They must have moved the power lines."

"Good," Will says. "I'm up for full destruction."

"They sure appear to carry power," Dave tells us.

"No. They're telephone lines." Jill states firmly.

Now I'm cooked. And then it occurs to me that this will be damaging the property of someone. What's happening to my morals? This is pure shenanigans. I've done art theft (a ceramic hand), come close to murder, lurked around with dead people, impersonated a medical professional, been hauled in by secret police, and continue to make them all think I am some kind of government agent. Why start behaving myself now? Thinking straight and petty crime do not go handin hand.

"That's right," I agree. "Right. Telephone lines, repeaters, communication, yes." I'm committed now. "OK."

"Let's time our jump together. A good three or four swings should bring them down." Jill assures us.

"Put your flashlights in your pockets," I ask.

Now, it's really dark. Just the stars are out, dotted between moving clouds. It's tough to see the wires just a jump away from us.

With an energetic voice, Jill says, "On the count of three, we jump and start swinging. Ready?"

"Must I?" Dave whines.

"One, Two, THREEE."

That's right, we all jump. But Nora just stays on the wall. We hit the wires pretty much the same time. Wump, wump, wump is the sound of our hands grabbing on. Makes jumping off stairwells seem easy. We hear the creaking and squeaking of the poles immediately. The lines start to sag, and the poles lean toward us. Where's Mitch? He's nowhereto be found until we hear the moaning.

"Mitch! Mitch! What's the matter?" Jill yells out. We're all hanging from the wire, and his voice is below us in the dark. Then a large bang assaults us. Sparks fly up by one of the poles. Oh no. I thought these were phone lines.

"Mitch!" Nora screams and shuffles her way back to the start of the wall. The poles are swaying, the lines are lowering, and more sparks fly up.

"Down here. Oww. I slipped."

"Abort. Abort." I yell out. Everyone drops to the ground.

Jill is the first to let go. By this time, the wires are really sagging, only leaving our feet maybe a yard off the ground.

BOOM! BANG. A series of noisy explosions ring out. I mean cherry bomb loud, followed by long flashes of light. Did someone just get electrocuted?

"Where is everyone?" Tom yells out.

Are these really power lines? Bursts of light and hot streamers from bottle rockets and fireworks of all sorts, including strings of firecrackers, explode around us and in the near distance. The heat from all manner of crackling and eruptions of fire and smoke envelop us, along with stinking fumes from smoke bombs. I'd seen plenty of World War Two movies, and now we are in one. It feels like a coup is starting up again.

"What in the world?" I yell.

The grass catches on fire in places. It's crazy. The waft of burning grass and exploding gunpowder fill up the air. I thought we had fried somebody, but this was like the attack at the roller rink. Not again? BAM goes another explosion. Pop, pop. Pop, BAM. It continues.

Mitch is up against the wall where he fell. We only see him when the strobes of explosions go off, but Nora yells out.

"E's head and feet - all wet *mit bloot*." Even sandals might have been better than those flip-flops. Jill joins Nora at his side, pawing all over him. "Vat's happening! Mitch!"

"Oh! My darling. Oh. Let's get some help," Jill yells.

We all gather around and determine we better get him home as soon as we can.

"You guys, get out of here. Get help. Get Bullet Head."

Tom and the others start to run back to the taxi corner to escape the growing fire and get a car. It's some distance away, where Bullet Head will still be on duty, leaving Jill, Nora, and me alone with a bleeding Mitch. Another explosion behind me erupts, and I turn to look. Two figures appear, clouded by a white and orange fog among the chaos. They move toward us like phantoms in a misty graveyard. I realize we are in trouble again. Could it be?

The larger figure emerges from the smoke. It can't be. The plumes of light reflecting off the fog tell us that it is. It <u>is</u> him!

"Tigran!!" Jill screams.

He just stands there, motionless.

Episode Thirteen

The End of It

416

Chapter Seventy-Six
Magical Mystery Tour

"How can this be? There's no way!" I yell.

Mitch just groans. "Nora, go. Get help."

"*Ja.* I get help fast," she scrambles away.

The phantom figure seems to float towards Jill. Fumes are choking us, swirling all around, they roll up, coming to take us away.

"Run, Jill!" I scream. She can't seem to get her footing as she rises, and Tigran grabs her hair. I rush to help, but the second figure stops me with a spurting flare in his hand, thrusting it towards my face. I fall and he restrains me.

Tigran now grabs Jill in a choke hold and his goon holds the flare close to my head.

A break in the smoke and the glow from the flare lets the visage of the figure become clear.

It's Tigran with a full nose.

"Tigran, how is this…? Leave her alone! This is not going to help you." I yell.

"I am Gor. You kill my brother." The phantom barks.

"You cheat us." I recognize the other voice – Tigran's knife- wielding goon.

"No, no. It was an accident," I yell.

From his massive body emerges a volcanic eruption, "Arrgggg. You lie!"

He pulls Jill's hair up higher and closes his vicegrip on her neck even tighter. I hear her gasping. I struggle as best I can to get free, but the goon waves the burning flare closer to my head.

It occurs to me; we won't have anyone coming to our rescue. No one follows us anymore.

"You have map, girl?'

"Yes," she gasps out.

"*Nerede?*"

"I <u>have</u> it."

Then he suddenly lets her go.

"Boss says, this was test. Next time, no test."

And they quickly disappear.

What? Fire burns around us in the grass. Together we stagger back to Mitch and drag him along the wall toward safer ground.

"We've got to get you up," I say. Jill and I get on both sides of him and quickly walk him out of the orchard to the street where we meet a frantic Nora. We hear fire sirens in the distance as Bullet Head pulls up and the others pile out. Bullet Head throws a blanket on the back seat. We get Mitch into the Taxi and Jill and I get in with him.

Jill gives Bullet Head Mitch's address.

"Shouldn't we take him to the military hospital.?" I ask.

"I'm not that bad. Take me home," he mutters. He seems kinda out of it, but off we go.

"Yeah, let's take him home first and let his folks decide what to do. Mitch, it doesn't look too bad," Jill assures him. He perks up a little on the way there. I would too with Jill caressing my head and holding <u>my</u> hand. I should be looking for fake blood, he is so sneaky. But he has a nasty cut on his head and scraped up feet and legs - this is not faking.

I guess his mom is a nurse of some kind. She takes him in to fix him up. They seem to know Jill. She wants to stay and doesn't live far away. They say they will get her home.

So, it is me and Bullet Head. His prayer beads swing wildly and clank against his rear-view mirror mimicking what's happening in my head. What was that? Why? Why do that and release us? These guys are serious arsonists. Makes Jill's embassy stunt seem like a firefly in a bottle.

"*Çok teşekkürler ederim, effendi*" I tell him.

"You make big trouble this night. *Çök fena.* Very bad. Why you like this girl? She not so *tatlı*, pretty."

"*Hiyir. Çok tatlı* to me. You're not using your best eyes. But, I'm not sure she likes me."

He takes down his prayer beads, "Then I ask Allah many times for new eyes - for you. But you know why this problem? You no bring cat for good luck."

Chapter Seventy-Seven
You Never Give Me Your Money

There is a flurry of notes passed the next day in class. In our first period, it was:

Athena,

What happened last night? Is Diablo Ok? I heard he was attacked by Chuk? Did he pull her tail? Fortuna better hide him next time Diablois over. Is that right?

Princess

How Chuk got into the conversation, I don't know. I have no idea how this started. Maybe I said something about Bullet Head's comment to me? I might just give money for what happens next. It's like reading the comics page, or, as the Brits say, the funny paper, and then it all breaks down. Our second period saw these passed in the halls:

Mr. Mustang,

What's this? I hear that Fortuna and Diablo got hung last night and then attacked an orchard. Were you there? Is that why a certain person was not in our first period?

Jane

Spitball,

What are we going to tell everyone about Diablo? I don't know how a cat got into the stories. Let's say some of us hung out together last night? Don't say anything else.

Athena

Danger 9b,

So, I think we just better say we were playing 'kick the can' last night. That would be a good thing to say at this point. Diablo just misjudged kicking the can. That work? Hey, by the way, did you know you can't hunt camels in Arizona?

Spitball

Sarge,

Princess said that Jane said she thought she heard Athena say something like Fortuna and Danger 9b were chasing a green-eyed cat with a flaming tail last night. The taxi driver thought it was Kemal Ataturk? You know that's not what happened. What's up? That was after Diablo was hurt. I saw the guys. Scary. Who were they? As you asked, I won't talk about them or the wall.

Lolita

Lolita is Nora or course. And here the folklore sprang up again. Many Turks still held onto the return of Ataturk as a green-eyed cat. So – cats roamed freely throughout Ankara, unharmed, just in case it could be him.

It was a shortened day so there was no lunch or third or fourth period. By fifth period, it had exploded.

Jane,

I didn't get any reply from Athena. Someone got hung? Fortuna is crying in class. I can't get to her. She is across the room. I hear there was someone who got stuck on a power line last night during a camel hunt? How in the world? And someone got caught smoking! I'm so worried. Was it Spitball?

Princess

Danger 9b,

Do you know what is wrong with Fortuna? Why is she crying? Why were those guys setting fires? Wild. What happened after you dropped her off at Diablo's? Did your taxi hit a cat last night?

Sarge

Athena,

I was not crying in class! What are they saying? I had something fly into my eye that really hurt. I miss not having lunch. I should have brought my rare PBJ for a snack, but I would be afraid I would be mobbed! I think I need some more excitement.

Fortuna

By the sixth period, it was completely out of hand.

Jane,

Diablo got kicked last night in the can by a guy who thought he was Kemal Ataturk? That must have hurt badly. Someone set a cat's tail on fire and exploded a taxi. I heard the sirens. Is that why he is not here?

Princess

Mr. Mustang

What is the kick the can story? Nobody told me. How did Chuk get into the Taxi with Danger 9b? Nothing is making sense. Was her bum clogged again?

Athena

Yeah. Jill had that skill – fixing Chuk's constipation.

Princess

Fortuna has had to do that before. Actually, Diablo I hear, got kicked in the bum by the Taxi driver because he called Ataturk a bald green-eyed camel. Or maybe the taxi driver got bald from the grassfire?

Jane

Sarge,

These half days are terrible. I can't get any straight news. There was a huge puff of smoke and a loud bang near Fortuna's desk last period. It really spooked Dirty Water. Danger 9b apologized for the disruption. Dirty Water sent him to the principal's office. Is that why Fortuna was crying?

Lolita

Athena,

I hope this gets to you. I had to slip it to Spitball on my way to the principle's orifice. I guess you know Fortuna did her chewing gum wraper routine in Mr. T's class. That's about the only class she hasn't done it in. I couldn't let her take the hit. Please tell her not to wory! I'm good at tall tails.

Danger 9b

It all got straightened out after school, without me. I was in the principal's office until he could see me. We stuck with the 'kick the can' excuse for our activities the night before. That is a game you played outdoors at night. What excuse do I come up with for the class disruption? I didn't have to.

"I don't know what's going on with you," Major Bean tells me. "But Mr. Tenney says you have detention now, so off you go. We'll talk tomorrow."

Oh. That's right. Jill and I got detention for coming in so late last week. He's finally getting around to it. She meets me outside the office, and we head for the history classroom.

"Why do you keep doing this for me? It would just go away if you said nothing."

"Then the whole class would be punished. No matter. Ready for some boring history assignment?"

"This is so silly. We're two of his best history students."

Tenney barely looks up as we enter class.

"Your assignments are on the table there." We pick them up and head to our desks.

I open the folder and freeze. It's a picture of the statue of Alexander the Great, with a scribbled caption, 'Where is he?' And a quote from the French philosopher Voltaire, *History is the story of all the world's crime.*

I look over at Jill. She flashes the same picture at me. The storage room doors then open, and two large familiar figures emerge. I jump up to run, but they move to block the classroom door. Tenney speaks up,

"Yes. The story of all the world's crime and oh how they love to pay for a piece of it."

Weird. He has no lisp. I move over to be with Jill.

"Or should I say, as Santayana, 'History is a pack of lies told about events that never happened by people who weren't there.' " But this time, the voice is weirder, like a fake woman's voice I'd heard before.

"It's her! Him?" Jill whispers loudly.

"Your grandfather was a fool. He did not deserve such a find. I authenticated the marble statue of Alexander. I knew it was real. I have the credentials. Your grandfather only dabbled."

He is coming toward us with an ancient sword we've never seen.

"Over the centuries, people wrote about rulers taking mementos from Alexander's tomb. Cleopatra was said to have taken gold to finance her losing war with Rome."

He now slides a desk in front of the both of us and sits on it, hovering with his weapon menacingly, waving it over our heads.

"Have any idea what this is?"

I gulp, "a Sultan's scimitar."

"It is whatever I say it is. And collectors will battle for it. Alexander's, Phillip's, Caesar's, Sultan's. Doesn't matter."

"You really think you can get away with executing us in our own history class?"

He laughs.

"Oh. That's not going to be necessary. And not my style. Far too messy and against the law."

Somehow this does not comfort me. He sounds so completely different.

"I was a CIA consultant at one point. That's how I know so much about Colonel MacGregor and their ways. They didn't appreciate my contributions."

"I'm not sure they are using Scimitars these days," I say boldly. "You

would be surprised." He rises from his desk, still admiring his artifact.

"So, you might understand now when I say how easy it will be for me to blame your father in the failed coup."

"He had nothing to do with it," Jill says tensely.

"Probably not. But it won't be hard to help the Russians implicate him pretty deeply. They're willing to talk." He turns to me. "And it won't be hard to include the sly Mr. Foster in the whole affair. I know about him as well. Oh, by the way, you all talk far too much and leave quite a trail of notes, Danger 9b and Fortuna. Whirling Dervish? You'reMr. H? He couldn't stop talking about it. Thanks for that one."

"You think you can walk out of here innocent and not have the school, the military, whoever take justice on you?" I blurt out.

"Oh. Well, what have I done? Nothing you can prove. I easily got this teaching position to you pathetic creatures so I could monitor you, Miss MacGregor, and your family. I don't think I want to endure such misery any longer."

He quickly turns and points his weapon right at Jill.

"So, let's get this over with. The map please." He clicks his tongue and gestures for Gor to get the purse. He dumps it out on a desk. This is my second glance of what is inside the forbidden zone. Perhaps another piece of the puzzle I can place? I ignore my curiosity for now. There is obviously nothing that resembles a map.

"So. You're up to your tricks."

"You think I would carry it in there?" She carefully lifts her shirt to reveal a piece of leather wrapped around her middle.

"Rick, help me. Hold this end."

I grab the part she holds out and she stands and spins slowly, unraveling the precious treasure. I gather it up. I look at her, she nods, then I reluctantly turn and hand it to Mr. Tenney.

"My, my, Professor Fontaine was quite thorough."

As if he were a Roman general admiring the latest spoils from his conquests, he practically drools over the piece for only a moment when his countenance turns really sour.

"This is incomplete."

"I have given you the map, as I promised. Just not the final piece."

"I'm not here to play games." He clicks, tilts his head quickly and Gor moves behind Jill and grabs her head. The other goon steps away from the door to cover me.

"I'll give you the rest, at some point, under my conditions."

"And what are they and why would I do that?"

"If what you say is true, you could still lie about my father and Mr. Foster after you have everything. Give us time to get him transferred to a different assignment. When he is safely out of your treachery, we'll re-negotiate."

"Hmmm. Interesting proposition." He opens a little black box from his desk and pulls out a syringe and bottle of liquid. "I might have a counter proposition for you," he warns, "I have some options here. You know I have contacts watching your brother. If you don't come through, I can make life… a… difficult for him and for you."

Just then, someone comes crashing through the door. It's Nora. "Mr.

Tenney, dis is not *rechts,* not fair. Dis make-up test is *zwei* times long as real one."

Tenney's goons pull rags out of their pants and pretend to dust off the desks. Tenney stashes the needle and whirls around to confront her with his sword.

"Extra points. Miss Schulte. What era is this artifact from?"

The lisp is back.

She looks around with a blank stare.

"Vat are you two doing here? Do not tell me, detention?" And she laughs hysterically. "Oh, *di* high *und* mighty *fraulein,* Jill MacGregor

is in *haft,* detention," she continues with her chiding. "Do you vant little Nora to give answers? *Ja?* You…"

"Enough!" Tenney shouts. "All of you, out. I've had enough of children. I'll be in touch, Miss. MacGregor."

Chapter Seventy-Eight
Helter, Skelter

"Is it true? You guys are leaving next week?" John asks after coming down our building stairs to see me.

"Maybe another American family will move in. Thanks for all the games."

"You didn't let me win enough times. I will be spoiled."

"Oh, by the way. You can pull up my walky-talky into your room – it's yours for the next guy. You want it?" I know what he is going to reply. Mom is in earshot. "Don't say it! Don't say it!"

"Heck yeah. That would be cool."

I show up at Jill's at the appointed time. I feel like I'm on a ride, when I get to the bottom I go back to the top and slide down until I see her again, over and over. We are going to make another attempt at figuring out the clues. Her mom and dad are gone for the evening. So is Billy B., I assume. The conversation pit is my favorite place. Feels a little cruel right now. I suggest the table in the terrarium, her glass enclosed jungle of plants off the parlor. Surrounded by a forest of green is good, where my lion can disappear if I need to.

"Has the re-assignment come through yet?" I ask.

"They're working on it. I'm just glad they believed us."

"I can't stand the history substitute. Tenney, or whatever his real name is, at least knew his stuff. I guess they are pretty sure he's beat feet out of the country."

"Something tells me he has eyes on us, not just my brother."

"You still have your security men on the house?

"I never know. If so, its scaled back. I guess the alarm still works."

"Good to know. I should have brought my scimitar."

That brings the laugh I've missed for so long.

"I made a chart of the Armenian numbering system. We'll need it."

"So, let's analyze this. He sent us all the way to Beirut for what?" I ask.

"I already knew about the expedition. I think meeting the elders was just co-incidental."

1	2	3	4	5	6	7	8	9
Ա	Բ	Գ	Դ	Ե	Զ	Է	Ը	Թ

10	20	30	40	50	60	70	80	90
Ժ	Ի	Լ	Խ	Ծ	Կ	Հ	Ձ	Ղ

"Maybe. But what he did after was not, and Beirut just made it harder for anyone to put it together. His passion for rare things got him that first edition copy. He wanted us to know that."

"Okay. But I've leafed through it, again, with cotton gloves. We've been down that rabbit hole."

"Let's look at the Armenian writing from the castle. Weird that Tenney didn't know about this and yet gave us the pictures. He told us the inscriptions just talk about who re-built the tower and walls for the great King Het'um."

"That's not particularly helpful."

"Probably not. But there are the numbers also. I didn't get them translated."

"Let's dig into it. Here's the first two symbols." I compare the figures with my Armenian number chart. Their numeric system is completely foreign.

"It's a 'one' symbol combined with a 'ten.'"

"Okay. Eleven."

"Here's a single number 'nine' and a single digit 'six'."

"Now another 'ten' with a 'six', sixteen."

We get to a collection of eight different numbers. Jill writes them on different pieces of paper and spreads them out before us.

"Okay grandfather. Where are you leading us this time? Maybe we are looking at numbers telling us chapters and verses, like chaptereleven, verse six?"

"Of what? You have scores of books in your library. Most don't have a chapter/verse organization. Even the Bible didn't have chapters and verses until long after these numbers were inscribed. That wouldn'tmake sense."

"How did you pronounce the letters on Tigran's back?"

"It was either, I mean, either Ne-Pi or Na-Fi."

"That doesn't match any title I know of in our library. Could that be a chapter of something with verse numbers?"

"There are too many variables with these numbers."

"Okay. Save that for later. But maybe we better look at indexes or title pages."

"Ahh. Well, let's see. A chapter or a name within a book. Wait. Wait. Why didn't this hit me before? Go get that Book of Mormon."

She's back in a moment.

"This doesn't have chapters or verses."

"Yeah. Not until decades later." I carefully open the book, a collection of writings by different ancient American prophets. "Look. Look at this first book. 'Nephi'. Armenians might pronounce this as Ne-Fi or Na-Phi."

"With no chapters and verses, how does that help?"

"But there are original page numbers. So, let's look at just the pages. What was the first number?"

"Eleven"

"Turn to page eleven. It's clearly in the first book of 'Ne-fi.'"

She carefully flips to page eleven.

"Nothing special. No markings. Nothing here that wasn't put there by the original printer. Jill, is there any other way your grandfather communicated with you?"

"You know, grandfather used to write me letters partially in his own mixture of invisible ink."

"Why would he do that?"

"For fun, I guess."

We then hear some scratching coming from the kitchen.

"We're about to find out. Wait a sec." She holds up all her fingers and her thumb scrunched together, pointing upwards and thrusts it in my face.

"Oh, yeah, Beirut."

She goes to the kitchen. In a beat, she comes back with a salt container.

"Chuk was scratching to get out. Let's try this."

On page eleven, she shakes this fine salt over the page.

"Wait. This book is worth a fortune!" I blurt out.

"It won't hurt it."

She then rubs the salt off the page. We look again.

"Look! Something here!"

A few faint marks appear on the top paragraph by some of the words on the page.

"Here – by this word – 'inheritance'." We both look at each other.

"Here is another one – 'precious'."

We hear some more sounds from the kitchen.

"Does Chuk want in again?"

"Ok, I'll get her. Just keep going!"

I look at our numbers again. I go to page 13 and apply the salt.

"Treasury! He's marked the word, 'treasury'!" I yell out.

Jill hasn't come back, and I hear muffled sounds from the kitchen.

"Jill? You okay? Chuk giving you grief?"

Still nothing. I get up and head that direction.

"Jill?"

I round the corner into their spacious kitchen.

There is Jill, in a headlock by a towering figure with his huge hands covering her nose and mouth.

It's Gor, the spittin' image of his brother Tigran. I think fast. I talk calmly, slowly.

"Hey. Just take it easy. It's all cool. It's Gor, right? Can you let her go and we'll see what you want?"

"She rich girl. My brother dead for you. Boss gone. Family need money."

"Oh. Well. We can get you money. Many *lira. Inchpeses?*" I throw the only Armenian word I know on him.

"That said to girl. I not girl. *Inchpesek* to man."

"Oh, that's how you say it?"

Jill is starting to turn blue her eyes bulging in panic.

"How do you say, Hello?"

He finally relaxes his grip but keeps his hand on her mouth, her nose flails trying to get air.

"*Barev*"

"OK. *Barev Gor*, I have money in the library."

"*Yes. gumar unem . . *"

"No. I don't need to know how to say it." I gesture, "Come <u>with</u> ME to the Library. We have money there. Girl will show you. Can you let her go?"

"No, let go," He starts to drag Jill to follow me.

"You like to smoke? Yes? Jill likes 'LUCKY STRIKE'."

Her eyes go bigger. "I like 'WINSTON' better. We smoke IN THE LIBRARY?"

"I no smoke. Bad for body."

"Oh, these are good smokes."

I'm walking backwards, stumbling towards the library, waving for him to come with me.

"Library is where we keep much *lira,* high up on wall with our LUCKY STRIKES." He follows me, dragging Jill along.

"*Kankhik?*" He says.

"Yes, *kankhik,* that money? Yes, much *kankhik.*" He drags her the last bit through the door when Jill catapults her leg up and 'lucky strikes' the 'panic' alarm button on the wall. I reach over and pull her fencing sword off the wall and toss it to her free hand. I then do the bestI can at a pathetic 'Winston' workout. It's enough to cause him to release her and defend himself, which he does, by delivering a pretty good blow to my body. I reel backwards to the floor. He turns to find a sword staring at his nose.

"You make Gor very much anger now."

"Gor, Tigran was very good to my grandfather. Much help." Jill reasons.

"Professor not good for Tigran. Family very poor now." He steps forward and she makes a swipe at him. He stops. The sword has a blunt end which he readily sees.

"This not weapon," and he grabs the blade and yanks it out of her hand. Still on the floor, I swing my legs violently across and catch his feet, throwing him to the floor, eye to eye with me.

"Ahhhh," he yells and lunges for me, catching my shirt, pulls me up and tosses me backwards. He pulls his massive leg back to kick me when from behind, two men tackle him and a third has a gun drawn pointing at him.

"Please don't hurt him!" Jill pleads.

Chapter Seventy-Nine
Fixing a Hole

Dear Danger 9b,

Finally, mother is arranging a trust fund for Gor and Tigran's families. I think that is the right thing to do. Father leaves tomorrow for his new assignment in Germany. Mother and I will stay behind to the end of school and arrange to move our household effects. These last few days of school are precious. I've got some leaks to fix. I know you can help keep my mind from wondering. As you suggested, I am sending you the rest of the words I discovered in the text. They don't make sense. Can we give it one more chance together to figure this out?

Your Fortuna

So, Danger 9b is going to be reassigned stateside, Fortuna, to Germany. Bringing down comm lines was our last mission. Mitch was getting better, but there were many questions about that final night. Not sure what that was supposed to accomplish. With Tenney gone somewhere and his goons not in the picture, it won't be raining dread on us anytime soon. Jill will, no doubt, be hearing from him somehow. She's not too worried about it. It means I can peacefully say goodbye to Jill and all the others. This is the hardest for me. I don't want to be forgotten as I disappear from their presence.

I assembled my puzzled ring – the gang, at my house after our last day at school for goodbyes. Tom shows up looking like a blurry-eyed sheep that is about to get shorn. "Well, bub. The jig is up. You guys want to tell him now?"

"Tell me what? Isn't goodbye hard enough?"

"I'm shocked. It all turned out just fine. This has been so much fun," Will adds, "Trust me, only Mitch and Jill knew, we didn't until today."

"I didn't want them to say anything," Tom adds.

"Okay…," I get out, expecting the worst. "So, what's up?"

"We know you don't work for the OSI," Mitch whispers.

I turn to Tom with an open mouth.

"Wasn't me."

"What do you mean? Look at all we've done!" I am thinking the 'trustworthy' thing may be in deep doo doo. May as well be now.

"I started to figure that out after our first caper," Mitch continues. "Marie's dad works at the embassy. He told us the CIA just does not do that."

Do they know about Jill and our real work? I think this is Mitch's last desperate attempt to take me down.

I turn to Jill, "You believe me, don't you?"

"Yes, sweety. I did for a long time. But Mitch kept bringing up questions."

"Yeah. Why couldn't you aim a gun?" Mitch remembers from scout camp.

"Where was all your spy stuff?" Will adds.

"A fake badge would have helped," Tom says.

"Spies don't carry badges or kids, weapons. Come on." Marie tells them, trying her best to defend me.

"But my dad, he is really a…"

"Oh, we believe that part. Our lips are sealed!" Marie reassures me. Jill takes my hand tenderly.

"Rick, they don't know what I know," she gives me a good wink. "It seemed really important to you. I think you needed it. I think I really needed it. So, I kept it going. It was so much fun we didn't want to stop!

You turned out not to be so boring after all, Danger 9b, and so imaginative!"

"But you weren't hurt by my lie?"

"Not hurt. Thrilled. Finally, someone was playing my kind of baseball. And yes, I did believe. And then it didn't matter, you know. Mitch convinced me to keep it going, and I agreed."

I turn to Mitch with disbelief. "Really? You?" I am trying my best to look like a repentant thief.

"You knew, Mitch? That fooled me," says Tom.

"We didn't know until today," admits the rest of the gang. "We believed."

"You all stuck by me with all those shenanigans? Who would do that?" I turn to look again at Mitch. "You didn't tell them?" He looks down a bit, then directly at me.

"Nah. I owed you that much. It was just Jill and me. We didn't know Tom was helping. Jill was probably more gung-ho about keeping it going than I was. She brought up that Rufus dude again to me."

"Rufus gave the King of Syria some advice one time I thought was pretty good, among a bunch of other good things," Jill tells us.

"Rufus told him the most important thing in life was to be magnanimous, you know, noble, worthy," Mitch recounts.

Then Jill adds, "The King thought the wisdom was so valuable, he was going to bestow quite the wealth on Rufus. And the only payment Rufus asked for was that the King follow his advice."

Well, after all, Mitch followed the 'a scout is trustworthy and loyal' far better than me.

"I thought maybe my loyalty might give me back Jill. You saw where that went," his voice almost cracking.

"Oh, yeah. About that," Jill interrupts. "You two are a big pain in my… neck. You know? You became impossible. Always battling back and forth. I couldn't make up my mind. So, Marie solved the whole thing for me. She distracted Rick to her, Nora to Mitch, and suggestedI enlist Billy B. to help."

"Enlist?" Mitch and I say together.

"Yeah. In the Post Office. Remember, I chose him? I told him my plan, and he came up with the idea for the ring just to make it convincing. Isn't he clever? I gave him a big kiss."

"What? You mean you and Billy B. are not the real things?" I ask with huge relief and hope.

"Well, he is a good and loyal friend, and he is very sweet, with a certain charm. No. Not the real thing."

The rivalry is back on! I get this surge of adrenalin or something. But wait. It dawns on me the three of us will be in three different locations. It's an even playing field. Who is on first now?

I look around at the faces of truly great friends I will probably never see again. Tom, Will and Dave, Karin, Aisha, and Marie. Jill is crying. I still get one more night with her tomorrow, my last before leaving. I guess she is warming up. I think Marie may be the saddest of all. Was she really pretending to have that secret crush on me? I get a big wet one from her, followed by hugs from the girls. Then typical Tom pipes up,

"Hey guys, Did you know…?"

"Tom, not now!" Jill interrupts through her tears. Tom quietly says,

"Hey, Danger 9b, did you know… we're really going to miss you."

439

The next day I help finish packing up the apartment, and Bullet Head takes me over to Jill's house for our last evening together. The fire and the conversation pit are now back on. Mrs. MacGregor has made my favorite Greek baklava. It's so nice to be back by the fire, enjoying the company of my goddess.

"Let's get down to work," she says. "I've written the words down on slips of paper we can move around."

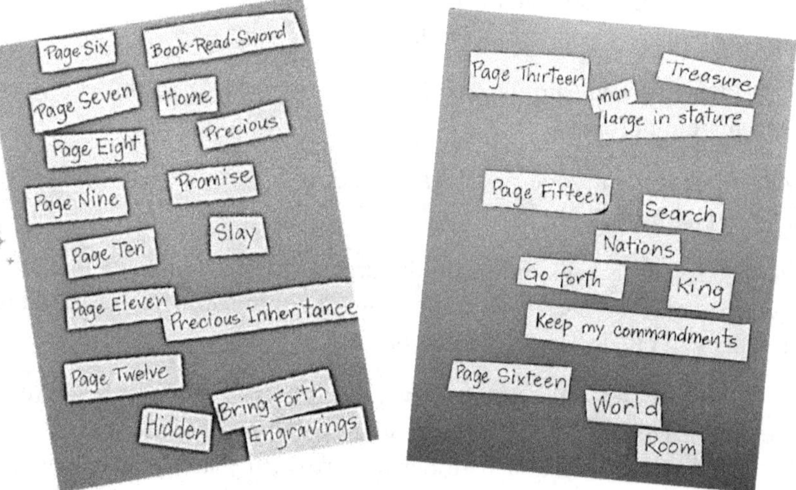

It's really unfair. Again, the scent of sweet jasmine and tulips is just overwhelming. I can hardly concentrate. The firelight is just enough to read the words, but oh, how it warms up her hair.

"Rick, I couldn't say it yesterday with everyone around. Our gang only knew a little about us. I did not share my problems with Mitch. Once you told me your secret, I hoped I had a comrade-in-arms, a real partner with whom I could share my burden. It turned out so right. What

can I say? Thank you. Thank you for all you did." She gives me a sweet kiss on the cheek. "You lie really well." It's a good start for the evening.

"Okay, Jameela. I'm on this. I think we both get the page eleven 'precious inheritance' reference. He's signaling to you."

"He is calling attention to a 'book.' We already have this book. It's a 'treasure,' and it's worth a lot if I sold it."

"That's way too obvious."

"'Room.' He is telling us there is a room."

"Page seven says 'home.'"

"Okay. Let's go in that direction."

We cut, rearrange the words and start to shuffle the papers around on the brass table in front of us.

"What 'room' in your 'home,'" I ask, "has a 'treasure' that is 'precious'?"

"And has a 'book' to 'read,'" she adds, "where you 'slay' something with the 'sword'?"

"Whoa. That's too close to home." She smiles at that. "Wait. Your 'treasure' trove of goodies in the library. It fits perfectly."

"Pick up the rest of the words, and let's go there."

We scramble to the library.

"Okay. What's left of the words? There are a lot of books here."

"'Search.'"

"Good. We'll look. For what?"

"'Slay' – 'king' – 'nations.'"

We walk down the two aisles, half the titles we can't read.

"'World' – 'engravings' – 'bring forth' – 'large in stature.'"

"Didn't you originally say, 'man' large in stature?"

"Oh. I must have cut that off."

I run my finger now across several of the more prominent books until I hit,

'*Historiae Alexeandri Magni*'.

"*Magni*. That's Latin for 'great.' It's been staring at us all this time. Who was the 'king,' who conquered the 'world' or 'nations,' and who was 'larger in stature' than Alexander the Great?"

"He was a short man."

"Oh. Good to know. But that's not what it means. Great and large, same difference."

I pull the book off the shelf. "This has to be it. The professor's passion."

We head back to the pit. We carefully leaf through the ancient volume.

"So, we still have 'hidden.' Yeah, that's for sure."

"'Engravings' and 'bring forth' and 'engravings' again."

'What about 'slay' and 'sword'?"

"That was to lead us to Alexander."

"But maybe those two words are not talking about Alexander, but the book, you know, 'engravings.' What about 'world'?"

"Didn't we just pass a drawing of their known world? Go back."

We flip back a few pages. There is the author's drawing of the world Alexander was slaying his way through. Nothing particular there.

"Throw some salt on it," I plead.

Nothing. It reveals nothing.

"We've come so close. Have we done all the words?"

"Wait. We've forgotten all about 'turn" and 'Whirling Dervish.' Did you do that math?"

"Why? It was a ridiculous number."

"Yeah. The whole thing makes me woozy just to think of it again."

"There is a picture of the dervish in the volume. Near the back."

"Really? No way. The inserted note here says this book was translated and printed around the third century. The sect of the whirling dervish wasn't formed until maybe a thousand years later. I remember that from Tenney's class. That doesn't make sense."

We excitedly turn to the picture.

"Jill, the page with the drawing seems slightly thicker than the rest."

She feels the page herself. Then looks at me.

"Hand me those scissors."

"What? You can't…" She reaches across and grabs them herself.

"I 'turn' to this page and will use my 'sword' to 'slay' and 'bring forth'…"

She carefully slices open the side of the drawing, "'engravings.'"

Two thinly packaged stamps fall out. She picks them up carefully.

"Philately – the study of stamps." She places them on the table and stares at them.

"We did it. <u>We</u> did it. You and me." She takes my hands in hers, then feels my puzzle ring. She slides it off my finger. It falls apart.

"I think I'll reveal another puzzle piece for you. *Boys* – we can't resist them."

She pushes me down on our cushioned couch and presses that luscious body across me and those uninhibited lips on mine. It's a celebration.

"I think this evens us up," she stammers and holds me for a long time. I will leave it at that. When we come up for air, she picks up my puzzle ring again and, in nine seconds, slips it assembled back on my finger.

"For now, this is just our secret."

"The stamps? Oh, yes. That too. My lips are sealed and well-polished, I might add."

Yes. That gets me my last laugh.

"I don't know what they are yet. But grandfather said to keep it to myself."

"You still have to figure out what 'go forth' and 'keep my commandments mean.

"Isn't it obvious? I have his legacy to follow."

Her grandfather clock strikes nine, the time when Bullet Head is to pick me up. Colonel and Mrs. MacGregor come downstairs.

"He's here, Rick. *Bon Voyage*, my dear," comes from a teary Mrs. MacGregor.

"You are an officer and a gentleman," the Colonel states, "but one crummy camel driver."

I take Jill's hands one last time. Her face is trembling. I reach up and push the sides of her mouth up.

"If you chance upon a frown," I begin, not sure how. "Do not let it stay, promptly turn it…" I can't finish. She gently pushes a pack of Juicy Fruit gum into my hands.

"Just in case," she whispers.

Güle, Güle Arkadaşer. Goodbye, my friends. Good and loyal friends never to be forgotten.

Epilogue
The End – She's Leaving Home

As was my habit, I secretly wrote a note with my name in a *flourish* along with my address and stuck it on Jill's piano (not under a rug), copying the first measure of her favorite tune, *"Claire de Lune."* Just my own special way of saying goodbye. I was here. Please don't forget me. It is an end. She'll always be in my dreams. I know the love I take with me is so much more than I can leave for her sake.

Even before Jill writes me, I get a note from Billy B. He says that he and Jill went searching for a beggar lady with a blue cane. Jill wanted him to make sure she got a five-lira coin dropped in front of her. And they were buying more fruit for various people at the Pazar from a particular vendor. We all change with time. Sometimes, that's what it takes – time.

I got this first letter from Jill two weeks after I got home.

My dearest Rick,

Grandfather somehow acquired two very rare stamps. The first is called the 'Sicilian Error of Colour' printed in 1859. Sit down. It is worth about two million dollars.

The second stamp is the 'Duloz Takse.' It was an Ottoman-era tax stamp from 1867. It's not valued as much as the Sicilian, but the national pride of Turkey gives it far greater interest for them. And the dig site is there.

How would you like to study Archeology with me here in Germany...? Brother Doctor Marshall?

You now have this book with all the great extras.

Now bring Jill, Rick, and the whole gang to life

with the recorded 14 hour theatrical audiobook

production version.

It features music by the Beatles and others with full sound design, and international voice talent.

"Danger 9b and his Goddess of Fortune"

Find it at:

Danger9b.com

Hear how it all started. National radio broadcast on:

NPR (National Public Radio) and CBC (Canadian Broadcasting Corporation)

The real story with a beat as told by the author on "Snap Judgment"

Danger 9b

https://youtu.be/F67FXXqkBvM

Podcast: Snap Judgement

August 2022

Acknowledgements

For a guy that's written hundreds of film and video scripts, this was far more challenging than I realized. My English teachers would laugh at me now if they knew I had earned my way largely as a writer. The writing coaches and books I read on Young Adult, and Children'sliterature beat me up on many of my early drafts. It only got better with time. At some point, you just have to walk away from a project and say,"it's good enough," or it will never be published. This being a highly personal story and project, I hope it's good enough.

Friends and family were so good to let me have the time to indulge in this vanity and frivolity. It was so much fun.

I was so impressed with the art work of David Erickssonn and especially for the additional book cover design work of Doug Stewart of dogstew.com.

I owe so much to the talents of many friends and international associates for their voice talent work, many as volunteers, on the audio production of "Danger 9b and his Goddess of Fortune" available through Audible.com. Primarily grateful for Benn and Hannah Dellenbach for bringing Rick and Jill to life and the multiple talents andsupport of friend, author and actor, Breck England.

Thanks also goes to my good friend and colleague, Noal Zabriskie for his sound engineering and music scoring and recording on the audio book production. It's a great piece of work. Check it out at Audible.com.

About the Author

Richard is a producer-director-writer of film and video with a 40-year career in the media business. He's written hundreds of produced film and video projects, ranging from historical, humanitarian, and biographical documentary stories to motivational and entertainment and dramatic pieces. His productions have won at the Chicago International Film Festival, the New York Festivals and numerous other film festivals and awards. He is the author of *Ain't Got Time to Die*, the script for a Broadway musical about Jester Hairston, an African American legendary Hollywood composer and actor. He presently has three self- published products in the new medium of multi-media eBooks. Check out his YouTube channel at:
https://www.youtube.com/user/RJHatchMedia

Or search for rjHatchMedia on YouTube.

Appendix

The Real Story

The journey for this book started when I found an old box in my storage room of things I had kept from my days long ago living in Turkey and Lebanon. I didn't want my heirs to worry about what to do with all my stuff once I was gone. I found a bunch of the notes from Jill(yes, she was real) and Marie, (yes, she was real, too) that they had sent to Danger 9b in seventh grade. There were letters as well, sent after I returned to the States. Unfortunately, I threw them away knowing no one else would have a clue what they were all about. I few weeks later, it dawned on me what a mistake that was but what a great story they would make.

My first action was to pitch my story to "This American Life" and "Snap Judgement". These are two radio drama programs that air weekly on National Public Radio in the US and Canada. Snap Judgement puts dramatic stories to a snappy, composed music track. They loved my story pitch, and we spent weeks recording. You can hear the result at this link:

https://youtu.be/F67FXXqkBvM

Or go to SnapJudgment.org and search for the title "Danger 9b". It aired May of 2022.

So, although Danger 9b and the Goddess of Fortune is a work of fiction with all the characters fictional personalities, they are based on real people I knew, real experiences we had, and the culture and history that surrounded us in the mid 1960s. These things took place when I was at the age of twelve. I aged up my characters for the story. The following pictures will give you clues how I crafted parts of the story from what was around me and what I experienced. What's true and whatisn't in my novel? Hard to tell, so I add these insights and real pictures in the following pages just for fun.

In case you didn't notice, each chapter is titled with a song from The Beatles repertoire. I can legally quote a title, not the verses. But, if you are a Beatle's fan, look for fun clues within each chapter to that chapter's title lyrics near the opening paragraphs. It's mostly seamless and they seem to work. I think they call that Easter Eggs in the video game world.

Richard J. Hatch

April 2023

Episode One
O! Fortuna

My first passport. Does this guy look like a typical spy?

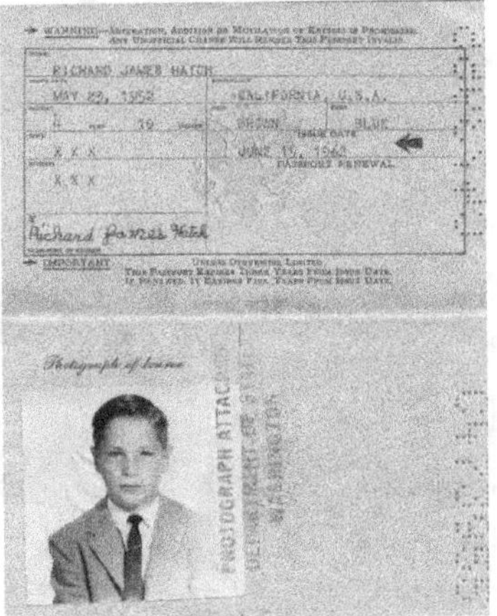

George C. Marshal Regional High School and Elementary School 1965.

454

The truth of the matter is, my dad was working in counterespionage in the latter part of his career in the mid-1960s stationedin Turkey. This is his picture as a captain before that career started with the Office of Special Investigations (OSI) with the Air Force. He was an arson specialist, but they moved him over to counterespionage when there was only one arson case. So, I knew this. I used it to my advantage to gainJill's attention. It worked for two weeks, I think.

There was a real Jill but the Jill I describe in the story is farfrom that Jill. But to my twelve-year-old eyes, Jill was abeauty, a real stand out. I wasn't so bad myself (this is my portrait at age 12) but I didn't make a very long-lasting impression with Jill. This was a simpler time for teens and pre-teens. Although my brother tells me there was quite a bit of "action" going on with his friends in high school in Ankara, I was a very naïve seventh grader. When I decided to age up my characters, I kept the idea of a more naïve and innocent (ie, moral) nature to the environment, true to my experience.

Turntable for playing vinyl records. The bigger records were called 33 albums (played at 33 rpm). They contained more songs on each side.

The smaller are called "45" records because they play at 45 revolutions per minute. It's what we danced to at Jill's parties. It's hard to describe

what a big influence The Beatles had on our lives. It still continues today.

Rare 1830 edition of the Book of Mormon. Some worth over 1 Million dollars today.

Bust of Nefertiti, Queen of Egypt, mother of King Tut.

This is Timund Persian Qu'ran from the 15th Century. It sold for 8.5 million dollars in 2020.

I had a fairly good collection of the "Hardy Boys" mystery series novels. It helped me, truly, come up with the lie to win Jill. The Beatles were in there, too. Add my dad's job, and I was in. So that part is true; a whopper, walking with Jill, and scoping out the embassy at night.

So, the Russian guard had on something close to this. Of course, with a gun. I have a confession to make. Although there really was a "break-in" at the Soviet embassyby the son of a spy and the daughter of the base commander, it wasn't Jill and I. It was my brother, Steve, and his

girlfriend at the time. They got some brochures and left. But my dad really got after him when he returned home. This helped give me the idea how to springboard the story.

Episode Two
Danger 9b and the Acrobats

I did actually climb a building much the same as the one in this picture. I did almost fall off a wooden ladder that was perched on the edge of the building at the very top, saved by my friends. The *kapaci,* caretaker, did chase us and we did escape just the way I describe in the chapter. I don't remember who was with me on this particular day.

This is a view off of our balcony down our street. We wanted a picture of an ashak cart.

Some of the older men wore baggy pants (called *"Shalver"*) as did our *kapaci.*

461

This man is selling *ekmek* or bread. This particular kind is called something like "*simiit*" They are round bread sticks. You buy things right off the street. Jill wanted 'smiit' with her peanut butter.

These are caves in Turkey where the early Christians would hide from their Roman enemies before Constantine converted and, over time, moved the whole culture into Christianity.

Episode Three Pictures
The Jillian Manuever

This is my mom, sister and me on the front balcony of our apartment on *Bestekar Sokak* (street).

This was a four wheeled ashak cart, drawn by a horse instead of an ashak (donkey). We really did hitch rides.

This is the real spy, my father Robert, demonstrating how to drink from a common jug. Leaning how to swallow and maintain a continuous pour is a fine art.

The real Banyo John and me playing the hot new game of 1964, "Spy Detective" with "Mousetrap" set up as well. "Crap yeah" is my invention. John was not part of the gang nor did he have dinner as I did with the caretakers of the building. That is where I learned a lot of Turkish, so I did speak some. I introduced Armenian chacters and some of their history based

on my association with many of them in my days living in Beirut from 1971 to 1973.

Jill's penchant for trickery is pure fiction but here are the one lira coins of the day.

We did have a constant flow of people past our apartment. Here are two men with their wives who customarily walk behind their husbands in public.

Episode Four
A Bad Combination

Forget the batter, look at that catcher. This overseas league was good fodder for more of the story to unfold.

Yes. That's me on the camel ride at our game, but that's not Jill. That's my team coach. The camel's name was "Clyde".

This is the real Tom on the far right. Notice the cast on my wrist, caused by Tom. The other guy I'm going to call Billy B. It's not him but he's my inspiration for the character.

The Dodger's awesome all-star catcher.

Ankara to Izmir on a train. It was anciently known as, Smyrna. It was conquered and expanded by Alexander the Great.

Yeah. We were first place consolation bracket winners in Europe in 1964.

Episode Five Pictures
Scouting Out The Enemy

The cover of our "Wizard of Oz" program. I know what you're thinking. Come on, it was sixth grade and they let a student do it.

I remember some of these people. But look at who played the "Wizard". Yes, and he was tiny. We all were in sixth grade but he definitely did not hit his

```
SCARECROW..............Bob Fernandez

WITCH OF
THE NORTH.............Sasha Squires

TIN WOODMAN...........Mark Hopper

COWARDLY LION.........Rick Hatch

SOLDIER...............Vance Anthony

WIZARD OF OZ..........Bill Beier

LADY..................Carla Fowler

WITCH OF
```

growth spurt this year.

I started out as a Cub Scout.

My brother, Steve and I did go to scout camp Egridir the summer of 1963 in the mountains of southeastern Turkey.

 This was the neckerchief
we wore
 around our necks.

You better believe there were "Hairy Mongers" aname my brother came up with. They sometimes covered our tents in the mornings. Steve was deathly afraid of them. It did work in my favor. I did not join the "Order of the Arrow", but it was a good devise to bring a complication into Mitch's life. The real Mitchwas not there. It gave me a nice setting to tell some ofthe backstory to Mitch which makes our rivalry work. There really was a Mitch, far different than the one I've created, who ended up with Jill, on and off even after I left. Jill stayed on for another two years in Ankara.

Episode Six Pictures
I'm Being Tailed

This was one entrance to the Ankara *Pazar* We did not go here often. Looks like a good place to make trickster Jill pull a stunt.

My dad snapped this picture in the market to give perspective on the booths. The image of this man gave me the idea to tail someone in this *Pazar*.

This is the best picture we took of the shoeshine stands. They were very prevalent and were elaborate structures made of brass. Seemed like a good place to keep Mitch occupied in the story.

Here is a Turkish traffic light of the 1960s, the guy in the middle of the street in the white structure. His

shoulders are in linewith the traffic. That means – GO for that street. There were no traffic lights in the city, and this gave jobs to a big police force. I'msure there are lights today. It was a nice detail that I came in

handy with Jill dashing away driving the cart.

So – dad really did run into two kids on a bicycle who were carrying a watermelon. Actually, they ran into us. And we all had to go to court. This is a collection of Lebanese *lira* and Turkish coin *lira* that helped us pay "buckshish" to the judge.

Okay. I don't know who the little girl is. She belonged to another tourist family but that's me in the suit with the Turkish guard at the *Topkapi* palace. Notice, her finger is on the trigger. Do I look like I fit in? What's with the suit? That was the way people traveled in those days. We dressed up.

The Blue Mosque, Istanbul

Topkapi Palace. Home to Ottoman Sultans

Jeweled Sultan's daggers.

Ferries in the Dardanelles – Port of Istanbul

This was our ashak cart diver who took us to the house outside of Istanbul. This was a trip I made years later with a traveling companion who wanted to visit his Armenian relatives out in the countryside. We took five different modes of transportation in one day. It was my inspiration for my "mission" with dad. My friend and I were on our way from Beirut to Munich by bus and stopped for a few days in Istanbul in 1973.

Episode Seven
Crusade to the Castle in the Sea

Kemal Ataturk, the founder of modern Turkey or Turkiye has a monument for his tomb in Ankara. The bookmark seemed a good way to sneak in some Turkish history without being too obvious and set up how much he was revered and rumored to come back as a green-eyed cat. How many people believed that? Who knows, but it was widely circulated during our stay in the mid 1960s.

I did have a magic kit very much like this one. I liked to perform for the family and friends. So I incorporated it into the plot

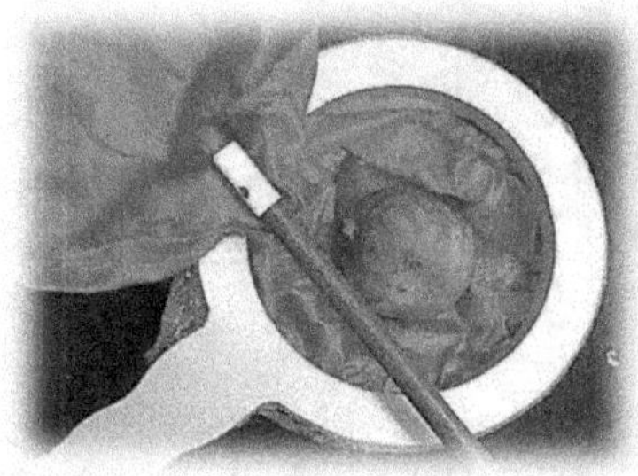

The Cheerios box trick was one I did make up and use.

479

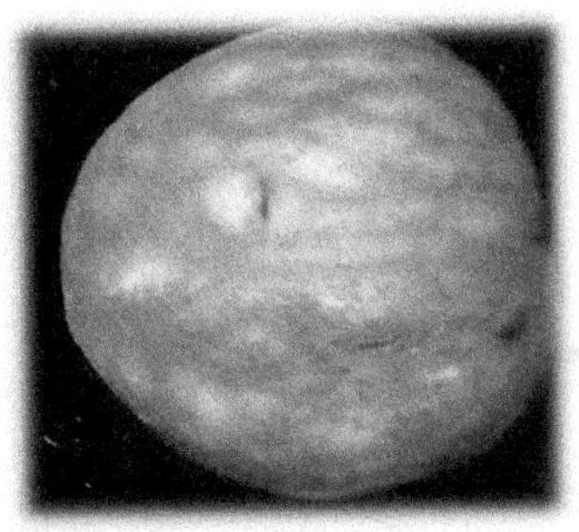

This is an Avacado pit, not Mars. It was a trick I saw somewhere. I thought it was plenty stupid and fit right in.

There really is a Kiz Kalisi off the coast of Turkey. My family and I camped out there a couple of days. And yes, we did paddle out there and explore. All of us got one whale of a sunburn. It was miserable driving home. My sister claims this was the trip where we hit

the kids on the bike carrying the watermelon. Good material for the story.

Salifke It is quite the beach in the summer.

Low and behold there was a movie being filmed right down the beach from us. My dad got close enough to take pictures.

There were two big Turkish movie stars in a romantic picture. Jill's character could not resist this one.

Looks like
Dad had a
long lens on
his camera for
this one.

We put in at a
rocky shore with
floating tubes and
kicked our way
out to the castle.

Kiz Kalise was in
ruins, but some of
the structures are
still in place.

Here are some Greek inscriptions we found at the bottom of the column.

Most of the towers were still intact, and you could climb up inside. Although I don't have a picture of them, there are Armenian symbols carved into one of the towers. Knowing this helped me put a clue here.

There really was a

Crusader's cross carved into one of the towers. My sister took this picture.

Here was my dad and sister on top of one of the walls.

This was
our
campsite on
the beach at
Salifki.

This is the other castle in the town of *Salifke,* about
15 miles from the shore.

In case you've never seen it, this
is a can of the eating kind.

Episode Eight
Skating Around the Issue

This is my real brother, Steve on the far right. He did
have a band
in High
School
playing all
the 50s and
early 60s
hits. It was
about the
only band
in school. I
portray him
a lot
dummier

than he really is – whoops, I mean – he still is a cool
guy, but I believe his guitar was a "Fender". There
really was a skating rink in our old gym which gave
me another idea for a setting to use.

There were two Turkish military coup d'etat attempts while I lived there. Fighter planes did swarm the air over our apartment, firing their guns at the American embassy, pictured here in 1965. The embassy was only two blocks away from us.

They also shot up several Turkish government buildings. It seemed a perfect event to throw Jill and Rick together to reveal more backstory and move the love story forward.

I do play the piano, so I included this as a way to compete with the character Mitch. I did have a pretty stern

Turkish piano teacher. Glad I stayed with it. Thepiano gave me a way to establish a tighter bond with my character Jill in the story.

I did have a "conversation pit" with a fireplace in my home in the States. I remember it as a very romantic setting that easily came to mind for Jill's house. She did have a larger house as I remember with a large glassed-in room for parties. It was not the mansion I describe but it was fun to imagine.

Episode Nine
International Escapades

There really is a sect called the "Whirling Dervish". I have two pictures of the time we went to their demonstration in the town of *Konya*. It provided another opportunity to weave in some culture and plot into the story. I did try to whirl. Lasted maybe one minute.

This is the "band" on the stage. It was very unusual music for a guy trained in classical piano and a fan of The Beatles. No one here played a "Stratocaster".

This is what the character of "Kilroy" looked like. It was no one artist. It just kind of grew out of some unknown incident, and off it went. We would say today it went "viral". I did leave notes everywhere I went.

Picture of the town square from our hotel in Iskenderun on the eastern shores of the Mediterranean. It was founded and called Alexandretta by Alexander the Great. He named a lot of places after himself. Iskenderun is apparently a derivation.

As you cross the borders and arrive in a new
country, you really do
get some nice stamps
in your passport
giving you
permission to enter.

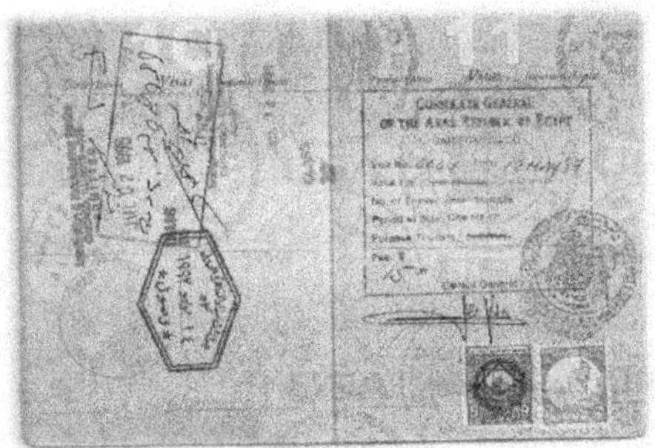

The Bedouin camel driver in Syria was wearing
clothing similar to this. He did object to his picture
being taken without buckshish.
So, Dad paid him. Don't know
what happened to those
pictures.

This is the Bekaa Valley in Lebanon, looking east to the border with Syria. It's a lush agricultural area.

Located in the Bakaa Valley is the ancient city of Baalbek, the site of ancient Roman Temples built to Jupiter and Bacchus.

 At that ancient time, it was a very large complex but had been damaged over the centuries by earthquakes and constant upheavals of battle. Much more has been restored since these 1960s pictures.

This is my 10 year old friend standing on a block of granite in the stone quarry where the material for building Baalbek  came from. It is still attached to the quarry hillside.

One of several Crusader castles still standing in Lebanon.

This is the Phonecia Hotel in 1964, where we stayed. It was destroyed in the 1970s civil war and has since been rebuilt.

This was the pool at the Phoenicia. It became a nice setting for the reunion of Jill and Rick.

There, indeed were windows looking into the underground bar from the deep end.

The Mediterranean Sea was just across the street.

Here is the
symbol of
Lebanon, a
Cedar Tree.
Notice the
snow in the
mountains.
You can ski in
the morning and swim in the Sea in the afternoon for
some months.

Jerusalem was
our next stop.
This is an 1836
lithograph from
artist David
Roberts. I
bought this in
an antique shop.
This shows the
Temple Mount
with the Dome of the Rock and the Kidron Valley.

This is the entrance to the Church of the Nativity in Bethlehem, as it looked in 1964. Nothing much has changed since. I could have recounted much history in this chapter, but it was not essential to the plot.

There is only one real spy in this picture. This was our family in the summer of 1964 posing on the Mount of Olives across from Jerusalem's Temple mount.

The Dome of the Rock, a
sacred space for Muslims,
Jews, and Christians, is the
most distinctive structure in
Jerusalem.

The old part of
Jerusalem is
completely walled-in
with stone walls
constructed in the
1500s by a Muslim
Sultan. You can walk
along much of the top
portion on the
ramparts. I cut much of this visit in the story short –
not essential to the plot.

The story took you back quickly to Lebanon. This is the main square of Beirut, as it existed in 1971. This is where all the bus lines and service cars converge. This is where I placed Tom, Jill, and Rick on their way to find *darrage massad* stairs. There are definitely hand signals and cultural gestures to learn. Some variations can get you in trouble. The juice shop I reference is right below the camera on the street level.

This is the lower half of the *darrage massad* stairs. And you thought it was fictional? What happened here was fictional, but the place is real.

Here is the sign at the street level just off the top of the stairs. Those are some real "Elders" that lived in the apartment and organized the congregations that met there.

Episode Ten
Ankara Home Games

While I like to think this is Mitch across from me, (there really was a Mitch) it is definitely me playing flag

football in seventh grade. This picture gave me the inspiration to write the incident for Mitch the Meteor and his tighty whities.

This game of spin the bottle may not still be in-play. It was for us. So, I used it to the best effect to tense up the rivalry with a bit of fun. I guess they don't have to play games these days to get in a little snogging.

So, for "Post Office", another game that has probably bit the dust bin of history, I found these notes from many years ago. Written by the real love of my life, they reminded me of the game we liked the best that moved the plot forward.

While this is the appendix for the book, this is the chapter I reference Jill's missing "appendix". This would have totally have been innocent me at that age.

The map of current-day Ankara said there was a Ferris wheel at *Golbashi* Park. I just took it from there and made up that environment and setting.

Episode Eleven
Resurrection

A lot comes together in this chapter. Not much visually to share. I never was in a Turkish morgue, so I had to do a little research. The idea for this chapter came from my daughter, who told me about some newcouple she had met who had invited her over fordinner. Unknown to my daughter, they had an apartment in a mortuary. This couple was so anxious to show my daughter around to every nook, cranny, and refrigerator like it was their own. Let's say it didn't help her appetite.

A number of details show up in this chapter thatrelates to so many other chapters. It wouldn't make much sense if it were the first thing you read. I mention 'periods' to puzzles, to baseball, to "Stratocaster", men in suits, wild ashak rides, a covered wagon, equestrian skills, a Turkish traffic light, a manual washing machine. It was fun to write.

Now on to puzzle rings. I really did have one. Never considered it for the real Jill, but it always created many questions when I got back to the States. I was the kid with the cool ring who stood up to answer questions and said, "Yes, Sir."

I did have a chemistry class in sixth grade. At the time, it was highly unusual for elementary kids to study chemistry. It made an impression on me to where I remember enough to make it a setting for the story.

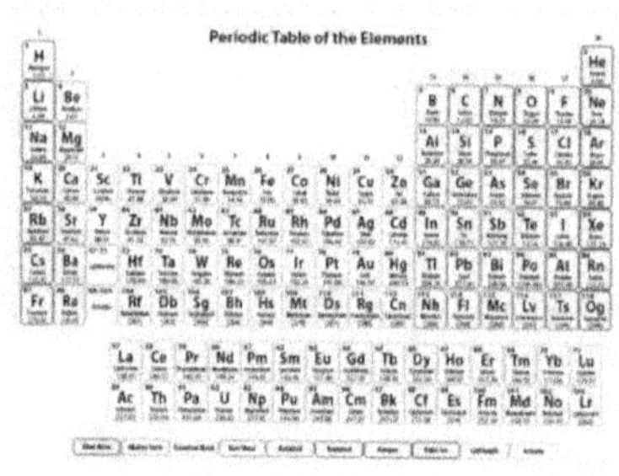

I remember, after all these years, the talk about valances for different chemicals. It became a perfect vehicle to get Jill to use for her dilemma between her two boys and concentrate on the challenges to her dad and future.

Episode Twelve
Reassignment

One of the things I worried about is how this generation of teenagers would have no conception about the use of phones in a stand or a booth and the being the only way to communicate. Pretty tough to cram two people in a box and hope readers understand you had to speak into a mouthpiece.

The 'mission' to take down the phone lines next to the government buildings may have seemed a little childish, but it was based on what John and I did in a field not far from our homes.

It was in an orchard rimmed by government buildings. There wasn't a lot for us to do, so we 'found' things to do. The surrounding walls were about ten feet high and two feet wide. Great for climbing and walking. And there were telephone lines sagging between poles we would swing on the right near the walls. So, it wasn't so ludicrous and actually something authentic.

I wish I had a picture of "Bullet Head" – Mr. Bey,
our Taxi driver. He was real, and we used him all the
time. I conveniently used him throughout the book
as a cultural hook and unusual confidant.

Episode Thirteen
The End of It

I was fascinated with the history of Alexander the Great. What a phenomenal character in history. He's not someone I would encourage anyone to emulate- very brutal times – but what he accomplished was astounding. So that is why he shows up so prevalent in the story. His lost tomb is kind of what I used as a MacGuffin – a literary device that helps drive the story.

Here is a picture of page 11 from an 1830 edition of "The Book of Mormon." Since I am familiar with it, it seemed a logical historical artifact that Professor Fontaine might want and easier for me to use. The Arabic script of the Qu'ran would have been harder to use. The vocabulary of the pages provided a convenient way to pose the clues. The word clues are from the actual pages indicated in the story.

FIRST BOOK OF NEPHI.   11

And it came to pass that after this manner of language did I persuade my brethren, that they might be faithful in keeping the commandments of God. And it came to pass that we went down to the land of our inheritance, and we did gather together our gold, and our silver, and our precious things. And after that we had gathered these things together, we went up again unto the house of Laban.

And it came to pass that we went in unto Laban, and desired him that he would give unto us the records which were engraven upon the plates of brass, for which we would give unto him our gold, and our silver, and all our precious things.

And it came to pass that when Laban saw our property, and that it was exceeding great, he did lust after it, insomuch that he thrust us out, and sent his servants to slay us, that he might obtain our property. And it came to pass that we did flee before the servants of Laban, and we were obliged to leave behind our property, and it fell into the hands of Laban.

And it came to pass that we fled into the wilderness, and the servants of Laban did not overtake us, and we hid ourselves in the cavity of a rock. And it came to pass that Laman was angry with me, and also with my father; and also was Lemuel; for he hearkened unto the words of Laman. Wherefore Laman and Lemuel did speak many hard words unto us, their younger brothers; and they did smite us even with a rod.

And it came to pass as they smote us with a rod, behold an angel of the Lord came and stood before them, and he spake unto them saying: Why do ye smite your younger brother with a rod? Know ye not that the Lord hath chosen him to be a ruler over you, and this because of your iniquities? Behold thou shalt go up to Jerusalem again, and the Lord will deliver Laban into your hands. And after that the angel had spoken unto us, he departed. And after that the angel had departed, Laman and Lemuel again began to murmur, saying, how is it possible that the Lord will deliver Laban into our hands? Behold he is a mighty man, and he can command fifty, yea, even he can slay fifty; then why not us?

And it came to pass that I spake unto my brethren, saying: Let us go up again unto Jerusalem, and let us be faithful in keeping the commandments of the Lord; for behold he is mightier than all the earth, then why not mightier than Laban and his fifty, yea, or even than his tens of thousands. Therefore let us go up; let us be strong like unto Moses: For he truly spake unto the waters of the Red Sea, and they divided

pose the clues. The word clues are from the actual pages indicated in the story.

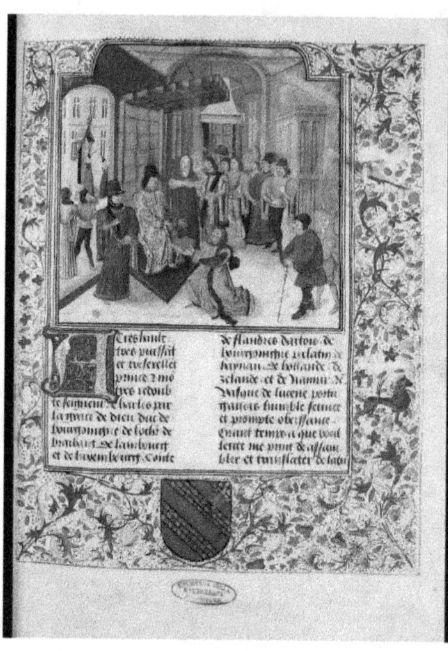

"Historae Alexandri Magni" was written in the first century A.D. by Quintus Curitus Rufus. The earliest known copy is from the 9th century, and numerous other versions were written through the centuries in different languages. Many had artwork included, which helped in the final reveal of Jill's treasures.

1	2	3	4	5	6	7	8	9
Ա	Բ	Գ	Դ	Ե	Զ	Է	Ը	Թ

10	20	30	40	50	60	70	80	90
Ժ	Ի	Լ	Խ	Ծ	Կ	Հ	Ձ	Ղ

Armenian is an ancient language. Here is a chart of their numbering system. It is so mysterious; it was an easy choice to make for building the story's clues.

A Primer on Alexander the Great

Perhaps the greatest general and conqueror of all time, Alexander the Great, looms as the greatest influence on the lands he conquered andthe myriad of leaders that followed him for centuries in the known world. In the span of only thirteen years, he conquered every land he encountered, from the present-day Balkans to modern-day Pakistan. He died at a very early age of 32 and did not designate a successor, which led to the breakup and continued chaos throughout his empire.

"In a reign of (only) 13 years, Alexander shot across the Greek and Middle Eastern firmament like a meteor, transforming whatever he — often brutally — touched and ensuring the ancient world and so eventually our world could never be the same again," wrote Paul Cartledge, A.G. Leventis professor of Greek culture at Cambridge University.

I used his overwhelming legacy as a driving force in the story and a source of intrigue. His official tomb has never been found. Perhaps it was destroyed and pillaged and will never be discovered. It could be in the waters of Alexandria, the city he founded in Egypt, or further inlandunder the modern city. The treasures are likely not there. Julius Caesar visited the tomb one time, 300 hundred years after Alexander's death. Cleopatra is said to have taken gold to finance her war with Rome. But the mystery of a golden sarcophagus permeates the thoughts of all archeologists. It is perhaps the greatest treasure next to Tutankhamen and is as elusive as the Ark of the Covenant.

Professor Catledge also felt that Alexander was perhaps the most famous human that ever lived in all the world until the age of the internet.

He was such a part of the country I lived in for years it was natural to lean into his fame in the context of events in modern Turkey.

Alexander and Bucephalus

514

A Christmas Carol by Charles Dickens

An award-winning full dramatic audio production combined with the complete, as-written text featuring original art.

email interest to: *rjhatchmedia@gmail.com*

Audio sample: *https://youtu.be/NKFoUQZdiMs*

Humanitarian Adventures in Egypt

Audio, Video, and Text detailing some of the work of two charity volunteers laboring in Egypt

email interest to: rjhatchmedia@gmail.com

Film and Video:

You can view a repository of much of the film and video work of Richard J. Hatch of rjHatchMedia by visiting his YouTube Channel:

https://www.youtube.co/@RJHatchMedia